RED/BLACK

RED/BLACK

Rachel Atherton-Charvat

Matador
9 Priory Business Park,
Wistow Road, Kibworth Beauchamp,
Leicestershire. LE8 0RX
Tel: 0116 279 2299
Email: books@troubador.co.uk
Web: www.troubador.co.uk/matador
Twitter: @matadorbooks

ISBN 978 1838594 985

British Library Cataloguing in Publication Data.
A catalogue record for this book is available from the British Library.

Printed on FSC accredited paper
Printed and bound in Great Britain by 4edge Limited
Typeset in 12pt Adobe Jenson Pro by Troubador Publishing Ltd, Leicester, UK

Matador is an imprint of Troubador Publishing Ltd

For Julian

ACKNOWLEDGEMENTS

There are many people I would like to acknowledge for their support in publishing this book.

My parents and Jackie, in facing their own adversities, especially at this time of crisis and isolation. My mother, for her infinite generosity to others and for passing on her love of books. My sisters, particularly Melinda, for her encouragement in publishing this novel. To my good and brilliant friends Wendy and Edward for their help and support in this endeavour.

For my nieces Clare, Megan, Jasmine and Eve, who in picking up the torch for the next generation of women, are breaking down barriers and pursuing their dreams. There can be nothing more noble and worthwhile. I hope they never lose sight of this.

Also, not least to mention Christiana for her professionalism and many years of unwavering support.

Finally, my husband Julian, to whom I owe so much. My love, my strength, my inspiration, who unceasingly holds a light up to the best of life's possibilities. For Miletus.

CHAPTER 1

SARAH SAT AT the roulette table anxiously rotating a chip through her fingers. The wealth that she was now staking, which had changed hands against the house over the last few hours, was to take a single spin. The time had come to make a single choice. Red/Black. After three consecutive wins at the table, it had to be now. A feeling in her gut, as with the last three spins. This was her opportunity. She had been right then, she was right now.

Others around her were already selecting their bets. After several hours having barely moved, her body ached, her head fragile to the intrusion of the people that came and went around her. The last few hours of her ever-shifting fortunes she had become exhausted by the spikes of ecstasy and the pits of desperation to stay in the game. But this was to be the last bet.

She focused on the table. Red/Black. Impatient with her own hesitancy in committing to placing her stake, she continued to turn the chip. Looking once again at the roughly stacked chips in front of her, she surveyed the amounts of her long-fought gains. Tonight, the luck had been hers.

The sum that she had coveted when she had taken her seat had been surpassed in the previous spin. But one more win would make good everything she owed, and set her up beyond her previous expectations. After months, this would be where it would reach its end. It would be over. She would never come back.

In choosing her bet, there wasn't any temptation to go to the fated numbers she had used so many times before. The numbers entwined with her past, dates, events, from her greatest fortune, love or happiness. Each had become meaningless in turn, as they had taken their share in her losses. As if they conspired to hurt her.

The people that she had lost, the people she had left, were in her mind gaining momentum in a relentless tide of thoughts. When she had been struggling to rebuild a swathe of losses she knew what they would say to her. Memories of them were becoming almost intolerable. After this turn, she would be able to indulge them beyond anything they had had before, to give them everything.

The croupier picked up the ball. It was now time to commit, her head buzzing with conflicting instincts as to where she should place the wealth of chips.

She closed her eyes. In a moment of certainty, the colour came to her. Black. The strongest feeling she had all night. In a swift move, adrenaline coursing through her veins, she urgently slid the stacks of chips across the green baize.

A man next to her, who had chosen the same colour, reacted to her move by spontaneously taking in a deep breath in admiration, then raised his glass in acknowledgement.

'Fortune favours the brave and all that.'

Unaware of the attention around her, she anxiously waited for the ball to set to purpose. Others around the table, whose attention she had quickly gained, joined in with the expression of excitement or anxiety. Two of whom then changed their mind from red, as if to be part of the big occasion that lay ahead.

The difference of a millimetre drop would release her from this torment. She blocked out contemplating the alternative outcome. Her stomach churned as the croupier set the ball in motion.

'*Mesdames et Messieurs*, no more bets please.'

Under the lights, the bold colours glimmered in the wheel's polished veneer, holding the attention of the surrounding gamblers. Those around the table gravitated to the thrill, now urging their favoured fortune, willing their deserved fate.

In that moment, she didn't consider that it was an amount she and her husband had paid for their first house. Or know that she would never see him again.

The numbers came into focus. The familiar metallic clank echoed around the bowl, as the ball bounced from one bed to the next. Sarah let out a cry as it came to rest.

CHAPTER 2

SARAH PICKED UP the neatly placed post from her hallway table. She passively flicked through an assortment of the usual bills and circulars before seeing a picture postcard from Cambodia. It was from her eldest son who had been travelling for the past three months, the photograph capturing a majestic image of the Angkor Wat at sunset. The grandeur of the ancient temple with its splendid towers cast an imposing silhouette over a serene lilied waterscape. An inviting radiant orange hue brought a flash of warmth to the cool hallway of their English home in winter.

> *Hey Mum*
> *Just to let you know. Having a great time. All is well. Amazing here. Anyway, love to Izzy and hope she is surviving her first term and turning up to some lectures. Hope the move is going OK. So, all is well aside from*

gastro-intestinal issues. It's probably breakfast time for you... I know. Will be in touch when we reach Sydney.
Love Seb

Making her way through to the kitchen she imagined how her son was doing on the other side of the world. She pinned the card on a board with the others he had sent. Alongside were various other photos of the family taken over the past year. How much had changed.

This would be the last month that they would spend in their house. In just over two weeks the removal company would be arriving to collect their belongings for a move to Germany. Over the last few months all arrangements had been made – removals, flights, passports and a multitude of other regulation forms that she was happy to leave to her husband, Graeme. After labouring through a German language course, she felt that she just about had the basics nailed down. Graeme, already near-fluent, had given her an incentive to improve hers, and not be reliant on him. The course entailed learning through the medium of phrases and stock images of various shops, animals and always unfeasibly happy locals pointing you in various directions. Along with this she had a rough grasp of formal pleasantries, shopping, driving signs and travelling on public transport. Impatiently, she had cherry-picked the language course, one that had been put together based around a limited stock image bank by a linguist equipped with what she interpreted as a modest sense of humour. It challenged her with basic questions such as how to ask the way to the post office, supermarket and wine merchant. Which she roughly accomplished. Other sections she swiftly skipped over, such as how to explain that penguins can swim but can't fly. Although at 10 p.m. on a night when Graeme was away it provided a little levity as she hashed through the complexities of German grammar and pronunciation. In frustration, after half a bottle of red dispatched, she appealed to the placid-looking penguin, krill in beak, in an exasperated plea as to why they hadn't been posted to France.

On her best days, she felt buoyed by their optimism of starting a new future, this being their first time living overseas since Graeme had joined the army. Germany was a 'great country', one of her friends told her, Berlin an exciting and cosmopolitan city. The Christmas markets, another one enthused, were 'simply magical'. Her friends' collective encouragement was offered in way of redressing the balance of the leaving party they threw for her. It was in recompense for being greeted by everyone wearing stonewash denims and mullet wigs, marking her entrance with a blast of The Hoff over the sound system. Her compliance had been non-negotiable as they put a blond wig complete with suspended plaits on her head. In celebration, they thrust into her hand a glass of wine, which she was grateful hadn't remained true to the national theme.

It was not a typical house move compared to the ones they had undertaken previously, which involved packing every piece of furniture under the roof, bar the redundant items for the car boot sale or dump, and moving everything else, lock stock. After that, the sum of her input had been standing on the periphery, delegating all to the removal men that she kept in motion with industrial quantities of tea and sandwiches, a mission that, albeit exhausting, was nevertheless straightforward in its criteria. This was a posting that entailed exhaustive amounts of mandatory paperwork and rules not allowing for deviation. What she had thought was Graeme being pedantic when describing the requirements was given clarity when he began reeling off a set of necessities and parameters that a military move would entail. The realisation that she was about to take on a life that revolved around allocations and allowances came when they were given a strict adherence on what their entitlement of square metres of belongings would be. Then followed the brutal decision-making of dividing up what they wanted to take and what to store.

Once that had been established, Graeme insisted on a clear division of responsibilities for packing. The kitchen, dining room, sitting room and bedrooms were her domain. He would do the rest, including his study and the garage.

Taking a notepad and pencil through the rooms she began two lists in two separate distinctions: items to go and items for storage, all of which were identified by corresponding stickers. There were things that had been earmarked for family, friends or charity. The TV and a few other white goods they were giving to their niece who was setting up home. Plants were for her next-door neighbour and good friend, Ellie, who had over the past month made several hints about how, given the high maintenance of most, they would need special care – a dubious point given that it was a collection of hardy palm and rubber plants, but she knew they would be left in good hands. Ellie had been a good friend, always there for the good and bad times over the past few years. For charity, there were two boxes of paperbacks and two cases of clothes that she had never worn.

Walking around each room she considered the home that they had put together over the past fifteen years. Finding the property had been a timely piece of luck, given their sudden decision to leave their previous home, a Georgian house on the outskirts of the town that had fallen into neglect. A shell of its original glory, they had bought it from an elderly lady who could no longer maintain the house on her own. It had been in her family for five generations, her grown-up children now scattered across the globe.

After she and Graeme were handed the keys, each plinth, wall and coving had been scraped down and rejuvenated. With each stroke of paint she wondered what had been before, and what the lady's family had been like when she had been younger and the house was full of life. Underneath the top layer of wallpaper, two more patterns were found, from what looked like the sixties and seventies. On the painted walls were dark patches where paintings had previously hung. Every room was testament to a history of her family's life: scuffed floorboards, worn brass door handles, dulled light switches and notably dusty high fittings that she doubted had been touched for many years. Later, when they began work outside, they discovered lost, corroded toy figures in the overgrown garden and two old bicycles stored in a far shed. Sarah imagined the joy, the successes, the hard times and finally the day that the elderly lady knew that her home was going to be whitewashed and consigned to the past.

Builders had been tasked only with what she and Graeme couldn't do, such as laying floorboards that needed replacing, and making good a roof in need of proper repair. It was shabby inside but attempts to keep it well maintained were evident. Peeling cupboards had been wiped down as best they could be, swept floors covered by ageing and worn oriental carpets. However, overall the interior resembled a vessel blowing increasingly more holes, the waterline rising. The lady's nephew, with whom they exchanged contracts, talked up the structural attributes. His aunt, who accompanied him on the day and handed over the keys, said very little. It was obvious to Sarah that memories being relived as she surveyed the house were not to be shared. At the time they had met she had felt partly guilty about buying the home. Graeme dismissed her concerns, saying that it would now be brought back to life instead of being some living tomb, and the price, the 'considerable price', as he would often emphasise, would keep her in comfort for the remainder of her life. As the lady departed the house she ran her hand with slow deliberation down the bottom of the balustrade. In what seemed a personal ritual, she examined her hand, murmuring something barely audible about it needing a dust. Her nephew gave an uncomfortable laugh, given what he saw as the obvious context of her leaving what was a rundown shell. A barely habitable, anachronistic testament to a lifetime. There were no tears and she showed no desire to engage with anyone. No wishing Sarah or Graeme well. Sarah watched her wait in the car whilst Graeme made some tactless remark about the monumental task that lay ahead. As they drove away Sarah put up a hand to wave goodbye, even though the elderly lady didn't once look back.

Each room had an intimate association for Sarah, where memories had been made as they gradually built up their new home. Every paint shade they had picked out, carpets acquired, curtains, furnishings. The door handles had come about by many searches in antique shops and at auctions, her husband happy to take the plaudits after he fitted them. But they both worked hard on the house, especially in the first stages of the renovations. They managed this around work and looking after the children. All of their energies channelled into the different projects, there was little time left to spend on anything else. Often, if she was waiting on a task, she went to a local auction house or other shops to pick out some new furniture.

On occasion, late into the evening on what became suddenly a task too far, they abandoned what they were doing and cracked open some wine. Sometimes they left their children with Graeme's mother and went to the local pub for the night. Coming back late, stiff-limbed they walked the mile back home, leaving the thoughts of the ditched task until the next day. Even though at times the reality of their huge undertaking felt overwhelming, it's what got them through, and amongst the dirt, dust, frustration and occasional chaos, it was what had kept them together after their world had fallen apart.

9

The interior was mostly her taste. It was the smallest pieces that she enjoyed the most, such as a pair of art-deco lamps, walnut bookcases that had been an unexpected bargain on a quiet day at the auction house, and ceramics from a favourite local potter. Books that had been in storage were brought out after six months, bringing with them a familiar comfort to the sitting room. In the winter there was nowhere she would rather be with a glass of wine and a book. In the summer she would open a set of French doors that overlooked their garden.

The garden had been an ongoing project for all the years they had been there. As with the house it had succumbed to neglect. It was a labour of love, and each time Sarah ventured into it she felt pride over what they had achieved. There was always something to be cultivated, planted or nurtured. At least once a week she would find time to go to the garden centre. In Graeme's office upstairs there was a side reserved for her books, a gardening section taking up an entire row. For the first two years they kept a photo album of the progress made. The digging, reseeding, planting were all catalogued in joyful if not weary poses. It was during this time that the lion's share was done. As the years passed Graeme became less interested, to the point that his sole contribution was occasionally mowing the lawn. Mostly his time spent in the garden would be taking a drink and indulging in a book whilst she worked. She had never told him but for all the good times they had laying the foundations, she enjoyed working alone in the garden – the multitude of scents, colours, and the gratification at the growing accumulation of wildlife. Instead of appreciating his input of the occasional mowing, she would notice the casual lack of symmetry in the cut. Or the fact that he never left his phone indoors, the grating sound of a novelty ringtone periodically breaking the peace.

Most of the furniture they had bought themselves, apart from some of the larger pieces in the dining and drawing room that had been passed on to Graeme by his parents.

Over the years, from corner to corner it had been her domain to upkeep, the details of which the others were oblivious, such as the splashes of coffee or wine near the dishwasher when the rest of the family had put in a glass or cup after what they thought was their contribution to housekeeping. Pulling out the fridge; maintaining the washing machine, dishwasher, tumble dryer, cooker. Once a month all the cupboards were emptied, wiped and re-sorted. Storage jars would be refilled and spices and condiments checked. Seb rarely commented, but her daughter, Izzy, gave her a continuing narrative on how she was betraying womankind. Sometimes it was light-hearted, and other times her provocation led to heated arguments. On one side, accusations of naivety and a lack of appreciation; on the other a charge levelled of living in self-induced shackles of domesticity, the latter coupled with a commitment to self-immolation rather than succumbing to being a slave to patriarchal rule. Faced with any problem, perceived injustice or dilemma, Izzy was head-on. She never let things fester. The opposite of Seb, she wore her heart on her sleeve. She had always been driven by a need for understanding, to find an explanation. Even if she didn't like the answer, she wanted to know every detail. But equally, if she had made her position, she would dig her heels in.

Sarah's routine was like clockwork. As soon as Graeme and the children had left the house she would start the housework. This usually took around two hours. Or two and a half if Ellie popped around for a quick chat or to request some advice that she invariably had already made her mind up on anyway. Saturday mornings Graeme would play golf and she used the time for preparations for the weekend. The afternoons were for her work, which began a year after they moved there after she

11

bumped into an old school friend who had opened a clothing boutique. At first she worked part-time, and some years later she would buy in as a partner. It was something that she had never considered but it gave her a life outside the home and once she began, she enjoyed the challenge of building up a business. After they closed she would often spend an hour or so extra after work talking with her business partner, Chloe, and recently a fledgling designer they had taken on, about new ideas that she had been mulling over, mostly when her head was in a fridge or pushing around the vacuum. In the previous year her hours spent at the shop gradually increased, with her sometimes not getting back until after 6.30. After Graeme began to increasingly complain about dinner being pushed back an hour by the time she had started it, she reverted to returning home earlier.

The maintenance of the house mostly went unnoticed by Graeme, unless she occasionally bemoaned his lack of gratitude. This would spark one of two responses: either that he appreciated everything she did or a thinly veiled dig at her having more time on her hands and so it should hardly be a cause for too many plaudits. The reaction was largely dependent on what type of day he had at work. The only time he made a great deal of effort was before or after he had been away. He picked out points such as the spotless nature of their home in whichever room he happened to be in at the time.

Now, as they prepared for the move to Germany, her usual methodical approach had been applied to the packing. In each room she wrote down every item to go, then placed the designated coloured sticker on each. Within half an hour she had covered the downstairs with efficiency, the kitchen taking slightly longer than the rest as she contemplated which utensils to include, and decided if she hadn't used a particular gadget for a year then it was staying behind. It was only when she began on the children's rooms that the consequence of the move really began to sink in. Izzy had selected the things that she wanted to take and packed them into two boxes in the corner. The rest was to go into storage. Seb had dismissively requested everything left to be 'bunged' into storage, but to take particular care with his vinyl collection, and a mate would be round to pick it up for safe-keeping. His bedding and clothes he had left in the drawers to be donated to charity. Packing up his belongings, she thought of when they had first moved in.

Taking out a record from his collection she placed it onto the turntable. A gentle crackle gave way to The Clash's live recording of 'I Fought the Law'. Turning up the volume she began a painful accompaniment that would have made Mick Jones' toes curl. Her awkward attempts weren't much of an improvement in thirty years. A couple of years before, when Seb was away at university, she had found a small quantity of marijuana under his bed. It had been a grim morning, having had a big argument with Graeme, and she had been busying herself with a deep clean of the house. Crashing to a halt at around 4 p.m. and post two large glasses of one of Graeme's favourite Burgundies, her inhibition disappeared. The little tin had the requisite tobacco and papers. As she rolled this bulging, uneven cigarette she thought how the family would react. Something along the lines of Graeme calling her irresponsible and embarrassing, Izzy laughing and saying it was long overdue, and the remaining family member most likely ready with a speculative request for reimbursement.

Seb's wardrobe had been commandeered by Graeme for his army uniforms. In a move ten years ago that had taken her by surprise, Graeme told her that he wanted to sign up after over a decade as a psychiatrist, telling her he now wanted to 'give something back'. His decision came after treating a soldier with PTSD that he had taken on as a patient in Gloucester. A shameful neglect of ex-soldiers, he said, a point that he would then bring up every time a news report came in about ongoing conflicts. Then one day, she proposed that he speculatively look into offering his services. He responded to her comment, and in so doing confirmed, as she suspected, that he had been awaiting her suggestion. A week later, he told her of a forthcoming interview to serve in the Territorial Army. Throughout the time he was advised to take to consider the commitment, he never wavered.

He was commissioned a year later after passing out from the requisite officer training at Sandhurst. After attending a shortened version for professionally qualified officers, she was pleased that it wasn't the full year that was usual for the regular courses, the measuring-up and tailoring for his numerous uniforms by the finest tailors on Savile Row accounting for nearly as much time. His number 1 dress was his blues, service dress and mess kit, his mess kit being his least favourite. After coveting a vibrant crimson and gold-trimmed high-collared cut he thought he might be attired in at formal mess dinners, he was told that his regimental colours were a rather dowdy maroon and blue. Laughing it off less convincingly by saying he had been sold a dummy after watching *The Four Feathers*, he took great pride in his place in the army and looked after every piece of kit meticulously, as he did with all of his civilian suits. In the time since he joined up, aside from the occasional frustration, he hadn't looked back. Then, finally, after a month's assignment as locum cover at a military medical centre the previous year, he asked her if she would support him becoming full-time.

Ever since he had been able to reconcile his salary to his tastes, he had his work suits made bespoke. He had previously told her that if he and his father hadn't seen eye to eye on many things, the necessity of a good tailor was a lesson that he abided by.

The organisation of her clothes was less fastidious, being chaotic in parts behind the concealment of the cupboards. The only part reflecting her husband's sartorial organisation was for her more formal wear. The dresses for the frequent dinners and drinks that his two jobs demanded were hung with greater care. Her shared ownership in a clothing boutique made the issue of acquiring the right dress straightforward. All of her clothes, shoes and accessories, bar one pair of Converse that she found in the back of the wardrobe the previous week, were testimony to how much she had changed since meeting him.

Adjacent to his uniforms were two shelves of kit, including the standard issue of various camouflage combats, and equipment. One item in particular, a gas mask, had to be retrieved one day from a young Seb, who was then given a lecture on why his little sister wasn't perhaps a fitting protagonist in a game of mutant alien invasion.

After doing a final check of Seb's room, she was relieved not to have made some unpleasant discovery of either an abandoned perishable, or some material that his father would espouse as the antidote to sexually repressed Brits. A logic that he didn't apply to Izzy and, much to her daughter's surprise, a contradiction that was backed up by her mother. With just Izzy's room to do, she took a break, opening up the window. 'Should I Stay or Should I Go' by The Clash began to play, a cue for her to turn up the music. In an exploratory, but ultimately unsuccessful venture, she did look with hopeful expectation for the same green tin.

The door suddenly opened behind her. 'Is this some sort of hint or just nostalgia?' It was Graeme, smiling at the sight of her midway through her rendition.

'Jesus!' She leaned over, turning the music down. 'How come you are home? You are supposed to be in London.' She walked up and kissed him.

'If you can believe it, I forgot my presentation. Anyway, I have Rich downstairs. Thought we would have a cup of tea then head off. So I can't stay long.'

As he left to go to his study she went downstairs to greet Rich. Rich was one of the few colleagues that Sarah had warmed to. Best of all she had made friends with him and his wife, Nikki. He was a doctor, who, like Graeme, had joined the army later in his career. But that was where the similarity ended. Rich was more outgoing, with an easy manner. Less hung up on the strict formalities of the army. They had to work closely as part of the same facility but he and Graeme hadn't become the good friends that Nikki and she had. Nikki confided in her that Rich thought it was because he was unapologetically too informal with 'the other ranks' he treated.

'Nice music,' Rich laughed. 'You missed a vocation there.'

'Yes, very funny.' She took down three cups. 'Tea? I don't suppose Graeme has offered to make you one.'

'Er. No, he didn't. Just as it comes. Thanks. So he still doesn't know his way round a kitchen, then?'

'You are kidding.' She retrieved a packet of Hobnobs. 'All that self-reliance drummed into you lot and not a thing carried back over the threshold.'

'Hey, don't cast me in the same light. I know the right end of a hoover and you should see my Sunday morning breakfast.'

'What a trooper. Anyway, Nikki's told me about your semi-conscious wanderings around the kitchen at the weekend, cremating everything within an inch of its life,' she joked.

'Is nothing sacred? God only knows what else you discuss. No, I wouldn't want to know.'

'You should try being married to a psychiatrist, everything is up for dissection.' She rolled her eyes as she began searching for a teapot that she couldn't recall making the 'to stay' inventory. 'I can't even watch *EastEnders* without him pointing out some Oedipus complex or sociopathic subtext. I mean, I just want to forget my troubles by indulging in murder, adultery and the weekly breakdown at the Queen Vic. How is that not healthy?'

'Who can argue?' he replied dryly. 'I don't think I told you this, anyway, I remember when I first met him. I thought as an ice-breaker it would be good value to pull his leg on psychoanalysis. He's not really big on deadpan, your husband.'

'Of his many attributes… er, no… definitely not receptive to deadpan.'

'I asked him what was the point of all that soul-searching, deliberation, a thousand distressingly fraught paths to find the underlying cause, etc. etc. When it basically boiled down to a repetitive whodunit, which always ends with the one who sports the hair rollers carrying the can.'

'Oh God, you sent up mummy issues. I'm sure he loved that.' She tried to stifle a laugh as she heard Graeme come down the stairs. 'Never mind when we take trips around art galleries… a whole host of artists whose work curdles before my very eyes…'

'You have my interest…'

'No, trust me, I will spare you, but even architecture gets the full treatment. You should have heard what he said about the Gherkin.' She then quickly concluded by whispering as the footsteps rapidly approached, 'I mean, the "bloody Gherkin".'

At that point Graeme came back through the door. 'It's a good job I checked.' He frowned. 'You forgot to pack my shaving kit.'

Both of them failed to suppress a laugh. 'Sorry, darling. It's nothing. Did you get everything else you needed?'

He hesitated as he looked to regather his thoughts. 'We can't be too long. So if that tea wasn't too far away it would be helpful.'

The atmosphere became more sedate as his mood changed. She poured the tea and placed the cups on the table. The plans for the meeting confirmed, Graeme hastily drank half of his tea and suggested that they get a move on because of the traffic.

'Oh and before I forget...' Rich turned to Sarah. 'Are you still OK for sharing a table at the Christmas ball next Saturday? Nikki said she had mentioned it. You have to go out in style.'

'I don't know about that but we would love to. Speaking of which, send her my love.'

'I'll be back tomorrow morning,' Graeme told her as he placed his cup by the sink. 'Don't forget the leaving drinks for work. I've picked up my dry-cleaning so no need to worry. Then we'll have dinner out. I've booked a table. Save us listening to a lot of old disingenuous drivel from the others.' He waited until Rich had made his way to the door. 'I'll call tonight. Just, don't worry about doing anything else. Put your feet up, you look tired.' He kissed her. 'I mean it.'

'Will do. Good luck and have fun.' She smiled wryly, as he had been grumbling that morning about the latest soporific symposium where he would be ticking down the minutes.

'Hmm. Joy of joys.' With that he closed the door, making his way down the hall before becoming engaged once again in conversation with Rich.

CHAPTER 3

THE FOLLOWING DAY, after finishing her set tasks early, Sarah decided to take the remaining three hours until Graeme's leaving drinks as an opportunity to spend some time in town. He had returned home early that morning for a quick turnaround before setting off for what had become his usual Friday routine: a visit to an old-fashioned barbers on the corner for a cut-throat shave. Before leaving the house, he pressed her for a decision on which tie and cufflinks, twice asking her to confirm, concerned that she hadn't given him the full attention as she was watching her toast under the grill. Then, as he left the house, she reassured him that she would be at his office at 6 p.m.

It was also a good excuse to take in some air and get away from the constant reminder of their imminent departure. Leaving Cheltenham was going to be the hardest part. Their move there had been a short one from Wiltshire and an opportunity to build a life for themselves and the children piece by piece. It was somewhere she and Graeme could agree upon. She had spent her childhood living just outside Gloucester, and the many trips to nearby Cheltenham had always been happy ones. The move hadn't been too far away, but far enough to allow them space and close enough to suit the demands of their respective families. Each place that they went to, club that they joined, friend that they made helped them take root in the community.

Not long after they moved to Cheltenham, Graeme set up in solitary practice, two years later taking on a partner. The children took up most of Sarah's time. To begin with, she only made a couple of friends that weren't part of a couple that she and Graeme socialised with. During the first year there, their next-door neighbour, Ellie, would pop round with post that had been left or an offer of a cup of tea. It was on one day when she had a flood in her kitchen and Sarah lent her a few things and offered to help her redecorate that they struck up a friendship. This had been the most enduring. Aside from socialising, when she wasn't doing the school run, she read, cycled and painted, and most of all she cherished her garden.

In the late spring and summer months the area came into its own. Music festivals, food and drink and historical festivals and, best of all, the literature festival held in Cheltenham. In the parks and on the waterfronts in Gloucester caterers, brewers, artisan goods laid out to be sampled. Basking in the sunshine, cool pints of local ales with their rich and honeyed hues provided refreshment, dulled only if clouds moved in, a point at which everyone headed for cover with the usual jovial bemoaning of the unpredictability of the English weather.

In the first year that they were there, she and Graeme went to nearly all the festivals that were nearby, the four of them making a day out of it, leaving the house early, to return later with two exhausted children and a fresh stock of local produce. They conversed with the farmers and craftsmen alike, about the harvest or the provenance of their wares, the children paying more attention to the chocolate than the goods put on display by the cheesemongers. A Bedlington Blue or a Stinking Bishop held no interest when the finest chocolatier in the area had a stand. Graeme and Sarah listened as they tasted a couple of the samples, learning about the cocoa beans' long journey from the exotic plantations in the valleys of Venezuela to the cottage industry amidst the rolling hills of the Cotswolds. Graeme would indulge as much as the children as they made their choices, delighting in the tastes of vanilla, almonds and fruits infused into each bite. Seb and Izzy excited as their father would always up the ante when being offered different weights. Graeme, being the most incorrigible, would inevitably feel the effects of the various mixtures of savoury sweets and hops later that evening.

On some days they would leave the children with Graeme's mother, to take the time to go out by themselves. Sometimes a trip out on their own, to their favourite music festival where they would spend a day lying out in a field, taking in the sunshine and food until the last songs were played.

Their best memory was the day, six months after their move, they had booked lunch at a pub in Cooper's Hill at the time of the annual cheese rolling event, when a swathe of fearless competitors would plummet down a deceptively steep hill to chase the prize of a Double Gloucester cheese, hurtling its way to the bottom. The usually sleepy village transformed into a carnival atmosphere with the anticipation of the event to come. With each race a melee of arms and legs would flail, in whoops of delight, exhilaration and fear, tumbling their way down, forging a muddy trail through the long, soaked grass to the bottom of the hill. Some with the misguided notion that they could keep momentum standing upright, until speed, gravity and over-confidence sent them bouncing and sliding their way to an eventual crashing halt. The elite runners becoming apparent, the winners would raise the prize cheese above their head. Some less fortunate competitors were attended by the medics on hand, ready and equipped for every eventuality. The day was extended into a long night as Graeme had stepped in to help an injured young Australian man when he lay in a heap at the bottom of the hill. As the young man's revelry was brought to a premature end by a broken ankle, his girlfriend offered them the room they had paid for in a local pub as a thank you. It didn't need to be offered a second time as Graeme insisted on a half reimbursement. A confirmation call was made to Graeme's mother and so began one of the memories she had treasured since. Drinking into the early hours and taking a walk through the village as the sun came up, it was the first time in months that they had been able to have some relief from the weight of grief that had taken them to breaking point.

When not talking of the past, they talked of a future, even though almost as soon as they had come back, the aspirations were buried in the usual routine. From making a commitment to going out nearly every weekend, as Graeme's work demands increased this soon ebbed away to every other, then around once a month. Sometimes he would surprise her, then on a couple of occasions in the following year he became fractious on the day before he had committed to going away. Since expanding the partnership, he insisted that she run everything by him in advance, as he didn't know what work would throw up.

The literary festival had a longer tradition with Sarah, having attended since she was a child. It was an event that she looked forward to every year, starting with her father taking her when she was six, then later going with friends, and it was an opportunity to have time on her own. Two weeks of the late autumn months, people travelled from their doorsteps around the world to that one festival set up in the elegant grounds of Montpellier Gardens and the Town Hall. Gathered under tents and the splendour of the Hall were some of the best contemporary writers, academic minds, artists, comedians and innovators. Mostly they had come to promote their latest books, some to contribute their knowledge and experience, most of which incited a thirst for knowledge from the crowds drawn to each and every different experience.

In the weeks previous to the event, she scanned a colourful, freshly printed programme that arrived at their house. Then the selections would come, along with a couple of telephone calls to people whom she knew would like a particular event. When she went with her father, they would go to the refreshment tent amongst the excitement and discussions on the events, and he would, without fail, grumble at the prices of the sandwiches and how they could possibly justify charging over £1 a time for a modest slice of fruitcake, unless it was baked by Mary Berry herself. 'A significant sum to a teacher,' he would impart to the busy person at the till. Sarah didn't realise at the time of the briefly cringeworthy experience that, later, after losing him so suddenly at twenty, she would have given anything to have him there with her, grumbling at the counter. Her father, having not succumbed to the extortions of the café, would take her to the booksellers. She could choose three books. This was given flexibility on the weeks that she had her particular interest in another of the speakers. As Christmas was not far away, they indulged in the same ritual of dropping hints at possible presents, which every year they opened expressing surprise at how they knew exactly what to buy. The ones that were signed were acquired when each took the obvious hint to go and look at something else for ten minutes.

Later, as a student, it was an opportunity to consume a couple of real ales, and soak up the atmosphere. On better days when it was warm enough, she would take them outside, along with a pre-bought pastry from her local bakery and watch the world go by.

In the years since she had been with Graeme that changed to wine, when it was just comfortable enough to order a Sauvignon Blanc that was the price of a paperback. Most of the time she went in for a coffee and cake where she would strike up a conversation with others who had been in the same lecture, or she wanted to hear about another that she hadn't been to. Most of the people she never saw again, aside from one woman who she struck up an acquaintance with and met up with for one day of the Hay Festival. Graeme wasn't interested in going, and she stopped telling him about some of the lectures as he sent up 'neurotic and depressed artists' as he had enough of those at work. And how they somehow managed to come out of their solitary and tortured existence spent in existential contemplation for a free piss-up, a wad of cash, and best of all talk about themselves for an hour – 'Heaven forbid I should be forced to endure the pontificating and self-adoration of some celebrity bore.' And he 'would rather be locked up in a dark room than listen to the patronising waffle of another overrated, pretentious windbag'.

Sarah savoured the festival and made the most of the spare time that she had. When the children were younger, Seb and Izzy enjoyed the children's authors. Most of all they found one of their few common interests, travelling and exploration, their imagination captured when Edmund Hillary gave an account of when he scaled Everest. On the drive on the way back, after a minor squabble between them over who would be Hillary and who would be Sherpa Tenzing, they embarked into a world of imagination. Rushing in from the car, they gave their father an exhaustive list of the kit that the three of them had speculated about requiring. Graeme teased them that at best they would probably just have their fingers drop off from frostbite, or be crushed in an avalanche, or even drop into a crevasse never to be seen again. But their enthusiasm was never dampened. However, he made amends by taking them all on a weekend's camping, the deluge and the midges on the West Coast of Scotland making her wish she had taken them to see the lecture in the Hall about one man's culinary journal from the Amalfi Coast to Rome. Graeme did not make it any easier by informing them that 40,000 midges will go for an uncovered arm in an hour, which he and the children found a great fact, especially as the three of them were immune. After hitting their teenage years their interest in going to the festival came second to things that were decidedly more 'cool'. But even up until they went to university they loved their holidays, where they camped in Snowdonia or went skiing in France, Izzy taking up Munro-bagging with a Scottish friend from sixth form.

Both she and Graeme loved theatre, so the Everyman in Cheltenham and having the RSC down the road was a bonus. Every Christmas when the children were younger she would take them to the pantomime. Later, when they were older, and with their friends or at an after-school club, about once a month she alone had taken to getting a ticket for the matinee performance, not giving a thought to anything beyond the closed doors behind her. A visiting company would present their latest play, in whose story she could become lost, watching actors following in the footsteps of the enchanting Lillie Langtry who captivated audiences a hundred years before, or the mellifluous recitations of Richard Burton who seduced audiences to another world. On her worst days when she just needed to get out of the house, she could sit through an entire performance and barely take in a thing. It was just the comfort of not having to be anywhere else and no one making demands of her. Her favourite escape was going to see a film at the Guildhall in Gloucester. It was something she had done since she was a teenager. Then it was going to see bands with her friends, which had usually ended up with them staying out until morning, the subsequent week of being grounded being an easy price to pay. Over twenty years later the ear-bleeding gigs swapped for a lazy afternoon film. Many of them she wouldn't get Graeme to sit through, and she didn't tell him that she went. When he would come home asking about what was for dinner, or reminding her that they had to be somewhere, or telling her about the day he had had, she was thinking of the film.

CHAPTER 4

GRAEME GREETED HER at the door of his practice. 'You look fantastic.' He kissed her on the cheek. 'Is that a new dress?'

'Don't worry,' She smiled. 'It wasn't expensive. It's one of Chloe's.'

'Even if it was, you deserve it. Gorgeous girl. Now, I promise you, this is going to be short and sweet.'

'It's the end of an era. You should enjoy it.'

'Hmm. No, I think short and sweet will be just fine,' he joked as he held out an arm for her to take.

For the most part, Sarah avoided going to Graeme's office. The last time she had been there was a few months before when they were celebrating taking on a new junior partner to the team. It had been a growing practice since he decided to join forces with another psychiatrist that he had known for several years. Not long after that he had taken on another partner, Jane, who, he had told Sarah, was to bring some fresh energy. Although he conceded that roughly translated as needing more money for extending their premises into another floor of the townhouse, which he knew was going to be up for rent. Then in an act of compromise, and anticipation of maximising their revenue, he agreed with Jane to take on two further psychotherapists, providing complementary treatment for their patients who required it.

Jane wasn't what Sarah had anticipated Graeme would have taken on as a partner. But, as he first described to Sarah, he saw her as a 'safe pair of hands' after learning from a couple of earlier unsuccessful attempts to expand his practice, his first partner ending up in rehab for self-medicating as a case in point. To all intents and purposes he and Jane had a comfortable and functional working relationship. Sarah had always had friendly exchanges with her on the times they had met. From Graeme, compliments about her were rare, but he said he respected her professionalism. Her officious nature in dotting every 'i', he told Sarah, meant that he didn't have to worry about a repeat of his first partner. She had brought in many new clients. That was at first enough to bridge their differences, such as her 'fluffy kittens' approach, which he had increasingly berated, having a disdainful view of her looping calligraphic platitudes and 'bumper sticker' inspiration.

The new changes for Jane's model of a twenty-first-century ideal of delivering holistic care soon came to be at odds with Graeme's comfort zone of straightforward clinical delivery. Then further suggestions driven by Jane, of trying to make the aesthetic environment more 'patient friendly', convinced the other practitioners, aside from Graeme, to adopt them. The new approach, which he derided as more of a 'hold hands retreat' than clinical, became a clash that had been one of the factors in his decision to leave the practice.

The new additions included a row of fluffy cushions and a gently flowing central water feature, which, as she recalled from last time during a long wait while Graeme was over-running with a patient, only served to prompt a visit to the bathroom. A wooden sign hung over the door, inscribed, 'Sharing is Caring'. How things had changed. As much as she thought that Graeme had a point, it was a world away from her first experience of a psychiatrist's office. And though being subject to what Graeme described as 'the assault of the cinnamon candles', it wasn't colourless and austere.

However, despite his and Jane's differences, the practice flourished, and so it came as a surprise to Sarah when he came back early one afternoon and told her about his intention, pending her approval, to accept a full-time army posting.

Now, as they entered the room, he leaned in towards her before they reached the people who were about to greet them. 'Two hours, tops. I promise. They want to present me with a gift. God knows what that will be if Jane chose it.'

'I told them that we could fit "Sharing is Caring" in the packing.' She winked at him as they began to greet people.

At his insistence, Graeme said that if they had to play any kind of music at work it should be classical, in view of the compromises that he had made to decoration, and it was non-negotiable. The early experiment of playing so-called inspirational tunes in reception had lasted for two hours and around one minute, and that was because Graeme had been on a call-out for two hours that morning. Fearing that one day he might come in to 'Wind Beneath My Wings', it had been agreed there would be no Bette, no Joni Mitchell, and anyone found in possession of any Vangelis would be put on notice. Chopin was playing gently in the background as they went over to the table to get a drink.

Jane came over to greet them. A half glass of champagne in one hand, she embraced Sarah. 'Good to see you! I hoped you would make it.'

'It's good to see you too.'

'Hmm. Started without me, then,' Graeme remarked coolly.

'I couldn't resist. Surely you know how much we are going to miss you.'

'My grief returned in equal measure.'

'So, cheers,' Sarah quickly followed up, raising her glass. 'To the end of an era. Any time you find yourself visiting Germany, Jane, please, you must drop by.'

'Not when I hear that you are next to the largest artillery ranges in North Germany. Seriously though, thank you for the invitation. It is appreciated.'

'Of course, Jane. You are always welcome,' Graeme responded flatly.

'Indeed.' Jane mirrored Graeme's disingenuous sentiment. 'Well, Sarah, I want to wish you the best of luck. Sorry to be so brief but I have to go and check on the caterers. If you would just excuse me.'

He leaned over to Sarah as she departed. 'Now I have a delightful fantasy of her wandering through an artillery range.'

'Now behave. You only have two, no, less than two hours. How you two have worked together for this long is nothing short of miraculous.'

An hour into the drinks Graeme was duly presented with his gift of the office photo, taken at a 'team-building day' a few months before – a golf outing at Wentworth, a pay-off for the next one planned, that of a zombie escape, for which Graeme made himself conspicuously absent at the last minute. It was a disappointment to the rest of the practice, as one of the primary motivations for going had been prompted by the look on Graeme's face when it topped the shortlist of suggestions. The golf photo, which was taken in front of the clubhouse, raised a smile to his face as he had won the gross prize that day. The other gift was a joke present of *Bette Midler's Greatest Hits* for his new office, which unexpectedly he seemed to take in good spirit.

Perhaps more in relief that the ordeal of the gift-giving had gone more smoothly than expected, he had another couple of glasses of champagne. No expense had been spared. One of the things that he and Jane had in common was a taste for the finer things. If there was a celebratory occasion to be had, they would do it properly. Every milestone in the success of the practice or additions or farewells had been the same.

Sarah had never fully enjoyed these functions and often found them laboured. Her decision to attend fewer came from one argument brought about after enduring a long dinner the previous year, during which one of the doctors gave an inordinately long-winded leaving speech full of double entendres and cryptic jokes about a couple of their regular patients, which most of the spouses missed, aside from his wife, who gave a barely disguised, knowing smile. During the time she and Graeme had been married, he disclosed very few details about his patients, a fact that she found frustrating when he would be called in the middle of the night. But she respected him for it.

Too late for her to avoid eye contact, Graeme's colleague Piers was heading her way with a bottle of champagne. 'Hello there.' Without prompt he topped up her glass. 'It's such a shame you are leaving. So are you going to miss us?'

'Thank you,' she responded as she took a sip of her drink, his obvious head start on the champagne clearly overriding the fact that they had only spoken on a couple of occasions. 'And thank you for your effort in the send-off.' She thought about saying that they would miss it but would have cringed at her own transparency.

As was usual at these events, Jane was making sure everything was going smoothly, directing the caterers, ensuring that invited guests were being hosted.

Sarah was grateful for Graeme's timely reappearance as he joined them. At the other end of the room, a distressed young woman came through the entrance, and was quickly intercepted by Jane who attempted to placate her. The room quieted down as she was becoming increasingly audible. Even the inebriated Piers glanced over. In a successful move, Jane encouraged the girl into her office. Graeme effected indifference to the disturbance as he gave Sarah a look which she understood as his intention to rescue her from Piers.

'Graeme! Nice speech, mate.' Piers broke the quiet as the conversation in the room gradually resumed.

'Hmm. Thanks. So tell me, how are you and Barbara getting on?' Graeme was making an effort to engage whilst keeping an eye on what was going on, discernible by the fact that he hadn't reacted to being called 'mate', one of his pet hates.

'Oh, good, yes thanks. She sends on her best wishes.' Piers looked over again as the door to Jane's office closed. 'Perhaps I had better go and help, we don't want one of the balloons souring the evening. It is your leaving do, after all.' Then, in a conscious act of gathering himself to present a sober and professional front, he placed down his glass and subtly checked his tie.

'I would just leave her. Jane will have this in hand,' Graeme responded.

'It isn't a problem. I insist.' He gave Graeme a strong pat on the back in a tactile and demonstrative gesture that Sarah knew he would like even less than being called 'mate', her husband's tolerance of which made Sarah smile.

'Goodness. You must be demob happy,' she laughed as Piers made his way to Jane's office.

Graeme turned his attention back to Sarah. 'Prat. Someone I won't miss,' he responded irritably. 'Now, more importantly, I hope you are looking forward to dinner. I've booked a table at that place that has just been renovated.' She looked over at Piers closing Jane's office door behind him.

'Who is she, the young girl?'

'Just one of the frequent fliers. One of Jane's highly strung students. Probably thinks that we are under-prescribing. It will be fine. Jane will just have to call her boyfriend and he will pick her up. She's a nice kid. So, anyway, I've heard all good things about this place. A new Michelin-starred chef, apparently.'

'You already told me that this morning.' She looked at him quizzically. 'I think you have been working too many hours recently. I hope she's alright.'

'Trust me, she is in good hands. Now, as I was saying, I have looked at the menu, you will love it. Great reviews.' He briefly hesitated as he saw Jane's door open. 'Even that pompous foodie from one of the broadsheets gave it four or five stars. I've forgotten his name.' He faltered as he noticed Piers re-emerge. 'You will love it.'

'You said. Are you sure you are OK? I understand this will be difficult. Letting go of this place. Perhaps the reality of all this coming to an end is really sinking in.'

'You know me, a slave to my emotions.' He smiled. 'Look, I think we should make our excuses to the others.' He glanced at his watch. 'We don't need to drag this out.' He saw Piers approaching, his previous jovial state having turned to a disgruntled expression.

'If that's what you want. You won't find any argument here,' Sarah replied, relieved at the cue.

'I appreciate it, you know. Everything that you have done… do… for me, for us. We have so much to look forward to. I love you. You know that.'

'Are you sure you are OK?'

Before he could answer, Piers rejoined them, immediately interrupting. 'Sorry about this. But you are required after all.' His frustration was evident. 'Jane's trying to calm her down. I know it's your last day but she is asking if you will help. The girl is threatening to shout the bloody place down. Anyway, apparently your assistance would be grounded with greater "clarity". I mean, the girl probably doesn't know what day of the week it is, never mind noticing my couple of glasses.'

'Sorry, Sarah.' Graeme leaned over and kissed her on the cheek. 'I think that I should go through.'

'That's fine. You need to go.'

'Rather him than me,' Piers began. 'Personally, I would just give her a shot of Haldol. Boom.' He clicked his fingers. 'Out like a light. Pillow, trolley. Sorted for a few hours. Save a lot of time and energy.'

'Seriously, you…'

He winked at her.

'Alright, yes, very funny.'

'Your chap. He will be a loss. Cases like this. Wayward delinquents. He makes anything like Robert Redford and a horse pale into insignificance.' He took another drink of champagne. 'I've seen him talk down more than most. Perhaps he's had enough of all that and that's why he is leaving us. Going full-time into the army. That we didn't see coming.'

'It's a new challenge. We're looking forward to it.' Sarah didn't respond to his enquiring intonation.

'And you? What about you? The officers' wives. We've had a couple of those on our books.' He rolled his eyes. 'One of them, well, almost came completely off her perch. After twenty years of doilies and the back of beyond, I can see why. Not that it will be like that for you… It's all a matter of…'

She interrupted him. 'So the office looks nice. You must have been on the committee that approved these cushions.' She picked up one behind her, wafting the peripheral feathers in mockery.

Her comment sparked a monologue about the unwelcome changes that had been made. Mostly about Jane's over-zealous approach to fabrics, and it being a wasted exercise in indulging the self-pity of the therapy patients, in turn then sparking a critique of every revisionist approach to talking therapies.

The disturbance gone, the drinks got back into full swing, aside from Franny, the receptionist, who she could see was also glancing over occasionally to look for signs of movement from Jane's office. Piers had now turned his attention to current affairs. The economy, with his forecast for higher taxes and the solution for benefit scroungers, then focused his diatribe on the Chancellor for being a fatuous twat who couldn't manage a budget for a fasting Buddhist.

From across the room, she saw a young man come through the entrance. He was met by Jane, who Sarah had missed leaving her office. The girl soon emerged from the room, considerably calmer. After what appeared to be her boyfriend put his jacket around her, she turned to look around the reception. She hesitated as she saw Sarah looking at her, at which Sarah quickly looked elsewhere, embarrassed that she had been caught in her curiosity.

While she made her excuses to go to Graeme, she left Piers, who soon attached himself to a group behind who were engaged in a boisterous exchange. The sight of the girl made her think of the times she had frantically had to call her own therapist, Tom, not wanting to entertain the thought that she been subject to some anecdotes by his colleagues. She understood Graeme's black humour. It was part of dealing with the stresses of the job. Not in a million years would she have wanted to be privy to what might have been said behind her back. Even ten years later she preferred to block out an occasion where she had turned up unannounced at Tom's office, tea and reassurance being offered by the receptionist as she waited for a chance to see him. The young woman had taken twenty minutes to calm her down whilst he had been on an emergency call-out. Beside herself, barely able to breathe, she hadn't cared about how it looked until she went for her appointment the next week, the young woman treating her with kid gloves. As she had previously informed

Sarah on her first appearance at the practice, this was her first job after college. Her desk was neat and tidy, a tiny framed picture of a young baby next to the phone, which looked as if it was half turned for people to catch a glimpse of. The young receptionist's confident demeanour and calm disposition made Sarah uncomfortable on her worst days. For all the help that she had received, there was an instinctive slight unease at her visits there, most acutely felt when being sympathetically ushered into the room by a girl who would be now only a few years older than her own daughter. Only a few miles down the road at home, she was the provider, the nurturer.

As Sarah made her way to Jane's office, she was intercepted by one of the therapists who wanted to wish her well, finishing with a couple of sentences in German which she couldn't understand. The language course seemingly evaporated, bar one sentence, prompted by the visualisation of a penguin complete with krill. The therapist and her husband, not knowing what to make of it, gave an awkward laugh, then offered her a language course they had at home, 'so long as she still had a tape recorder'. One of the younger people in the group began mocking them, asking if it was stored with the VHS collection. The ensuing inter-generational counter-mocking gave Sarah an opportune moment to take her leave, thankful that Graeme was just as eager to avoid what would most likely descend into drunken 'we'll miss you's and commitments to visit that would never be kept. The table was booked for 8 p.m. Looking at her watch it was only a few minutes to.

In a move to remind Graeme of the time, she walked towards Jane's office.

She opened the door to find he and Jane were arguing. The confrontation ceased immediately. Graeme's tie loosened, his anger thinly veiled, avoiding immediate eye contact, he tried to effect composure as Jane said nothing.

'What is it, Sarah?' Graeme snapped. 'Can't you knock?'

'Knock!' she retorted incredulously, taken aback by his outburst. 'Why should I knock? What's going on?'

Jane gathered up her bag and keys. 'It's nothing, Sarah. Just work.' She turned to Graeme. 'Ask Franny to lock the door before she leaves.'

'No, wait, Jane.' Sarah urged her to stay.

'I'm sorry, I have to go. I have to go to a call-out. Really, Sarah, it's just been a long day. It's been resolved.'

As the door closed Graeme quickly talked over what would be her inevitable questioning. 'It's nothing. Just a minor issue. There is a discrepancy in the books. I should have told you. What with the move. Everything that was happening. I needed a little extra money for some additional expenses. It was just £5,000, for heaven's sake.'

'You took money from the practice?! Why on earth would you do that? We don't need money. What about the payment from the army for moving?'

'The "disturbance allowance". Seriously, that doesn't come anywhere near to covering everything. You know everything, all the investments we have are tied up long-term. Which was your idea. I'm just saying...'

'No. Absolutely no way. This is not on me. Oh my God, Graeme. What were you thinking? That's fraud. No, it's theft!'

'Don't be so dramatic. I told her about it. She was OK. It's just the bill for this damned refurbishment has come in. I just took a little more than I needed. I didn't tell you. But it was one thing after another. The car we sold. Well, the gearbox went. I had to refund them, then I had a few bits of kit... Look, I didn't want to worry you. It's in hand. She's deflecting because the cost ran over.'

'Why didn't you tell me? I don't understand. I have the money from the shop.'

'I'm sorry. I should have given you more credit.'

'This is so unlike you. You know how I feel about things like this. Jesus, Graeme, I thought there was something seriously wrong. Let's just get this over with and go.'

They returned to the drinks, Graeme not breaking stride as he wrapped up his farewells before they left for dinner, during which he reassured her that it was more of a miscalculation. He had taken his eye off the ball. Then, after they got home, when she brought it back to the subject, he told her there was nothing else to it and to call Jane if she needed to. If it would put her mind at rest, then she should do it. There would be no issue, no comeback about the money. The matter had been settled.

Unable to let it rest, she later confronted his incredulous unwillingness to share her embarrassment and was frustrated at him making a joke of what was a considerable sum, saying it wasn't like him. Then, he brought up the matter of the money she had insisted on sending to Seb, a new computer for Izzy, new items for Germany, the new suit that he didn't even need for his new job and the two nights away in London to see *Les Mis*, which, in all honesty, she could have spared him. Their final words on the matter were that he was conscious of the stress the move was already putting on her. It was the first time since the news of the posting that he had directly addressed her depression. Something he had been ever vigilant to since they had been together.

Her paranoia was put to rest the next day when she went to retrieve a scarf which she told Graeme she thought she had left at the party. On the drive back she felt foolish for doubting him. Jane had said to her that she was angry about the money, but so long as it was paid back as they agreed, it was OK. Then, as she took her cue to leave, Jane sympathetically asked how she was doing, and reminded Sarah to look after herself. Before the inevitable polite rhetorical offer of any help if she needed it, she made her excuses and called Graeme to see if he wanted her to pick up anything for dinner. That night, as an end to the matter before they left for Germany, she told Graeme that she insisted she take money from the shop to give him to pay Jane. Even with that and a few other unforeseen expenditures in making the house right for the new tenants, it left her with a good amount to reinvest in perhaps a new venture when she came home.

CHAPTER 5

THE DAY OF the ball arrived. They had decided to make use of the time beforehand to continue with the preparation for the move. The process had been all-consuming and the idea of escaping boxes and itineraries was a blissful proposition. By the early afternoon they had achieved a sizeable chunk of their respective tasks. The last thing on the agenda was to tackle the loft.

'I don't want to be late getting ready.' Sarah hesitated as she prepared to scale the ladder up to the loft. 'Why we can't take a day off packing I don't know.'

'You'll thank me in a few days. You were the one that insisted on the loft. Anyway, just another hour or so, Mrs Hughes, and that's it. That leaves us with about two hours, which should be enough, even for you.'

'Ignoring you,' she said dryly.

He smacked her backside as she moved up the ladder. 'Christ, try to kill me why don't you,' she laughed. 'Onwards and upwards.'

Surveying the loft space she contemplated the enormity of the undertaking ahead. She put on her headphones, a compilation of music thrown together that morning to distract from the task. The air was musty in the enclosed space, which she found a little claustrophobic. Making her way cautiously through the beams she looked for a place to start. She began with the furthest point away from where the toughest decisions were to be made. Stacked around her was a testament to fifteen years of memories, keepsakes and a damning indictment to the knee-jerk, and ultimately superfluous, purchases, a point immediately brought home when she tripped over an ab-toner that was half concealed in a thick run of fiberglass, one object in a miscellaneous hoard, including boxes of books, old toys, sports kit. There was a tennis racquet that would probably last about three return shots before giving way, but it was one she had at school. As was the hockey stick, leaning against various gym contraptions that had had about three uses. Next to those, a rowing machine with a cumulative distance of around 5 km, which had been thrashed out when they bought it ten years ago.

Everything had to be sorted for storage, as new tenants were moving in for the time they were away. There were things that she knew she wouldn't win the battle to keep, as she was under strict instructions to carry out a significant cull. Committing to this promise the previous night in a hypothetical sense, over a bottle of wine, it had been easier than the reality. She decided that a good start would be the rowing machine, which hardly had good memories. A £500 purchase that had had the initial novelty factor and a 2 lb weight loss was outweighed by £400 in chiropractors' fees and two weeks of excruciating pain. A red sticker signifying charity was placed on the seat. The same with a tape deck, food processor, DVD player and an old games console that belonged to the children and she knew wouldn't be missed. She picked out one of the games.

It brought back fond memories of the constant battle for supremacy between Seb and Izzy one Christmas. Only a few months ago Seb had been laughing in recollection of the memory of their old consoles. Apparently, it was prehistoric and had less than the memory of one of his thumb drives.

At the other end, which she had been avoiding, was the box that had belonged to her son Ben. Set aside from the other belongings, it sat concealed by other possessions, which had been subsequently stacked in front of it over the years. She placed the pad down on one of the other boxes. Carefully, she began taking away the barriers in front, feeling her stomach churn as she caught a glimpse of it. On the surface it was an ordinary plastic tub, with a set of dinosaur stickers adorning the top, slightly worn, in the same condition as it had been when she first sealed it. Graeme hadn't noticed it in the move, and although it was the first time she had seen it in years, it had been there if she needed it.

Sarah sat beside it, slowly unsealing the lid, which caused a thin layer of dust particles to be released into the air. Neatly packed inside were an array of her son's possessions. What had been his favourite toys, that for years she had secreted away, rescued from the suggestion she had resisted from others for it to be a part of a cathartic moving-on process after his funeral.

It had been over five years since she had opened the box, at which time there had been no connection to the joy he had in his life, but it had been too difficult to part with it. In the chill and damp atmosphere, all she could think of was the life that could have been. How he was taken from them. Going back to the day of the accident fifteen years before. These toys were not as they were to him, as they had been packed away, stored like artefacts. She picked up each one with slow deliberation, recalling happier times when they had been thrown around the house, enjoyed, battered, as he was indulging in adventurous possibility. Then she uncovered the most important item: his favourite, a transformer, which she had cursed more than once for tripping over it. A toy that had been lost and, in a great show of relieved emotion, found and rescued from a muddy outside expedition. As his favourite, it was the last thing that he held onto. She carefully placed it down. At the bottom lay the last two possessions: a jacket and a woolly hat that had belonged to him. She lifted the soft quilting to her face. It was cold and musty but she still was able to pick up the faintest of scents. The smell brought him in a rush suddenly closer, more acutely, as if he was there.

Overwhelmed, she pressed it to her face to muffle her sobs, aware that Graeme was only a short distance away. She sat there for a few minutes alone, as regrets resurfaced and what-ifs induced a suffocating grip on her senses. Pulling her knees into her chest, she struggled with the recollections flooding back. There were no photos downstairs aside from a couple of albums kept in a drawer. A five-year gap had no representation. It was Graeme's way of dealing with things. Not long after his funeral, every picture had been taken down and soon after that the house was on the market. Everything went, aside from this box. The children kept one item belonging to their brother, then began a systematic process of closure initiated by Graeme. The move to the house was defined as a new start. Every stroke of a brush, wallpaper sheet hung, tile precisely placed.

She then heard Graeme on his way up. She quickly wiped her face, placing the items hastily in the box, trying to push down a lid that was stopped by the rearranged contents. Quickly standing up, she moved to busy herself restacking some nearby boxes.

'Hey, I was just on my way down.' She spoke loudly to try and negate the tremble in her voice. 'No need to come up.'

'I'm here now.' He noticed that she had been crying. 'Don't tell me you are getting sentimental about this junk.'

'You know what I'm like about hoarding.' She avoided making eye contact.

As she moved he caught sight of the box. 'What's that?'

'It's nothing. An old box.' She felt guilty, as if she had been caught.

A look of recognition came over his face. 'Oh. I see,' he said placidly. 'I thought we dealt with everything.'

'Dealt with?' she snapped angrily at his matter-of-fact response.

'Come on, Sarah. Don't be obtuse. You know what I mean.'

'Why is it so difficult for you to understand?'

'You aren't the only one that misses him. He was my son too.' He hesitated. 'But we had to move on.'

She looked up at him as he waited for her to say something. Instead she returned to gather the box. Taking the lid off she carefully began to replace the items as she found them in the box.

'So what do you plan to do?' he said calmly.

Initially ignoring him she carefully placed the lid back on. But she could see that he was waiting. It would be like before. He wouldn't let it rest until the issue had been settled. 'I don't know. Perhaps leave it with your mum.'

'You know that will upset her. Why don't we just let these things go? He is always in our memories.'

She turned to look at him. 'It's good to hear that you do actually think of him from time to time.'

'You knew I was coming up with a cup of tea. Have you considered that this is some sort of cry for help, abstaining from responsibility about making a decision? Do you want me to take care of it for you, is that it?'

'Stop,' she snapped. 'Just shut up. For Christ's sake will you stop being a fucking shrink for just five minutes.'

'He isn't coming back. You should deal with it. This isn't healthy,' he continued, as he could see that she wasn't responsive. 'You have to be realistic.'

'I'm not you.'

'It's been fifteen years, Sarah.' He handed her the mug of tea, gently touching her hand. 'I understand. Now come on. Let me take it.'

She quickly intervened. 'Don't touch it. I will sort it out. Go downstairs. I'll finish the rest of the stuff up here.' She wiped her face again. 'I'm fine.'

'Alright. But I'm here if you need me. Just talk to me. Don't make yourself ill again. I'm just trying to look after you, that's all.' He leaned over to tentatively kiss her on the cheek but she pulled away.

'I'll be down in a while. Let me finish this.' Tears once again began to well in her eyes.

'Put that down and come with me. Take a break. Just for a few minutes. Seriously. Just follow me.' Graeme didn't wait for her response as he made his way down the ladder.

At first she resisted his request and instead sat down on one of the boxes. After a couple of minutes of hearing him moving around in the kitchen, she heard the back door open and close. The house fell silent as she took a long look at the stacks piled from beam to roof. Aside from the box, inherited belongings from her parents and the things they kept from Izzy and Seb, she suddenly had an overwhelming urge to be rid of everything else that surrounded her. The superficial junk crammed in stacks to which she professed a sentimental attachment, which had been far exaggerated since their previous use. Abandoning the task, if not to see Graeme, just to get some air, she made her way downstairs. Taking a drink from a half glass of water she had previously left there, she could see Graeme in the garden.

Sarah leaned through the door. 'What are you doing? It is freezing out here.'

'Just get your coat on and stop whining. I want to show you something.'

45

'This had better be worth it.' Donning a coat and scarf from the back of the kitchen door, she went out to meet him, wearily anticipating that a diversion was about to be introduced, one of half a dozen that he had used to deflect from having to talk about the time of losing Ben and how she had to move on. Swearing that if the theme was going to be new horizons, or possibilities were given air, she wouldn't be responsible for her actions.

Pulling in her coat tightly, she walked over to Graeme, who was making his way down to the end of the garden.

'Where are we going? It's freezing. Can't we do this over a tea at least in the kitchen?'

'Stop moaning.' He came to a standstill waiting for her to join him. 'What do you see at the end of the garden?'

'Oh for heaven's sake…' Stopping mid-sentence, she turned about to go back into the house. 'I knew it. No, actually, this one I'm not sure what metaphor this is going to be but, come on…'

'You don't even know what I am going to say. What have you got to lose? Are you going to feel any better going back in there?'

'OK. Fine,' she snapped impatiently. 'What do I see? The garden. The gate at the end, next door's cat, probably wondering what the hell we are doing.'

'Start with the gate. Do you remember when you first saw this place? You came to do a recce because you couldn't wait for the appointment with the estate agent the following week. How he was a busy man and she had to patient. The old lady needed his guidance.'

'Twerp.' She smiled. 'Yes, waxing lyrical about the wide-eyed wonder of its potential.'

'You recall what he said about that decrepit Aga? What a wonderful kitchen for the lady of the house to bake to her heart's content, telling me, "They are the must have."'

'And you said, "If the carbon monoxide doesn't kill her first." But seriously, the place was a complete mess. Poor old girl. There was no way she could have managed that.'

'And the gate was nearly rotten. The beds and the lawn were overgrown. I don't think she had anyone except that parasitic nephew.'

'Funny how he was able to be round in a moment's notice when we wanted to discuss terms. I often wonder how she was after that.'

'She was fine once she settled into the home. I said she would be.'

'You never told me that. How did you know?' Sarah responded in surprise.

'I had a call-out to the care home. I stopped and had a chat with her. You must be getting old, darling. I came back and told you. She told me it was a relief and she looked as if a weight had been lifted.'

'How do I not remember that? But then again, I wasn't in the best place.'

'This is what I'm trying to get you to realise.' He took her by the hands. 'You were a shell when we lost Ben. I barely slept, I was checking on you, always. I was so frightened I was going to lose you.'

'And then I left.' She broke away. 'Why are we going over this again? I'm sorry. I know what I put you through. I don't want to go back there, Graeme.'

'No, stop. I didn't say it because I want to rake up the bad things. When you came back and we put things back together, we found this place. When you stood at that back gate, you said that if, just if we were to move, that it should be here. It was the first positive thing that you did since losing Ben. The first real hope I got from you that I saw a future for us.'

'You didn't give me much of a chance to think about it.'

'If we had stayed in our old house we would never have moved on. We wouldn't be together now.' He gently retook her by the hand. 'I understand. But, how you were up there, just now, it took me right back. You as a shell, all consumed by his

47

memory. Ben isn't that box. He is with us. Always. Who ran us ragged, loved life, loved us, his brother, his little sister. You were a great mother to him. He adored you. Nothing you did or could have done would have kept him with us.'

'Enough.' Sarah's voice trembled. 'Please don't.'

'Listen to me, those things up there aren't Ben. The life he brought to them was in him. I don't need photos or old toys. I have the memories inside. We just cope in our own way.'

'You held it together for Seb, for all of us. I know.'

'That isn't what I brought you out here for. I've got something for you. Well, of sorts.' He smiled. 'All those years ago, when you stood at that gate you could have walked away, given in. But you didn't, you created a home for me, for Seb and Izzy. Think of the times we had here, because you made it so. This will always be here for us. Our home. There is something else. Yes, wait for it…'

She raised a smile at his attempt to lift her mood. 'Let's hear it then.'

'I have enlisted a gardener. He is a member of RHS and has even won accolades at the Chelsea Flower Show, no less.'

'Seriously, what…'

'You have a meeting with him next week. Whatever your instructions, he will work to that. Comes highly recommended, good bloke all round apparently, but anyway. There. What do you think?'

'No way. You are joking.'

'On my life. It was supposed to be a surprise. Not just that. He has said that he will give you regular updates, and Skype if you want to know how things are going. He won't change anything without expressly asking first, and give you a tour when you want to remind yourself of the garden that you will be coming back to.'

'I can't believe this. How did you meet him and what about the tenants?'

'He's Franny's brother. The upside of having someone in the office that leaves nothing of her personal life to find out. The tenants? Delighted. Who wouldn't be?'

She put her arms around him. 'I can't believe you did that. Thank you, wow. I don't know what to say.'

'I would do anything to keep you happy, you know that. Look at me. I love you more than any job, above all else. Any time you want to come back here, I will hand in my papers. We keep looking forward.' He put his arms around her and kissed her. 'Just remember the good times. I've heard you and Seb laughing about the times he and Ben had together. That is how to honour him.'

'You rarely joined in, you know, when Seb asked about Ben. Before you say anything, I understand, I wish you felt differently but anyway.'

'So what are you going to do?'

'What do you mean?' She gave him a quizzical look.

'With the garden? You know, with your own personal Monty Don. I thought another bed of chrysanthemums.'

'Did you now. You haven't planted a bulb in about ten years.'

'I know. This is what I mean about more time for us. We had a good time putting this together. In Germany, we will have more time for each other.'

'Hmm. All that time off and those possibilities?' She smiled. 'Don't say any more. What you have done is amazing. Thank you.'

'Anything you need I am here for you. You gave me this life, my children. I've loved you since the first time I saw you. It doesn't mean anything without...'

'Alright,' she interrupted. 'You really have to stop there. I'm fine, I'll be fine. You're right, I know. We should look forward. But let's just leave it at that for now.'

CHAPTER 6

ARRIVING AT THE officers' mess, the revellers were steadily making their way through the entrance. The flurry of activity that Sarah had engaged herself in since she had found the box had come to a halt in the cold evening. It was a relief to have escaped the suffocating confines of the unsettled house. She now even embraced the freshness of the sharp frosty air. For everything that Graeme had done from the minute she had taken off the lid of the box she had felt burdened by her frustration at not knowing what to do with it. Dealing with emotions that had taken her aback with their intensity, realising that she wasn't prepared for them. The things that had given Ben such joy were now, as Graeme had told her, just morbid hooks to something that was shattered. Graeme's offer to take responsibility replayed in her head. Any creeping temptation to give in to this was quickly dispelled. It was all she had left of him.

Graeme took her arm as they approached the door. 'I know that was tough for you today,' he whispered. 'Now try and enjoy yourself this evening.'

Sarah squeezed his hand in recognition. 'I will. Thank you.'

Around them elegantly dressed guests chatted as they prepared to present their tickets. In front of them a lady pulled her shawl a little tighter against the chill whilst her partner grumbled an utterance about the hold-up. A number had chosen the option of fancy dress in the theme of the Titanic, who were, as usual, more extrovert in their behaviour than most. One of the men was attired in black tie, with seaweed hanging from his shoulders and wearing a white homemade period lifejacket. He was engaging with those around him who were complimenting or sending up his efforts. One person, who he seemed to know well, placed a wager that given an hour under the lights and in a packed room, that was surely to be a short-lived prop.

A fire juggler had been positioned nearby to entertain the arriving guests, a warm and exuberant welcome on a cold December evening, designed to offer a taste of the long night of festivities ahead. He drew appreciation from the guests as the flaming batons were tossed with precision high into the air. The bright flames ripping bursts of light through the backdrop of the dark skies.

As Sarah and Graeme made their way down the corridor, the lively hum of conversation drew closer. The cavernous hallway to the anteroom was lined with military paintings. Vast canvases in ageing gilt frames depicted battle scenes fought throughout the centuries. A fierce cavalry charge that she had observed during her first visit was from Waterloo. Then, as they progressed further, muskets were replaced by machine guns, horses by tanks. It was a place that she knew well from dinners and events since Graeme had joined. However, it still felt like an alien environment to her.

The community to her seemed tight. Although made welcome, it appeared that everyone knew everyone else, which most did. To Sarah, they were undertaking a well-versed routine, in harmony to the same refrain. She didn't notice many awkward or faltering exchanges. She had once put it to Graeme that if a person was picked up from one end of the room and dropped into the other to converse with a relative stranger, the same metronomic discourse would commence. Or her exact words were: 'It's like a string is being pulled in their back.' The only prerequisite was to ascertain with whom you were talking. Then the appropriately pitched narrative could begin. Everyone knew their place. Like sections of an orchestra. For the serving members, senior ranks occupied the key positions. The CO commanding the baton, the 2IC taking their place at first violin. Most others in the pit aspiring to be noticed, and waiting to be afforded the responsibility of being given a solo. Others content to underpin the score such as the older reliable second or third seats, where they could efficiently see out the concert, just longing for the post-performance drinks. As for the young members of percussion, they weren't really noticed until one member became errant and banged the cymbals loudly and out of time. Then, finally, the wives who were made busy setting up the chairs and stands, and provided the sheet music to hum along to, were graciously presented with flowers as the audience left the room.

The functions that she had attended did nothing to abate this view. She considered herself as a johnny-come-lately to a party, as if wearing the wrong thing and having brought the wrong dish. At best she was the party kitchen dweller. These reservations that she shared with Graeme were only rebuffed by telling her that she hadn't given it a real go.

Aside from making friends with Rich and Nikki, she had made few other acquaintances in the mess, which was another reason why she mostly dreaded these functions. With the demands of her work and running the home, she barely saw enough of her long-established friends, which she had made during their time in Cheltenham. In an attempt to reassure her, Nikki had told her that she wasn't missing anything and it was a clique she was better off out of.

They were greeted at the door with a choice of drinks. Neatly presented on a pristine linen-covered reception table were rows of gin and tonic, red or white wine, champagne, or orange juice for those not partaking. The room was decked out with Christmas decorations and the Titanic theme – an idea conceived from one of the young subalterns, which was then approved by the committee. The previous day the same committee worked to put it together, along with an army of wives eager to impress with their efforts. Not quite the same opulence of the liner but a decent effort nevertheless. The intent was if they couldn't replicate it to the same grade, go for tongue-in-cheek nautical naff. The consensus all round was that it delivered: lifebuoys from the garrison pool hanging on the walls, crafted portholes with high waterlines, oars from the rowing club crossed above the door and the string quartet seated on stacks of old leather trunks. To complete the atmosphere, a light blue light filter in the chandeliers. The idea of suspending mannequins from gym ropes was seen by the CO as 'over-egging it' and they would offer too much temptation for the raucous young subalterns in the early hours.

Graeme introduced Sarah to one of his colleagues who they had first bumped into in the dining room. She warmly exchanged pleasantries, which were repeated as she was introduced to the other people in the group. Their names went in and out of one ear as she made all the polite overtones, including praising the set-up of the ball, unlike Graeme who stated that it looked cheap and just the sort of tacky rubbish he expected from the current committee, who turned every one of their endeavours into a 'bloody cake and arse party'.

A welcome intervention came in the form of a young waitress who approached them with a tray of drinks, from which Sarah took an inviting glass of champagne. Graeme gave her a familiar look, a suggestive glance she knew translated as 'For God's sake, don't have too much.' His encouragement for her to take one of the tasty canapés further translated as 'especially not on an empty stomach'. He had already displayed his disapproval at the double gin and tonic that she had finished at twice the normal pace. She hovered over the canapés then politely declined, raising an eyebrow mischievously at her husband who failed to disguise his irritation. A woman next to her deliberated over the pastries then made her selection. As she did, the waiter gave an answer to her enquiry that they were cheddar beignets. Declining the complementing chilli dip, she gently put it to her mouth, discretely placing her other hand underneath in the event of the possible debris. Graeme, who had previously been in mid-flow of conversation with one of the other officers about the disgraceful diminishing pay allowances, took the nearest one, dispatched it in one go, then swiftly regained his thread. The events of the day had preoccupied her since she first opened the box, their voices filtered out as she mulled over recollections, the smallest items that she had forgotten she had packed in there.

The sight of a room full of mostly strangers, or at best acquaintances, made her consider if this was going to be a significant part of her life once they reached Germany. Nikki had already warned her that it was something of an isolated posting. But Graeme allayed her fears by saying that Nikki was confusing it with a camp fifty miles away. This location, according to him, was a darling, idyllic town that would mean they had more time to spend with each other. The job, he said, was a pipe and slippers posting that he apparently could do with his eyes shut. They could travel and perhaps rent a ski lodge for a few holidays in the winter. She suddenly broke away from her thoughts when one of Graeme's colleagues made a polite enquiry as to how many children she had, her inattentiveness making her stumble a little on her answer. Sarah's hesitation was noticed by Graeme, who made a joke about it being a long day because of the packing, her mind too easily able to wander in the face of the ubiquitous practice of the standard enquiries made to wives. In her limited experience so far they consisted of how many children did she have, how was the shopping – assuming that she was on a posting – and then frequently being given a patronising expression of sympathy for being married to a soldier, as if she was in need of a boosting validation of the 'important role' she was playing.

As a couple broke from the group, Sarah gave Graeme a subtle cue to go through by suggesting that they had better check the seating plan. The dining room maintained the continuity of the Titanic theme. The tables were precisely set with the requisite silver and glassware. Polished candelabras and various pieces of silverware were catching the light from the overhead chandeliers. Similarly spaced along the table were finely sculpted military figurines of soldiers or horses, which, in keeping with mess tradition, adorned the tables of every dinner. The room was divided into specific areas, arranged in groups from first class to steerage. Even though it was just of nominal importance, she overheard a passing couple who sounded disconcerted that they weren't in first class.

Sarah was relieved to see Rich and Nikki at the back of the room. It was good to see a familiar face, as thirty minutes of offering superlatives, listening to military anecdotes and their work conversations from that week were wearing thin. Her concentration was flitting in and out, half a mind on when to pick up on when she should join in with the consensus or have to respond to a question. But she was in good company. The woman opposite spent much of the time looking around the room, and seizing one of the canapé waiters' attention every time they passed.

'Hey, Nikki! How are you? It's good to see you.'

'I'm fine. You look gorgeous!' she replied demonstrably, touching the sleeve of her dress.

'Thank you! Not so bad yourself, darling.'

'One of yours, I take it.'

'Absolutely. Well, I say that, it is one of Bridget's designs. It was only finished last week.' Sarah embraced the compliment, taking pride in her dress. It fitted her perfectly. The contoured, black, full-length gown, complemented by a pair of shoes Graeme had bought her a few months before, made her confident about surviving the night ahead. 'She is a bright talent that Bridget. Not sure how long we…' she hesitated, '… she, I mean, Chloe that is, will hold on to her. But, thank you for noticing. More than someone I know,' she replied jokingly, tipping a nod in the direction of Graeme. 'I'm not saying he wasn't attentive but he did say he had always liked this dress.'

'He's completely hopeless.'

They broke off as they watched a woman walk by dressed as a corpse. She was attired in a cool aqua sequined gown, her dishevelled hair pinned up, and wearing blue grey lipstick for authenticity. 'Now that is what I call style.' They laughed as the woman jokingly acknowledged their attention by pulling a deathly face.

'Now why didn't I think of that?' Nikki lamented. 'You would certainly be spared keeping up this appearance for eight hours.'

'I know. After the last one, my calves wouldn't flex for at least twenty-four hours. I did suggest as a joke going in fancy dress to Graeme. One of the stowaways in steerage. You should have heard him!'

'Yes, I can imagine how that went down.'

'I don't know how I kept a straight face. He told me I would either look ridiculous or it would be seen as some passive-aggressive gesture, given my aversion to blending in.' She rolled her eyes. 'It isn't as if I could feel more uncomfortable at these things.'

'Oh God. Going as a doomed passive-aggressive on a sinking ship. That would take some pulling off. So, anyway,' she changed the subject as Rich arrived with some drinks, 'tell me, how is the move going?'

Her momentary diversion dissipated. 'Don't ask.' She took another sip of champagne. 'I have never seen so much paperwork.'

'The first is always the most difficult. Don't worry, you will soon have it nailed down.'

'First? Ha! First and last. This is only for the short-term. After this we will be back to Cheltenham.'

Nikki laughed. 'So that's what he has told you.' Seeing her expression change she quickly followed up with, 'I'm joking. Come on, you know I'm joking.' There followed a slightly awkward pause before Nikki suggested looking for their table.

The dinner was a procession of courses greeted with mixed responses, from appreciation to criticism. The beef was too dry, the jus too rich. The man opposite closely peered into his dessert to emphasise its modest portion size, grumbling to anyone that would listen about 'damned jockey rations', as he had with every course. He proceeded to ask the harassed waiter if the chef thought any of them were riding in the 3.15 at Cheltenham the next day.

During the meal Graeme spent most of the time talking to the lady to his left. She couldn't really hear what they were saying against the backdrop of lively exchanges and the clatter of cutlery. For the rest of the time a young army dentist offered a range of anecdotes from his time in the service, delivered with the assumption that she had no issues with discussing extractions and the general state of the soldiers' teeth over the dishes. The final tale of a burst abscess made her place down her spoon in resignation, close to the end of her dessert, a hint which he took up on, and the conversation turned to enquiring about her husband's position in the army. Mercifully, for the time had come where it was permissible to leave the table. Having seen Sarah's discomfort for most of the evening, Nikki firmly led her away.

'Come on! You will enjoy this!' She took her by the hand and guided her across the room.

'Well it can't be any worse than hearing about the perils of neglected gingivitis.'

'Sorry, what?'

'Never mind. So, where are we going?'

At the far end a group of people were standing around a table, initially in attentive silence then emitting a mixture of groans, and a cheer spontaneously erupted. Sarah looked at her quizzically, still unable to see what was going on.

'It's roulette! Have you played much?' Nikki enthused.

'Roulette?' She stopped in her tracks. 'That's nice but not really me. I don't gamble.'

'Well, I know I won't get you to dance, so you leave me with little option. Come on. Just give it a go.' She gave a gentle tug on her arm. 'It's all very tame. It's just playing for a holiday. It isn't as if you are going to lose a fortune. Everyone is allocated a free set of chips.' She gave her arm another soft tug. 'The prize is a holiday in Greece,' she teased. 'You know how much you love the sun.'

'Alright, alright.' She looked over at Graeme who had stayed at the table talking to the woman he had been sitting next to.

"Oh, ignore him. She's another doctor. They will only be banging on about their credentials and their gift for saving us mortals,' Nikki mocked as they watched them in a serious exchange.

'You're right, I suppose. Nothing to lose.'

They acquired their chips and took a place at the table

where a couple had just left. At first Sarah was a little tentative. Nikki immediately jumped in with a healthy wager on red, as if to encourage her friend to take the plunge. Sarah watched a couple of spins in a quick study of the layout and options for placing her chips. Despite the cold outside, the stuffy atmosphere was intensified by the people closely gathered around the gaming table. The croupier overseeing proceedings was dressed in an immaculate white shirt, with a neatly tied bowtie, his slick ebony hair neatly combed to the side, a flawless reflection of the calm and orchestrated function of the process he was overseeing. Unaffected by the warm surrounds, he struck a contrast with many of the excitable revellers. Some of the men had removed their jackets. One lady, having taken off her silk gloves, had placed them neatly on the edge of the table. He coolly observed each play, monitoring where the chips were positioned, ensuring that none exceeded the time for placing their stake. When the ball was firmly set, he promptly began paying returns, and restacking the lost chips. When she was ready, Sarah wagered only four chips at a time on a colour, and four additional ones on dates. Graeme's and the children's birthdays.

Within half an hour Nikki had blown her chips and was following Sarah, who was also depleting her funds. The prize of the holiday that was being offered for the overall winner at cards and roulette was tantalisingly displayed on a large vibrant poster behind the croupier. An inviting vision of a Mediterranean idyll on the sun-soaked Greek island of Santorini. Blue azure church domes beside brilliant white houses looked out over the warm cerulean waters of the Aegean below. Lying beyond, the surrounding tranquil islands of the archipelago that stretched into the horizon. They had missed out on a summer holiday this year. A last-minute commitment for Graeme had meant that they had to cancel, with the promise to rebook as soon as he got back. However, with work and other engagements, and the shop experiencing a few issues, the promise never held.

Holding her last twelve chips she placed three of them on the usual and the last four split equally between 5 and 36. She picked up her purse ready to leave, light-heartedly bemoaning the fact that she had spent over an hour, only to stove in, announcing that she was better at cards as there was some skill in that. Hesitating to see it through to its conclusion she pessimistically took a last glance as the ball bounced to find its place.

'Red 5,' the croupier announced. 'Red number 5.'

'No way!' She placed her purse down again on the table. 'Ha! I'm a gambling genius!'

'Good girl!' Nikki whooped. 'Now do that again and I will be back with some more drinks. Oh and Rich's allocation.'

A sizeable pile of chips was gracefully slid over to Sarah, who had been waiting in anticipation of the scale of her win. She marvelled in the fact that such a victory could be achieved so quickly. There was almost triple what she had been haemorrhaging since she had taken her place. She beamed as she registered the envy of the man next to her. From nursing what she now considered a miniscule amount, this gave her a renewed energy.

Now speculating on the high of the previous win, she placed double her average bet, this time staking on which third of numbers would come up. Her first, the third 12. To her delight it won. Then the same amount on third 12. Another win. She joyfully stacked the chips, eager to place her next bet. She then placed double that amount on the first 12. Along with three additional counters on red 5. The wheel spun, her gaze fixed with anticipation. The ball came to rest. Second 12. The sight of the ball nestled in the wrong bed made her feel disappointment bordering on irritation.

In defiant perseverance, she gathered her thoughts as a

woman next to her reaped a substantial bet that she had on red. At the time the woman had taken her place next to Sarah, she had loudly bragged about her good night at cards. Her husband, looking the worse for wear, took a large sip of whisky before claiming the credit by way of his tips. This made Sarah more determined. It was her night, and not to be usurped by a person who was going to have a lucky couple of 'all-ins' at the end. Scanning the table she rapidly deliberated over the numbers. Should she go for thirds, colours, odd or even? The raucous, self-assured woman placed all her chips on red. This would have left Sarah just up if it came in. There was no chance in her just wagering a smaller amount on red to stay ahead. She had to focus on her game. In a gesture of confidence, the woman joked with Sarah that she should go with her choice, as she needed someone left to make it interesting. Initially, she gave a light-hearted response by giving her a conciliatory smile. The woman then responded with a wink, smiling at Sarah, making it obvious that she should know she was playing her.

Sarah took one look at the halcyon Mediterranean vision overhead, then made her choice. 'We'll see,' she announced. She placed all her chips on black, everything that she had been playing for all night on one spin of the wheel. The croupier evenly confirmed the bets as he set the wheel in motion. The man and the woman laughed as if she had taken the bait.

The players fixed all their attention on the two women and the competing towers of chips stacked next to each other, that in less than ten seconds would be heading in opposite directions. Proliferation or end game. The ball bounced along the slots. As it was at its end, momentum was urged or demands were whispered for it to stop. After clipping red 5, it landed dead in black 10. Sarah cried out in delight.

'I did it! Yes!' She was about to mock the woman next to her in an adrenaline- and champagne-fuelled reaction. But the woman, after a gasp of disappointment, congratulated Sarah, albeit begrudgingly, on her win. The response made her a little embarrassed as the people on the nearby card table and the immediate surrounds turned around to see what the fuss was. Most had gone all in with their chips on red, perhaps backing the woman with the implacable confidence. As such, there was almost immediately an exodus of people from the table.

At that point Nikki came back, exclaiming disbelief as she looked at the numerous chips that she had accumulated. 'Look at you! I don't know, I leave you for an hour.'

'An hour?! What time is it? You are kidding? It can't be that late.' She didn't confess that she had barely noticed her leave the table. She checked her watch. 'It's 3 a.m.! I've been here what…'

'Four hours! You seemed to be enjoying yourself so I left you to it.'

'Where's Graeme?'

'Oh there are a few of them that have spent most of the night at the bar. You must cash it in…' Nikki urged her, '… now! You should come and sit with a few of us.'

'I don't know.' She pointed up to the poster. 'I want to give myself every chance.'

The croupier, who was now looking a little weary, took a sip of coffee that a colleague had bought him ten minutes before. 'Madam, the table will be closing in five minutes.'

'Just once more. I haven't seen anyone else do as well but…' She then glanced over at the card table. 'What about them?' she said anxiously, putting her hands behind the chips ready to ride her luck once more.

'Not that I would try to tell you what to do, of course,' the croupier began sedately, 'but you do have an awful lot of chips there, an awful lot.'

Sarah withdrew her hands from the chips. 'Yes, of course, I see you wouldn't influence me.' His genuine but amenable expression gave her the belief that she wasn't just being fobbed off so he could close the table early. 'I understand, just an observation,' she replied excitedly. 'Yes, I do feel a little tired. Silly to try and ride more luck.' She turned to Nikki. 'I'll just go and see how Graeme is then I'll be over. Oh my God! I so hope I have won. Oh sunshine. There's a thought.'

'If you wait another fifteen minutes they will be calling the result,' the croupier told them as he began preparing to pack up the table. 'Best of luck,' he smiled. 'Send me a postcard.'

For what she saw as almost certain affirmation, Sarah exuberantly expressed her gratitude.

She turned to Nikki. 'Thank you! I had a great evening! I have to go and tell Graeme!'

'No hope of taking me then.'

'How about a magnet of the Acropolis and lunch at Zorba's in Gloucester.'

'OK but a decent bottle, not that anti-freeze retsina they serve,' Nikki joked as Sarah elatedly went in search of her husband.

'Done.' She turned back towards Nikki. 'And thank you again. I mean thank you for tonight. It was just what I needed.'

'You're welcome. I'm glad you enjoyed it!'

She found Graeme, who was now sat with some of the other male officers. He was semi-slumped in a leather armchair, a glass of whisky dangling loosely in his hand.

'Hey, how are you?' She leaned over to kiss him on the cheek. Her buoyancy was met with irritation by some at the noisy intrusion into their quiet conversation.

'It was great,' she enthused, still oblivious to what she had interrupted. Another officer then came and announced that thank God the survivors' breakfast was being served in ten minutes. A ripple of contentment greeted this particular news as one declared that he could murder some bacon.

Sarah then continued, 'What a buzz. No, you are right. Going out took my mind off things. Now, I don't know yet but we could have won that holiday.' She hesitated, waiting for him to react.

'Oh that.' He rolled his eyes replying flatly, 'Well done.'

'The holiday,' she repeated as if he hadn't quite understood what she had said. 'I mean, I'm not sure but let's just say that in ten minutes' time we will know!'

'Yes, very good.' He placed his glass down on the table. 'You do realise that it is one of those donated cons.' He sighed. 'Here's a free hotel for a week and by the way you have to pay for breakfast, lunch and dinner because we are ten miles from the nearest tiny village. No doubt they have timed this offer during some sort of religious festival when everything is shut,' he continued, encouraging the others that were listening. 'You can borrow the donkey but it will only get you halfway there.'

The man sitting next to him laughed. 'You're right. Andrew here won it last year. It cost him an arm and a leg.'

'You see,' he said dismissively.

At that point the announcement was made. 'The winner of this year's holiday is Mrs Sarah Hughes.' A combination of applause and groans came from the flagging guests who were still braving it in the early hours. 'Now, breakfast is served.'

Everyone in the group took this as the cue to get to their feet. A relieved murmur was expressed by most, particularly one re-emphasising his relief at the prospect of a large serving of bacon. Graeme got up to join them. 'Are you coming?'

'No, it's fine, I'll be through there when you have finished.' With that he left for the dining room.

CHAPTER 7

As the moving day grew closer, the more her anxieties of leaving their life in Cheltenham came to the fore. Nearly every day for the past month Graeme had been coming back with more information on the new posting. When she had a moment of doubt, he would talk of opportunities and fresh adventures for them to re-energise, to gain perspective on all the things that they had. They could always return and nothing was set in stone. Cheltenham wasn't going anywhere and he could always re-open a practice and Chloe would most likely welcome her back. The boxes could be unpacked as easily as they were packed. But as each contract was signed and possessions loaded onto the removals, reversal seemed improbable.

A week after she had left work at the shop she went back to say a final goodbye. Seeing Chloe and Bridget at the counter, she felt a stranger. A delivery of couture used to have them bristling at the expectation of the sales they would make. Knowing which customers would be drawn to which.

Positioning them in the best place and light. The debate about how they should incorporate them into the window display. Mrs Forbes would be passing the following afternoon on her way to the historical society lunch and, according to Chloe, who took it off the rail as it passed through into the back store, the odds on her not purchasing the latest Jacquard jacket were slim.

Near the door there had been positioned a modest set of new designs, a style that Sarah had previously expressed doubts over. When they saw her notice them they said that they were just testing the waters. The fact is that they did look good and she said she thought that they would be a great way to bring some fresh clientele. Wishing that she hadn't come back in so soon, they all engaged in a flat conversation. There was nothing to say that hadn't been said before. Sarah declined Chloe's offer that they have a last lunch out. Giving them a final hug she left, not looking back, imagining that after nearly fourteen years since she first stepped through the door, there might be, perhaps should be, something more of a wrench or a chasm as she made her departure. After the ups and downs, progress, setbacks, people she'd met. The worries she would take home with her or the elation of a big sale, even just everyday ties that had been so much part of her life. But instead of the grief that she anticipated, she felt very little but out of place.

The distance-learning diploma in business management that she had chosen to do whilst in Germany was something that she had picked from a range of courses from the Open University. A course that she had settled upon after narrowing it down to three roughly similar options. Graeme was happy that she would have a purpose. It was over two decades since she had graduated with her maths degree and she felt apprehensive about getting back to studying.

CHAPTER 8

THE FAMILY GATHERING was the last event before they left for Germany, two days prior to them boarding their flight. It had previously been decided that the goodbyes to family and friends would have to be combined due to time constraints. They hosted it in a private room at a local restaurant. With the house packed up, it was the logical choice, the venue having the added bonus that it would also be on neutral ground. If they had accepted an offer from one of the family members to host the occasion, it would inevitably have been seen as a snub by the others. As nearly twenty returns came in, it was something that they anticipated would have to be got through, rather than indulging in anything as fantastical as something to relax and enjoy. As each person confirmed, the visualisation of the families converging on the same venue would, as Sarah put it to Ellie, come together with all the harmony of a game of KerPlunk.

The keystone of Graeme's family was his mother, Lydia, his father having passed away when Graeme was young.

Since the decision to go to Germany, she had waged a steady campaign to undermine the move, telling Graeme she was old, her health was failing and, when all else failed, that she didn't want to spend her last days alone, and questioned just how many winters she could endure. To Lydia it was no matter that the longevity of her relatives for at least the last three generations tended to be around the ninety aggregate. Not to mention, Lydia had barely seen the inside of a doctor's surgery in years. Nor did anyone allude to the fact that every day she took her two spaniels to the point of exhaustion over the steeper gradients of the Cotswolds, or crack a stiff pace at her twice-weekly round of golf, or of her exertions in running a tyrannical tight ship over her ladies' church group. Instead, Sarah reassured her that the time would pass quickly and they could come back if there was a problem, and a flight could be purchased in a day, laying slightly less emphasis on her final reassurance that she was welcome to visit any time.

On Sarah's side of the family, having lost both parents she was left with a couple of aunts and cousins, an uncle she barely saw who lived in Australia, and three other cousins that she hadn't seen in eighteen years. Izzy and Seb's offer to come back if they wanted was, from their perspective, gratefully not called in, Seb being on the other side of the world, and Izzy, having seen them a couple of weeks before, was now holidaying with a friend and had promised an extended visit to Germany once they had settled in.

A lifetime of having nearby family and a network of friends they had acquired over the years was about to have a fundamental shift. For two years she would be living over 650 miles away. Relationships that she had taken for granted suddenly came into sharp focus. Ideally, they would have made it round to see everyone before they went, but in the last couple of weeks the move threw up unanticipated commitments or tasks that left them with fewer opportunities for meeting up with people.

Her reservations about a long-distance move were met by numerous positives from Graeme and also Nikki, who had recently come back from a two-year posting in Cyprus. There were many common factors in a life overseas. There would be no being drawn into partisan squabbles in the family. Most conversations over Skype were happy or positive, either no one wanting to burden her, or, as she cynically put it, in the case of one of her sun-seeking cousins, jeopardising their next visit. All the time she was out there, there was no being asked to join in or arbitrate in disagreements, or someone dropping over to the house to lend a sympathetic ear, who then turned you into the whipping boy the next week. Or, as she put it succinctly, as far as she was concerned, family hostilities turned into a two-year Christmas game of football over the trenches. In Sarah and Graeme's case, their families took on a more periodic pattern to their conflicts, more medieval in turning out for seasonal campaigning only at the larger get-togethers, rather than Nikki's protracted Stalingrad. In smaller groups, where avoiding personality clashes could be swerved, she had formed some good relationships.

At any appearance by Graeme's mother, he rarely relaxed. She would always find the most conspicuous spot, ready with a tale of the latest health misfortune, thus giving herself a prompt to talk about her eldest daughters, who, should she ever need it, were both surgeons, and further, how they were leaders in their field, flying the flag in the Hughes family tradition of pioneering surgeons. Although, his sisters would often telephone to say that they had been called in at the last minute, or on a plane to a conference, somewhere or other. He had a younger sister who had died when Graeme was a teenager.

Sarah's favourite members of his family were his cousins Hannah and Sam, who broke with Graeme's family tradition of going into medicine or becoming financiers. Hannah was an artist and coffee shop manager, and Sam a dry-humoured landscape gardener, who she got on well with, Sam being a kindred spirit in all things horticultural. The three of them would often watch from the sidelines as the numerous personality clashes sparked around the room. They affected voiceovers for the repetitive disagreements taking place at a distance, recurrent feuds which had been reignited from the last gathering.

Graeme and Hannah had little time for each other. One memorable Christmas Hannah made a comment to Sarah from out of the blue as they had been catching up. Sarah had been going through the routine highs and lows of getting ready for the school holidays, a couple of issues with Seb and the school, an impending trip away for Graeme. With no prompting, Hannah asked her when she was going to allow herself to be happy and do something just for herself, a remark that nearly made her choke on her drink, not least because Graeme was standing next to her. The rest of the conversation had been notable for two reasons. First, Hannah was impervious to Graeme's retaliatory passive-aggressive psychoanalytical observations about her. Her answers to his accusations of her being detached from the real world, selfish and existing for ephemeral pleasure were casually laughed at. She replied to each accusation with, 'Thankfully', 'Possibly' and 'Certainly'. Then she began to turn it around on him. Her flippancy infuriated him as she seemed to know what buttons to push. The confrontation was only broken up when his five-year-old nephew, who had been listening in as he chomped through a left-over mince pie, loudly piped up to his mother, 'What is a "fermeral" mean?' As she gave her brother a disapproving look she led her son away, but not before he could splutter one more crumb projecting frustrated enquiry as to what was a 'narsik tosser'? Then Lydia, having also overheard the exchange, came over to intervene, telling them they all should know better.

Sarah's family consisted of a range of backgrounds, mostly teachers, academics and artists, with a couple of exceptions, including an aunt who was a speech therapist, and another one, Aunt Lizzie, who was a spiritual healer, an eccentric who pursued a relentless mission to extol the virtues of her work, in particular her ability to telepathically communicate with animals. She had a son and a daughter, the latter a performance artist who had gained brief notoriety in the family after chaining herself naked beneath a local underpass to symbolise the vulnerability of man and nature's existence to the relentless tide of urban sprawl. Except no one at the local news desk picked up her email, and she was only spotted later by a coach of senior citizens en route to Stonehenge, and had to be rescued and treated for hypothermia. Much to her mother's relief, her fame was confined only to the family and the residents of a certain Sunny Willows Retirement Home. Her aunt's son, Joby, who was even less popular, was a semi-professional musician who once got them thrown out of a restaurant for smoking pot in one of the toilets. There was always the inevitable clash between her aunt espousing her unorthodox hypotheses and a cynical conventional medical consensus on Graeme's side. 'Spiritual luddites' versus 'try wafting your hands to perform a triple bypass'. Which was almost preferable to when politics came up. Sarah's other aunt, Penny, being a Green Party councillor, would inevitably clash with the more conservative factions of Graeme's family, which accounted for nearly all of them. Unflattering epithets usually abounded between the different factions, ranging from 'capitalist lackeys' to 'tree-hugging pinkos'. Every year the world was going to hell in a handbasket.

The starting point for discussions was usually instigated by Graeme's elderly Great-Uncle Hugo, according to whom the blame was put squarely at the feet of 'freeloading single mothers and soap-dodgers'. As the appointed family

71

demagogue, he had a stock set of phrases that were the solution to the country's moral decline. There needed to be 'more tube tying and a return to National Service' and the towns of this country were lawless and degenerate, drunken women staggering the streets in next to nothing, like baby giraffes. His description was more akin to Hogarth's *Gin Lane* but few took the bait, and most took the path of least resistance, offering an empathetic acknowledgement, or an 'agree to disagree' tactic, before seeking a quick exit.

The timely departure from Uncle Hugo's crosshairs usually came swiftly after his first reference to 'in my day', and just before the anticipated 'political correctness gone mad'. No one invited his spluttering indignation, pointing out that he lived in a sleepy hamlet in Wiltshire, a place where the most raucous happenings, post-war, amounted roughly to two events. The first in 1998 was when a postmistress, in protest at the rural closures, barricaded herself in her post office, and the second was the vicarage once getting egged on Halloween. Needless to say that the tide of insurrection was nipped in the bud by the naming and shaming of the delinquent 'eggers', who were then frogmarched off by the vicar with buckets of soapy water and a few punitive and salutary biblical lessons.

On the other side, Aunt Penny often gave allotment metaphors for the economy and achieving world peace, saying everyone needed to calm down, then, effecting a deep breath, telling them to create a 'safe space' to converse. This had, for the last two meetings, provoked the same comment from one of Graeme's cousins, that Penny might want to take that 'safe space' and a couple of beanbags to the Kremlin, and, in gentle refrain, ask Putin to shift several thousand tonnes of armoured steel perched on the edge of the Baltics.

However, Hannah was a different matter, Uncle Hugo having made the assumption of her being a socialist on the basis of her being an artist. In truth, she held the belief that nearly all politicians were shifty bastards, regardless of party, angry slogans calling for social change always diminishing into ever-decreasing fonts once the baton was in hand. With her easy manner and immunity to the machinations and intrigues of family politics, she was the person who Sarah got on with best.

Ironically, during the whole of that last evening, it was Uncle Hugo who brought about the only spontaneous demonstration of unity between them all, when everybody's eyes closed in collective resignation after he picked up a menu and suddenly noticed a safety warning that stated that the walnut cheesecake 'may contain nuts'.

However, that evening of their leaving do turned out better than expected, given the potential for dysfunction, and it was with a sigh of relief that Sarah and Graeme made their excuses around 10 p.m. All wished them well, each with their own parting message, one of Graeme's cousins saying of course they would love to visit, but perhaps meet in Berlin instead. But during the evening she felt moments of sadness about the life that she would be leaving. Despite the confirmation of contact details and promises to visit, she was already feeling the sense of separation.

CHAPTER 9

THE LAST MORNING had already been set aside by Sarah for one last purpose. Graeme didn't want to go with her, but she had made the suggestion anyway. Given the inevitable tension that would follow, it was something that she preferred to do alone. To take a last visit to see Ben who had been laid to rest in the cemetery of their previous village. A half hour's drive through the Cotswolds from their house was enough time for her creeping anxiety about what she felt as a kind of abandonment.

Tucked away between vast and gentle undulating arable lands, the church stood not far from their last house. Arriving at the cemetery, she was thankful that it was empty. The skies were once again darkening as the threat of rain hung in the air, the day having fluctuated between breakthroughs of sunlight and sudden downpours.

The bench on which she took her place was the same one that she had sat on early on the morning of his funeral. On it, a dedication to a warden that had given fifty years' service. In the wet weather during her visits since then, she brought a waxed blanket to protect her from the soaked and mossy timber, its poor state further emphasised by the regularly polished brass plaque. The trees swayed to the unrest of the swirling wind, shedding residual drops from the previous deluge.

In the past, many of Graeme's family of previous generations had marked their christening, marriage and burial since the sixteenth century. The village was where they had made their home after they were married, Graeme being the only one of his siblings to move back after his training.

In the spring the village held a gathering. It was to get everyone together to celebrate the past and present of the community. Many of the villagers would bring their gardening tools, spending the morning weeding and tidying up the cemetery. One elderly lady, who made full use of the fruits from the hedges, would bring everyone a pot of homemade jam. The vicar made an elderberry wine as a thank you to the volunteers, and one year, one of the more adventurous locals made a distilled blackberry vodka, an offering Sarah noticed was discretely given its full potential by kick-starting the barbeque.

Food and drinks and hampers all laid out, each person made their own contribution. A nineteenth-century farmer, Thomas Crabtree, had the distinguished honour of his crypt being the drinks table. A gesture, according to his descendants, that he would have fully appreciated.

They brought the children to midnight mass on Christmas Eve and Easter Sunday, the two biennial attendances serving to pacify Granny Lydia, who would have everyone hopping into line if there was any sign of mutiny. Along with Remembrance Sunday and an Easter egg hunt for the children, these were the annual commitments. The latter was always a source of concern, as a young Seb would terrify the vicar's grandchild, saying that the ghosts were watching. His antics were brought to an abrupt halt when he took the lower arm of a model skeleton from his science classroom and placed it sticking out of a narrow gap in one of the crypts. The following admonishments seemingly had little impact as Graeme, who was struggling to keep a straight face, held up the offending extremity and a digit fell off. Sarah left them to it, as it had been a while since she had heard her husband laugh.

Years before, at Ben's christening, Ben watched wide-eyed as people made a fuss of him, with some of Sarah's friends cooing at the sight of him, although joking by saying she was a glutton for punishment having another so soon after Seb. Sarah's best friend at the time, Pippa, winked at her husband, informing him that it was about time they had another. Sarah had anticipated that Ben would grumble when the water was placed on his head. He didn't. Instead, he began to scream the place down. The vocal eruption was then accompanied by a frantic thrashing around of little legs and arms, his piercing outburst reverberating around the vaulted ceilings, a seismic rupturing of the serenity that took everyone by surprise. The vicar then accelerated to the conclusion of the ceremony. The guests were mostly laughing, with the exception of Lydia who tried to rapidly restore order. Sarah apologised to the vicar as a means to excuse her and Ben from the final proceedings. She decided that the best way forward was to take him outside for some air. There began some inevitable ribbing and offers for help as she made her way down the aisle, one of Graeme's sisters patting her on the back saying that she didn't realise it was an exorcism. Halfway down, Ben's anxiety was then expressed in a more involuntary sound from the other end. So the last rows of pews now rolled in laughter as he flew past in Sarah's arms as she tried to make light of it whilst trying to pacify Ben, telling everyone, 'It's stage fright… it must be stage fright.'

Graeme's mother, less keen to see the funny side, however,

submitted to the fact that the commotion had to run its natural course. But she did insist that they remain for the last hymn. As the elderly organist struck up 'All Things Bright and Beautiful', Sarah found the fresh summer air a welcome relief. Pulling out a little hat for cover she rocked him in her arms.

'What was all that hullabaloo, little man?'

The sound of Sarah's voice began to soothe him. His cheeks were red and his eyes still teary. She wiped away the last residue of the water before raising him up to kiss him on the forehead.

'You know what Granny's going to say?' She took a quick instinctive glance just to check that Lydia wasn't behind. 'She's going to say "this has never happened in our family".'

The second verse of the hymn forcefully prompted by the organist, she could just about hear Graeme's mother, whose exertions in singing just a little louder were failing in their intention to lift the malaise. No doubt their minds were focused on the imminent reception.

She looked down at her son, smiling. 'You think that's bad. You wait until "Come All Ye Faithful" this Christmas. Let's see if we can dodge that and play the "teething card", shall we, my darling?' She swayed him gently.

Ben, now quite settled, was more alert to his surroundings. She took him for a walk around the perimeter. The ripe blackberry bushes were laden for harvesting. It was no coincidence that the grass had been freshly cut. Lydia had organised a thorough tidy the previous morning. An array of wild flowers, camomile, knapweed, a vibrant scattering of poppies provided a colourful border at the back of the church grounds to a neighbouring field, a picturesque cover for the rusted fence that acted as a barrier to various livestock. The current residents were a herd of dairy cattle, in whom Ben took great interest. He showed no fear as he reached out his arms. As she edged as close as she dare, the peace was broken as people began to filter out of the church. One of the cows snorted at them, startling Ben, who then was only further encouraged to touch them.

Later that evening, once the guests had gone, Graeme's mother delivered a lecture on the indignity of the day, further making the point that 'moo cow' was not a healthy way to develop his vernacular. Even Graeme teased his mother on how a six-month-old is supposed to have decorum. The conversation then descended into sniggering farce when, once again, Ben, now reactive to the latest batch of puréed apple, gave a similar contribution to the one earlier when they had dashed under the holy vaultings.

Five years later, as the sun rose on the morning of his funeral, Sarah had quietly left the house while the others were sleeping. Graeme had fallen asleep on the sofa only a couple of hours before, after succumbing to exhaustion after barely a few hours' sleep that week. Lydia had shouldered the responsibilities of finalising the last-minute arrangements for the wake. They had spent the day consoling Seb, after they thought it was best for him not to go to the service. He was picked up by one of Graeme's sisters to look after him and Izzy until the next day. Sarah had spent little time with Izzy since the accident. As she was still very young, she didn't want her at the hospital.

For once, Lydia's calm coolness proved to be a positive influence. For all the comfort and attention that Seb received from his parents, Lydia helped conceal their intense grief, which Sarah was unable to fully suppress in front of the children. If Granny took Seb out riding or out for a walk with the dogs, it shielded him from the blackness and visceral anxieties of their home. And for that time Sarah was grateful.

On the morning of the funeral, she had sat on the bench wanting to remember how things were, to make sure everything was kept locked tight in her memory. She couldn't go to the other side of the church, where they had prepared to lay him to rest. The skies bright overhead, feeling the warm sunlight on her face, it was difficult to conceive that it would be the day that she said goodbye to her son. She remembered her anger, the rage that she felt at God. He didn't exist because there was no reason for her son to go. It wasn't the devil or God she raged at Graeme's mother, the night before his funeral. The accident had been at the hands of a drugged-up teenager, high on the multitude of substances they later found in his system, running a red light.

Later during the service, she was barely able to contain herself as the vicar talked of His mercy, contemptuous of Graeme's mother's faith, her abandonment to a higher power, believing there was a plan. 'What fucking plan?' She countered Lydia's attempt to console her by telling her Ben was at peace. 'How can there ever be peace?' Why had he spent two weeks in a hospital bed when he was never going to wake up? She wasn't aware that she was shouting at his mother until Graeme came in and found them.

Earlier that morning, Graeme had gone to the churchyard where she was sitting, to walk her back to the house to get ready. Without saying a word he approached her, embracing her as she got up to meet him.

'I can't let him go.' She began sobbing, holding Graeme tightly.

'He will never leave us. He will always be part of us, Sarah.'

'I need more time. I'm not ready. Just one more minute.'

He got her through, when they went home to dress. She said nothing else until she made ready to leave the house. The quiet passage of the solemn procession marked a pace as they brought her son up the pathway. Behind her she turned to see Lydia, her face drained, her composure betraying her grief. It was the first time that they had really connected, as they exchanged a look of mutual loss.

Since the accident, she had replayed the crash over and over in her head. Day and night. Her helplessness as she was unable to reach Ben in the back of the car, shouting his name as the car lay on its side. Her ears ringing from the impact, the aftermath bringing the terror of silence. The twisted metal trapping her into her seat. Calling out to the people who had rushed over to the car. Screaming at them to get to her son. But most of all, ingrained in her memory was the look on the face of the woman leaning in to grasp her hand as she begged for a sound from Ben. The fear the woman failed to conceal as she took a glance at the two men who were trying to reach him.

For two weeks he lay in the hospital bed. Sarah spent day after day talking to him about everything they had done, the places they had been, holidays they would have. How his brother was waiting for a game of football. Reading his favourite stories. But often the memories of when they had read them before just emphasised the state of his motionless body. That once leaving the room distraught, that reading after reading, he didn't show any response. But the blank walls, monitors and intrusive lighting were inescapable.

The odorous linger of disinfectant and the sight of strangers was a world away from his bedroom at home, the playground of his imagination, where the stories came to life. A room set under a galaxy of painted stars that she and Graeme had created for him. In the centre, a planetarium mobile that had been painted and measured to detail. They had taken the day off to prepare it as a surprise for when he came home from school. Reluctant to the task at first, Graeme threw himself into it. Halfway through the afternoon, Graeme had mocked her depiction of a planet which had an infeasible amount of craters, and she had painted Mercury to the colour of Mars. It had been one of the best afternoons spent and Ben loved it. As she settled him to sleep with his favourite stories, he would nearly always engage in relentless questioning on why did this or that happen and if not why not. 'Why can't we fly?' 'Why do worms want to come to the surface when we jump up and down?' 'Can you play football in space?' 'How do astronauts brush their teeth?' Announcing that if he couldn't be a transformer, he would be an astronaut, or a pilot, or a football player. The latter aspiration came generally after football club, where the questions were fewer, and the sleep easier to come by. At the time a not unwelcome brevity as she heard Graeme in the kitchen opening a bottle of wine.

Watching Ben in the hospital bed, she would have given anything to have just a moment of those times back. As he lay there she talked about everything and anything. Vigilant for any signs. Praying for him to just wake up, a smile, to say one word. Hour after hour, there was nothing. Sometimes after leaving the ward, she would sit on the wall outside, dreading going home. The worst times were when Seb came to see him and tried to stir him, telling him about his school day and how he had a new game that he was going to beat him at. And when he didn't respond, he would leave in frustration as if he was failing. She would get on to Graeme for any perceived slight hint of despondency, whether imagined or not. Ask the nurses if he had moved, telling them she was sure that she felt something.

Then late on a Friday afternoon, the consultant gave them the news of the results of Ben's latest tests. His face confirmed what she had seen in the face of the woman at the accident. Their boy had gone.

There had to be more tests, or treatments. Whatever the cost. The doctors had to be withholding options because they were too expensive on the NHS. After scouring medical journals, she sited every tenuous study, every anecdote about people waking up from a coma, sometimes years afterwards. Insisted they consult someone overseas, every piece of research undertaken. Why didn't Graeme have more contacts? Pacifying God, promising anything, just to see his eyes open, his beautiful blue eyes, to wake up, to have him back. At every turn Graeme failed to get her to accept what she saw as him now being complicit too.

As they switched off the machines, a terror enveloped her. He slipped away and there was nothing but a black void, a darkness that she had allowed her son to slip into. When the doctors left, Graeme sobbed as he broke down, bringing her around to his suffering that she had neglected to comfort. They stayed for a while, each looking for the other to take the strength to leave.

The next morning, after they said goodbye, she was overcome by wanting to go back. Just to see him one more time. When her bargaining and anger succumbed to reasoning, she sought oblivion. Nothing else mattered. Until that moment she had refused any medication from Graeme, feeling she needed to be alert when he woke up.

In the days after his death, she couldn't bear to be awake, and when she became conscious, she thought, just for a moment, a very brief moment, that everything was normal, as it had been before the accident. Then began the long days, the void, the what-ifs.

Being in the house with daily reminders of Ben was unbearable, at first not being able to go into his room, then she would spend the day lying on his bed. A week after the funeral, she was coaxed out of the house by one of Graeme's sisters, during which Graeme boxed up all of Ben's belongings. Aside from the plastic tub of a few of his possessions that he said she should part with when she was ready, he took the rest to the charity shop. Afraid that she would try to retrieve his things, he told her that he had sent the best to a charity shop a distance away and 'taken care' of the rest.

One day, on an impulse, returning from the supermarket,

she drove to the estate where the mother of the driver of the car was living. For an hour she contemplated whether to knock on the door. All the things she considered saying were lost when his mother opened the door. Against the dark hallway, her pallid complexion exposed by the daylight, her eyes hollow, she frowned in hostility at the sight of Sarah on her doorstep. Was she police or a social worker? Stammering over her words, Sarah said that she was Ben's mother, a revelation that didn't mean anything until she explained further. The accident. We lost our sons. Instead of the mutual empathy that she expected, she just looked her up and down. What did she want? Was she asking for compensation? As she leaned in, the smell of stale sweat and tobacco was overwhelming. 'You don't look like you need it.'

Sarah listened, chilled by the woman's indifference to her loss. Her son's life, their sons' lives, had been relegated behind the concern of where the next fix was coming from. The stench of the flat brought her face to face with the neglect and abuse that had come into their world so violently.

Before she could finish, the door was slammed in her face. That night she went home, not telling Graeme where she had been. She thought of the woman's son, the monster who she had imagined, and how that was his life. At the time she didn't think of how the woman had ended up where she had, just the seething hatred for what she saw as causing the death of their sons. A year later Sarah read in a newspaper that the woman was reported to be found dead from an overdose in a local park, the connection to the story of the young junkie from the fatal crash a more marketable commodity for the local rag. In salacious detail it described how she was a survivor of an abusive father who was in prison for the manslaughter of her mother.

As time went on, the conversations between her and Graeme became less frequent, apart from explosive arguments, until one day he came out with what she knew he had been desperate to say. Was she concentrating that day? His anger turned to apologetic reasoning, because how could she not see him? Wasn't the road clear? She should tell him. But it was OK, he was often changing the radio channels, or taking a call from work. But he just needed to know. After that they made the effort in front of Seb and Izzy, but between themselves they used excuses to spend time apart, until the day she packed a bag and left.

CHAPTER 10

SARAH AND GRAEME arrived at their German apartment on a cold January morning. There were few people to be seen as they waited for the estate warden to arrive. They kept the engine running as the temperature outside had hit -8°C, according to the BBC. Since stepping off the aeroplane late the previous night, Sarah was beginning to understand why Graeme had been making such a point about the heavy woolly winter wardrobe, as he had already had to surrender his gloves that morning. They had spent the previous night in the officers' mess, in a warm room, periodically disturbed by the water coursing an antiquated piping system in an attempt to fend off the North German winter. At breakfast she sat next to a young captain who welcomed her to the garrison as he tucked into a healthy-portioned cooked breakfast. It was, as he informed her, to set him up for the day on the firing ranges. As he finished the last of his coffee before getting up to leave, he quipped that it was not a place for the faint-hearted. As she wished him well for his day ahead, she got the impression that this was probably a standard welcome for all the winter newcomers.

Instead of concerning her she took it as a challenge. Her home would be her home and they could shape it how they chose. Her diploma would keep her busy and it was a chance for her to do things that she hadn't had the time for in the UK. If she needed a trip back then, as Graeme had reminded her in her moments of doubt, the flight was a matter of an hour.

They had only been waiting a matter of minutes when the estate warden arrived. After a brief exchange of introductions they purposefully headed for relief from the elements, during which they light-heartedly collectively bemoaned the freezing temperatures.

A squad of soldiers marched down the road past them, forging a pace into the stiff wind, their faces red with the exertion and the cold, and warm breath bursting into the freezing air. Each carried a heavy backpack that bumped along with each stride. It made her feel exhausted just to watch them, particularly seeing two heavy-legged individuals at the back that were being cajoled by an instructor.

As soon as they entered the building the warden began a list of admin, consisting of things that needed to be checked and signed for. The drab communal hallway was austere and cold, even in a comparative sense to the outside. A functional, concrete, cavernous space, with a metal railing leading them up a staircase to the front door.

'Don't worry, sir,' the warden remarked to Graeme after catching Sarah's concerned expression. 'It gets better when you are inside. Now, the heating hasn't been fully switched on but that will be rectified this morning. I can assure you I will personally see to it.' He jangled a few keys in the lock before finally finding the right one, smiling as if he was at some sort of unveiling. 'There is no possible way you could fill this apartment. You could even set up a set of stumps in this hallway.'

Sarah tried not to react as the apartment was revealed. The sight was one of a complete wash of magnolia. At the end of the hallway a solitary brown table with a clipboard and file resting on top. As the other two began to talk practicalities, she made her way down the corridor. Magnolia kitchen, dining room, bedrooms, sitting room, bathroom. A layer of glossy magnolia up to shoulder height stretched the length of the hallway, in what she joked to an unreceptive warden must have been a rush of blood by the decorator. In her mind sprang a number of their paintings currently in transit, that were now being designated places.

Continuing with his itinerary, Sarah winced as the warden shared a moment of what was an attempt at male empathy with Graeme, by explaining that there was an office above them for him to get away from it all. Conversations with Nikki came to mind on the subject and her parodies of her observations on the army's ideal familial dynamic, and she had a good idea what her friend would be saying at that moment. The warden meant escaping 'er indoors'. Her friend's opinion was roughly surmised in a succinct universal stereotype. It was the poor husband suffering the hardship of having to spend evenings and weekends within an enforced domestic confinement. In being forced into a suffocating existence having to spend about four and a half hours housebound during the week – about three and a half when counting her absence in the kitchen for dinner. Where was his downtime and space? Not to mention when he got back from playing sport on a Saturday, then in the afternoon watching others on television do the same. 'But to be fair...' She smiled as she could hear Nikki say, '"Well, love, you have more time on your hands than me. You don't have to go on exercise or get sent away and I work all day, but Sunday after golf, now that is sacrosanct. I do it all for you. You know that..."'

Remembering the conversation as having little relevance

aside from giving Nikki a morale boost at her latest frustration with army life, she was now beginning to understand. The anticipated bland army furniture that she had given her a heads-up on occupied every room. To her amazement it was as Nikki described it to near exact detail, even though it had been nearly eight years after her and Rich's posting to Germany. She took out her phone to take a photo to send, accompanied with a single expletive typed underneath, an adjective that was a frequent flyer after the watershed, and would lighten the day of a woman sitting in an office a thousand kilometres away. As Graeme was confirming the final details she came back to thank the warden.

'You're welcome, Mrs Hughes. Don't worry too much about the history. If Number 12 starts telling you she's seeing ghosts, it's because she has too much time on her hands.'

Graeme intervened. 'Well, thank you again. You have been very helpful. If there is anything else I will call your office. I can appreciate you are a busy man.'

The warden took the cue, handing over the duplicate copies of paperwork, then made his way out.

'The history? What does he mean?'

'Oh, that is nothing. I will get to that in a minute. Firstly what do you think? Roomy, isn't it?'

'Roomy?' she laughed. 'Well, I don't know quite what to say! It's different.' She looked around the hall. 'And to think that your mum believes we are living some Raj-like existence.' Peering out of the window she saw a couple of soldiers running around the grass opposite with a spike collecting leaves. 'What on earth...'

'Oh that. They're on a punishment for something,' he laughed.

'You are kidding.'

'This is the army, darling. I'm sure it's preferable to polishing the outside brass or painting the curbs.' Before she could answer, he continued, 'I know this place doesn't look like much.'

She raised her eyebrows.

'OK, a little bare. But once we put our own stamp on it...'

'It's fine. Stop worrying. I should have been a little more prepared. But the magnolia. Jesus. There have to be a few more options. No, and please don't say a blank canvas.'

'You should see what the junior ranks have to live in before you complain.' As she watched the soldiers in their fruitless task, he put his arms around her. 'Well, I suspect it won't be dull.'

CHAPTER 11

Two weeks later their belongings had arrived. Her familiar possessions were a welcome sight. The earlier earmarked watercolours of the Cotswolds, she made a priority to hang in the hallway. The beautiful rolling green hills of home transformed the 'hospital ward', the moniker given to the hallway. It was the day after they arrived that Graeme had revealed the dark past of the block. It had served as a relieving hospital from the liberation of nearby concentration camp Bergen-Belsen. In the place she now made a home had been people who had somehow made it through hell or perished. In the place where she slept had lain shattered souls who had endured unspeakable evil at the hands of the worst of humanity. It was a horror that was almost impossible to get her head around, which in a perverse sense made it easier for her to reconcile herself to living there, although she made a point of avoiding the cellar, after her first and only excursion into it when Graeme informed her that it had served as a mortuary.

Now, almost seventy years later, the block, still with the original assigned number emblazoned in large writing on the side, MB86, had been transformed into a twenty-first-century British officers' home and the relative comforts that came with that. Being honest with herself, its history wasn't an image that she wanted to venture into too deeply. Her visit to the remains of Belsen brought a tangible darkness, which touched her to the core. In her mind, the indelible accounts and images she saw at the museum, she knew would stay with her a lifetime. One consoling remark about living there came from Graeme when he suggested that they wouldn't perhaps see this as a violation. It had been the British that had liberated them. Despite knowing that they were coming from different perspectives, it nevertheless held some resonance, whether they would have seen it that way or not. Finally settled in her home, she felt safe and impervious to the purported apparitions that were woven into urban myth. The given name of the 'hospital ward' stood in the spirit of the black-humoured yet reverent reminder of those before and what it now had become.

Each room provided more than ample space to meet their needs. The kitchen had space in abundance. The carefully sorted utensils and wares were methodically unpacked. Aside from two breakages, which were a ceramic salad bowl and a couple of glasses, mostly things had arrived in good order. Within a week she had fully unpacked and organised a routine. There were compromises that had to be made and things that had to be purchased. Their limited allowance of twelve cubic metres covered the essentials, a sizeable chunk taken up by Graeme's golf bags, two bicycles and skis. When accruing staple provisions for the pantry, it proved more of a task due to the differences in diet but essentially she felt that she was back into a routine. Within a fortnight she had signed up for an aerobics class once a week, and joined an indoor tennis club within a month.

The army camp itself had a harsh and brutal functionality to it. Uniform angular and block buildings that she had learned had been built to accommodate the formidable and fearful numbers of the army of the Third Reich. From a black and white photo little had changed, the numbers to the buildings repainted along with the paving stones lining the roads. In the winter, the grim barracks presented as an inescapable reminder of the all-encompassing military environment. It was a long way from the leafy boulevards of Cheltenham and all the familiar comforts of her previous life. But this was now her home for the next two years and would be a part of her life to make of it what she could.

CHAPTER 12

IN THE FOLLOWING months, as the thawing winds brought spring, she frequently visited the nearby beautiful medieval town of Celle. The research that she had undertaken back at home undersold its charm and character. The lively market square was graced on each side by medieval half-timbered, gabled houses, tightly built in high, narrow storeys. Decorative facades set with diminutive windows and topped with peaked angular roofs, which she considered gave them a fairytale quality. Their previous long-departed occupants had left legacies to boast of the status that they held in the town, each carving and design inviting you into their past – lions rampant, coats of arms, mythical creatures contorted in purpose, effigies from gargoyles to the devil. A splendid architectural guard of honour lined the worn cobbled streets below, these thoroughfares which had brought forth splendour, deprivation, religious turmoil, innovation, war and reconciliation. Dwellings that were now home to restaurants, shops, boutiques and cafés. When winter turned into spring, the vibrant blooms of window hangings and flower markets breathed fresh vitality into the town. With the arrival of the warmer climate, café and restaurant owners moved outside, showing off their latest menus to shoppers and tourists alike, the rich aromas of sweet baked pastries and freshly pressed coffees passing through the air. At night the main attractions were a raft of beautiful restaurants, many with aged, dark beamed dining rooms, warmed by wood-burning fires. On winter nights they provided a welcoming sanctuary from the harsh North German climate, something that she greatly appreciated when set in comparison to the bleak military camp.

On market day, armed with pre-prepared phrases and a pocket-sized dictionary, she gathered supplies, with nearly always a few superfluous additions. The sight and smells of the produce provided by regional farmers filled the square. Vegetables, herbs, regional and particularly the national cheeses that she sampled each visit. Dozens of types made around the country – blue bries, Emmentals, from the North to the mountainous regions of the Alps. At each visit the cheesemonger, who spoke reasonable English, would explain their origin. She listened and learned of their history, from their beginnings in monasteries or created by German immigrants living on the Russian Steppes. Most of these she enjoyed, with one exception, whose consumption felt like the longest five seconds of her life: the brutally odorous Limburger, a cheese that perhaps, if wafted under the nose of one of those carved effigies behind her, may have brought the very thing to life. Graeme had little interest, saying she had been sucked into a sales patter to a gullible tourist, and instead always requested French varieties. In sum, he would tolerate it as long as it sat well on a biscuit and didn't kill the port.

Two events that had been played up by most people there were, firstly, the much anticipated asparagus harvest, and secondly, the Christmas market, which she wasn't aware at the time she wouldn't be there to see. An invitation to join a book club had been taken up. This took place on a Thursday once a month. Wednesdays there was a coffee morning that she was persevering with. On Friday, more often than not, Graeme went to end-of-week drinks in the mess. Saturday he played golf and she would occasionally join him in the clubhouse in the afternoon, after which they would often go out for dinner. Sunday they would take the car out to explore somewhere. The little German that she had learnt had come in handy and she was able to negotiate her way around the shops and bank. The rest of the time she spent studying.

Everything had a place, everyday a purpose.

CHAPTER 13

IT WAS WEDNESDAY. Wednesday was coffee morning, an event that she had come to like the least, considering it to be a vortex of gossip and unruly toddlers. But there were a couple of ladies that had become friendly acquaintances, and in a couple of months there was a new battalion coming in, and Graeme had encouraged her to stick with it. After a leisurely breakfast, she read her emails, especially looking forward to those from Seb and Izzy giving her updates on how they were doing, and taking time to catch up on the early news in the UK. At a continued pedestrian pace she took a long shower, during which she failed to find a plausible excuse for not attending. When she had been woken up that morning by the turbulent weather outside, she had considered not going. And if she hadn't confirmed to one of the other women she bumped into in the NAAFI the previous day that she would be there, she would have probably stayed in. Grey skies overhead cast a dark gloom across the estate as she made her way out to the car. Divine intervention by way of a long-shot phone call from one of the women to say that the NAAFI roof had fallen in had failed to materialise. Graeme had been away the past few days and his early evening return flight, and her saying she would collect him from the airport, gave her little excuse to avoid going.

Pulling up outside in the car, she hesitated in order to steel herself before walking in, deciding that if she spent an hour there she could then come back and finish her due submission for her tutor. The meeting took place in a room within a converted building that had served as the officers' mess when it had been part of the Wehrmacht base. In keeping with the other buildings of the period, it was another imposing structure with a labyrinth of cavernous rooms that now facilitated the functioning of welfare services, concession stores and administrative offices. On the outside, a reminder of its past in the form of a stone emblem sat above the keystone of the entrance – an eagle with a space underneath that had been chipped away, which she had since learned had been a swastika. Over seventy years before, the same arch underneath which had passed people carrying out sadistic plans of a malevolent ideology now facilitated a steady stream of British Army wives for a cup of tea and a slice of sponge cake.

Walking into the room she was greeted by the sight of the usual crowd that attended. Most were still in the process of pouring their tea, with some taking one or two of the biscuits on offer, a couple of them making a show of declining and offering self-deprecating comments about their weight. Katerin, the CO's wife, noticed that Sarah had just come in. A native German, she had helped Sarah with some tips about the local area. A genial woman who Sarah got on with, it was apparent that she was the glue for the group. Running most welfare events, she had a subtle and skilful way of getting people to volunteer before they were even aware of being asked. The other wives respected her, but behind her back they mocked what they perceived as her inherent cultural compulsion to have everything running like clockwork, although irony and sarcasm were mostly lost on her, and she found the habits of British understatement and perpetual apology baffling. In a meeting, if she didn't like an idea she would be straightforward, which rendered some, who could only communicate in duplicity and passive-aggression, bewildered and frustrated. A range of unflattering epithets were assigned to her, of which she seemed blissfully unaware. Such things were an endemic sport amongst the group. No one was given a free pass in avoiding scrutiny. Some were light-hearted, but others, according to Graeme, in a discussion she wished she hadn't started, were a way of countering their anger or frustration at their unofficial status allocation, which underpinned nearly every aspect of their social life.

No one openly challenged Katerin. She didn't come across to Sarah as a person who suffered fools. What she had come to realise was that the army family didn't like turbulence. Opt in or opt out, but if you choose the latter, do it quietly. Most of all, a state of equilibrium and propriety had to be maintained. 'Happy wife, happy life.' But there was also the company that could break the loneliness of a husband being absent for months at a time. And there were those that were simply happy-go-lucky or thrived on the structure and stability it gave. In Katerin's absence a few would speculate about her life, her marriage, her parenting and most of all enjoyed scrutinising her dress sense. Having observed from a distance, it gave Sarah enough caution to not become too involved. The benefit of being the shrink's wife was that it would put off more than a few. She knew that she had been subject to the usual character study.

One of the majors' wives that she was on good terms with volunteered the information, before she could tell her that she would rather not know. Sarah considered that it could have been worse, as it was mostly about Graeme because of his profession. And one cutting joke was apparently made by Millie, a fusilier's wife from Glasgow, with her usual dour acerbic wit, which made Sarah affect mild offence on behalf of her husband, but make a mental note for future use.

Sarah had so far only made a modest contribution in volunteering. If she had thought herself skilled in organisation, she had to take her hat off to this current ladies' committee for their proficiency in how they operated, all delivered with the efficiency of a Formula 1 pit-stop crew. From charity events to day trips, everything was planned to the letter. The next event was a families' day. When she realised that she had caught Katerin's eye she was already preparing to bat things off. Sarah had so far contributed to two events, one of which was a lunch, the second a previous families' day and, as she had witnessed, they were exhausting affairs. If she got roped in it would be several hours on her feet, start to finish, working on a stall. At best, the pitch for guessing the amount of sweets in the jar, at worst helping with the bouncy castle. She had needed two paracetamol after just helping for two hours at the last one, affirming in her mind that if she was firm there was no way she could be forced. She was her own person. A middle-aged woman, for heaven's sake. She steeled herself as she watched Katerin striding over with purpose.

'Sarah, how good to see you! What about this weather?' Katerin embraced her.

Another habit that Katerin had adopted from the Brits was to be able to overcome any problems with ice-breaking, or shyness. Indeed a pretext to any conversation was to talk about the weather.

'Awful, isn't it. Ugh. The storm yesterday.'

'Yes, Larry, you know our spaniel, he had a terrible night. The poor thing.' She sighed in exasperation. 'These big empty houses. The noise.'

'Poor Larry.' She remembered trying not to smile when learning his name, deciding not to ask how this unfortunate dog had been saddled with it. Larry was an adorable black and white Springer Spaniel with an ever-inquisitive dappled nose, who revelled in the attention he drew, always making a beeline for anyone in possession of a sausage roll. Katerin's attempts at telling everyone not to indulge him so much mostly failed, the previous week giving the group a polite reminder after the prolific baker of the group, Beatrice, pointed out in a fit of pique that Larry had accounted for around 70% of the traybake she had spent two hours making and he was 'of course, no doubt, a lovely dog' but could everyone desist. To which nearly everyone took collective action in ignoring the request.

'Oh, it is terrible. It is these storms or the artillery ranges,' Katerin continued, 'rattling through every room.'

Millie looked over. After seeing she had overheard, Sarah knew that a huddled conversation was about to take place regarding the relative merits of living in their respective accommodation, a five-bedroom detached house in a leafy avenue versus a one-bedroom flat, whose state the young woman had previously bemoaned to some of the other wives, who 'did nay live at the arse end of camp by the gates'.

'Still,' Sarah continued, 'hopefully the weather will soon improve. We will be getting some much warmer fronts through.'

'Absolutely. Now, I wanted to ask you about the families' day coming up.'

'Oh. Katerin, I have to stop you there. We are going to be

away, otherwise I would love to help. The last one was great fun.'

'I see. Well, that's not a problem.' She smiled. 'Where are you going? Somewhere nice, I hope.' The weather topic exhausted, it was on to holidays until she hoped Katerin would make her excuses and she would be roping someone else in.

'Actually, we are off to Berlin for Easter. I am looking forward to the break.'

'Easter?' A joyful look came across Katerin's face. 'How long are you away for?'

'Oh, the entire period.' Graeme had told her the event was on the previous Saturday. It was the one social event that he had expressed an aversion to, on account of it being the last one they attended when she had unwittingly volunteered. It hadn't been entirely at odds with a heads-up that someone at work had given him, who described it as a migraine-inducing experience, consisting mostly of a demolition of luminous junk foods which fuelled roughly six hours of frenzy, although not just involving the youngest members of the family. After accusing him of being a snob and insisting that they give it a go, she later conceded that perhaps they were a bit past it, too long in the tooth for these things. Especially after her stint at volunteering.

Sarah had made sure that she had covered the dates to be away. 'From the week before Good Friday.' She considered that had to be belt and braces. 'Ugh. That's a shame. You will have to give me some recommendations. You are from Berlin, after all.'

Ignoring the last part, Katerin eagerly responded, 'But the families' day is a week earlier!' At this time they were joined by two of the committee, who had arrived on the flanks. It was a move she had seen before in a film she couldn't recollect, except these were two Laura Ashley-clad majors' wives, not velociraptors. Sarah felt an awkward silence as no one resumed the conversation. After just three seconds she buckled. 'Oh. That's good. I wouldn't want to miss it.'

'I'm glad I can count on you! What shall I put you down for? Your choice, of course.'

'Well,' she began in resignation, 'what about the sweet-counting one?'

One of the majors' wives checked her board. 'Ah. I'm afraid that's taken.'

'Bric-a-brac?'

'No, we have Susie and Lisa covering that.'

'The tea and cake stall?'

The woman scanned the list then shook her head. 'Taken. There is one that we can give you. It would be very much appreciated. You are exactly what we need. Good with numbers, you will be fast with the transactions...'

'And that is...?' She steeled herself in resignation.

'It isn't that glamorous. But... Aside from keeping the till, all you will have to do is take the money, and make sure they don't take on any ice creams, of course, and be careful if you see them have too much fizzy,' the woman failed to suppress a giggle, '... and when they start to look a bit peeky...' She then regained her composure. 'But not to worry, Tracey will be there to help.'

'Yes, good, the bouncy castle, who wouldn't want to?'

However, she knew Tracey would be more of an ordeal than six hours of dozens of manic under-tens catapulting themselves in all directions. Tracey, being an exponent of the raw food diet, would take any opportunity to give people the state of the nation's health, and the ticking time bomb of a dietary apocalypse. Despite putting Sarah off a Chinese lunch when they were on a group outing, she couldn't help but be impressed at her knowledge of almost every additive in existence. Upon examination, like a barcode reader she could identify nearly every synthetic ingredient known to man. Useful to a degree but if anyone deviated from something that hadn't just been pulled straight from the ground, dropped off a tree or been swimming in the sea that morning minding its own business, then they would be in the crosshairs. It was after the same lunch on the drive back, as everyone had been informed, to the point of exhaustion on genetic modification and Frankenstein colourings, that Millie was quizzed by Tracey on the contents of her children's lunchboxes that she prepared, and condescended to inform her that the imbalance in her diet could ultimately shorten her life. 'It wasn't rocket science.'

Millie coolly responded by saying to her that the bottle of carrot juice she was drinking had less plastic than the tuna she had for lunch. 'Oh and by the way, the effects of that and the half pound of minging raw cabbage' she was digesting, were 'posing more of a threat to life in the confines of this wee minibus'. It was, everyone agreed later, a more measured response than they were expecting from Millie, specifically relating to Tracey's own immediate prospects of longevity. Those on the bus that had headphones promptly searched for them, unlike Sarah who was then called upon to adjudicate. As E numbers and food fascism abounded, for Sarah the minibus had suddenly become a lot smaller. It was the last lunch that she committed to. That was the plan.

At Sarah's compliance to the families' day task, one of the women scribbled something down on a clipboard, expressing their gratitude, and left, having spotted someone who appeared to be making their way to the exit.

Out of the cold and back through the front door Sarah slumped down on the sofa, trying not to think of the exhausting prospect of several hours of listening to Tracey's irascible monologue on genetic modification and food intolerances, praying that they would be set up a good distance away from the candyfloss stall. She picked up her laptop and turned her thoughts to the essay that she had to complete and send – a welcome diversion. Baulking at the thought of more tea she poured herself a glass of water as she waited for the laptop to switch on. When she returned she noticed that the screen was not coming up. Checking that she had it plugged in she tried once again. Nothing. The deadline for the assignment was in forty-eight hours. Although having given herself a day extra in the planning she was already having anxiety about the latter part of the submission. In her usual meticulous routine, she had made a back-up memory stick. There was also Graeme's computer upstairs. He hated any intrusion and would reluctantly let her use it and always grumble when she asked to do so, which is why she gave up bothering long ago. Saving herself the grumbling encounter on the phone with Graeme about his privacy, she retrieved the key to his office from a drawer.

The study that Graeme had put together at home bore little resemblance to the one before her. He had made many improvements to the dusty shell that he had inherited at handover. It appeared as if this bolthole for the domestically overwhelmed male had been surplus to requirement, for possibly at least the last two occupants. As soon as he had seen it, Graeme immediately requested it be repainted, as it was the priority room for him to place his belongings when their things arrived. The main addition was a new desk, which had two German deliverymen muttering what she perceived as expletives as they eventually tessellated the large oak frame through the door, not helped by Graeme encouraging them forcefully every time they encountered an infeasible gap.

Even after several weeks, the faint smell of paint remained prevalent in the air. It had lost its cold, austere appearance as Graeme had arranged his belongings. She sat down, resting back in his chair with its oxblood-red, supple leather seat, which she had bought him when he had set up his practice. The same clock to which he had worked to time for all the years she had known him rested above the door, and hung around the room were his formal army photographs. The surface of his desk was kept immaculate by means of tidies, pots and a letter rack. Placed alongside, two inkwells in perfect symmetry. Lying neatly in front of these a black fountain pen, which had been a gift from his father. It never left the desk. The sole family photo was of her with Seb and Izzy two years ago on holiday in Wales, everyone smiling as they had just come to the agreement that she and Seb would rather be in a nearby inn, about 1,000 feet below, that was doing a promotion on a local ale. Izzy and Graeme had been content to crack on at a stiff pace having been freed from the shackles of the reluctant half of the family, who kept reminding everyone that there was a cool drink within half an hour's walk, and talking them through every increment in gradient. She and her son had hatched the plan half an hour before, deciding that repetition in the conversation of the issue of heavy legs, mentioning the time walked and distance to go would be enough for the others to gleefully cut them loose.

She thought that it would be a good time to send Seb an email before she started working but with explicit instructions that any photos sent back should not be of the beach, at least for another month. She smiled to herself as she looked outside at the gloom, knowing that would be the first thing he would send, no doubt with a cold beer in hand. How much she missed their time when they were all together.

The only notable change to his office over the years was the subsequent upgrades of his computer. The screen illuminated with an invitation to type in his password. It wasn't something that she had been expecting, as no one else had ever used it. Graeme, being a creature of habit, usually went for passwords using either family, psychiatry or military association. For their joint accounts he had assigned her 'Allenby', 'Montgomery', 'Wellington' and 'GlynHughes', a famous military namesake. 'Zulu', used for his email account, dropped in favour of 'Isandlwana*' when it was hacked. For the next five minutes she typed in a series of guesses, including her name, the children's names, the places they had lived, his university, his army number. She attempted to get him on his mobile. There was no answer. She slumped back in the chair in frustration, missing valuable time working on her essay. Twirling the memory stick between her fingers deep in thought, she sought inspiration for the password to come to her. As she scanned the room again she noticed a picture taken a few years ago on board a Royal Navy ship, an invite for drinks in honour of the Queen's birthday. It had been docked in port where Graeme had been attending a course. He was standing on the blustery deck with a few others that had been given a privileged tour, a glass of wine in hand that looked as if it was grasped rigid against the Baltic wind. The name of the ship, HMS *Lysander*, was posted underneath along with the date. The date and name she typed in, as with the other photos, then HMS Lysander, then just Lysander. To her surprise and great relief the screen opened up. The desktop picture was a palm tree casting a shadow over a beach and a sunset, which evoked memories of a holiday that they had taken a few years before in Italy, and the anticipation of the trip to Greece they were yet to take.

For the next four hours, bar a break to make a coffee, she worked to virtual completion of the essay. At the end of the last paragraph she brought up his music account and found one of the few mutual bands they both liked, then stretched back into the chair, enjoying the relief of finishing the assignment. Without distraction, it had come together with greater ease than she thought. There were only the footnotes to add, and she had over a day to do that. Looking at the desktop and the idyll of the sunset over the beach, she recalled the evening of the ball. The thrill of the win. Outside the usual sound of troops marching past could be heard even in the rafters. The overcast skies opened as it began to rain, a heavy downpour beating against the glass. The light obscured, she flicked on the desk lamp that brought a comforting radiance to the room. It would be another forty minutes before she had to leave to pick up Graeme. There was plenty of time for her to see how the tennis was going. Albeit a far-off tournament, it was a sport she keenly followed. Just a quick check and then she would prepare to leave.

Every summer, watching Wimbledon was sacrosanct. The family knew that if there was anything that they needed her attention for, before and after the close of play was the time to ask. At her boutique the radio in the back room broadcasted the excitable tones of the BBC commentators riding the rollercoaster of each match, usually culminating with a lamentation of the falling away of the latest plucky British tennis player who had been outplayed. Listening to the news that morning it was the turn of the latest British challenger that had reached the fourth round, an unknown from the West Country whose potential had been talked about since reaching the same stage last year.

After tuning in to a radio station on the internet, she joined it as the match was already into the first set. Even accounting for the inflated optimism of the partisan British commentators, the player was holding her own. Clicking onto the match stats she had been strong in holding her serve and dominating at the net.

The second set went to her opponent. To the side of the

screen a bright advertisement was flashing. It was a betting site. Two odds were flashing and evidently changing in response to the outcome of each point. The young player was 11/4, which, having a basic grasp of odds after a couple of outings to Cheltenham races, was a surprise to her, as the contest seemed quite evenly matched. The third set had the match in the balance. The British girl was now 30-0 down in her service game at five games all. The odds went to 6/1. Sarah scoffed in surprise. She had seen her fall behind early in games several times in the past year in the third set, only to recover.

If it were initial nerves, she had overcome them quickly. Her previous weakness had been her lack of domination at the net. On what she had heard, 6/1 seemed widely disproportionate. The sound of the contest could be heard through the commentary. As anticipated she recovered to take it to 40-30. Game point. The roar of the crowd gave away the fact that she had taken the game, the delighted commentator confirming the rocketing ace that had flown past the outstretched backhand of her opponent. She looked at the screen. It had dropped to 6/4. When the match point came on her serve with her advantage, the odds, having dropped to 1/100, had disappeared off the screen, as a long rally ended in triumph for the ecstatic teenager. It crossed her mind that a £20 wager would have paid for the new jacket she had just ordered. Closing down the computer she checked everything had been left as when she had come in and locked the door behind her.

Re-entering the hallway, pleased the local girl had progressed to the quarter-finals, the sudden recollection came to her that she should be picking Graeme up. Quickly locating her mobile, she saw that she had missed a call and a couple of text messages from him.

'The flight is on schedule. Can't get hold of you. I land at 6.

Love you.' A subsequent text repeated the same message but with the addition of 'Please don't be late. Exhausting trip.'

Sarah looked at her watch. 5.55. Knowing the airport was at least an hour away she grabbed her keys and bag in a panic. Not wanting to get caught speeding in the camp by the officious and ever vigilant RMP, she pushed it to the limit, before reaching the gate. Once out on the autobahn she could put her foot down. At the junction, there was a steady stream of traffic. She edged forward in anticipation of a gap, tapping the steering wheel impatiently as she was waiting for the opportunity to leave a message for Graeme when he landed. She looked at her watch once again. 6.00. Her wipers were now at full tilt. After another four cars a gap appeared. Accelerating away, she calculated that she could get there in around fifty-five minutes if it was clear, less if she really put her foot down. That would be, given the parking etc, 6.50. This was one of the few occasions that she had been thankful that Graeme had insisted on the Mercedes sports car. It was capable, as he boasted at the salesroom, 'of something ridiculously quick' in 0-60, a point she conceded as it was now cutting through traffic like the proverbial hot knife. The autobahn was her opportunity to make up considerable time, as there was no speed limit. On the outside lane she accelerated to a hundred miles an hour, but even then had to pull in twice to faster drivers. Soon she was able to estimate she was about twenty miles away. 6.25. Another fast-gaining sports car sped past her, throwing spray against her car. With ten miles of the motorway to take advantage of she pulled out to follow in his wake, roughly gauging the distance in between by the distorted glow of his rear lights. Unaware that a car had veered out a hundred metres ahead she suddenly found herself heading rapidly toward their sharply illuminated brake lights. In an instant she swerved into the inside lane narrowly avoiding a truck, her heart in her mouth as the penetrating horn thundered through from the rear. Gripping the steering wheel tight she regained her breath in the inside lane. The traffic had picked up again as it passed her. For the next minute or so she regained her composure. Looking again at her watch, carefully this time she pulled out once again, not least to get away from the truck driver who was still remonstrating at her, twice having driven up close behind to flash his lights.

A little behind her calculations she prepared for the turning for the airport. Checking the clock it was now 6.55. It wasn't a disaster. The rain had begun to ease off as she sighed in relief at reaching the airport. After the adrenaline had seeped away, she was annoyed at herself for taking such a stupid risk. At most he would have been waiting twenty-five minutes. It was more than likely he would have been held up, as they had been on their first flight in. Passport control, as she recalled, had had a long queue last time. There might have been a delay in taxiing the aircraft. Overhead a plane was descending to land. The skies were now clearing and the sun breaking through the clouds. The afternoon's downpour glistened on the saturated road. That night they would go out and celebrate him coming home.

Pulling out of the junction she prepared for the excuse that she was going to give him. The traffic, perhaps, or something a bit more inventive like there were random checks going on at camp. She dismissed that, as he would no doubt bring that up at work the next day. Traffic was the most plausible. In an instant the phone rang next to her. As she looked on the seat she was slammed with a tremendous force. Her mind caught in confusion and panic, her body froze, no control of what was happening to her, overwhelmed by the loud and violent contortions of grinding metal and shattering glass. A second crunching blow sent the car over to a ditch. The last thing that she felt was her car sliding down the bank. For the briefest of moments before blacking out she thought she saw a motorbike heading in front of her.

CHAPTER 14

'Thank God you are awake. Do you have any idea how much of a fright you gave us.' Sarah heard Graeme's voice before she could open her eyes. She strained to focus on him as she was lying in bed. He leaned over and kissed her tentatively on the forehead. 'We've been so worried.'

'What happened?'

A nurse who had been attending a patient in a bed opposite came over. Sarah didn't fully understand what was being said in her broken English but Graeme took over in German, after which the nurse departed. Sarah looked down to see her right leg fixed in plaster. A searing pain shot through her side.

'Jesus!' She reached for her side. 'What's going on?' She leaned forward, wincing. 'What happened?' she repeated anxiously. But before he could answer she had a sudden recollection. 'Oh God. What did I do? No,' she stammered. 'Something just hit me. Just from nowhere.' She attempted to sit up. Her neck weak she recoiled back to the pillow. Her body ached, weighing her back down.

'It's alright.' He held her hand. 'Calm down. It wasn't your fault. You were hit side-on, someone overtaking at a junction.'

'Was there anyone else hurt?

'It wasn't your fault. We can talk about it later. You have to concentrate on getting better.' He held her hand. 'You do realise you are getting the best stuff, you know. Some serious morphine,' he responded with a flippancy that she wasn't convinced by.

'This is important. Was anyone else hurt?' she repeated urgently.

'Sarah,' he gently squeezed her hand, looking attentively into her eyes, 'you have broken your leg, a wrist and two ribs. You had some internal bleeding and have just come out of a long operation. I promise you, there is nothing else for you to worry about. Once the consultant has seen you we can talk.'

It wasn't long before the police came to question her about the crash. Their inquiries prompted some intermittent memories before she blacked out, reassuring her as she failed to remember all the pieces. The driver in the first car that was hit was a businessman on his way home, who seemingly had had one too many in-flight drinks. What they were later to discover was about half a bottle of Scotch. He was unscathed from the accident. Then, with efficient explanation, the *Polizei* informed her that he would be facing prosecution. For a moment they broke from a gentle formality to offer an empathetic gesture in trying to console her that he was remorseful in accepting his culpability. Wishing to hear about the others, she interrupted her husband's flash of anger at this disclosure, by asking them to tell her the rest, needing the answers to the questions that she had been seeking since she had come around. The other vehicles in the accident were a car driven by a mother, with a young child in the back – the mother had suffered whiplash and was shaken up, but otherwise OK – and, the policeman informed her, a motorbike ridden by a young man. However, they would not comment on his injuries. Their ineffectually veiled reticence led her to burst into a barrage of questions. Then an instantaneous image of the motorbike came to her.

As she began a disjointed explanation of her last conscious moments she took in every piece of information that they could give her regarding how the crash had unfolded, the most surprising being that the car had ended up on its side in a ditch. One of the policemen, who had been taking notes, paused briefly to tell her that she was lucky. It was an obvious ploy to get her to slow down with her frenetic enquiries. Even though they refused to further divulge any details of the crash she persevered, only ceasing when Graeme reassured her that he would go and find out later.

After they had left, she pieced together everything they had said and tried to reconcile it to her own recollections. She didn't share with Graeme all the 'what-ifs' of her timing of being there. She knew what he would say, giving her anxieties short shrift. He had told her too many anecdotes of anonymous patients of whom he had expressed contempt for their weak, irrational frailties. When she called him out a few years ago after what he described as a laborious day with a depressed self-indulgent woman. He was indignant that it wasn't the same with her. It was never the same. But he helped her through with his calm reassurance. True to his way, Graeme began a detailed medical explanation of the motorcyclist's trauma, until she snapped at him in frustration. He then confirmed in a nutshell he would make a full recovery. He said that he heard he had even joked about when he could get back on a bike. It wasn't until she heard this that she began to really contemplate the recovery that she had to undertake.

After having to remain in bed for what seemed an eternity, she had waited eagerly for the doctors to pronounce her fit to go home. Graeme had been there as much as he could fit around work, but the visits had felt short. She tried not to show how she dreaded the solitude after he left. The long hours on her own, the familiarity of the ward and the same repellent smells began to bring back memories from the crash with Ben. Failing to become engaged in the books and magazines that she had been given. Staring at the pages, frustrated and restless to leave. Having asked Graeme for her purse under the pretext of needing cash for the shop, she regularly took out a photo of Ben. Despite the medication, she had been unable to get much sleep. Drifting in and out of sleep during the day and night she went over and over the accident in her head.

CHAPTER 15

Upon returning home, Sarah breathed a sigh of relief as she crossed the threshold of the apartment. What had previously not felt truly like home was now a welcome sight after several days in hospital.

However, like at the hospital, the nights remained the worst of times. Lying in the darkness, there was no escape. Every time she turned, or moved, a wince of discomfort served as a reminder of the accident. When she closed her eyes and eventually slipped into sleep, terrifying, fatal images of both crashes, imagined and real, became merged in her head. A concealed faceless terror always bringing the horror back to her, to the point in time where she had a choice, where she could have changed her direction or path or not looked away, in a split second, and where she would still have her son. Fractured memories came together of being in the car when she spoke her last words to Ben, then the motorcyclist before they collided.

On the first three nights when she couldn't sleep, she woke

Graeme and he would sit with her, attempting to hold her to logic. It wasn't her fault. On the third he suggested she might need some extra help, to get her through as it had before. Just for the short-term she could start with a low dose. She met him halfway, no antidepressants, but agreed to a different sedative. The next couple of nights she was thankful for them. The nightmares remained but she slept through at least until dawn. He left a box of antidepressants in the bathroom cabinet, suggesting she give them consideration, as these were better than the last ones. Just 25mg to start, then gradually build up to see how it went, reassuring her that several of his patients in Cheltenham had responded well to them. Instead, she batted him off, half-joking with a comment about whether this was the latest pill to peddle because he wanted another freebie hotel conference from the pharmaceutical company. At the third attempt to get her to reconsider, he said he would leave them in the cabinet. She was reluctant to acknowledge how at times they had kept her head above water before, and even though she could see him holding back from reminding her, they both left it at that. Instead, she was comforted for the time when he told her that they were in this together.

On the sixth night, despite the sedative she woke up sweating, struggling for breath, and contemplated just for a moment waking up Graeme, who didn't stir. Now she wanted to keep to herself the violent chaos in her head. It was hers alone.

Following two weeks of being back, she was coming to terms with the frustration of her physical confinement. Graeme had made several modifications to accommodate her lack of mobility. And after her initial protestation that he had gone overboard, she soon began to appreciate his efforts. Once settled in, he told her of a work trip coming up, that he had been pinged for at the last minute. A week's course in Edinburgh, followed by two days in St Andrews. Despite his offer that he could miss the weekend he had pre-emptively told her that this was a one-time opportunity to play at St Andrews. A friend of a friend was a member and had offered a few of them a round on the Saturday. At the first utterance of her saying she would be fine, he kissed her, saying that he would make it up to her. He had booked leave for two weeks in late July, and they would take the trip to Greece. She responded by firstly venting her annoyance at him being sent on another short-notice trip, and then conceding that a week without his fussing might not be a bad thing, confirmation of which came later when, listening as his taxi departed outside, she slowly released a cork from a nicely chilled bottle of Chablis, with a bowl of pistachios and *The Shawshank Redemption* cued up.

Everything had been put in place that she might need whilst he was away. On the table Graeme left a list of telephone numbers she should call if there was a problem she needed help with. It began with a number for his unit support and finished with the details for a cleaner that would be able to come round on the Thursday if she called to confirm. He cooked two sauces and a curry for the freezer, stacking them alongside some ready-meals. Judging by the photo on the sleeve, she conducted a quick confirmation that the pizza house number was still in the letter rack. All that she had taken for granted before, even taking a shower, was a considerable feat. She was unable to fully cook a meal, and not able to drive. Even just 'keeping the damned cast dry', as she moaned to Nikki on the phone the previous week, was an encumbrance. On the most sleep-deprived nights her days were exhausting and foggy.

The children weren't told about the extent of her injuries, as she knew they would come home. Seb was now working in New Zealand to cover his travel costs and Izzy was in Greece, on a break from Cambridge. She missed them. Every time they received a phone call or email, or a postcard from Seb, as he said he didn't mind doing retro, she was reminded of the void that they had left. The life and vitality in their lives had taken flight.

Various people had been round to visit. Of course now she had no excuse for not reading the latest sci-fi novel proposed by one of the group. A twenty-fifth-century fantasy that had been written by a cousin of one of the ladies from book club. Six chapters in and the search for superlatives was still ongoing. One of the women called to offer her take, which was that it was *Brave New World* meets *Mork and Mindy*, all in a slightly off South London vernacular. In the week Graeme was away she agreed for the meeting to be held at hers. A combination of the pushiness and the eagerness of the group to come around and help made her acquiesce.

CHAPTER 16

SARAH CRIED OUT as she violently awoke in the near pitch black of her bedroom. In her mind, her car was about to go into the ditch. A searing noise of twisting metal, with the inevitable collision awaiting. But this time, she could see the motorbike in her path. With the deafening impact, terror enveloped her as she prepared for the imminent inevitability of her life being ended. In her nightmares she felt he was close, within the blackness hearing the chilling cries that she couldn't get to. Her body paralysed unable to make herself heard. Every detail, now most of all the stench of the overflowing gully that she previously had no conscious recollection of.

Hastening to get out of bed, her morbid thoughts were overwhelming her, the fear not relinquishing its grip. She frantically fumbled for the lamp, knocking it to the floor. The room was silent, her heart still pounding in her ears. Her first instinct was to get out of the room, to escape this judgment. In her waking moments the visceral wickedness prevailed, the shadows concealing a malevolence conspiring to keep her there. In her confusion, she desperately sought clarity, and to find a familiar sanctuary from its suffocating grasp. After reaching to open the curtains, a low-lit streetlamp provided just enough light into the room to orientate herself.

With hurried deliberation she winced in pain as she guided her way along the side of the bed, taking a crutch to steady her as she reached for the door. Slowly her eyes adjusted in the silence of the hallway. At every point there was a light switch, which she turned on – the dining room, the kitchen, the hallway. In the sitting room she put on the television. The monotonous tones of the night-shift news presenter broadcast the scores of the previous day's matches, a beaming Rafa Nadal giving an interview on his latest win. The normality of this provided some comfort, drawing her back to the world. From the adjoining dining room, she listened as the delighted player was being given a playback of his roaring moment of triumph. She poured herself a large whisky, her hands trembling as the smooth spirit eased into her body. She opened wide the curtains to see the street below. A group of inebriated soldiers passed by. One of them, noticing her up at the window, whistled as the others laughingly hushed him. Immediately she stepped away in embarrassment. But the sight of others and reconnecting with the real world was a further separation away from the nightmares. It was a normal night. Like any other, this would pass. She replayed Graeme's words in her head. To focus on reality. Closing the curtains, she began to feel the chill of the air on her sweat-soaked nightdress. Unable to face going back into the bedroom she brought the duvet through, leaving the news on, where another few measures of whisky saw her drift off until morning.

The sound of the doorbell roused Sarah from her sleep. Initially disorientated as she found herself on the sofa, she could see from the breakfast news it was past 10.30. The bell rang again. She groaned as she lay back down, hoping that in a minute they would take the hint and go. Picking up the TV controller that had dropped onto the floor, she turned down the volume. Her head splitting, she recoiled as she met with an unwelcome waft of the half-drained whisky glass that rested nearby on the coffee table.

The doorbell went for a third time.

'Sarah?' The bell was replaced by a sharp knock. 'Sarah, it's Katerin. Are you OK?'

Sarah sighed as she pulled back the duvet in resignation, bemoaning that of course this morning it would be her making a visit. There was no point ignoring Katerin, as she wouldn't be deterred. Since Graeme had been away a few people had popped round to show support, offering sympathy, reading material, films, empathetic medical anecdotes, a lopsided Victoria sponge – nevertheless gratefully received – and a pitch from one of the coffee morning ladies to promote the therapeutic properties of cross-stitch. This was accompanied with a magazine of a woman displaying what appeared to be an unnaturally exaggerated expression of delight over a tiny tapestried angel, which, she regrettably joked to the offended enthusiast, appeared to have unfeasibly tiny wings and disproportionately large feet. But the fact that this had become a topic for debate was making her more aware of her need to venture out.

'I'm just coming. Give me a minute,' she called out, knowing that as soon as she stepped into the hall her movement would be detected. Catching a sight of herself in the mirror she put up her hair into a band, before wrapping herself up in her dressing gown.

'Katerin, it's lovely to see you.' Sarah kept herself mostly concealed behind the door. 'Sorry, I'm not being rude, I would invite you in for coffee but I think I might be coming down with something. I wouldn't want you to catch it.'

'Pah! Let me worry about that.' She edged a little closer to the door. 'Did you remember about the book club tomorrow?' she continued before Sarah could answer. 'Now, everything is in hand.' She paused momentarily. 'I thought I should just go over a couple of details. It won't take long. You are still OK with this?'

'Of course. If you give me a moment I can put some coffee on.'

'I wouldn't hear of it. You go and sit down! Leave that to me.'

Sarah opened the door fully to let Katerin in. Her neat appearance was complemented by a faint scent of Chanel No.5, catching her as she passed. Pulling her dressing gown tightly in, she left Katerin to start the coffee before disappearing to find something to throw on. Her percolator would give her at least a few minutes to keep her occupied. There was no point in trying to subtly hint that it wasn't a good time. As she knew too well, Katerin was always direct with people and assumed that they would be with her.

'So how are you managing?' Unwittingly she looked Sarah up and down as she went to hand her a coffee. 'It must be such a struggle.'

'Oh, it isn't so bad. Thank you for making that.' When she was getting changed she noticed her hands were a little shaky from the combined effect of the whisky and lack of sleep. 'Could you just pop that on the side and I will get us some biscuits. Chocolate OK?'

'Wonderful. Now you are on board for this book club, I think it will do you the world of good. We have the sandwiches and cakes accounted for and you leave the drinks to us. Everyone is looking forward to it!' she enthused. 'Well, in spite of that book. Dear God. Anyway. But at least then it will be over. Aliens spawned in Croydon. This is not funny. Nor interesting.'

'You might want to brush up on your superlatives.' Sarah smiled.

'And Graeme. You will be missing him, no doubt.' Before Sarah could answer, Katerin's phone began to ring in her bag. 'No, it's fine. It can wait.'

'No, really, please take it in case it's urgent.'

It wasn't urgent but it did prompt Katerin to make her excuses after she finished her coffee as Sarah tried not to show her relief to be getting back to the duvet.

'Thanks for coming round and I appreciate what you are doing.'

'It is not a problem at all.' She stopped briefly before leaving. 'Just one more thing, Sarah. I think that you are incredibly brave. Everyone thinks this. I am always here if you need to talk. You have been going through such a lot.'

'Oh. Well, thank you,' she replied, feeling a little perplexed. 'Nothing that a significant course of wine therapy and physio won't fix.'

'I know. Of course you will be fine. Now, chin up and I'll see you tomorrow.'

CHAPTER 17

THE NEXT MORNING, Sarah wearily silenced the blast of music from the alarm. She had been awake most of the night. The sedatives Graeme had given her seemed to have little effect. Even taking an additional sedative worked for only a couple of hours. At that moment she was annoyed that she had agreed to the book club. The bedside clock ticked around to 8.00. If she hadn't this to get up for then she would have taken double the dose and a couple of extra measures of cognac. Opening the door with bloodshot eyes and a puffy face would give someone the cue to hold some kind of inquiry.

Allowing herself another ten minutes in bed, she listened to the usual weekday routine going on outside. The engine of the neighbour's car kicked into life as their teenage son was being reluctantly ushered into the back. Like most days, he was enacting his usual futile rebellion against the tight morning schedule. The much younger children of the neighbours the other side were squealing in their usual indefatigable mania. After having their football swiftly confiscated, they were now finding another diversion as they were herded into the vehicle.

After an hour of tidying around and taking out the required crockery, she sat back in anticipation of the frantic activity to come. At least two would be bringing toddlers. Although she was out of practice on making a house toddler-proof, she had been given a heads-up from one of the other ladies regarding one particular tiny offender who had a penchant for shoving anything of appropriate size into CD players or plug sockets, or generally gravitating towards anything that looked off limits.

They arrived nearly all at once, with the exception of Tessa, the mother of a young toddler who made an entrance in a flurry of activity, with the young child and new baby in tow. After the initial bluster and rundown of everything that had inconvenienced her or held her up that day, she began to take in Sarah's apartment.

'Well, this is nice. Most people don't like minimalist, but I am not one of them.' She then paused for close inspection of her photographs on the table. 'So this is your husband?'

'Yes, that's Graeme.'

She picked up another photo for close scrutiny. 'And these are your children I take it?' Her inquisitiveness and overfamiliarity caused Sarah further irritation with her.

'Seb and Izzy, yes.'

'What a good-looking family.'

'Thank you. That's kind of you to say so. How about we go through.' She could see Tessa focusing her attention once again onto Graeme, no doubt making swift calculations and evaluations as Sarah anticipated the next question.

'You met when you were young.' She picked up a wedding photo. 'Judging by the dress, quite a few years ago. But then again, we all had a meringue, darling.' She regained her thread. 'Yes, you are very young there. How did he manage that? A pretty girl like you.'

'I wouldn't say that was fair,' Sarah replied, aware that the flattery was intended to divulge more details. 'Shall we go through?' A look of frustration from Tessa was barely suppressed as she extracted her child from his pushchair. The young boy seemed to have Katerin's dog Larry in his sights, who was bounding down the hallway after hearing their voices. The boy called out to the dog, who duly obliged, springing towards him, then began licking the child's face, which made him let out a squeal of delight. He then attempted to lick Larry back, which made Sarah burst out laughing.

'Thomas! What have we said about this! No licking Larry! Dirty!' At that moment a call to the excitable pup came from Katerin in the sitting room, who must have heard the commotion. Dog and child headed off, one leaping ahead, the other making less pace in giddy and unsteady pursuit.

'That's a first,' Sarah laughed. 'Still, he will be building a formidable immune system.'

'He's usually well behaved. His nursery said he is ahead of his peer group in cognitive skills. It's a sign of confidence. He is going to be an extrovert, they say.'

With Larry now in the other room called to heel, the child was attempting to get his mother's attention, calling out from the end of the hallway by looking back through his legs, the feat making him topple over.

Tessa quickly continued, 'They say that he can solve problems beyond his years.'

'Well, yes, he does look a livewire. That's good.'

Interpreting Sarah's remark as insincerity, she turned back to the photos. 'We find a less formal environment will foster his creativity. We didn't want to be the typical military family. All that stiffness and convention.' She gave another glance back to the photos. 'But perhaps that is the comfortable option, perhaps works for most. Nothing wrong with that.'

'Indeed.' She wanted to make a joke about slipping one

of Graeme's sedatives into their spaghetti hoops to get them through the unruly times, but knew that would be round the coffee morning in a flash, and rather than being said in jest, it was disclosed by means of a meaningful confession. 'Now, shall we?'

At the beginning of the meeting, everyone expressed a mixture of empathy and admiration. They were soon catching up on who was doing what, holidays, husbands, schools. Sarah was inundated with offers to help with various tasks, errands or invites, all appreciated bar one who suggested that she could recommend a cleaner whom she might find 'a little more intensive' than the one she was employing. But she took it with a pinch of salt. It was Tessa. A woman with an encyclopaedic knowledge of the personal lives and circumstances of nearly every person that happened to fall into her sphere, possessing a remarkable memory that could vividly describe any incident witnessed, which could be considered fodder for gossip. One of her favourite pursuits was to create a psychological profile on someone by analysing the interior of their home.

During the meeting Sarah found herself in and out of the conversation. Fatigued from the lack of sleep, the sound of cutlery against cups or plates reverberated through her head. Despite the high ceilings the noise echoed in sharp clashes from wall to wall.

Since the crash many people had been around to help. It was a relief that no one wanted to talk about the accident aside from how she was feeling, telling everyone she was fine and listening to a few of the same anecdotes that they wanted to pep her up with. It was noticeable to her that everyone was seemingly more attentive that morning. She wondered if Katerin had said something about her dishevelled state the previous morning, and speculated if there was more behind the comment about the housework.

The discussion about the book mercifully lasted only half

an hour. Even the person who had recommended it conceded that perhaps it could have been better.

'So, Sarah,' the voice was Tessa's, 'I have to say,' she announced audibly during a slight lull in the conversation, pausing to ensure that she had gained the attention of the others, 'you seem to be taking all this in your stride.'

'Really, I'm fine. Thank you for your concern but I am on the mend. You know, you have all been great. This has been a real help.'

'And it could have been a lot worse for you,' Tessa encouraged, 'and you shouldn't feel guilty, not at all.'

'Tessa,' one of the other women cut in, 'perhaps Sarah would prefer a diversion rather than going over it again.'

'OK,' Sarah responded, confused. The women were suddenly very awkward. It couldn't be ignored. 'I'm not sure. Am I missing something?'

Tessa was about to cut back in before Katerin pre-empted her. 'We know that it wasn't your fault. No one thinks that.' A few of the other women murmured in consensus.

'Look, I'm not sure what you mean.' she responded irritably. 'Sorry. I didn't mean to snap. What do you mean?'

'The young man…' Katerin began awkwardly, having realised that she didn't know what they were saying.

'Sorry, what…? I don't understand.'

'On the motorbike. You surely know.' Katerin momentarily flushed as Tessa leaned a little forward.

Sarah's anxiety suddenly escalated as she noticed the unease and evasiveness on the women's faces. 'No, I don't know what you've heard.' She threw a look at Tessa. 'He is fine. I know he had an operation but they said he was going to make a full recovery.'

'Sarah,' Katerin quietly continued, 'there is not a good way to say this. I'm so sorry but he's dead. I…' she looked at the others, '… we assumed that you knew.'

'Oh God.' She slumped down into the chair. Her head began to spin. 'I don't understand. He came through an operation. Graeme said…' She stopped. 'Was it something the hospital missed?'

'They wrote that he died in surgery the evening of the accident. He didn't regain consciousness.' She then turned to the rest of the women. 'Perhaps we should give Sarah a little space.'

A suggestion that they were keen to accept, they quietly took their leave as Katerin took hold of her hand. 'I'm so sorry. It was in the garrison magazine this week. It had been in the local newspaper a while earlier.' She then corrected herself. 'Of course you probably wouldn't have seen that.' She then stopped as she could see that Sarah wasn't listening.

'I thought he was OK. Christ…' The recollection of the conversation with Graeme at the hospital reran through her head. 'But…' she went back to the crash, '… I didn't see him, Katerin. I didn't even see what he looked like. Do you have a copy? What was his name? How old was he?'

'Do you think this will help?'

'How old, Katerin? Please just tell me!'

'OK.' She attempted to hold her hand in comfort.

Sarah immediately withdrew. 'I have to know.'

'He was twenty-one.'

Katerin stayed with her for an amount of time she wasn't aware of. Nor did she absorb the consoling advice being given, just the details of the motorcyclist, Andreas. After a while, when there was little else to be gleaned from Katerin, Sarah told her that she needed to rest, as she was in need of a sleep. Seeing her out, she repeated her request for the magazine. After the door closed she processed everything that she had been told, bewildered as to why Graeme didn't tell her. She wondered if he had thought about what had happened in the accident. If he really thought it was her fault. This then escalated in her mind. What if there was doubt on this, if she could have done something? Why did he give such detail to his lies? All of the time, she questioned how he had been so calm at the hospital. In the subsequent time that had passed since Katerin had left the apartment, she thought of the exact moment she had sent him off to find out about the motorcyclist. She recalled that he even complained about the coffee in the vending machine. After several times of considering if she was confused, she was certain that had to be the time.

However, the flood of images that came to her mind were once again of the accident. Most of all the loss of the young man that now had a name. Andreas Mueller. He wasn't anonymous. Thinking how young he had been, quickly following in her mind a comparison with her children's age, a young soldier walking past below joking with his mates drew her attention, like him. She thought about how at that age she was just embarking on life.

Mostly she was plagued by the thought of what would have gone through his mind as he saw her. His last conscious moments. He must have known that he couldn't avoid her, the terror of facing his impending collision. When did his pain cease? She thought she had a sudden and consuming dread, not knowing if it were real. Was there a shift in the weight of the car pushing him into the water? It was her that had condemned him, her actions. As in her dreams, she imagined the scorching engine of the car crushing him as he lay helpless, suffering in final terror. Whether he knew there would be no escape as his eyes closed for the last time. If he did, my God, if he did… She pushed herself to further imagine his life, how his parents must be feeling, hating herself for wishing in that moment she hadn't found out.

It had been two days since the book club. She spent the nights playing movies that she drifted in and out of. It was on the third that she took out a pen and writing paper. What if she wrote to his parents to send her condolences? If they knew that she was sorry...? That she understood what they were going through? They would be beside themselves with grief, and would feel that their lives were gone with his. Katerin delivered the magazine as promised, which was when she told her of her intention to write to his parents.

Sarah began her letter. As she pondered what to say, she slowly wrote the date and her address, wondering if they had preconceptions, or dealings with the British garrison. Whatever that may or may not mean. It was the only thing they may know about her – occasional conflicts between soldiers and young local men. She then thought, what if he were one of them? Whether they had seen one of the Brits in the supermarket bellowing in impatience at a worker's inability to understand English, or wanting to know why their brand from home wasn't stocked. She knew how she would feel if she were them, if she only saw that side. Was this why the police were so reticent to discuss his condition? Was it the family's anger? What if they knew she understood their loss, if she told them? That she knew that a day wouldn't go past where they wouldn't think about him. Knowing that every memory would be replayed, desperate to make sure that he should be remembered in every detail.

Sarah began her letter.

'Dear Herr and Frau Mueller...'

For three hours she searched for the words. After four hours she had written and rewritten what amounted to half a page. Nothing seemed right. Every time she reread it she found it wanting. Too formal, too familiar, too weak.

By the following day the letter was finally ready to send. It was the best she could put together after a dozen abortive efforts. Having read the content, Katerin reluctantly agreed to translate her words, asking Sarah again whether she thought it was a good idea. Instead of her usual forthright and laconic responses, she tried to persuade her of the possibility of this backfiring. As she echoed the words that she had been told time and time again – it wasn't her fault – she cut Katerin off. After Sarah insisted that it had to be sent, Katerin talked her into sending it through a third party, instead of sending it to the house. At least she should see if they were receptive to reading what she had to say. They decided on leaving it with the police not with the hospital.

Sarah stayed in the car as Katerin went into the station alone. Avoiding the lumbering effort of negotiating the station's steep steps, and the further possibility it would be a cramped wait, was the deciding factor. It was a disappointment, as she wanted to hand it over in person. She watched as numerous people made their way in and out the station, the uniforms of the *Polizei* taking her back to the day in the hospital. As she contemplated getting out of the car to ease the discomfort that was intensifying in her back, she saw Katerin coming out of the station.

Impatient for her report she began as soon as she entered the car.

'What did they say? Will they do it?'

Before turning on the ignition she turned to Sarah. 'You shouldn't get your hopes up. I understand, Sarah. Really. I would not wish this on my worst enemy, but you should try to move forward now.'

'But they will know that I care about what happened.'

'Oh, Sarah. They are grieving now. You understand this. Now, please. This is a good opportunity to close the history. Now, you are coming to my house. It is not good to spend too much time alone. It will make you very unhealthy. We are not young and need to look after ourselves. You look terrible and you are as pale as a ghost. So. I will make lunch.'

'Thank you, Katerin, for everything and today. Yes, lunch would be nice.'

'Not at all. Larry will be very excited to see you. Ugh. These wretched storms again last night.'

Returning to Katerin's, they spent the afternoon sitting in the tranquillity of the garden, a freshly cut lawn in part shaded by an arrangement of fruit trees that were only gently disturbed by a cooling breeze as she relaxed back with a post-lunch cup of tea.

'Your garden is beautiful. I miss mine very much.' Sarah had been there before but it had been at night, when it was filled with people at a drinks party – the usual conversations and semi-formality. It seemed more a blur of people that Graeme either worked with or spouses she 'must meet'. Three times hearing Graeme repeating the same anecdote of how a patient really had come in with a pair of pants on his head and pencils up his nose. She doubted it was true but it seemed to go down well, and she played the part as if the story was a distant recollection, her being the straight man in the duo. A one-hour 'show our faces' appearance turned into six as a few stayed on, and she was stuck with two of the wives that were giving her a host of examples of their tongue-in-cheek domestic woes, bemoaning the military, the impending visit of their offspring from boarding school, a good school always given the honour of at least three repetitions. Or the discussion became one of the parental or social deficiencies of those who had made their exit.

The garden was Katerin's pride and joy. They had a similar shared perception of the beauty, but Sarah hadn't assigned the same philosophy as Katerin as to how these were a collective symbiosis. Her approach had always been more of practical and working aesthetics, and she wondered how her herbaceous freestyling Jackson Pollock would go down with her. When Katerin struggled to explain *Pflanzensoziologie* in greater detail, in frustration she would break into German, explaining how gardens and their cultivation were like a community, not individuals. What Sarah thought was going to lead to a joking comparative metaphor of the coffee morning instead turned into sharing their love of gardening, relaying their own stories of the projects and labours of love they had undertaken over the years, and the varieties they planted. For two hours she felt some respite in the warmth of the sun as they talked of the plans she would make, each promising they would visit when they were both back in their homes. But she would never meet up with Katerin or see her own garden again.

As Katerin was in the middle of telling her about a recent visit to the botanical gardens in Brunswick, and how they should go once she was better, a sudden tumultuous boom sounded from the ranges.

Katerin threw her arms up in exasperation. '*Oh mein Gott!*'

From the end of the garden a panicked streak of black and white fur, tongue outstretched, bolted past them in search of cover.

CHAPTER 18

THREE NIGHTS PASSED before Graeme called to say he was on his way back from the airport. Three days of her waiting to confront him. On the phone she had found it hard to keep things together. As he relayed the events of his day, she struggled to contain her emotions, finding it hard to keep her patience with him. He seemed oblivious to her distraction, even when twice she failed to effectively respond to confirmations that she was following him. The most trying time was as he talked her through his golf round, which culminated in him telling her in emphatic style about a shot that he had made to win the round – a rollercoaster narrative of his success. Ten minutes of trying to hold her in suspense as to whether she thought he would prevail, which of course she knew he had, otherwise the story wouldn't have been told. She was already on her third glass of whisky when he arrived home. As the keys turned in the door, she prepared herself for whatever she might have to hear.

'I've missed you.' He kissed her as he dropped his bags. 'Wow. Have you been at my single malt?'

'Just a couple. How was the flight back?' She walked ahead of him into the dining room before he had a chance to answer, trying to conceal the anger building in her.

'It was fine. But I could do with one of those. Ugh. Some bloody typically overfed American blocking me in. But what a weekend! I know I told you about the shot I made coming back up the eighteenth. A hundred and seventy yards to within two inches. What I didn't tell you was we had a £500 pot on it. Not only that, Harry – I told you about him – he was almost timed out. A ten-handicapper. Anyway, I have brought you something nice back. You would have loved it. What a spectacular place.'

Most of the time she paid lip service when he would say something such as this – 'You would have loved it' – but unable to know where to start she had little tolerance for letting this pass. 'Why would I have loved it, Graeme? Why exactly is that? I hate golf, actually no, mostly golfers and… God… why do you say such things?'

'Alright… I understand that you are not thrilled about me staying the weekend. But I'm back now. Here to look after you and make it up to you.' He continued as she failed to respond, 'You know I appreciate it. A one-off.'

'Graeme, I don't care.' She stopped him abruptly. 'Will you just shut up!' she burst out angrily. 'I don't care about your bloody golf game.'

Taken aback he said nothing, waiting for her to finish. Instead she poured a whisky for him. Having his full attention she initially failed to find the words that she had imagined confronting him with when he returned.

'What on earth has happened?' He accepted the glass she handed him. 'Is it something from home?'

'Where to start? The hospital seems as good a place to start as any.'

He looked confused. 'I don't understand, you are not

making any sense.' A sudden look of anguish came over his face. 'Oh God. The children.' He urged her: 'Sarah, is it Seb or Izzy?'

'What?' she quickly interrupted. 'No, they are fine. Don't you think I would have called you with something like that?'

'Oh thank God. Don't do that,' he responded irritably. 'So, what is it? Nothing too serious, then.'

'I wouldn't say that. Would you?' she continued before he could answer. 'The crash. The motorcyclist.'

'Oh that,' he replied in a matter-of-fact manner. 'Someone told you.'

Incredulous at his tone she began to shout at him. 'He was twenty-one years old, Graeme. Twenty-one. That's younger than Seb. What I find incredible is the deception. The details did give it an authenticity. How do you do that?'

'You know perfectly well I did it for you.'

'For me?'

'Well, just look at the state of you. I did what was best for you. If you hadn't found out you would have been better for it.'

'And there we have it. The shrink steps in and takes control. Do you even know what his name was?'

He didn't answer.

'No, I didn't think that you would. It was Andreas. He was an engineering student. In the German newspaper they showed a photo of him and his girlfriend. They said that he was a really talented athlete. You should see the picture. His whole life ahead of him. I have the article... just look at it and you will see...'

'Honestly, no I don't want to see. What would be the point? It was a tragedy but... Look, you have to let this go. You didn't kill him. Now, you need to calm down and we can go through this step by step. You don't look as if you have had any sleep. I can help now I'm back.'

'Have you not listened to a word I've said? A young boy

died.' Tears began to fall. 'I don't understand you. What is wrong with you?'

'Alright. I'm listening…' He put down his glass. 'Why don't we just sit down, talk this through.'

'I don't want to sit down!' She broke down in tears. 'I've been going out of my mind. In this place. It's every night. I think of Ben.'

'This has nothing to do with our son.'

'No, Graeme, it never does.'

'We have been over this time and time again. What about if you call Ellie and invite her over? I know this is a difficult time but I think that you are going to need something to get you through this rough patch. We can just go with a low dose, only for a short time.'

'For fuck's sake, Graeme! I don't need more medication. I need to deal with this in my own way. Having a husband that doesn't lie to me would be a start.' She stood up to look out of the window. 'Life goes on as normal out there. I'm not part of it. I'm sorry, I think we made a mistake. I made a mistake. I have thought that perhaps instead of increasing medication, I could see someone, find a counsellor. I wish I had Tom here, but there must be someone. Not on the camp, of course, but I have asked Katerin, just speculatively, if there might be someone. Before you say anything,' she continued defensively, 'I haven't committed to anything, you…'

'You did what?' He turned on her angrily. 'You shouldn't have told her anything, you know what these women are like.'

'You really don't know Katerin very well, obviously.'

'What did you tell her?'

'Oh well, Graeme, I told her that I sit with my head wrapped in tin foil all day and…'

'Don't be facetious,' he snapped at her. 'You don't need another counsellor, if you just did as I said. What else did you say to her?'

'Nothing! She brought it up because she knows it has been difficult since the accident. Don't worry, I didn't tell her anything about my depression. I remember the brief.' She affected a mock salute.

'You have to hold it together. Christ,' he continued in exasperation, 'I have more compliant adolescents when it comes to taking their medication. Don't you think that other people will begin to notice? With my position, if I can't...' He hesitated.

'If you can't what? Control your wife? You didn't keep it from me about Andreas to protect me. You did this for yourself. Oh yes, we know that you like to play God, Graeme. Casting out judgments on soldiers, on wives. I do hear, you know. Half of them are about people you don't even meet. Treat people? You keep them quiet and save the army money and inconvenience.'

He flared up in temper. 'You need to get over yourself and stop this self-pity. We are in a goldfish bowl here. Do you want this played out in front of everyone?'

'Oh and there is the raw nerve...' She tailed off, seeing the anger in his eyes. 'You are more worried about work.' She sat back down. 'Do you know how I found out? A gossip who wanted a cheap rise. In here. In our home... Look, that doesn't matter... not as much... I know what his parents must be going through.'

He regained his composure, softening his tone. 'I know. I was trying to protect you. There was nothing you could have done to avoid him. The police told you this. He wouldn't have known anything about it.' At her lack of response, he failed to conceal his impatience. 'Look, I'm not being unsympathetic but do we have to go over this ad nauseam?'

She cast a look of disbelief at him. 'I must have heard him. I know I heard him.'

'What are you talking about? You are just punishing

yourself. How many times do we have to tell you? It wasn't your fault. We have got through worse. Much worse. Let me help you.'

'You aren't listening to me,' she cried out in exasperation. 'Why won't you listen! No, I hear him. At night. He was under the car. He was conscious. I am certain of it.' She looked imploringly at him, her voice trembling. 'I can't get it out of my head. If I hadn't looked at my phone. That split second. It was me. No, don't say a word. If I hadn't been there...'

'You have to stop this. You are just having nightmares. How much of that have you been drinking this week? Knocking that back isn't going to help.'

'It would help if I was just a bloody robot like you.' She lifted her head. 'I should be logical, is that it? Rational? No. That isn't the way. We can sit down and go through a load of psychoanalytical bollocks, find something that vaguely fits.' She took another drink. 'What will you come up with for this one? No, that isn't your specialty. No, that's giving a chemical compound that will make me have a philosophical view on this. To have closure. To move on.'

'We aren't getting anywhere if you won't listen. I've had a long day. I'm going to bed and we can talk when I get back from work.' He casually picked up the near-empty decanter. 'If you are going to drown in self-pity, don't make it my best single malt. I'd prefer it if you joined me but that is up to you.'

Not answering, she watched him go to leave the room and then stop to make a final comment. 'I don't want to argue with you. It's difficult for me to watch you do this to yourself. Do you ever consider that? You seem to forget, but you know how this can go. We can get through this.' Seeing that she wasn't going to respond he concluded, 'It's your choice, I can't force you.'

Sarah sat up for an hour, then another. Graeme was long since asleep. He had been asleep about fifteen minutes after going to bed. After an hour of lying awake in bed she went over the argument with him. She hadn't expected him to show contrition and knew he would tell her that he was doing it for her benefit. But she had imagined he would understand. She didn't want to sleep. The idea was suffocating. She sat up in bed, her head still groggy from the whisky that she had been increasingly cutting into since Graeme's return.

In the fallout of their argument, she now privately contemplated Graeme's suggestion that she go back on medication. Even though it had helped make her well again in the past, and his objective diagnosis had made her see reason, she was still resentful of him. Despite the many thousands of prescriptions he had written, he couldn't ever feel what it was like to be pulled into what could be a living hell.

To Graeme it was a matter of clinical objectivity and deciding the best-fitting drug. At the start this was good, but when she wanted his empathy, he couldn't see why she should have such 'resistance to taking something that is going to make you feel better', the exception for her being the sleeping pills, which, when they worked, spared her the long drawn-out waking nights. But for the rescue with the medication provided came a compromise, the downside being the laboured days where she had to tolerate her fatigue, because it was the best option against what was the alternative.

From the beginning, when she agreed to treatment, came the apprehension of the trial and error of finding the right drug because the last one had made her nauseous, shake, and even when it was the right one, it would come at a cost. All the time she knew that she was being checked up on by Graeme and would be lectured every time she forgot or refused to continue with the tablets, protesting that they were making her ill, or they would disagree when she said she was certain that she was feeling better and didn't need to take anything. Even at the refill of one glass of wine too many, he would give her a reality check on her limitations.

But most often before an episode, Graeme would see it coming before her, when her depleting reserves of energy would make her frustrated, angry and feel close to breaking point, and she refused to acknowledge what she knew was coming. Then she would feel suffocated by his intervention, wracked with guilt over her inability to get herself out of what would cut her off from her family.

She hid her medication from her children in a locked cabinet early on when they were young, then out of sight when they were older. Despite her best efforts, they knew when she wasn't well. It was impossible to hide. She was desperate to not have the children go through any feeling of responsibility or thinking that they might in some way have the key to make it stop. In an attempt to reassure them when they were young, she would tell them it was just like having flu, or a broken arm, and just needed time to get better. But, it was always there, never far away, when the insidious, consuming blackness would close in around her.

For the greatest part of her life, there were the days where she opened her curtains in hopeful expectation or resilience to whatever lay ahead. On the worst ones when the illness took over, her life was suspended as she withdrew from the world, retreating to a loneliness that she had seen in her mother, but never understood until it happened with her. The days and nights when she couldn't sleep, staring at the four walls. Then listening in the morning as she heard others go out into the world she had no desire to engage in.

But after they had left, when the door closed, she felt relief that the house fell silent. When Graeme would telephone from work to check on her, she would sometimes become fractious, on occasion hostile at the intrusion.

At university it had been easier to hide, a depressed student hardly a stand-out novelty, and when previously she felt that no one noticed, it was a surprise when one day a tutor asked her if she needed to talk. Brushing it off as a late night, she had sat through his lecture not taking in a single word, leaving the hall as people seemingly moved around her. As they were talking or laughing about their day, she was a spectator, separated from the rest of the world. When a friend asked her if she was OK, except in a more direct way than the tutor, she joked it off. She was in a student environment where scores of people were hitting nearly every condition on the diagnostic scale, from bipolar to Asperger's. A girl two rooms away from hers, a self-harmer, had dropped out only the previous week after a complete breakdown, just one of a whole host of undiagnosed disorders freewheeling around campus.

Another reason for mostly concealing her lows was remembering how disclosure had played out when people discovered her illness. From well-meaning cups of tea, to 'pull yourself together', she had done them herself and witnessed them. Her mother's friends, who thought that she should be jollied up or she should be avoided. One thing that Sarah did eventually accept from Graeme was that you can't just find your own path out without help, something that her mother never acknowledged.

When her mother chose to interact with people she had the darkest sense of humour. One day a friend of hers began reciting an article from a magazine on the power of positive thinking, telling her it was most likely in her case mind over matter. Her mother, who had clearly reached her tolerance level as the woman took an inhalation for the beginning of the umpteenth paragraph, told her that there had been an article in *The Lancet* confirming in a recent study that, given the right conditions and exposure, her illness could be contagious. As Sarah was passing outside the door she overheard, then instantly had to put her hand to her mouth to suppress a sudden burst of laughter. However, the joke lost its shine when the woman's daughter, who Sarah had struck up a friendship with, began to make excuses to not come over to her house after school.

For Sarah, there had been one bad experience with a psychiatrist as a student, when she reached breaking point. It had been enough to vow she would never step back in another shrink's office. If it hadn't been for Graeme, she probably never would have done.

The psychiatrist in Cambridge, whose help she sought as an act of desperation one day, had become swiftly intolerant to her reluctance and instinctive resistance to taking medication. As she struggled to communicate and articulate her fears in her dulled confusion, he just talked over her scepticism. She was 'a maths student not a doctor'. Then he contemptuously dismissed her 'anecdotal evidence' of side-effects, his derision thinly veiled with an affected smile as he wrote the prescription, which he punctuated by saying, 'It might all seem a little daunting but she shouldn't read too many scaremongering articles.' Noticing his eyes flick to the clock, she realised that she had been in there for eighteen minutes. Hesitating to move, she considered that she hadn't said a single thing about how she felt. The clock ticked over to another minute. He put his pen down and placed his hands together on the table, looking once again at the clock. 'I won't keep you any longer, Miss Young. Make an appointment if you have any problems.' As she left his office, stepping out into the street she felt that it was the most formal way she had ever been told to fuck off in her life. Another ten yards down the road, she tossed the prescription into the bin, retreating back to her room, until three days later she was finally coaxed out by her friend to go to a party. Waking up on her back having been sick kept her from drinking until a couple of weeks later. After walking out of the middle of a particularly soporific lecture one day, she suggested to her friends when she got back they should all go to the Baron of Beef for a few pints. The lunchtime went through to post-closing drinks at a friend's house until the next morning. She never went back to the doctor, and never again contemplated it.

Her first experience of seeing the effects of medication was when she was a child, witnessing her mother suffer from bouts of sickness from lithium and ultimately raging against having to take anything prescribed. Then there were the following arguments between her parents, and when her mother refused and the subsequent rollercoaster her illness sent them on, until what seemed like her inexhaustible reserves of energy came crashing to a halt. Her first real memory of one of her mother's episodes was when she was about seven. At the time, Sarah thought it was the most fantastic day, not knowing that her father was fretting when he got a call from the school to say that Sarah hadn't been dropped off. All she knew was that instead of going to school they drove to the coast. It was a beautiful day in which must have been at least early summer. Her most acute memory was of flying a kite her mother bought from a local shop, the largest one they had. Looking in from outside as it hung motionless in the window, it begged to be given flight in the strong prevailing winds blustering around them. After hurrying down to the beach, the red, white and blue riding high through the wind, they thrilled at its soaring heights in the bright sky.

After eating fish and chips on the seafront, they clambered their way to the end of one of the rocky headlands, where her mother told her the tales of Odysseus and his journey home from Troy. The white horses riding the turquoise waters, glistening in the radiant sunlight. Above them was a covering of the lush green grass on the higher outcrops, patches of delicate pink flowers swaying in the wind. Before getting into the car they collected a bunch of whatever flowers they could find. As she selected each one, her mother listed all the flora and fauna, which Sarah was unable to keep up with. More acutely than the memories of the vibrant colours, the crimson, yellows, purples, she remembered the scented ones above others. The coconut smell of the gorse most of all.

Years later, when she had begun telling Izzy and Seb about it during a visit there, Graeme was passing a yellow flowering Alexander plant and quickly interrupted to pick one of the leaves and then ate it. Immediately it caught the children's attention when he told them of how the Romans brought it to Britain, conjuring images of menacing legionnaires ascending the beaches from their triremes, evidently a better subject matter than a story of fish and chips with a granny they had never met.

During that visit with Graeme and the children, they had reached the base of the same headland where she and her mother had sat. When she told them about that day, Izzy and Seb wanted to go out to the same far point, she and Graeme immediately affirming a no. As Graeme rebuked her for putting such an idea into the children's heads, it was then she saw the danger, the relentless tides of the Cornish coastline breaking onto the rocks over the swirling interchanging currents.

She hadn't seen it that day as they delighted every time they were hit by the spray of the breaking waves. She was sailing with Odysseus as his tumultuous voyage was brought to life. His trials and triumphs in overcoming the wrath of Poseidon, fighting off the Cyclops, and his eventual return to Ithaca to reclaim his kingdom. The magical day had come to an end as they arrived home after dark. After falling asleep on the way home, she awoke once they pulled into the drive, to be wearily confused by her father's ire, relief and exhaustion.

From that day with her mother, she had pressed one of the buttercups into a wildlife book she had given her as one of her previous birthday presents. When Izzy had been about the same age, she took the book to school as a project without asking Sarah. It was when she came home to boast to her mother about the show and tell that Sarah saw the flower was missing. At first she felt upset as Izzy became profusely apologetic, but outwardly played it down.

Later, when she next went back to the coast, she thought of the dried, scentless flower crushed between the pages, that she had held so dear, but without giving it as much thought, took greater comfort in the sight, but more the smell, of the fresh, growing flowers that would take her back to the joy of that day in a moment. It was one of the most treasured memories to which Sarah held on tightly, after the day came when her mother had no fight left.

After the highs came her mother's withdrawal, and in the aftermath her father took on a different kind of vigilance as she retreated to her room. A gloom prevailed in the house, despite her father's best efforts to distract and reassure Sarah. Any early attempts Sarah made to 'cheer her up' were met with little response, until the day came when she would once again slowly ease back into their lives. Sarah became adept at following her father's instruction in not overwhelming her, despite every instinct to hug her mother and tell her she had missed her. She would just go and sit next to her on the sofa, and they would watch a film together. But she didn't share with her the occasional hurt she felt as to why she couldn't be like other mums when she didn't feel up to coming to a school sports day or parents' evening. Or when she was only just given a reprieve from suspension for breaking the nose of another girl in the gym by throwing a medicine ball into her face when she called her mum a nutter. Sarah recalled sitting outside the head teacher's office after her father had been summoned to the school. Being beside herself with guilt should her mum find out and putting her proud father through what she knew would be an embarrassment. After he walked out of the office, they said almost nothing until he reached the car. Once they closed the door he calmly told her that she would be grounded for a month, along with no pocket money. As he started the engine he offered his final droll and sincere words as he kept his gaze ahead, saying there was some consolation that in being called away from work it hadn't just been 'for a milder transgression, such as deploying a lesser-offending netball'. Knowing that wasn't a cue for an invitation to laugh, she just reached across to squeeze his hand.

It wasn't long after that in her teenage years, Sarah began to suffer with what she recognised too well in her mother's downs. She would get angry with her parents, particularly her father, who she saw as becoming too intrusive. After seeing her mother's resistance and struggles with medication, she said that there was no way she would do the same, mostly because of fear of the side-effects, but also because of the certainty that it would define her, label her for life. For the most part she was able to cope, and instead of her father forcing the issue, he reluctantly accepted her choice.

It was only later after Ben died that she fully committed to taking regular medication. It was a course of antidepressants, along with a sedative that Graeme had first given her. He gave her no choice, leveraging Seb and Izzy as her incentive. The tablets that she had long seen as the enemy helped get her back on her feet. But when she forgot about the place it kept her from, she would stop taking them. For periods that worked, until the next time. She also sought the help of a counsellor, and it proved to be her best decision.

For seven years she worked with Tom, a therapist who she found by mere chance. Graeme had shortlisted three female psychotherapists that he thought would be suitable. On the way to see one of them, she bumped into a man outside the door to the building where she had arranged to meet the new prospective therapist. Since leaving the house, her head was filled with what she should say, what she shouldn't say, preparing to make a bolt for it should she be presented with suggestive inked stencils, or if the therapist consistently repeated her name in insincerity. She also didn't know if she was ready to talk to a stranger. Five yards before the door she was at the point of turning around, but instead of doing so she walked quickly towards the entrance, contemplating that once she was in reception she would be able to get a better picture.

Sarah didn't see a man coming from the other direction, who was also heading towards the door. She knocked into him, dropping her bag to the floor. Simultaneously a pastry bag he was carrying was dislodged, its contents spilling onto the pavement.

Accepting her nervous apology, he picked up her bag. Seeing her anxiety he immediately put her at ease, by joking that he wished everyone was as keen as her.

As she took her seat in reception she spent the next ten minutes waiting on her appointment, after the receptionist apologetically informed her that the therapist was stuck in traffic. With each minute ticking past, she once again questioned her decision to come. As her doubts built up, along with imagined bad omens at the therapist being delayed, she began to convince herself that this wasn't right for her. Picking up a magazine she flipped through the pages with her eyes set on the clock. The second hand moved in plodding, audible increments which exacerbated the slow passage of time. She continued to flip past a dozen pages of which she had retained almost nothing. A few minutes later the receptionist once again offered her apologies. This time she elaborated by saying that the therapist would be delayed indefinitely, as she was in a tailback on the M5 due to an accident, and would have to reschedule. It was then that Sarah asked to see the man whose lunch she had sent flying. After a wait, during which she assumed her request was being cleared with the other therapist, he opened the door to ask her to come in.

After inviting her to take a seat, he took a chair opposite

hers. The chairs were placed in front of a desk that was mostly clear, aside from a file and some papers stacked neatly with a pen placed beside them. No photos, no clue as to anything about him. A painting hung on the wall opposite of an ocean pier. Bringing her attention back to him he began.

'So tell me about yourself.'

'OK. My name is Sarah Hughes. I'm twenty-seven. I have...' She hesitated at the invitation to start immediately talking about her family. '... So, I live not far away.' She faltered in the silence of the room, feeling a weight of pressure to break it. She could feel herself go flush. Struggling in her reticence, her eyes cast up again to the painting. 'So, what's that meant to be? Don't tell me, we are to think of new horizons, happy times, ugh. I bet, yes, it is a thank you present from one of your depressed artists.'

He didn't respond.

'Yes, I knew it. You therapists have to remind yourselves how brilliant you are.' He remained quiet, leading her to feel instantly remorseful. 'Look, I'm sorry. I don't know where that came from. I don't think I am doing the right thing, you know, being here. Again, I'm sorry, I will pay for your time, of course.' She picked up her bag to leave.

'Are you going to let me tell you?'

'What?'

'About the painting.'

'Oh. OK.' She sat back down, keeping her bag close on her lap.

'It was painted by a former colleague, and I'm sorry to say, he jumped off that pier last year. It actually has a lot of meaning for me.'

'Oh shit! Wow, I didn't...' She stopped, as he had a small detectable smile across his face.

'Of course you're joking, right.'

'If you want to know, I picked it up in an antiques shop

last year. It isn't sentimental, or personal, I just really like it. I find it relaxing.'

'Oh right.' She broke into an embarrassed smile. 'So making a joke about suicide, are you even supposed to do that?'

'Sarah, you seem to have preconceptions about what therapy is. This isn't about me, and it never will be. In this office I will listen, not judge, nor offer you answers to your life questions or attempt to sell you magic fixes. You should understand that when you come in here and close the door, whatever you say stays in the room.' He anticipated her about to make a joke. 'No, it's not Vegas. But, you can say what you want to, and the decisions after that will be yours, this will all come from you. However long it takes.'

After giving her a moment on what he knew would be the definitive decision as to whether she would stay or leave, he continued, 'Now, shall we start? Do you want to tell me about yourself?'

After composing her first few sentences, thereafter followed a flood of thoughts that spontaneously came out in broken sentences. They were mostly about Ben, Graeme, her guilt in feeling that she hadn't been a better mother to Seb and Izzy, breaking down in tears as she brought Ben into the room. She surprised herself as to how much she unloaded to someone who had been a stranger only an hour before. It was Tom that had to gently remind her that her time was up. The first breath that she took outside in the street was a moment of release.

Being in his office, she was glad that she had shared her memories of Ben. Nearly everything that she had held back from Graeme, from anyone, she gave air to in that room. When she was ready, she was able to once again enjoy the good times. But, no matter what was said, what reassurances were offered, she could never accept his loss. She repelled at the notion of 'moving on', shutting down the possibility of acceptance that she was certain in her mind he was waiting for. They were all waiting for.

She saw Tom twice a week for the next three months until she was content with just once. It was a retreat where, when she couldn't disclose how she was struggling to Graeme, she felt safe in the confines of his room. Graeme's office could not have been more different, with bright lights and a clinical display, with stiff functional patient chairs that rested a couple of inches below his own. If Tom's office was reassurance in disclosure, Graeme's offered reassurance in chemicals. Over the years that they had been together, she never liked to go to her husband's work. Designed for brevity of visit, it was a utilitarian space for finding applicable diagnosis, and the subsequent and expedite explanation of delivery of treatment.

Everything in Tom's office had an order, a projected calmness. An aesthetic replication of whale music. A lamp whose bulb was twenty watts shy of its regular purpose, with a sandalwood bowl of pot pourri underneath. Later, having seen an identical decorative bowl in a craft shop, she bought one for Graeme's office, which lasted about a week before it could be found on one of the shelves in reception.

Tom sat in a high-back chair, one that mirrored hers, as he walked the fine margins of inviting disclosure wrapped up in supportive rhetoric. Occasionally leaning to make notes, she knew behind this projected serenity he was digesting, reflecting and working to facilitate her path. It was not an aspect of the process she wanted to give too much thought to, especially at the times she pushed herself and fell short of articulating her feelings. Something that for the first few months she berated herself for. Tom didn't have many books on display, as he said clients would often use them as a distraction. Unlike Graeme, with two full bookshelves of academic texts, which he once told Sarah were less for reference than to put off an amateur, self-defining Freud wasting his time. Tom's office, despite mocking it on her angry and disjointed days for possessing crap paintings and scented empathy, was her safe haven and he had got her through times when she could barely see beyond the next day.

For seven years his office had been her sanctuary until at the end of one session he told her he was moving to America. Six months later she said her goodbyes, making a promise that she would send the occasional email to say that she was OK. A year later when she became ill again, she made two abortive attempts with other therapists, the longest being a month. Neither clicked and she decided to stop looking for a replacement.

CHAPTER 19

THE FOLLOWING NIGHT after her argument with Graeme, once again she lay awake restless in the silence. They had barely spoken that day and he had made his excuses in the evening to go to the mess, arriving back late, only to go almost straight to bed.

The relief of the morning felt far away, as it was only just past one o'clock. Taking her dressing gown, she went into the sitting room where she picked up her laptop to read the news from home. Firstly, she checked her emails, but as she hadn't sent any for the last couple of weeks she wasn't expecting any. The previous day's lottery winner was announced – a ticket from Birmingham worth £10 million or thereabouts. She smiled as she waited to read the story of the announced winners on the following week. Mr and Mrs So-and-So popping a bottle of fizz and saying that they would still live in the same semi-detached and continue working at their ordinary jobs. When reading these stories of tremendous windfalls she thought of what she would do. It didn't need much imagination. A glorious binge of all binges. Travelling the world first class. Sod humility and a magnanimous acceptance. Hand over the cheque and then bugger off to the Bahamas. Instead, she had always lived to budgeted means. Ellie teased her when she was showing her latest splurge on credit. Life was for living, accusing Sarah of using her exacting calculations for her finances as some sort of substitute basket weaving. And all that self-denial wasn't healthy.

At the bottom of the sports report, once again the betting website came up. Sports, casino. Odds flashing. She went to close the laptop. Once again it caught her eye.

Out of curiosity, she opened up the webpage, bringing an illumination of sporting fixtures and casino games upon which to place your stakes, odds constantly changing on an array of sports, which she barely knew existed. From continent to continent, it was as if she had tapped into a frantic world of money changing hands. On the front, a football game taking place in Australia caught her attention as everything was suddenly suspended. A roar sounded as the word 'GOAL' flashed across the screen. Not realising the sound was up, her heart skipped a beat as the roar echoed through the silence of the room. Listening out she couldn't hear Graeme stir. She felt a strange exhilaration as she had no idea about what else was going on. But it was Sydney FC v Melbourne and the half-time whistle had just sounded. On the far side of the world cold bottles of VB were being joyfully consumed, and others downed in commiseration. She imagined the celebrations as the chants rang out in the stands. Beneath the football was the cricket, baseball and basketball. Home runs, baskets sunk, all to no doubt the same rapturous applause, jeers, groans and elation. Further down minor tennis tournaments were being played in Asia. As she clicked through different pages the options presented as near endless. This along with the dazzling enticements for the casino lighting up the drab room.

There were several hours to go until morning, and the hands on the clock seemed to have barely moved. The Sydney FC v Melbourne game was just beginning the second half. Looking at the top of the page it displayed a sign to log in for an account. On the advert £10 could be staked for free. An opening gift. There was nothing to lose. It wouldn't even be her money. To stop thinking about everything for just one hour.

It took her a matter of minutes to set up an account that welcomed her to their club, wishing her the best of luck, a sentiment that she doubted somehow. Then a message popped up with a code. The match was into the fifty-fifth minute as she pondered what to bet on. Not just a simple matter of win or lose. Dozens of different options, too many to go through. When the next goal would be, how would it be scored, who would it be, how many cards, corners – the list was endless. It was 1-1 and the odds weren't that different. Goals. There were bound to be more goals. You could select under or over four goals. They had to think there were going to be more as the odds were even and it was already ten minutes into the second half. But were these odds calculated on money already placed or probability on their form? Sarah's mathematical instincts came to the fore, frustrated that she didn't have more facts or knowledge on which to make a better-informed choice.

She decided to place her bet on goals over, not under. Otherwise the time might seem like an eternity. As she typed in her £10 stake, she hesitated. It seemed a lot, even if it wasn't her money. The odds then changed. 11/10. Even better. Without giving it further thought she placed the bet. A countdown began. 3-2-1. The confirmation came. An electronic display of a betting slip. A world away from the paper slip that held the annual Grand National bet. It was also double what she would have bet on any horse that day. She clutched the betting slip in her hand for the duration of the race, until ten minutes later hope was transformed into a redundant scrap. Aside, she remembered the one time that she had put 50p on Maori Venture in 1987 at 28/1. A small fortune which, after much consideration, was weeks later turned into a much looked-forward-to 12" record and lunch with her best friend at *Pizza Hut*, although retrospectively, for her memory, and her record collection, she wished that Rick Astley hadn't been Number 1 at the time.

Nothing happened in the football match for the next few minutes, and the pang of regret crept in. What had possessed her to do such a thing? The odds were steadily going out. Her focus then drifted to a tennis match and prompted her to wonder why she hadn't at least stuck to a sport she knew. Her attention was then suddenly drawn back to the match, which was showing all bets suspended. Then came the flash across the screen. 'GOAL.'

'Yes!' She quietly restrained her celebration. Then she looked at the clock. Sixty-three minutes. A quick calculation told her that there were twenty-seven minutes to go. A cinch. She prepared to go and get a coffee. At least this would be interesting. One goal. That would be all it took. Tucking her laptop under her arm she made her way through to the kitchen, impatient to reopen the game, not wanting to miss a goal in the thirty seconds or so that she had the screen closed.

Making the coffee she waited as the only movements on the screen were the periodical changing of odds as the time passed. At the eightieth minute, halfway through her coffee, she once again considered that she should have just left it alone. Ten more minutes. Then, with barely a moment of it being suspended, the word GOAL flashed up again on the screen.

Suddenly Sydney FC had become her favourite team. Before the final whistle went she saw the amount register in her account.

She told herself that she would have cashed it in but for the regulations of her having to play the stake three times. It was still another few hours until sunrise. If she just played this through she would cash it in or fail. Onto the screen a fresh fixture appeared that was about to commence. This was tennis. Her game, and she had an immediate gut instinct that was too good to ignore.

When the free bet ran its course, and with another match that she had a good hunch on, she decided to take a small amount from the account with her remaining money from the sale of the shop, in which there was just under £24,000. Tonight she was taking a mere £25. Tomorrow it would be replaced with interest. Sarah duly made the transfer.

Over the next few weeks, she began spending most nights, placing a series of bets, sometimes singular, but often many ran concurrently. If she had a loss she sought out why. In a further distraction, often during the day, she began researching many of the sports that she was staking a bet on, intensively observing and taking in information on three main sports: tennis, horse racing and cricket. The terminology and complexities of the latter two she had been blissfully unaware of and had barely known the basics. She had been absorbing it all – an unfolding, glamorous, high-stakes, intense, gruelling and sometimes gut-wrenching drama.

Mostly, this was on the radio and websites, in which commentators, statistics, pundits competed with gut instinct in making her choices. A variety of sports that mostly she had known nothing about now became a challenge to become proficient in understanding its plays and trying to formulate algorithms. Her degree in mathematics she was certain was giving her a significant advantage. It had been a while since she had challenged herself by working out similar formulas and complex probabilities, but now in the fresh pursuit of bringing about a new way to success. In cricket, which bowlers would be suited to which pitches, the weather conditions, which trainers did well at which tracks, which horses had dropped up or down in grade, which team had a good home or away record in a match, the form of a particular pitcher, striker or batsman, who was injured, who was on a winning streak.

CHAPTER 20

It was past 1a.m. Restless and waiting for Graeme to fall asleep, she got out of bed. He didn't stir as she quietly closed the door behind her. It had been a long day after significant losses at two race meetings and she was impatient to recoup her money. Taking a glass of cold water she felt the relief of leaving the darkness as she immediately made her way to her laptop.

She then began betting on a series of fixtures around the globe. Tennis, football, rugby sevens, boxing, horse racing, now basketball. All of which she had continued over the weeks to take in as much information as possible, including the rules, the players, the form. Sometimes paying off after much research and calculation, other times placing random blind bets when waiting on her next preselected fixture. What she knew about tennis was set in contrast to the other extreme such as handball, of which she only knew the basic rules. But, whatever the time of day or night, it was all a click away. There was always a clock beginning its countdown, always a shot being lined up or defended, a fence to be jumped, or not, a finish line to be strained for, a boxer ready to succumb, a last gasp of hope and expectation as the victors gained the spoils.

Oblivious to the time, she only became aware of morning approaching as the first light began to radiate through the curtains. The account balance showed £487 by the time she heard Graeme open the bedroom door. In the middle of a crucial stage of a wager, her focus returned to the screen. A time-out was being taken in the last quarter in a basketball game featuring the San Antonio Spurs v Denver Nuggets.

Overall, the points average for Tony Parker, the prolific point guard of the Spurs, had gone up in the last couple of weeks. Requiring more attention than a hunch, she quickly accessed records as the commentator confirmed what she had read before the game started. In the last game he had a winner from a long field goal as the buzzer sounded. He had watched what was the winning three points with a perfect shot. The net barely rippled as the ball passed through, prompting the team to celebrate in unison. He was one of the best, and instinct had told her that the minute he lined up the shot, it would be in, along with most of the fans surrounding the court as they held their breath as the ball was in flight. The sight of the basket had sent £850 coming back her way. An amount credited within a few brief minutes. Revelling in the sight of the boosted balance, she had listened to the post-match interview as if she were part of the celebration. It was that game that had made her so confident about backing them again today.

Sarah heard Graeme close the bathroom door to begin his usual routine.

Now, the animated coaches called the plays as the team leaned in. Exhausted players took their orders as behind them the sweat of their labours was being swept from the court. The sound of Graeme had made her miss the number on the latest foul count of the opposition's star player. Just under a minute on the clock, an eternity in basketball. Each team had two time-outs remaining. San Antonio were one point ahead. The next play would be for two shots. Most likely they would be three ahead.

Resuming play they duly completed the penalty shots. The following seconds ticked down, Nuggets losing possession. She gripped her hands, damp with sweat, into tight anxious fists. The Spurs player Tim Duncan followed up with what looked like an all-too-easy lay-up. Five ahead and the Nuggets coach called a time-out. £1,290 was twenty-two seconds away.

From the restart, a fast move was executed well and a two-pointer for the Nuggets was scored. In what looked like a moment of distraction, one of the Spurs players was dispossessed. A breakaway down the court made for an easy two points. A mildly fractious exchange between two of the players was short of the expletive that Sarah made as the play recommenced. A resulting basket from her team went partway to recomposing herself.

The bathroom door opened and she became irritated as she heard his footsteps along the hallway. Keeping half an eye on the screen, her hand was ready to close the lid as she waited until she was sure he was going back into the bedroom. Another basket scored by the Spurs to take them to five points ahead the clock ticked down to three seconds. The Nuggets made a deliberate foul to make the Spurs take the shots. In what seemed an inexplicable bout of nerves the player missed both attempts. Buoyed by their glimmer of hope a confident point guard secured a long-shot. Two points in it with only 2.6 seconds on the clock. There was no way that Spurs could lose it.

The last time-out was called by the coach. After the restart the ball was launched down the court. A tie would send them to overtime. Instead of making sure of the overtime, one of the

Nuggets players lined up a three-pointer. Sarah, along with the rest of the arena, held their breath, adrenaline coursing through her veins as the ball seemed to take an eternity in flight. It bounced off the rim away from the basket. She let out a yelp of delight. However, the ball was caught off the rebound and, in a flash, a teammate grasped the ball and deposited the basket for just the two points. For a second, her anger and disappointment came to the fore as overtime loomed. Then she caught the dreaded sight of the referee calling an additional foul against a Spurs player. An extra shot would be awarded to the Nuggets. The colour went from her cheeks. Less than three seconds ago she was ruing not putting all of the account on a Spurs victory. Now the enormity of the sum that was in the hands of a man over 8,000 kilometres away began to sink in. If it had been her player that was lining up for the shot, he would have looked tired. She would have been certain his nerves would get the better of him. But the tall, athletic man calmly lining up the shot looked fresh, confident and as if there was not a single doubt in his mind about sinking the penalty shot. He duly fulfilled her expectation and his team were in raptures.

Sarah clicked onto her account, bringing up the amount left. £45.23. Her anger surged inside. Why hadn't that idiot defender just left it alone? It would be overtime. She was certain that she would have at least split the stake to make sure that she at least recouped her losses. Her lesson would have been learned. The ecstatic Denver captain was now being interviewed as she heard Graeme approaching. She turned down the volume, turning the screen away from the door. The next fixture she immediately focused on was a minute away. As she quickly assessed her options Graeme walked in, to which she took off her headphones.

'I'm just off. I thought that you might want a coffee.' As she failed to respond he continued sympathetically, 'Have you been up long?'

'No. I'm fine. Thank you. And no I don't need a coffee.' She tried to suppress her irritation as her eyes flicked back to the screen. 'I'll see you later. Have a good one.' Looking down once again, the match kicked off.

'Sarah, you need to try and get more rest.' He walked towards her, prompting her to conceal the screen. 'I think that we should talk. How about lunch?'

'OK, sure. Lunch. How about the NAAFI?'

'I've got the afternoon off. How about going into Celle?'

The tennis would be on and Federer was imminently scheduled in the order of play. Firstly, Sydney FC was about to kick off. 'I'm not sure that I'm really feeling up to going into town. It will probably be busy.' Her fingers tapped impatiently as she sought to place her bet.

'You need some air at least. You want to try opening up these curtains. It's stuffy in here.'

The betting odds on the game suddenly suspended. 'GOAL!' flashed up on the screen. 'For goodness' sake, Graeme!' She snapped down the lid of the computer. 'Stop fussing. I'm not a child!'

Her outburst stopped him in his tracks. 'What has got into you?'

'I'm sorry. I'm just tired. Yes, perhaps we should take the afternoon out. That would be great, book a table for about 1.30.'

'OK. It will give us a chance to talk. I'll pick you up at one o'clock.'

'Whatever you think.'

He looked at his watch. 'Make sure that you are ready.'

Sarah waited for the door to close as instantaneously she turned her attention back to the laptop. Although she knew she had missed the boat, she still placed a handicap bet on Sydney FC to win. Before the game, the odds were 10/11 on an outright win. Even though they were 2-0 up she placed the remainder of the account on Sydney to win by at least two goals. Within twenty minutes the opposition team had hit two successive quick-fire goals, as Sydney had done at the start. Five minutes from the end, a towering defender ranged upon the goal and powered in an injury-time winner. Her resentment turned to Graeme. If he hadn't come in to nag her, she would have the return in her account. In the aftermath of the match, she felt dehydrated. The account balance at zero, she placed another £200 in the account. The guilt was fleeting as she eyed what she knew would be a winner in the next match. £100 placed, she took a deep breath and left the computer as the players commenced warming up on court.

The next three matches went well and she had £435 in her account as the last match was coming to an end. A comfortable win for Federer, his opponent looking all at sea. Demoralised, his unforced errors racked up, shot after shot finding the net or called out. She had been right about the fact that he didn't look fully fit in the last game, and if it hadn't been for the tantrum of his opponent who effectively threw the game, she doubted his staying power. She had been right. Two games shy of what seemed an inevitable rout the trainer was called on and then he conceded. A player that when fully fit would have made a contest of it, as he had been when recently winning her a healthy amount at one of the minor tournaments, she was now breathing a sigh of relief at his being beaten by fatigue.

Waiting for the amount to appear she stood up, stretching out. £730 appeared as she refreshed her account. An ODI cricket match was mid-innings. It was Australia playing in Bangladesh. The money had to go with Australia, but would have to be a handicap bet. They had made over 270 runs. How many would Bangladesh be bowled out for? She considered that it had to be less than 240. But, what was the pitch like, what were the weather conditions? She waited for the stats page to open and also the commentary feed.

Opening up the curtains to the bright sunlight, she noticed next door's son walking past. It took her a moment to compute that it must be lunchtime. In a panic she looked at the clock, which was showing 12.43. Throwing open the curtains and windows, she made her way as quickly as she could to the bathroom, cursing as she rapidly attempted to cover her casts. Her frustration got the better of her for the second time that day as she eased herself into the shower. Dropping the shampoo and forgetting to take a towel from the cupboard, she felt the anxiety of the time ticking down until Graeme would be back. In momentary relief from the panic that had set in, she gave in to a moment of mild hysteria as she dropped the bar of soap that flew like a toboggan around the back of the toilet, appearing out the other side. By the time she made it back to the bedroom it was only five minutes to one. Her mind removed from the rollercoaster of the last eight hours, she noticed that Graeme had pulled up outside. Not sure whether she would look closer to getting ready by being midway through drying her hair or halfway dressed, she plumped for grabbing the hairdryer. It quickly occurred to her that having the full extent of her casts and fading bruises might garner some sympathy and quell his annoyance.

As she heard the door open she briefly switched off the hairdryer to call out, 'Sorry, I'm running a little late. The water went off this morning. I'll be ten minutes.' She swiftly turned it on again as he came into the room.

'Don't worry. There's no hurry.'

She switched off the hairdryer. 'What have you done with my husband?'

'They're never busy at this time.' He walked over to her, moving her hair back, kissing her neck. 'What about a late afternoon lunch?'

'Graeme, I don't think that is a good idea. It isn't that...'

He withdrew. 'Something else to blame on the car crash.'

'Seriously, look at me.' She let out a laugh to ease the tension. 'Really, at least wait until the casts are off.'

'Sure. Of course. It isn't as if you are here most of the time anyway,' he condescended.

'What is that supposed to mean?'

'You never spend any time in our bed anymore.'

She turned her attention back to getting ready. 'Do you have the slightest idea what I am going through?'

'It was weeks ago, Sarah. I think it's about time you started to move on.'

'Just leave me alone, Graeme. Some of us can't switch off like you. It wasn't you in the crash with Ben. And it wasn't you in this crash. If you had been, you might have some idea.'

'And here we are again,' he responded in cutting exasperation. 'Wallowing won't give you an excuse not to make a life here. Just like then.'

Her heart racing, she put on her dressing gown and followed him out. 'What is that supposed to mean?' she called out angrily. 'Like then?'

'You've always stayed in the past. You never wanted to move on. You filled cupboards, cooked meals…'

'Where has all this come from? I don't understand.'

Her look of anxiety made him check what he was going to say first. 'Forget it. I've just had a difficult day. Let's just go and get some lunch. We could do with getting off camp.'

As she finished getting ready, his words replayed in her head, thinking how she was going to salvage the day. When she was finally ready, she went through to the sitting room where she wasn't sure what she would find. Whether he would be holding onto this or, as she hoped, put it behind them.

When she saw him in the sitting room with her laptop, a moment of dread seized her. 'What are you doing? That's my computer!' She rushed over, closing the lid.

Her outburst of anxiety took him aback. 'Alright. Calm

down! I was only going to catch up on the news. I didn't know that you were into cricket. Although, I wouldn't expect anything from the BBC, except everyone sending in their shots of watching it on a beach somewhere or other.'

'Sorry, what?'

'You. Reading the cricket. Why, what did you think I was doing? Checking your emails?'

'It's just a privacy thing. Nikki sent a personal email. I didn't know if it was still open. Not that I think you would read it, of course.'

'As if I would be interested,' he replied nonchalantly.

'We should get going.' She looked at him to see if there was any hint that he had gone beyond the first page, and noticed the betting site in the bar. Her habit of keeping a dozen pages open at the same time had most likely obscured the name of the website.

Graeme's comments about her not moving on, and the close call with the website, made her preoccupied over lunch. The exhaustion began to catch up on her halfway into their meal, accelerated by her second glass of white wine. The noise of the restaurant grated through her head as she made every effort to stay on top of things. Turning her attention to Graeme's work, she left the bulk of the conversation to him. The topic came to its conclusion when it was obvious he couldn't say any more.

'What did you mean, back at the apartment?' Sarah began.

'About the move, I take it.' He lowered his voice. 'I didn't mean anything by it. I should apologise, I suppose.'

'You suppose?' she replied irritably. 'I'm not interested in an apology, Graeme. I want to know what you meant...'

'Here?'

'There is no one within twenty feet, Graeme. Why did you say that I stayed in the past? I thought we made a wonderful home before. It was everything we said it would be.'

'This isn't about Cheltenham. It was a stupid comment. I just worry. I know that this has been hard for you.'

'I've joined three clubs and before this did I miss a single dinner, or even one of your chronically soporific work drinks? But yes, I miss my friends, my work. I thought that the business course would be enough. You keep telling me how lucky I am that I don't have to work... so, perhaps... if I took some more work.'

He interrupted. 'There isn't any work that's suitable. Not as my wife. You know this. Once you get over this bad patch, it will improve, I promise. You just need to give it another go. This is a once-in-a-lifetime opportunity, make the most of it. We will take that holiday and when you come back we can make a fresh start of it.' He leaned over and held her hand. 'It will get better. If you let me help you concentrate on getting better. As soon as the cast comes off, I will take some leave. Of course, work commitments aside. How about we just take it one step at a time? One day at a time. If you aren't happy by the beginning of the summer, I promise we can do things your way.' Not pressing him for what her way would entail, they spontaneously acknowledged that they should call a truce on the topic. Soon after, Sarah asked for the bill, suggesting that they cut short lunch and go back to the apartment.

Later that night, waking up at 2.30 a.m., the commitment to get things back to normal began to evaporate as she lay awake. Weighing heavy in her mind in the dark silence of the room was the world of possibilities that lay forty feet away. Taking a sedative she attempted to go to sleep, then when that failed she took another before they eventually took effect. It would be six hours before she awoke. Her first thought led her back to her laptop.

CHAPTER 21

TODAY WAS GRAND National day. In an hour's time Sarah and Graeme's guests were arriving to watch the event. Something of a double celebration, as her casts were now off, giving her the relief of being able to move around with greater freedom. A gradual progression with her physio allowed her to get back to doing the things she had missed. The everyday pleasures that she had taken for granted, such as cooking well-prepared meals, taking walks out and not lumbering around every time she chose even to go out just for a coffee. The downside was the expectation that she would rejoin the social scene in full capacity, not least from Graeme who just the day before was giving her a rundown of impending events. The resumption of joining a ladies' poker morning where the stakes were a token £1 for the victor drove her to distraction. Before leaving the house she would place a couple of bets that would run concurrently. When the winner of the poker game was being congratulated, she would be discreetly checking her wagers, looking on the players around the world who had been championing her stakes. If the bets came to fruition or her teams lay vanquished during the time she was there, even in the event of her nursing a loss she felt a quiet satisfaction that the other ladies didn't detect a flicker. This was hers, and at the conclusion when they went their separate ways she would be able to gain more details.

As Graeme was out at the shops gathering last-minute items, she had taken the opportunity to tune in to the tennis. With her earphones in, she was watching the men's tennis championship title, which could be decided on the next point. It had been played out over four hours with £270 riding on the outcome. The crowd hushed in anticipation of the delivery of the serve. It was the first break point opportunity against his flagging opponent. Five gruelling attritional sets where every point had been hard fought. The defending champion wiped his brow, his focus unwavering. He pulled out of his routine as an overexuberant member of the crowd shouted encouragement, only to be swiftly hushed by those around him. Regaining his composure he bounced the ball, once then twice. After a slight hesitation he tossed the ball up. Every sinew to his fingertips extended in motion to deliver the full force. At full stretch the opponent returned with a cross-court backhand. But he was ready. On the front foot he greeted the ball with a more ferocious backhand. Having partially recovered his position the opponent set himself, anticipating that an accurately delivered repetition deeper into the corner would have him wrong-footed. Sarah saw it, as did the crowd who gasped as they also wondered if the telegraphed move would be his downfall. The ball headed deep into the corner. The champion didn't move, helpless in having to watch. Was this his title?

Sarah suddenly felt a hand on her shoulder. 'Could you not hear that I was calling you?' Graeme remonstrated as she took off her headphones.

'Wow! Do you have to creep up on me? I was just watching the tennis,' she responded irritably before quickly taking a glance at the screen. The champion was lying on his back, his hands over his face as the camera panned around to an appreciative crowd, his racquet some distance away in what she imagined had been a great release of the moment of victory.

'What a win!' she exclaimed in delight. Her annoyance dissipated as she knew that she was now over £470 better off. 'What a game! Sorry, you were quick! I thought you would be a while yet.'

'I've been over two hours,' he responded, perplexed. 'I had to go into the town. If you can believe it there was no chilled champagne. You do know that they are going to be here in less than an hour?'

She quickly looked at her watch. 'Oh sod it. Where did the time go?' She swiftly closed down her laptop. 'I'll be ready in no time. Don't stress so much.'

The previous night at a mess dinner, at 2 a.m. to be precise, Graeme had invited around half a dozen of the other officers to watch the Grand National that day. The offer had come in response to a drunken contest between a few of them about who had the best insight into the race. She and Graeme had been to a few previous race meetings at Cheltenham, Sandown and Ascot where the racing itself had been a peripheral event to the socialising. At the dinner, all of them embellished their knowledge with a plethora of anecdotes on previous wins, shameless name-dropping of trainers and owners and an in-depth tale of meeting the Queen at Ascot. Aside from the odd painful clang of a well-connected name, she listened to what was being said about the race. What was congruent with other information she had heard over the past few days.

The guests arrived almost all at once. A couple of the men who Sarah didn't know were swiftly introduced. In buoyant mood, she enthusiastically welcomed them, offering a range of drinks as Graeme took them through to the sitting room. Given the dinner parties that they had hosted since being there, this was a breeze to organise. Canapés and drinks. In her head, she had almost a rolodex of canapé recipes that she had accrued over the years, ranging from smoked salmon or sea bass blinis, to beetroot and goat's cheese crostini and asparagus wraps. Given the amount of times that she had prepared them over the years, Chloe joked that she wouldn't bet against her doing them on a ten-minute clock, blindfolded. However, today they were being served crispy chicken, cheese straws, a throw-together plate of carrot-heavy crudités with hummus and Kettle Chips. She sensed when she told Graeme that morning what she was doing that he held back on other suggestions. Her late night and being less than impressed that he had invited so many at short notice would have resulted in him having a pinny launched in his direction. As usual, the drinks she left to him while she was in charge of keeping their guests supplied with food.

The room buzzed with anticipation of the main race. The preceding races gave a couple of them the opportunity to impart their knowledge to the others. When Sarah came through with the latest tray of pastries, one in particular, Paul, a young major, asked Sarah what horse she had chosen. 'So, Sarah, will you be having a bet? Tell me, what's the housewives' choice?' he joked to her, playing up to the room.

'I thought Donald McCain's horse.'

'Just because he is Ginger McCain's son? Interesting choice but this is no Red Rum,' he laughed. 'But the checked colours are pretty, I suppose.'

'Yes, very funny… actually I was told that if the going was good to soft he stood a great chance. Apparently, he's the right weight, age and he did well at Cheltenham last year. And yours is?'

'Er, as a matter of fact it's Chief Dan George. A solid outside chance. A very nice horse.'

'You could be right, however my concern would be that he fell at his last outing at Cheltenham. But hey, I'm sure you know what you are doing.'

Graeme looked at her in surprise.

'You know that Nikki has a friend that's a trainer. She gave me the tip and a bit of a rundown on the runners and riders.'

'OK. If you say so. I'll put a call in. So the McCain horse for you. I'll put you down for a quid?'

'Go crazy Graeme, make it £1 each way.'

He duly obliged as the bookmaker took his call after placing £50 on his selection. As he waited in the phone queue he put his hand over the receiver. 'I wouldn't put too much stock on Nikki's advice, she just knows the trainer's wife. No, this is AP McCoy's year again. Greatest living jockey on last year's winner... from Jonjo's yard.' He spoke loudly enough to impress the others, doubling his initial stake after hearing that Paul would be wagering that same amount.

She smiled as he confidently boasted his knowledge. He was repeating the exact words from his friend at dinner the previous night. She thought about responding to his comment. He was right about the trainer, one of the best. According to one of the radio hosts he had state-of-the-art facilities for his stables, from a solarium to a swimming pool. In curiosity she had looked it up. Indeed there were horses living in better conditions than some of the soldiers. As Graeme rejoined the conversation, upping the ante on his claims, she knew that he wouldn't know 'Jonjo's yard' if he was in the pool swimming alongside the recovering runner from the 2.30 at Sandown.

In the lead-up to the race they talked up the chances of their horses, over a near demolition of the snacks that she had been making earlier. She was now wishing that she had just emptied a couple of bags of crisps for all the appreciation. Her efforts in baking pastries and making dips had barely raised a comment. One of Graeme's friends, Crispin, that she had heard in the general discussion, talked of an up-and-coming horse that had also been strongly fancied by one of the pundits on the radio station that morning. It began to set her in two minds. Money was coming in for the horse as the race became closer. With five minutes to go she took the opportunity to go and place her bet.

Her horse was now at 14/1. What a price! The horse fancied by Crispin was 8/1. Money had come in for it that morning. Her account stood at £557, with two pending bets on matches to take place that morning. She heard Graeme call through for more Kettle Chips, which she acknowledged as she hovered over the keyboard. She put in her earpiece to hear the commentators. 'This will be one Donald will dedicate to his father... His horse...' Without delay she made the selection. £100. To win. Click. She then listened as the other pundit jokingly accused the other of being sentimental as he reaffirmed his choice. She then put £50 each way on the other horse.

The excitement in the sitting room intensified as they urged the starter to get a move on. She heard another cork popping. 'Sarah!' Graeme called out. 'It's starting. Hurry up. Oh and better bring another bottle of champers as well.'

It was a gut feeling. In a rush she put another £300 to win on her choice, Donald McCain's horse. Her stomach flipped at the sight of the amount that was now being placed. In a flap she had a sudden change of heart. But the money was down. In her account sat £57.

A variety of comments were voiced as the starter lifted the tape, all of which abruptly turned into a cheer of approval, echoed by the 70,000 race-goers that roared through the speakers. Her heart raced as she looked for her horse, one of two wearing identical colours, bar a difference in cap. The commentator's voice increased in tempo with anticipation of the first jump. The thunderous pack reduced by one as the race had its first faller – a brief and anxious moment for all in the room as they checked to confirm that their horse was still racing.

The blink that it had taken her to place the bet now felt like a drawn-out eternity. Two fallers at the next then two more at the fourth. The tension rose as they approached Becher's Brook. One of the worst fences, an awkward monstrous obstacle that, even when cleared, a near seven-foot perilous drop awaited the competitors on the other side. A stomach-churning moment gripped her as several horses were claimed. They all collectively gasped as they saw the carnage unfold, all in differing expressions, hoping that they would quickly get to their feet, a souring moment as the relentless contest continued. The commentator gave a swift assurance to viewers that all the horses and riders were up on their feet. She took her eyes off the screen to pour herself another glass of champagne. Her horse had been ever present in the front ranks. She waited for the name of her horse to be called out as the latest casualty. The highs and lows continued to be echoed by everyone as they cheered on their pick. Some familiar terms from the radio were being expressed. A dozen fateful adjectives to say the same thing – your labouring horse has no chance, 'being ridden off the bridal', 'falling back', 'treading water', 'struggling to keep with the pace' – all of which she anticipated to be attached to her ride. Of all the horses backed by those in the room, one by one they dropped away, including the strong tip by Crispin, which saw her second wager of £50 each way evaporate. No one could see her with her back turned, looking at the ceiling, wishing this agony would end. Already trying to justify that it was only winnings that she was playing with. Nothing lost. A mantra that was failing to make any impact. She could hear her horse being mentioned with greater confidence. Lifting her glass to her mouth, she was unaware that she had drained it completely.

A cry went up as there was the announcement of another faller. 'Well, that's Sarah's horse,' Graeme grumbled.

She quickly turned to the screen. 'What's happened? Oh no! Is he out? Is he alright?'

'Alright? Of course! He's got plenty in the tank. Only two fences left.'

Paul muttered something barely audible about an injustice and it being a lottery. But Sarah was now transfixed. Graeme was right, and those that had now joined the consensus that she was looking the most likely. He had led for most of the way. She thought that surely his luck wouldn't hold. In pursuit was Graeme's horse ridden by AP. The hero of a win for a fourfold triumph at Sandown, and a 16-1 runner in a steeplechase at Newbury in the past month, she was now willing him to drop away. That all his skill and judgment would abandon him.

The others, aside from Paul, who had seen their horses fall away one by one, were now cheering on hers, Graeme also forlornly trying to will the unbridgeable gap of a dozen lengths. In cheers and adulation the jockey rose triumphantly out of his saddle.

'It's the McCain family back with another winner!' the commentator cried out to the backdrop of the roar from the stands.

Nearly everyone congratulated Sarah on her victory, which soon turned to groans as Graeme announced that she had only wagered £1 each way. She felt numb. Not wanting to do the calculations before now, she waited until the race was confirmed, even accounting for the dreaded stewards' enquiry that had sent down a modest bet the previous week.

'Still, what does that equate to, a new lipstick?' Paul scoffed. 'No. I should say congratulations,' he continued, feigning magnanimity. 'Great luck. Well done.'

In the background she saw the result confirmed. 'Well, some of us have it. But hey, there is always next year. Assuming yours has finished by then.' The amount came into her head. £5,600. No, of course, stake back. £6,000. £6,000!

One by one the guests filtered out. She could barely contain her excitement. The bottle that she had brought in at the start of the race was now empty. Before going to retrieve another, she put on some music at a volume that was immediately turned down by Graeme.

'No need to go overboard. Fifteen quid is hardly a lottery win.'

She popped the cork of the bottle. 'But don't you just love it when you win something.' She turned the music back up as her thoughts turned to how she would spend the money. It crossed her mind to tell Graeme and surprise him with a holiday or a new watch, but the fallout would be greater than the reward. Some could be put away for a later date, when she felt enough time had passed so as to avert the lecture on taking such a risk. This was her finale. She would send £1,500 each to Izzy and Seb. She decided to take up one of Graeme's ideas after another of her sleepless nights a few weeks ago, that she should take a spa day to relax. His suggestion came from seeing a notice on the board in the NAAFI for an organised ladies' day out. However, after the win she had just had, she decided on a hotel in Berlin that Katerin had recommended. Anything at that moment to escape the darkness, the long nights and to give herself some perspective. Once away from the place, it would be a chance to reset, to come back and attempt to put everything behind her. This was the high that she would finish on, committing to herself that that would be the last bet. After Berlin, the account would close and this would be the end of it.

CHAPTER 22

THE DRIVE TO Berlin was well over three hours, and she hadn't driven outside of the camp during her short time back behind the wheel. The obvious choice to her was the train from Celle. Graeme agreed that it would be a good idea to stay overnight. Before she could put it to him, he suggested that she go alone, spoil herself. Despite it being months since she had been away, she felt guilty about her solo indulgence, especially when Graeme insisted on paying for the room.

Once on the train, the greater the miles between her and the camp the more relaxed she felt. A half-empty carriage allowed her to rest back with a paper and coffee as she sped through the countryside. At the sight of the city coming into view, her thoughts turned to the happy prospect of being in the capital at her own leisure. She then took a swift cab ride to the hotel, where she exchanged a few words of English with the taxi driver about her trip to the city. Upon arrival, she delighted at the sight of the opulent façade of the hotel, certain of its ability to deliver on every expectation she had hoped for.

At the hotel reception desk, the people at the counter next to her were checking in, their Louis Vuitton cases resting with an attentive bellboy awaiting his cue. The reception, set in Rococo elegance, featured smooth and imperious marble columns that reached high into the decorative ceilings. A few hotel guests were sitting in soft, luxurious sofas drinking coffees, which were being delivered by quietly courteous waiters.

'*Guten Tag. Mein Name ist Sarah Hughes,*' Sarah began with slow deliberation, knowing that it was highly likely her linguistic efforts would have to be extended beyond that.

'Hello, Mrs Hughes.' The receptionist quickly broke into fluent English. 'Welcome.'

'Thank you. I have a reservation for this evening.'

'Let me just check that, madam. Yes, you have a deluxe room on the fourth floor.'

'Deluxe?' Sarah pulled out her paper. 'I booked a standard.'

'Yes, that does appear to be the case. But, the standard rooms are booked up, I'm afraid.' She double-checked the computer once again. 'Yes, all taken until tomorrow.'

'Can I just ask what the price difference is?' she enquired quietly.

'This is our mistake,' She smiled. 'We would be happy to offer the upgrade by complimentary means.'

'Well, when you put it like that… Then I gratefully accept.'

'I will just prepare the key for you.' As she went through the check-in process she listed the amenities and services on offer. Rounding off, she handed her the key. 'I hope you very much enjoy your stay with us. I think that you will like your room, you have a beautiful view of the cathedral. My name is Celia, and you can call and ask for me. We can help you with anything that you may request.'

'Thank you. As I am here I'd like to book in for some treatments this afternoon, please. Could you tell me what you have to offer?'

The receptionist presented her with a glossy leather-bound file, with an array of pampering, massages and indulgences, including Reiki, Thai, Shiatsu, manicures, pedicures, as demonstrated in the photos, where many of these were being experienced by impossibly beautiful women, often in languorous recline. None of them were evidently undergoing the deep tissue massage that Graeme once suggested be used as a potential method for breaking recalcitrant guests of the CIA.

A woman next to her peered over as Sarah opened the menu. 'I have to recommend the organic detox and the reflexology. You couldn't have found a better place.'

'It seems so.' Sarah smiled, flipping through all the treatments. 'It all looks wonderful.'

As she turned each page, she found every conceivable way in which the body could be purged, scented, cleansed, painted or tinted. Some conjuring up an enticing allure of complete relaxation, others in contorting manipulations she assumed came with complimentary painkillers. Eventually, she decided upon the organic detox ritual which the woman had first recommended, then a manicure which she calculated would leave her enough time to take a gentle walk out for a light lunch in the city.

As she was led down to the spa she was sold a philosophy of nurturing, mindfulness. In serene and quiet seclusion she was shown an amphitheatre sauna, an ice fountain, heated recliners, all of these placed around a tranquil marbled pool. Below was set gentle lighting under the warm azure waters, drawing you up to a soft celestial skyscape in the domed ceiling. It was, as described in one review, a temple that seduced the body into releasing the mind.

Introducing herself as Anthea, the pristine young masseuse, with her svelte figure and flawless skin, began with a rich narrative of the healing properties of the luxuriant creams and oils that were then slowly and methodically being applied down length of her body. A selection of the finest natural products, composed from the purest ingredients harvested from all corners of the world, at the completion of which, she closed her eyes and gradually succumbed to total relaxation amidst a backdrop of subtle floral scents and a gentle sleep-inducing soundtrack playing behind her.

During her manicure, she found it was a good opportunity to gain suggestions of a nice place to eat. Without giving offence to the local cuisine, she showed a preference for French or Italian. Not far from the hotel on Gendarmenmarkt, there were many good ones to choose from. Last of the recommendations was a highly rated Italian. However, this was caveated by its exclusivity. Sarah recalled the name, as Katerin had mentioned it as a place that her husband had taken her for her fortieth. In recognition of the name, the manicurist said she would ask, but she re-emphasised the slim chance that Anthea might be able to help. Her older brother was the maître d' and he might be able to accommodate her. In parting, Sarah thanked her and made a few inevitable purchases that would be sent to her room, in particular a pot of aromatic organic botanicals that were going to do well to retain their romantic magical effects in the austere barrack-style bathroom. She also awarded her a generous tip on the receipt in tribute to her miraculous, therapeutic powers. In response, the young woman wished her a good stay, confirming that she would try to get her a table for that evening. Sarah accepted the gesture but anticipated her chances were slim of such a short-notice opening.

She lay back on the bed dialling Graeme's number, to which she had no answer. Instead she sent him a picture of her with the message, 'There is a heaven and it smells of sunflowers and chamomile. Cleopatra would never have had it so good... Speak later! Love you xxx'.

Perhaps prompted by the enticing aromas of almond and

marshmallow from the pot of cleanser, her thoughts turned to lunch. Time having passed quickly it was now nearly 2 p.m. A new dress that she had bought for an upcoming drinks at the mess was the perfect choice. Admiring herself in the mirror, she wished that Graeme could see her. Checking her purse she eagerly left her room, happy in the prospect of taking a seat at one of the outdoor restaurants lining the plaza. Walking into the lobby she felt a renewed energy, preparing to escape into the delights of the city. A transformation from the tired early morning start and feeling the effects of a couple of hours on a stuffy train. Her thoughts were interrupted by her concierge, who intercepted her by the door.

'Mrs Hughes! I'm glad I caught you! The table that you requested, you can be accommodated at three. If you wish to take it? It is the only time that we could arrange.' He said it with a hint of jovial affected regret, happy in the expectation that the offer would be well received.

'That's wonderful.' She looked at her watch. 'Is it far? Should I get a taxi?'

'No need, madam. It is just a few minutes' walk. You have plenty of time.'

'Thank you so much! And please thank…' she quickly searched her mind, '… Anthea. Yes, Anthea,' she confirmed with relief. 'What an unexpected bonus.'

Sarah buzzed with excitement as she recalled Katerin's certainty that it had to be booked well in advance. It was where the rich and famous came to be seen. Nikki would be green with envy. It would also pay her back for the endless teasing about how she had lunch at the table next to Kristin Scott Thomas at The Ivy. Oh for at least one household name. George Clooney, perhaps a bit too much to expect, but Katerin had been told he had been there on several occasions. The last place she had been for lunch was the NAAFI tearoom, a white-sliced sharp cheddar and pickle sandwich to the backdrop of manic under-fours competing with each other and their mothers' attention. The boisterous weekly parents' and toddlers' group had been cancelled in the nearby hall due to redecoration and that was the fallback venue. It had been a long while since the veil had been lifted on her own imperviousness to her own children's capacity for mayhem. Middle age and grown-up offspring had brought that sharply into focus.

Entering the restaurant, she was taken aback by the grandeur, marvelling at its splendour as she was escorted to her seat, and subtly looked around the restaurant at the other diners. One in particular caught her eye. Was it Isabella Rossellini? She glanced over discreetly. If it wasn't Isabella, then over there was definitely Meryl Streep, an actress that Graeme would always grumble about whenever she put on one of her films. He would spend at least all of the opening credits listing her worst performances, nearly always replicating what even she had to admit was a dodgy Dutch accent from *Out of Africa*. He effected a long drawl of 'I haad a faarm in Aaafrica…' A near riot ensued with the release of *Mamma Mia*. She happily recalled the screening in the house with her and Izzy, who sang every track that echoed, or rather warbled, through the hallway and up to his office.

It was Meryl! Would Nikki believe her? No chance for a photo but she was close enough to overhear parts of a conversation – something about the film festival.

The waiter arrived attentively, handing her a menu and giving the day's recommendations. She smiled as she listened to him wax lyrical about the magnificent creations that the chef had conjured up that day, wondering how many times he had to suppress the actual words of a harassed and highly strung chef ordering him to push the slow sellers that needed to be shifted. As he pressed on with the nuances of that day's specials, she discovered, like the spa, this too had a particular philosophy. It seemed these were two conflicting ones. Purity and respect for the body was about to experience a sharp reversal. Looking at the menu it was going to be a retox of ample proportions. What had been worked out was to re-cometh in what was likely an even greater spiritual experience. It was easy to blot out Anthea's informative instruction on the destructive nature of what alcohol and sugar did to one's wellbeing. Even quicker than that, she blotted out her commitment to heed the words and she was a changed woman. A brief glance at the prices of the antipasto menu, she knew this would not be a frugal meal. But holiday rules dictated that the prices were to be ignored.

She considered how many courses she would have. Three would suffice but the fish looked wonderful. In particular, what caught her eye was the roast monkfish. She hadn't had that in such a while. But to start, the Sardinian cured ham. No, the scallops, or a delicious-sounding dish, given her poor grasp of Italian, that was something with tomato, ricotta and olives. She was in a dilemma between them, falling on the side of the scallops as it was easier to pronounce than 'Fiori di zucca freschi ripieni di ricotta e pistacchio, serviti con pomodorini al forno e olive taggiasche'. For the meat dish she chose the lamb. Not the beef fillet flambé, as tempting as that was. The last time that she had something flambéed at the table, she felt a compulsion to give awkward intermittent superlatives during the cooking, which Graeme later reproached her for. For dessert she had an easier choice in mind, plumping for an old classic for later. A tiramisu.

The waiter acknowledged her order, repeating her requests. 'And for the wine, madam?'

'What would you recommend?'

'Our sommelier would be delighted to help.' Within a moment an ebullient gentleman arrived, his hands clasped together in expectation that he would be about to impart his considerable knowledge. After quick consultation with the waiter he duly began to match the appropriate wines to the dishes.

'Do you have any preference?'

'Well, preferably red. Oh and before that could I have a glass of champagne, please? The Blancs de Blancs would be fine.'

'Of course, now for a selection.' He ran his finger down the list. 'May I suggest the Barbera d'Alba? Or perhaps this,' he pointed out the selection, 'the Barbaresca Barbaresco Albesani Santo Stefano? Or a Volnay-Santenots-du-Milieu, Première Cru?'

She looked to another wine that caught her eye, as she had heard Graeme boasting of his in-depth knowledge of the best years for this particular wine. 'This Chambertin,' she pointed to a bottle on the menu, '… would you recommend this one?'

'The 2005? A delight. A great year for the region.'

'That sounds perfect then. Yes, thank you.' One thing flashed into her mind about 2006. A freak weather phenomenon. 'A shame about the hail storms in 2006.'

He tried not to look surprised but delighted in concurrence. 'Perhaps you are being too modest about your knowledge?'

Before she anticipated he would continue and discover that was indeed the extent of her knowledge, one of the waiters signalled for his attention.

'Excuse me, madam, and I hope you enjoy your meal. Any further assistance on a dessert wine perhaps, I will be very happy to advise you.'

Each course came out. A succession of beautifully crafted dishes she considered masterpieces, each cooked and assembled with precision. A manifestation of the no doubt hard-fought, blood, sweat and tears Michelin star displayed at the entrance. In perfect and harmonious symbiosis with the wine, she savoured every mouthful, prompting a flood of superlatives straight from the usual pretentious reviews in the broadsheets. A particular pompous bore on a BBC cooking show came to mind, which she reluctantly conceded would just about nail it. It was a meal which she felt would be a long time in replicating.

Instead of her usual amaretto and espresso, she substituted the amaretto for a cognac. Time stood still. At that moment there was no other place to be, just that restaurant. Everything else could be left back at the camp. Even Meryl had been relegated to the background. In fact Sarah hadn't even realised that she had departed, and also she would never know if it had been Isabella Rosellini as the table was now occupied by a group of businessmen. If there hadn't been a no-smoking policy, she probably would have partaken in the rich, velvet extravagance of a slow-burning Havana. But neither health and safety nor her non-smoker lungs would tolerate. But it was a thought.

The bill arrived in a neat leather stitched case. If she could have just handed over her card without looking, it would have been preferable. She opened it carefully, fortifying herself for the total. A couple of hundred pounds would have been worth every penny. Scanning quickly to the bottom, she reread it to check it was right. Four hundred and twenty euros. Instead of what would have been her reaction on nearly every other day, that of more than slight angst, she broke into a smile. Mostly she imagined Graeme's face, telling her she could have saved one hundred and fifty of that on a wine that she probably didn't fully appreciate.

The late afternoon cooling breeze greeted her as she left the restaurant. She had a momentary regret over the cognac and decided to take a photo of the outside of the restaurant to send to Graeme.

'Me again… what a lunch! Wish you were here. Now walking it off!!! Love you darling xxxxxxx'

Another burst of sunshine broke through the clouds, illuminating the busy market square. A far cry from Katerin's description of an outdoor concert she attended there, the concert hall flanked by the French and German churches whose domes were visible from the heights of the hotel. Unlike the quaint architecture of Celle, there were three dominating neo-classical buildings. It was difficult to visualise the carnage and devastation that they had been subjected to over the years. Whilst admiring the glistening gilt dome of the German church, a dark covering of cloud gradually obscured the sunlight. A few people who had been basking on the surrounding benches gazed to the heavens. A woman next to her smartly folded a newspaper up after taking a long look up at the skies. Two advertising posters for a forthcoming concert were caught in the increasingly strong breeze. The brief show of sunshine upon leaving the restaurant looked as if it had made its last hurrah as the clouds quickly moved in.

In her pocket her phone notified her of a message. She smiled in anticipation that Graeme had finally got her messages.

'Have you been drinking? I said a break, Sarah, not a new mortgage. Busy day for some of us. Speak tonight. I will be at home after 9. Will call.'

Wrapping her raincoat tightly against the stiff breeze she decided to go back to the hotel, wishing that she hadn't texted him in the first place. The thought of home was a sobering one. Since stepping onto the train, it had barely warranted a thought. There had been so much to take in. Now, the mention of the apartment brought its proximity back to her. Graeme's job. The camp.

Walking briskly along the pavement she hurried back to the hotel. As she moved to place her phone quickly back into her pocket, the device slipped out of her grasp and clattered to the pavement. Her previous commitment to buy a protective case was brought sharply into focus as she saw it split apart. A man in a smart suit briefly broke his stride to pick up the casing, which she then managed to refit. Even though it was physically intact the screen was dead. She had often remonstrated with Graeme that it was due an update but always conceded to the argument for economising. Why spend money on something that she wouldn't use half the capability of? They were for spoilt teenagers and yuppies. The latter term he stopped using after being mercilessly ribbed by Izzy and Seb.

As she placed her phone into her bag, her attention was taken by a glamorous boutique in front of her. A few carefully positioned Chanel and Dolce & Gabbana bags had been placed on stands set apart to make their own statement, the rich supple leather and gold clasps of the Chanel designs shown off under the soft lighting set within the display. The flamboyant Dolce & Gabbana collection fronted with an extravagantly embroidered palladium and crystal was a dash of ostentation much too far for her tastes. A bag that would launch a thousand speculations of her having a mid-life crisis should she have it on her arm for one of the garrison functions. Underneath there was a row of bold street artist designer wares with a $7,000 price tag, which she speculated were from the line of Emperor's New Clothes for overnight internet whizz kids. She considered that the difference in commercial terms between naff and garish and the must-have accessory was the addition of two extra noughts on the price tag, and most crucially being seen perched in the crook of a suitably famous elbow.

Her eye was drawn to an elegant clutch bag on a shelf she could just see through the window, unaware that a woman was passing her to enter the shop, who then stopped to address her.

'Kommen sie ein?' The woman held the door open for Sarah. 'Are you coming in?'

'Um...' Her German once again abandoned her. 'Sorry... OK, yes.' She took hold of the door. 'Thank you.'

The woman appeared to be a regular, judging by the

familiarity with which she was greeted by one of the shop assistants. It wasn't long after initial pleasantries that they were discussing the attributes of a handbag that she had picked up from a nearby shelf. Having noticed the price tag in the window on the way in, Sarah was looking for a swift exit. She hesitated as she watched the woman now comparing a second bag. It was so matter of fact, the assistant keen to flatter. It had been the same when she had her boutique. The importance of the experience of the purchase, as if the union was destined, with a couple of exceptions, primarily the significant differential on price.

As she turned to leave, she took another glance at the bag that had caught her attention on the way in. In her hesitation she hadn't noticed an assistant approach her.

'I think that this bag would suit madam perfectly.' The assistant picked up the bag from the shelf.

'Beautiful, yes, but I don't think so.'

'You will not find a finer, more elegant bag. The stitching is immaculate and there are few better than this.' She latched onto Sarah's hesitation as the words had taken hold in her mind. 'Every so often we are all deserving of indulging ourselves. If you do not mind me saying you have the posture to carry this off. Please, have a look.'

Embarrassed by the compliment, she took the offer of inspecting the bag more closely. 'Yes, it's beautiful.' She placed it on her arm and turned to the mirror. 'But perhaps not.'

The customer who had walked in at the same time then passed her as she left the shop with two parcels in hand. 'That is perfect for you. I have one just like it.' Sarah smiled in acknowledgement, not wanting to give the assistant, or herself for that matter, the encouragement to cross the Rubicon of price-tag blindness.

She and Ellie would often joke about it, when Ellie had relayed a story of her latest splurge. Sarah would tease her friend about her being impervious to the temptation of the excesses of the glamorous and seductive world of luxury designers, all of which was orchestrated by stylish assistants who waxed lyrical about glamour and possibility. Sarah had done it many times herself in her boutique. When the harmonious, serendipitous union of the coveted exorbitant luxury was brought together with a final tactile caress and smell of fresh leather, there is a complete failure to withhold the three words that would later lead to regret.

But as Sarah now stood at that crossroads as the assistant offered another superlative, and certain that the bag would match a dress she had seen in a passing window of a boutique fifty yards before, she blurted out, 'I'll take it.'

In an imperious subsequent campaign, Sarah stopped at several other boutiques. After making a few more purchases, she returned to the hotel, not before calling into a men's couturier to acquire a perfectly matching shirt and tie which were displayed in the window. Once back in her room, she put down the bags on the bed with relief, then ordered another bottle of champagne before putting on some music. She thrilled at the crisp and neat parcels now sprawled across the pristine duvet. Which to open first? The restraint shown in the store was now released. Waiting until the champagne's delivery, she toasted the day.

Appraising her vast haul of purchases she decided to go in ascending order as she unwrapped the first top. Even though the tissue paper was about to be cast into the bin, she took great care in the opening. Holding the top up against her body she buzzed at the thought of where she would wear it, for which occasion. It was similar to a top that she and Chloe had been admiring during a flip through the Harvey Nics website a year ago. No, it was better, the cut was flattering, the stitching flawless. In the penultimate acquisition of the bag, then came the shoes. A floral pair of pumps that she instantly coveted the moment that she saw them. However, it didn't stop her trying on another six pairs before she confirmed her purchase to the assistant, the young attendant that had caused Sarah to show every bit of restraint every time she said the word pumps, or rather 'poomps'. They were a perfect fit. These surpassed anything that she had had before.

The hotel phone sounded next to her as she poured herself another glass of champagne.

'Good evening, Mrs Hughes. We have a call for you. It is your husband.'

'Oh! Thank you.' In a swift moment Graeme was patched through.

'Sarah?'

'Hey, darling! What a day I am having! Why didn't you call me on the mobile?'

'I have tried,' he replied in barely restrained frustration. 'The first receptionist couldn't find you on the system. Anyway, could you please go and find your damned phone.'

She reached down into her bag, taking out her cracked mobile. 'Oh God, I forgot! The stupid thing broke.' As if in confirmation, she gave it a couple of forceful taps on the bedside table. 'At least I can get a new one.'

'Sarah!'

'Sorry. But, hey, I have to tell you about the day. Oh the food, Graeme.'

'It sounds like you have had quite a time.' Although his voice was more conciliatory his manner was curt, which put her a little off stride.

'I'm sorry about the phone. How was your day?'

'Not as fun as yours, obviously. So what damage has been done to my card?'

'Your card?' she responded more soberly. 'It was money from the shop, if you must know. I want to tell you about the day, Graeme, don't spoil it. I want to take you to this restaurant. You will love it.'

'Then it will be time for my card, I suppose. About money, I'm doing this for your own good. I understand the difficult time you are having. Just don't go overboard.'

She hesitated. 'No, Graeme, heaven forbid. Tell me about your day. How was work?'

'It was pretty much the same. There is one thing I have to ask you. I know it is short notice but wanted to run something by you before you got back. You don't have to go. I completely forgot to tell you that it is Crispin's dining-out at the mess.'

'Tomorrow?!'

'I thought it might help take your mind off things.'

'Jesus, Graeme. I'm not sure,' she replied, knowing full well he had already said that they would both be attending.

'All you have to do is put a dress on. It will be a chance to show off that one I bought you at Christmas.'

'It's OK. I will put you out of your misery. I'll come. I won't be back until the early afternoon. My train doesn't get back in until four.'

His mood was now more buoyant. 'That's plenty of time. I will be there to pick you up. Do you mind if I crash? I am knackered. You can tell me about your day when I see you tomorrow.'

'Sure. I will see you then. Love you. But don't worry about picking me up. A taxi will be no bother.'

'OK, if you like. Sorry if I was spiky. I was just worried when I couldn't get hold of you. I'm glad you have had a nice break. Night. Love you.'

She turned off the music, taking off her dress before laying out on the bed. Pouring herself another glass of champagne, she relived the whirlwind of a day, knowing that in the morning some of the extravagance might be seen in a different light. Closing her eyes she put the sober reckoning out of her mind, thinking that in a moment she would call Graeme back, feeling guilty that she should turn the invitation of dinner out the next evening into such an ordeal.

In the silence of the night she awoke in terror. She reached out for the light and switched on the television. The decline from the heights of a few hours before was taking her on a familiar journey. Her discarded dress lay cast over a chair, the shoes strewn underneath. Her heart pounded in her ears as she adjusted to the darkness.

It was still another five hours until sunrise. Her skin was cool and she reached to wrap a bed cover around her. From the high window she looked over the city and to the square beneath. In the late hours a few people were making their way home. No one looked up as the gentle flow of intermittent traffic passed by. She briefly entertained the thought of calling Graeme, then Ellie, but it was past one o'clock in the UK. What would she say? Ellie didn't do things in half measures and she would probably then come over to see her. In the pit of her stomach she felt the reluctance to have to tell her everything.

How could she tell her about Andreas? She feared the possibility she would side with Graeme on this. They couldn't understand that she was still desperate to fill in the remaining gaps of what she had to be subconsciously blocking out, all the time having to withstand Graeme's continuing irritation to what he saw as her irrationality. Lecturing her, offering logical reasoning, the motorcyclist was gone. His frustration boiling over as he wrapped it up in the same meaningless words, 'accident', 'terrible, tragic misfortune', to which she had become immune.

The bedside clock was showing it was still only just past two o'clock. The clock hadn't moved. She took a sleeve of her sedatives from her purse, popping one, then a couple more with a remaining half glass of champagne on the side. Curling up into a ball under the covers, she drifted off as the newsreader faded away.

CHAPTER 23

Sarah awoke to loud knocking. Her head spun as her unsteadiness made her relapse back onto the pillow. A voice could be heard over the television.

'Madam.'

Her body ached as she pulled herself up. Hoping to get to the door before the knocking continued she quickly grabbed the dressing gown from the back of the bathroom door. Not even making any attempt in German she responded with irritation.

'I'm coming! Please give me a moment.' Opening the door her eyes were almost in full focus as she was met with the sight of a cleaning lady, who seemed to hesitate slightly before she spoke to Sarah. 'Sorry, but you have to go to checkout.' At Sarah's perplexed look she continued in polite firmness, 'Checkout is 12 p.m. I must clean the room.'

'Checkout?' She looked at her watch. Straining to focus, her stomach turned at the realisation that it was nearly 1 p.m. 'Oh my God. I'm sorry. *Entschuldigung*, ten minutes. I'll be ten minutes.' She held her hands up in numerical demonstration. *'Zehn Minuten.'*

Closing the door, she tried to organise her muddled thoughts, the first being of the train. She gathered her things together, pushing them into her case, including all of the purchases, excluding the bags, which she tossed towards the bin. Pulling her train ticket out from her purse she could see it was leaving in thirty-five minutes. With no time for a shower she rushed into the bathroom, cursing as she stumbled over one of the errant shoes, giving herself a target of getting down to reception within five minutes. In the short time, she made a swift effort to remove last night's make-up. The soft lighting in the bathroom did little to disguise the puffy bags around her bloodshot eyes, and pallid, drawn complexion. Once back in the lobby she felt exposed against the smartness of the other guests. One who passed her gave her a look of mild disapproval as he signalled to a promptly attentive concierge. Her fresh clothes did little to conceal the smell of stale alcohol that she felt was oozing through every pore. Her hands trembled as she signed for the bill, apologising for being late out of the room. She then hurriedly made her exit, all the time checking her watch.

With a couple of minutes to spare, she got on the train. It wasn't until she sat down she felt a raging dehydration. Sweating after running to make the departure, she searched in her bag for a half-drunk bottle that she was thankful she had forgotten to discard the previous night.

As the train pulled away, her thoughts turned to returning home. Forging through the countryside she sat back in her seat in exhaustion, her head too delicate to listen to music and the rush of the journey doing little to abate her fragile condition. Yearning to sleep she hoped a couple of hours would be sufficient to recuperate. Anxious that she may miss her stop, she set an alarm ten minutes then another five minutes before she was due to arrive.

When the train came into her station, the flurry of activity of the disembarking passengers around her reignited her fragile disposition. She accepted the help of the young woman next to her, who retrieved her case from the overhead rack. In her haste she didn't stop to check around her, as she was anxious not to miss her stop. The same passenger made a quick pursuit of Sarah, who, after catching her at the door, gave her her handbag, which she had left behind. She briefly raised her sunglasses, expressing a spontaneous outburst of gratitude, followed by a moment of dread had she lost it. As she alighted the train, a young child ran past her on the platform, squealing with delight as she broke from her mother's hand and running into the open arms of an elderly couple who offered reciprocal encouragement. The child's piercing voice cut through the unabating state of Sarah's fragile skull.

'*Oma! Opa!*' The child embraced the couple, who enveloped their granddaughter in a hug.

Making her way through the stream of travellers, Sarah, still feeling nauseous, once again began to sweat. The sight of a commuter tucking into a crumbling pastry became acute to her senses. Passing a patisserie she caught a smell of roast ham. Speeding up to take in the air outside the station, she passed a burger stand as she had almost reached the doors. Before she had even looked over, she was assaulted by the smell of meat juices and a woman at the counter calling out for an order, most likely a delayed one, as a group of teenagers let out what came across as a sarcastic cheer. She knew that she shouldn't have looked but then, in a spontaneous and instantly regrettable act, she glanced over at the booth. On the tables were a few discarded remnants of previous customers. Greasy fries and a burger box lay open, stuffed with its half-eaten contents. Her stomach churned. The last sight before she abruptly looked up was a child picking at an egg bun, not troubled in offering an open-mouthed mashing prelude to imminent digestion, accompanied by the mother attempting to address a runny nose with one of the napkins.

Having made it outside she embraced the fresh air, but it did little to ease her precarious condition. After seeing a drinks machine she searched quickly in her pockets where she found enough change for a chilled can of cola. Then after shakily cracking it open, she drank it down with quenching relief. It was a reprieve that soon dissipated, as her stomach seemed less impressed with the gesture. She discreetly leaned against the wall. The taxi rank had a glut of cabs so she decided to take a moment to settle. In an attempt to combat the fluctuating flushes in temperature she removed her coat.

'Sarah? Heavens, are you alright?' Graeme had suddenly appeared. 'You look awful.'

She tried to keep a distance but he had already moved to kiss her. His sympathy turned to recoil. 'Ugh. You reek of wine. What have you been doing?'

'Please, Graeme,' she began quietly as a means of placating him and attempting to nip in the bud any escalation that she would be ill-equipped to deal with. 'I overindulged. It was alright, I wasn't out late. But anyway, I wasn't expecting you! Thank you, wow, it has felt like a very long journey...'

His expression remained hostile, however his voice significantly dropping in volume. 'It smells like you had, no I don't think I want to know. No disguising it was red anyway. You...'

Before he could continue she desperately interjected, 'Please, for the love of Christ don't mention alcohol. I'm really sorry but let's just get back.'

Once they were inside the car she prepared herself for the anticipated lecture that would inevitably commence. Whilst he was packing up the car, she pulled down the visor mirror in front of her. The harsh light offered no favours as she examined her puffy and drained reflection. Realising that Graeme had a point, and with her increasing nausea, she saw her best ploy was to show complete contrition. She snapped up the visor as he re-entered the car.

'So. OK.' He placed the keys into the ignition. 'I have to ask what the hell you were thinking.'

'I am absolutely, well and truly sorry.' His demand for recollection fought her resistance to focus on anything else. 'Truly. I'm sorry. Can we just leave it at that? It really isn't as bad as it seems. I was fine, it was more to do with the carriage being so hot. I'm not even convinced the seafood I had last night… Oh no, that's another one not to mention. Really.'

'I'm assuming you took your tablets. You know you shouldn't be drinking. This has to stop, Sarah. We need to talk about this. I'm going to have to insist.'

'Insist? I don't think so, darling.' She had forgotten about the extra tablets and the remaining wine that she had washed them down with. She turned the heating down a notch and wound down the window. 'Why don't you tell me about your day instead of lecturing me like I am a child?'

'If you didn't act like a bloody teenager given the run of the house…'

Her system's revolt to the cola and lack of food was gaining momentum. She said nothing as she mentally focused on the passing journey, deciding that the best strategy would be to tick off familiar landmarks, one at a time.

'We have to go to a dinner in three hours and I have to swing by the office to pick up my mess kit.'

'I'm not being funny, but look, Graeme, really, please stop talking,' she replied sharply.

'So, I should be on eggshells, you are the one…'

'Oh God,' she frantically implored him. 'Please, no eggs, please, Graeme. I mean it. I'm not joking.' Without warning she suddenly burst out in a moment of involuntary laughter. 'Shit!' She quickly tried to recover to her previous show of remorse. 'I really didn't mean to do that.'

A car overtook them at speed. Without saying anything Graeme responded with a sudden acceleration, following in the car's wake.

'What are you doing?' She sat up. 'This isn't funny.'

He continued to speed, passing the other car as it pulled in.

'Graeme, slow down, for fuck's sake.'

After a few seconds he began to decelerate.

'Stop the car.' He didn't immediately react to her plea. 'Please! Stop the car I'm going to be sick.'

She noticed him take a look at her then the interior of the car. 'Oh, for Christ's sake. Just hang on. We will be off the autobahn in a few minutes.'

'You have about thirty seconds.' She held her hand to her mouth.

He brought the vehicle to a swift halt on the hard shoulder. Within a second of stopping she made a dash for the back of the car. Before she could gain the discretion of cover she vomited. Leaning against the side of the car, she convulsed once again. Then a third and fourth time. The wet road, smell of fumes and the soaked verge brought another convulsion. Her head spinning she waited, still using the car to steady her, until she was sure that it was over.

She stood upright as he was about to get back in the car. 'What was that back there?' she confronted him angrily, her hands shaking as she took out a tissue from her pocket. The traffic continued to speed by. An articulated lorry rumbled past, then another. 'Are you out of your mind?' she shouted over the thunderous sound. 'Why would you drive like that? Do you know what I have been going through?'

'Don't be such a drama queen.' He prepared to get back into the car. 'When you are ready.'

'Do you have any water?' She made the request in reluctant desperation, her voice hoarse, her body still trembling.

'No.' He just looked at her, making sure his contempt

registered. 'You'll have to wait until we get home.'

Sarah took in some deep breaths before preparing herself to get back in the car.

'I was miles away from anything. There was hardly anyone on the road.' He hesitated before continuing. 'I was paying attention.'

'Are you trying to say something?' she replied incredulously. As he got in the car, she quickly followed.

'Of course not. That is your issue. In your head.' He wound down the window before casting a glance at her shoes. 'Disgusting.'

They exchanged few words for the rest of the journey. Her anger towards him failed to abate, dehydration making her head begin to throb, sensitive to every acceleration, vigilant as he overtook every vehicle. The landmarks passed in what seemed like an eternity until they reached the apartment, the last being the camp's gates, marked by Graeme's sudden change of demeanour as he presented his ID card, smiling with his usual quiet satisfaction as the private soldier saluted him as he pulled away.

Taking her case from the back she saw a bottle of Evian tucked behind the first aid box. She was about to challenge Graeme but instead gently closed the boot. Hauling what seemed to be a case that had doubled in weight, she made her way up the stairs. The dusty austere stairwell was as usual bleak. Following Graeme into the flat where he had already disappeared into the kitchen, she noticed the overbearing heat. One unpleasant consequence of the uniformity of heating in the entire block was that it effected the temperature of either peak-hour laundrette or a chiller cabinet. There was little in between. Aware that he would be watching her in the kitchen, she tried not to display the urgency she felt for a cold drink. Taking out a sparkling water, she went to retrieve a glass, her arms so fatigued that she felt a momentary loss of control as she brought the glass from the top shelf. Unable to sip in moderation she gulped down the water, satiating her thirst. They continued to avoid an exchange with each other, and without any comment he left the room.

Once he was gone, she in part recovered after the boost of a slice of bread and a vitamin drink. It was the most stable she had felt all day.

After discarding her clothes onto the floor she walked into the shower. With little intention of doing anything other than sleeping she roughly dried her hair, only to tuck herself under the soft covers of her bed.

It had taken her most of that time to finally get to sleep, drifting in and out, when in what felt only a moment later her alarm sounded next to her. Once again she had sweated through the bedclothes. The house was silent as she eased herself out of bed. It was past 6 p.m. One of her dresses was hanging on the back of the door, a post-it note next to it. 'I've been called into work. You need to be ready by seven. I will be back to pick you up.' She switched on the TV as she nursed a cup of coffee. Flicking through to the sports channel, a tennis match on the APT tour was about to start. The fourth seed was warming up in the quarter-finals against an opponent that the commentator had commented in his previous match had never reached a semi-final. The strong favourite was 4/6 on. Odds on, but still a great price for what would be such a one-sided match. With less than an hour to get ready, she put the TV on in the bedroom, turning the sound down to put on some music. An occasional glance at the TV saw her player power to a 6-2 first set. Halfway through the second set at 4-3, Graeme had arrived home to collect her. As there was no chance of following the rest of the game with Graeme harrying her to get ready, she turned off the match at the last possible moment. Her player had to hold his service for a two-set lead.

CHAPTER 24

As THEY DROVE to the mess, Graeme's mood, as in the same manner earlier at the garrison gates, switched as soon as they arrived. A parting shot from him as he turned off the engine, about pulling herself together, was soon changed to the earlier gregarious persona, when he recognised someone from his unit pulling up in the next space in the car park. A transformation from the short drive there, where there had been a reignition of the argument that had been sparked at the train station. This time asking her where she had been, and then in an enquiry that was angrily rebuffed, who she was with.

Once inside the mess, she sought out a gin and tonic from the table, despite her lingering nausea. It wasn't long before that was replaced with another before the five minutes' call was announced. Sensing that Graeme was trying to hold her back before they went into the dining room, she took, as was tradition, the invitation of the arm of the officer seated next to her, who had come to escort her into dinner.

One of the officers next to Graeme struck up a conversation

about a key game for the rugby play-offs that evening. Graeme's team, Worcester, were playing Gloucester. She watched as he goaded his friend Simon, who was a Gloucester fan, about the crushing defeat they were going to suffer.

She didn't have an in-depth knowledge of who the players were for those clubs, or whether or not they were right when they discussed the relative merits of who had the better line-out or advantage in the scrum, nor did she care.

She waited until the toasts before going to the ladies'. It was her first opportunity to check the result of the tennis match that she had bet on. Her player had lost the second set in a tie-break and then capitulated in the following two sets, angry about his pathetic display where he wimped out after a 6-2, 6-0 loss at the end – a *coup de grâce* of a final twenty-minute set that had lost her £250. If she hadn't been in such a rush, she would have remembered that the player her money was riding on, although ranked twenty places above his opponent, had played a four-and-a-half-hour game two days before, and hadn't been 100% before that. She was annoyed at herself for not remembering or seeing in the blatantly obviously generous odds that she had secured on him. Instead she should have saved her money for the later game she had been waiting to start as they were on their way to the mess – an underdog at 3/1 who she had a strong gut feeling for. Next to the other result was confirmation that the 3/1 shot had won in straight sets.

In the cubicle, she brought up the betting site. As a few of the women exchanged brief conversation, she brought up the market. If Graeme was wrong, and the Gloucester fan was right, then she could make something good from the day. Unburdening herself of the added guilt of her spending spree would be a start in putting the two days behind her.

During the dinner she had repeatedly got the attention of the waiter as he refilled her glass. She hadn't been taking stock of the amount she was drinking. Once back at the table, she managed to sneak a look at the game on her phone, within the confines of her purse on her lap under the table, becoming increasingly irritated knowing that it would be another couple of hours before Graeme would even contemplate leaving. As she once again discreetly checked for the rugby score on the match she had been following, the final whistle blew.

A second round of port was being offered by the man sitting next to her, which she was unaware of as she calculated that she was still ahead on the day. Just. All thanks to Gloucester. Previously unnoticed by Graeme, her inattentiveness was exposed by the fact that she was holding up its progression. 'What are you doing, darling?'

'I thought that you wanted to know about the rugby?' she quickly responded, embarrassed by being caught out with her phone.

'Not now, Sarah.'

'OK.' She reacted to his chastisement. She closed her purse. 'But just in case you are interested, Worcester lost. Stuffed… Well, that will teach you not to support your local team,' she continued as she saw Graeme's growing annoyance. 'Yep… they were hopeless, pummelled…' She took the last sip of her port.

'Yes, thank you.' Graeme turned his attention back to Simon, from whom he was clearly about to have to listen to an 'I told you so' for the points he had been right on.

Before he could start, Sarah continued, '… thrashed, mangled, annihilated… Sounds like they ran out with their boots on the wrong way around…'

'Alright, Sarah. I get it.' Graeme gave her a perplexed and disapproving look, and looked fleetingly at her glass.

'Darling,' Sarah raised her glass, 'are you trying to hint that I have had enough?' She winked as she picked up the port.

The officer next to her swiftly but politely attempted to intercept the decanter to pour it for her. 'Please, allow me.'

'No, thank you, I can manage.' She took the decanter and poured herself a top-up. 'Anyone else?' An offer no one took up. 'OK. I know, we ladies aren't supposed to touch the port.' She took a sip. 'Funny that. You know. Which traditions you keep and which ones you don't.'

None responded as they assumed her comment was rhetorical. Which it would have been had Graeme not turned his back in what she knew to be his way of preventing any further remark from her.

Sarah took another sip from her glass. 'Now, I'm pretty sure that a long, long time ago, you had to purchase your commissions. Am I right?'

'Thankfully, that has changed,' the officer next to her responded.

Graeme quickly followed up, affecting indifference. 'Sarah is still finding this all a bit new. But come on, Simon, let's hear it about Gloucester.'

'And…' Sarah interjected, '… let's not forget that years ago women weren't even allowed to join. Right, so we have two good changes right there. But still they aren't allowed to serve as combat troops, is that right? Infantry and such like, on the front line!'

'To be fair, Sarah,' the officer said, two seats away, 'it isn't really a suitable place for a lady.'

She turned sharply. 'Hmm. Not suitable. But suitable enough for significant numbers risking their lives in other ways – covert operations, medics and pilots. And what about in wars, to end up being tortured and a having a meet and greet with a firing squad?'

'Well, perhaps not all,' he responded patronisingly. 'There were some important contributions.'

'Very generous. Certainly I've seen a fair few much fitter than some of the male plum duffs that they wedge into a uniform now. Didn't you say, Graeme, that they should be put through a ring like an umpire and a misshapen cricket ball... and if they get wedged... whoosh... stick 'em on a wheel and half rations for a month. Oh... there's another thing... I'm just going to say if I might...'

'Yes, why stop now?' Graeme resigned himself to her following thoughts being given air, hoping his apathy wouldn't provoke an extended continuation.

'I remember something on the news a few years ago about openly gay people not being allowed to serve... those crusty old retired generals in a rare panic that there would be anarchy, mutiny in the ranks, PT performed to YMCA, soldiers edging their way around the wall to their bunks, sleeping with one eye open, and the mess would be awash with pink gins and scatter cushions.'

'And few batted an eyelid,' Simon laughed.

'Exactly, and who knew that most people serving were more concerned with the ability to rely on their fellow soldiers to have their back. So to speak. Anyway, I digress. So, returning to women... Hang on, where was I?'

'Firing squads,' the wife of a visiting colonel joined in, smiling, having now latched onto their exchange.

'Yes, firing squads. Or perhaps we should move on,' as she winked at Graeme. 'I think he is imagining one right now. So... tradition.' She took another sip of port. 'I can't touch the port? That is one of the line-in-the-sand traditions you have decided to hold on to?! Well, I tell you something else, when Wellington celebrated Waterloo with his officers, they didn't drink a bulk buy on a deal from the local supermarket.' She made a point of inspecting her glass.

Simon smiled in agreement, mirroring her appraisal by putting his nose to his glass. 'You do have a point there. It's the new mess manager, a civvy.' He rolled his eyes. 'Wouldn't know a good port if he fell over it.'

'... and I'm pretty sure if that lieutenant over there,' Sarah continued, 'had turned up in Wellington's mess with that clip-on bowtie, which I think you will agree makes him look like he is about to pull a rabbit from his hat, he would have been ejected with one of those famous boots up the arse...'

'OK, Sarah.' Graeme was now breaking through his previous state of restrained irritation.

'Speaking of Wellington,' the colonel was now engaged, 'apparently chef has to do a vegetarian Beef Wellington now! An abomination. Vegetarians. Now there's an insidious dissention we should have nipped in the bud.'

There was a jovial murmur of consensus.

'Communist infiltrators, I'll bet. With their green tea and sensibly coloured trousers,' Sarah teased, looking at the colonel. 'I think I know someone you would get on well with.' As she attempted to regain her thread, for the first time she noticed that she was slurring. Given the looks from the others, she was the last to make this observation. 'Do you know what else, and perhaps on a slightly different note. They wouldn't have carried out risk assessments on soldiers getting up ladders to change a light bulb for the same soldiers that they send out into minefields. I thought I'd heard everything with that one...'

A groan came from the colonel. 'Trust me, there's more.'

The conversation broke up as one on the waiters made his way down the table to take away any remaining glasses. 'Anyway, to the rugby.' Graeme turned to Simon. 'A great win for Gloucester, then.'

Once the colonel had departed, Graeme took the first opportunity to suggest they left, taking up the offer of sharing a lift with one of their neighbours.

Once they closed the apartment door behind them, an argument erupted, Graeme initiating it as he slammed the keys down on the hall table. 'Why did you have to be so embarrassing? What has got into you since we moved here?'

'Perhaps I was a bit off. Sorry. Let's just go to bed. It's late. I'm tired.'

'A bit off?! Your parting words to that other colonel were, "No offence about the cricket ball comment. Graeme didn't mean you." Brilliant, thank you for that, then you suggested that one of the paintings was a war crime, and got your heel caught in one of the drains outside.'

'OK. Perhaps not my finest moment,' she joked.

'This isn't good enough, Sarah.'

'It was just a bad night. I'll be fine. I have a few things to do tomorrow, fresh start, I have an essay due, lots of stuff, things...' Despite trying to show restraint, the memory of the CO's face came back into her mind. She broke into a smile as she saw the transparency of her disingenuous commitment. 'Sorry. I mean it. I promise.'

'Clearly, it isn't enough. You know what I am going to say.'

'Yes, no doubt, "Let's try another medication." Have you been offered a load more goodies from the pharmaceutical reps?' she laughed. 'Which one are you peddling now?'

'Fine. So, what are you going to do? Let's hear it,' he snapped back. 'What are you going to do to make yourself feel better? How about as a start making more of an effort with people?'

'People? Who are you talking about?'

'The other wives. They keep themselves occupied, why can't you? It doesn't have to be spectacular, take up another hobby... there are plenty of things that you can do. They have day trips, classes...'

'Another hobby. Yes, great idea. I joined the tennis club, aerobics, a coffee morning, God knows, I should be in line for some sort of decoration for that...'

'Which you are going to less and less.'

'You try going to one of those coffee mornings. If Marx thought religion was an opiate for the masses, the army took notes and set it to tea and sponge cake. Keeping wifeys quiet,' she said in exasperation. 'I miss working, Graeme. I miss my friends. And no, don't tell me to invite Chloe. It isn't the same. I miss the shop. Talking to people. I mean… look, it's different.'

'The shop? We have enough money. Take the time to enjoy yourself, or try something new.'

'New?' she scoffed. 'New? I think that they are quite thin on variation here. It's just the ordinary things, you know, like going for a coffee where there isn't a possibility of running into the crack troops of a wives' committee, fundraising for the local charity, needing help with a families day or having to negotiate coffee mornings whilst navigating away from the latest intrigue of the neighbour or neighbour's husband. No rank-conscious…'

'Oh God. Here we go.'

'Just hear me out.' She regathered her thoughts. 'No rank-conscious community based on who it is appropriate to form bonds with and who should be kept as a polite acquaintance. Apprehensive at seeing the seating plans for dinners, where we have to endure the same anecdotes. To have to be aware of who writes which reports for whom, should we be about to drop a clanger. Or…'

'Oh, poor you. All these dinners that are laid on…' he interrupted as she sought her next words.

'Please, just listen! To not be Sarah "the shrink's wife", "Lt Col Hughes' wife", or like at the last coffee morning, batting off being quizzed by one of the other wives, who was certain that her neighbour had "AD… what is it… HP or DD", so she could give validation to circulate rumours about her at the mother and baby class the following week. To not have to see soldiers "beasted" underneath our kitchen window every morning, or do anything without one of the other goldfish in the bowl being witness. To not suffer hint-immune people who just drop around for a coffee or quick chat, knowing that there was little possibility of pretending to be out, to those who view army homes meaning being army community accessible. To be back to how things had been before you had joined full-time. To be able to breathe again…'

'Christ,' he countered dryly. 'It's like listening to an alterative version of Kipling.'

'It's not funny, Graeme. You have to listen to me.'

'There's no point talking to you when you get like this. Do you know how many people would love this opportunity? The wives that you are so clearly contemptuous of, some of their husbands are away for six months, they have young children to look after.'

'Because the army is so receptive, so bloody caring about these women. Ha! And who thought that you would be the champion of the downtrodden, Graeme? What, now I'm trying to think of the last description of a patient. "A hysterical squaddie's wife who should be grateful that she has been spared the rough end of Glasgow." You exude compassion, empathy… I'm sure these women are queuing up for your sympathetic ear.'

'You are taking that out of context. You have to pull yourself together, for Christ's sake. We will talk about this when you sober up.'

'Well, I look forward to that. Can't wait.'

She waited for the sound of the bedside light clicking off before opening up the laptop. Impatiently, as the page loaded, she tried to recall how much would be in the account. Quickly signing in, she delighted in satisfaction at the sight of the total of £600. She took a quick glance at the match report on the BBC. Charlie Sharples sprinting to run onto a well-timed chip and scoring a brilliant try. Brilliant Charlie Sharples. The usual live games flashed around the board. She poured herself another drink. No fixture attracted her attention, but at the side the roulette wheel caught her eye. Red/Black, Odds/Evens. She began with her first deposit. The first stakes placed, the wheel started to spin.

CHAPTER 25

THE MORNING WAS a slow start. Graeme had already got up when she finally arose. It had only been nearly three hours previously that she had slipped into bed. Throwing on a pair of jeans and the first T-shirt that came to hand, with slow deliberation she prepared the percolator. Being only warm to the touch, she didn't need to look at the clock to realise that it was late morning. The sight of a greasy pan left by Graeme, thick with the smell of bacon fat, made her nauseous. He sat eating his breakfast without saying a word, only distracted once by his phone on the table notifying him of receipt of a text, to which he smiled and glanced up at her before quietly placing his phone into his pocket. Then, neatly stacking his crockery into the dishwasher, he left the room. A minute later, as the pot was near to boiling, she went to follow him in a desire to break the tension, but once in the hall stopped short, for fear of reigniting their argument. Her head was not ready for a blow-by-blow account of the night, and what he had already told her the previous night was an embarrassment.

Returning to the kitchen, her thoughts were interrupted by a knock at the door. Being in the hallway, there was no chance of either of them ignoring it.

As Sarah approached to answer it, she could see the woman through the glass had long blond hair. Initially indistinguishable, she took a deep breath in recalling that she had said to Katerin that if she was at a loose end to call in, forgetting completely that Graeme had taken a day's leave in anticipation of the late night. The bonus to this visit she was confident of was that at least it would force him to snap out of his brooding.

Opening the door she cried out in joy as she was greeted by Izzy, sporting a backpack which she dropped down to hug her mother.

'Izzy!' She threw her arms around her. 'Oh, sweetheart! How wonderful! What are you doing here?'

'Long story. It's just for a short visit. Anyway, I thought I would surprise you.'

'Wow! You have certainly done that!' She wiped her tears away, hugging her again. 'How I have missed you!'

'Alright, Mum!'

At that point Graeme came through. 'Hey you.' He walked over and kissed her. 'This is a surprise. Run out of money?' He gave her a wry smile. 'That would explain you ransacking the rails of the charity shops again, I see.'

'Yes, very funny. If I can't visit my mum and dad without them being suspicious... Oh, I can smell coffee... and... ew... bacon. Dad, since when have you started eating fried bacon again? You know Mum hates that.'

'Never mind bacon.' He hugged her. 'It's good to have you back. A short stay, I suspect. How did you get onto camp? I'm surprised they let you in looking like that.' He smiled.

'I told them I was your long-lost love child.' She smiled at her mother.

'Hmm. I believe that you might just do that,' he replied dryly.

'So this is the army quarter. It's nice.'

'Do you think so?' Sarah laughed.

'Well, no, unless you are into the sanatorium meets 1950s IKEA look. Speaking of hospitals... Wow, Mum. You look terrible! Heavy night last night?'

'Lost none of your cheek, then.'

Izzy looked around the hallway and peered into one of the rooms. 'Blimey. I'm half expecting Nurse Ratched to appear. So what time is pill-popping call?'

'Alright, you,' Graeme responded. 'Come on. Let's go through and you can tell me about what you have been up to. Not just Greece, I want to know how your studies are going.'

'Is it OK if I go with the nurse?' she joked to Sarah.

'It's fine. Go on, I'll bring some coffee through. Izzy, it's so good to have you here.'

'Yeah. Good to be here too, Mum.' She turned to her father as they made their way to the sitting room. 'So you would not believe some of the things, Dad. Athens, Delphi. I know you've been there but, wow. Anyway, it wasn't just there, we have just been in Turkey, incredible...'

Sarah went back through to the kitchen. She could hear Izzy telling her father about her recent exploration to Greece. The quiet apartment suddenly seemed to have transformed in a moment. The happiness of seeing her daughter held an unavoidable comparison to how they had been for the last few months. Life being breathed into the place for the first time.

The next morning Izzy was already up making breakfast. 'What's this? My daughter truly knowing her way around a kitchen. Who are you?'

'Yes. Ha ha. Dad said something had come up and he had to pop into work for a few hours, and I thought you deserved a lie-in. Now, I've made pancakes, fresh orange juice.'

'Pancakes?'

Sarah went up and tasted a piece of one of them. 'Oh! This is good.'

'Don't act so surprised. A friend of mine I met in Athens – he was from Chicago – anyway, he taught me how to do them. The real ones.'

'Friend? He…?' She raised her eyebrows to her daughter who began busying herself with setting the table.

'Well, they look an improvement on mine. Can you do waffles,' she affected an American accent, 'and eggs on rye?'

'Mum…' she groaned. 'Do you want them or not? There are some hungry-looking soldiers over there I can always give them to. By the way, what on earth are they doing?' Sarah walked over to see a soldier chasing a food wrapping across a pitch with a pointed stick.

'Don't ask. Anyway, I am taking you into town today to buy you lunch. Seeing as your father monopolised you last night, I want to hear all about it. More about where you have been, how you are and if this friend has a name.'

'Lunch sounds great and I can tell you all about it. Firstly, how are you? Aside from your luxury pad, there must be some other real benefits to life here.'

'It's Nirvana. Excitement and fly-by-the-seat-of-your-pants stuff here. They sometimes do two for one on the scones in the NAAFI. No, I'm joking. Before you say anything. There is a good social life, the local town is beautiful, there are some good ski resorts only a few hours away.'

'That's great. You can take me with you next time. Whereabouts did you go to?'

'We haven't quite got around to it yet, but how about we start with the town? We can go for a look around then have lunch.'

They took their seats in a café on the square. It was a quiet morning as a few people were milling around, many taking a mid-morning coffee at the outside tables, the bright sunshine enticing people outside, albeit in warm jackets. Sarah sensed that Izzy had some sort of disclosure, as she seemed distracted and usually would have suggested they go inside. Her tolerance to cold, when she wasn't running or hiking up some hillside, had always been low. Sitting at the table she pulled her sleeves down over her hands, which Sarah was sure she was about to clarify was the sudden differential between there and the Mediterranean, anxiety or a bit of both. On the way, Izzy had asked about the apartment, the garrison and general questions about living in Germany – the people, the food – and seemingly anything that deviated from discussing how she had been. But knowing each other, it was an unsaid expectation that a more in-depth conversation would be forthcoming when the time was right.

'Are you sure you don't want to go inside, darling?'

'No. Fine. Absolutely not. It's good to sit and watch the world go by.' She pulled her sleeves a little further over her hands.

A waiter approached the table to take their order.

'*Ich mochte zwei Kaffees bitte. Oh einen Moment, wir nehmen zwei Stück Schichtkuchen!*'

The waiter nodded in acknowledgement.

"Ha! Are you impressed?"

'You're doing really well, Mum. I'm proud of you.'

'Don't be too impressed, asking for two coffees and two slices of cake, that is about my limit.'

'No, I mean with everything. It can't be easy with leaving your friends behind, Chloe, the business and the house. I know that you must miss your garden. Don't take this the wrong way, but I have to ask. Are you happy?'

Sarah was taken aback at this frankness. 'Where did that come from? I'm fine. What made you say that?'

'You don't look the same. A bit tired, no, knackered. You and Dad, are you alright?'

'Izzy! What a thing to say. Of course.'

'It's just. He's my dad and I love him. But really he can be kind of an ass sometimes. I'm just seeing that you are OK. You haven't emailed or Skyped as much. Seb said the same. Which is fine but… it's not like you.'

'Ass?! Now that is it! I have been so busy with studying for this course. It's a long time since I spent that much time at the computer by the time I have finished an assignment. You remember what I am like with typing. Pen and paper when I was last studying.'

'Missing that Tippex and smudging, when you were a student. Not that we hear much of your student days. Being a mathmo you had to be a bit of a geek, I bet. Camped in the library while your mates are having a few pints at The Mill.'

'Hmm. Something like that. Now, I've ordered us a cake with ten layers to it. Obscene but quite delicious. So, to your news. For a start, I want you to tell me about this person who is ruining that expensive English vernacular we invested in. So what is his name?'

'Ignoring the last. His name is David. So no, it isn't Chuck or Brad.'

'And don't tell me, I'm going to love him,' Sarah joked.

'Good grief. Do you want to know or not?'

'Go on. I'm just teasing.'

'So, David,' she re-emphasised his name, 'is an archaeologist… well, in training, but it isn't serious. We just are… you know, enjoying travelling.'

'As far as euphemisms go…'

'Mum!' she quickly interrupted. 'Please… yikes.'

'I have to say that I expected something more along the lines of a struggling musician, or surfer dude. That's a bit conventional.'

'Oh my God. "Dude"?!'

'Ah, the power to embarrass your children. I've still got

219

it!' She winked at Izzy. 'It seems like such a long time since we last saw you,' she lamented. 'Come on, tell me some more about David and your trip. You were saying last night about the Aegean. How was Turkey?'

'Oh it's beautiful, Mum. It isn't what I expected at all. It's why I didn't come sooner, we spent an extra couple of weeks there. David met up with a friend he studied with in Boston, anyway I'll get on to that. I'll show you a photo when we get back that we took in a bay near Ephesus. It is the most beautiful place. The waters. Stunning. It's opened up a whole new world. I don't want you to laugh. But I feel like this is my niche, I was meant to find this. I wish I could really explain.'

'I'm not going to laugh. I promise. Although the idea of you in a dusty pit with a trowel in a pith helmet and a pair of empire-builders, sorry, darling. I'm listening.'

'OK, so we were in a place called Miletus. There was no one there. Ruins, something that you might take a passing interest in. Do you know what happened there? Western philosophy was born. No, not Athens, what is now a dusty ruin, occupied by a couple of attendants and a trinket seller. You don't want to know really, do you?'

'I do! It sounds fascinating. Keep going. We have all afternoon. I want to know about your life. We have seen so little of you, I want to hear everything you have been doing.'

'There is something else. Please don't go mad, there is something I need to tell you.' She took a deep breath as her mother flashed a look of anxiety. 'I'm thinking of dropping out of medicine.'

'What? When?'

'I have already had a lecture last night from Dad about my lack of enthusiasm. The thing is, I don't want to go back just yet, actually if ever.' She then quickly followed up. 'Please don't tell him yet.'

'I won't.'

'No, really, I mean it.'

'Izzy, trust me. I just wasn't expecting that. Wow. I want you to do what is best for you, but you need to think this through carefully. Take your time. But don't, whatever you do, base this on David. I know this might seem...'

'Oh no! Seriously!' she swiftly replied indignantly. 'Please don't think that this is all about a man! Come on, Mum! You know me better than that! He has asked if I want to go back with him to Turkey. So, in a nutshell, his friend has asked him if he wants to spend six months on another project down on the west coast. They are uncovering a theatre that has been submerged in earth for nearly 2,000 years. Can you believe that? The last people to see that were the ancients.'

Sarah looked at Izzy, smiling.

'What is it? Why are you smiling? You're angry, aren't you. I've really thought about this. But you know your gut instinct. It just feels right. The idea of going back to study medicine, ugh. Do you know how many medics I have met at uni who talk about parents or grandparents who are doctors, or of their ambition to invent a cure for a host of diseases. Perhaps they will contribute to a future cure, become a celebrated surgeon. But, that's not me. I think that there are plenty of people that can do what I could achieve. When I think of going back, I can't face it.'

'It sounds like you have already made your mind up.'

'I'm sorry, I wanted to make you proud.'

'You always have. I remember when you made the decision to go into medicine. I should have realised.'

Izzy passed over her mother's last comment. 'I'm not saying that I will be an archaeologist, I have no idea, but for the first time I feel on the right path. This has opened up a whole new world. I don't want to do fashion either. No offence, Mum.'

'None taken. I think I have been prepared for that bombshell. Do you know what I think?'

'I'm bottling it. You think that I should go back to give it another go… because I will listen to what you have to say.'

'No, I don't think that you are bottling it. That would be the last thing that I would say. I think that you should go with your gut.'

'What! Are you serious?! I can't believe you are saying that,' she laughed. 'Dad would have a fit.'

'I'm not saying you shouldn't think about it. Would it help speaking again to your tutor about this? Have you spoken to them? You can always go back to university and see how you feel then.'

'No! I mean, I have done, but no! I don't want to go back.' Her outburst made her mother raise her eyebrows as if she had anticipated her reaction. 'When you say that… no.'

'You know what you want, then.'

'Yes, I do. It can't be as simple as that, can it?' She didn't wait for Sarah to answer. 'I suppose it can. Is this happening? Will you be with me when I tell Dad? I don't think he will be so understanding. I thought that if I told him I was pregnant then tell him the real reason I'm dropping out it might soften his perspective.'

'I wouldn't count on it, darling. I wouldn't count on it.'

They returned home about an hour before Graeme was due back. Most of the lines they had rehearsed in order to break the news gently had succumbed to the judgment that he would see through it, or have a ready answer. They were still deliberating when they heard the car pull up outside. Having cracked open a bottle in anxiety, they were nearly at the end of it when he came through the door. Sometimes the suggestions descended into farce as they tried to ease the tension. But the sound of the door prompted a sobering tone.

'It will be OK, I promise you, sweetheart. I can't believe I am saying this to you of all people. But be sure of yourself. If this is what you want it doesn't matter whatever anyone else thinks.' She kissed her on her forehead. 'As much as I hate to admit it, you are an adult now. Your life is your own. I'm so proud of you.'

'Stop being a goose, Mum. I know you are. And thank you for supporting me. I mean it.'

'Hey, Dad, you are home. How was your day? Come and sit down, I will make you a cup of tea.'

'Alright. This can't be good,' he responded suspiciously as he placed his hat on the hall table.

'What do you mean?! It's just a cup of tea,' she said, surprised at her father's response, unaware of her blatant transparency. 'I don't get to see you very often, that's all. I just thought that we could sit down and have a chat, pick up from yesterday.'

Graeme looked straight at Sarah who rolled her eyes at her daughter's floundering attempts. 'I think it is best that you tell him. You shouldn't undersell your father, he is a reasonable man and wants what's best for you.'

'Blimey, Mum, and you thought I was struggling to say the right thing.'

'Izzy, be serious. I think we should all go through and sit down. Take a deep breath and let her finish. Now, Graeme, you have to hear her out.'

'Oh God, you are not pregnant, are you?' he stated in a more clinical and sober tone than they expected if he thought that he was facing that prospect.

'Well, as it happens…'

'Izzy!' Sarah quickly interjected. 'Come on now, be serious! Let's all sit down, I will bring us something to drink.'

Sarah headed for the kitchen, Graeme and Izzy to the sitting room. Preparing the cups and listening to the first percolations, there was little but a faint sound of an exchange going on in the sitting room. Assembling the tray she noted the voices had gone quiet. Leaning on the counter wondering if she should wait, she hoped that Izzy was doing the right thing, if she should have encouraged her to take more time. She knew that Graeme was going to find this shattering. In his eyes, in both their eyes, they didn't think that she had considered anything else. It had endured all the years beyond the junior doctor's set she had asked for when she was barely five, that they thought would probably be a passing phase – as with Seb, who had said he wanted to be a helicopter pilot or run out at Twickenham to play for England – and from when she was starting senior school and announced that she was going to be a doctor. It had been barely a year since they had celebrated her acceptance to Cambridge. She thought back to that night when the anticipation and dreams were played out at their favourite Indian restaurant. He had never faltered in his faith or expectations of her.

The coffee rumbled on as she waited in anticipation, expecting tears from Izzy and what she was certain would be Graeme's initial lack of acceptance.

She heard Izzy come down the hallway. 'That was quick! How did he take it?'

'It went OK, I think,' she whispered. 'He's not really asked too much about the actual dig, but baby steps, I suppose.'

'I would settle for that for now.' Her statement had come as a surprise, as she wondered if it was just shock or most likely a delaying tactic so she wouldn't dig her heels in.

'Thank you, Mum. I have been worrying so much. Like I told you before, I know what I am doing. You can't believe the relief. You know when I was telling Dad, it just convinced me even more I was doing the right thing.'

'I think you're very brave. I wish I'd had your confidence. Self-awareness.'

'You could never tell you were married to a shrink,' Izzy teased. 'Listen, I thought I would go out and get us a bottle of wine to have with dinner. I'm not sure he has taken it well…

I don't know, he was a bit quiet. Do you think that he really is fine about it? I've never seen him like that. I expected,' she paused, 'well, a bollocking and a "you are throwing your life away" speech. I thought I would have a real battle on my hands.'

'You knew he'd be disappointed and will probably need a little time to digest it. But it will be fine.'

'I don't think champagne would be quite right. There is a place near here, isn't there?'

'Um yes, the NAAFI,' she replied distractedly as she wondered how Graeme was. 'Save your money, Izzy.' She reached for her purse. 'Here.' She handed her twenty euros. 'And here's a ration book. Just show some ID and say that you are Colonel Hughes' daughter. I'm sure there won't be problem.'

'Rations?' Izzy laughed, her mood buoyant. 'Oh, Mum! I can't tell you. It feels like a weight, a great big staggeringly whopping weight has been lifted. I can't wait to tell David that I am coming with him to the dig. What are we going to unearth? I mean, it could be anything. I could just be the next Howard Carter! I'll be sending you and Dad photos. When I get back to Turkey, I will call you all the time.'

'It's OK. Really, I'm pleased for you. Your dad will come around, I promise. He loves you very much. Now, there is a sign at the end of the road if you go left. In fact there is a museum on the camp just before there. Go and have a look while you have the chance, it will be open for another hour. There are some photos of excavations that have been done on the camp.' The coffee rumbled to a conclusion. 'Now, you go and I will see you later. Take your phone in case you have any problems.'

As soon as the door went Graeme came through into the kitchen.

'How are you feeling? I'm sorry, I know you are going to be disappointed.' Sarah attempted to console him.

He calmly took a glass from the cupboard, filling it with water. 'Was this your idea?'

'Why on earth would you think that?' she responded, confused. 'She seems very sure of herself. Actually I've never seen her so sure. I think we should be proud. Izzy's gone to get something to celebrate. Don't make her feel that she has to make something up to you. It's hard, I know, but it has to be better than her realising this a year or two down the line. Let's go through and talk about it. Calmly and soberly, Graeme.'

'Ha, that's rich coming from you. The state you have been in recently.'

'Let's keep this about Izzy. She needs our support.'

'So when exactly did she tell you?'

'About three hours ago. This is as much a surprise to me as you.'

He looked at her disbelievingly. 'Whatever you say, Sarah. Don't worry, I know exactly what is best for my daughter. This David, no doubt a drifter. His best prospect is as a circuit digger. Did you know that? No guarantees. Even if he makes it, my corporals earn more than he probably ever will. I have it in hand.'

'You have it in hand? What is that supposed to mean?' He turned away from her, going back into the sitting room. She followed him down the hall. 'Graeme, what do you mean?'

'I have a contact in the faculty. We can sort this out. Give her a month in that Anatolian shithole with no money and she will come around. When she does, she will have a place to go back to. If I can't talk some sense into her, her tutor will.'

'I should have known when she said that you had taken it well. What was I thinking? Don't you dare interfere, Graeme. She is an adult. It is her life and medicine isn't the be all and end all. You didn't even bother to listen to her plans. Just calm down and hear her out.'

He picked up his phone.

'Put it down, Graeme, and we will talk when Izzy gets back.'

Closing the gate outside, Izzy turned to walk down the street, looking up at her parents' apartment. She caught the eye of her father as he began to scan his phone contacts. Knowing his sense of propriety, she made an extravagant wave at him as Sarah came to the window.

'You can't do this. She will resent you, no she will not trust you again,' Sarah implored. 'Just take a moment to think.'

'I have thought about it. It is a ridiculous thing for her to do. It's Friday. I will be able to catch him at work.'

'I mean it, Graeme. Put the phone down. We will talk. You will come to understand her. I would have thought the same as you but if you listen to her, she...'

'Don't you patronise me! You have no idea what she would be throwing away.'

'What, because I'm not a doctor?'

'Or ever really had any ambition, to be honest,' he responded cuttingly.

'If she is so happy, why would she being doing this? Has it not occurred to you that she went in for the wrong reasons?'

'What the hell are you talking about?'

'Why do you think that she went into medicine?'

As Izzy continued down the path past the gymnasium she watched a PT class being put through their paces. A couple of the soldiers were increasingly struggling to keep up with the rapid squat thrusts that the rest of the squad were keeping in time to. A white-vested PTI suddenly shouted a change of moves to press-ups, to which they duly shifted. Not without a groan from one of the two men at the back, a complaint that had caught the attention of the instructor. Izzy smiled as the ailing soldier displayed a sudden burst of energy into the task.

An RMP car passed her on the road. She watched the driver in full conversation with his colleague. The sight of the police immediately reminded her of what Graeme had said that morning about keeping some form of ID on her and she wondered if she had brought her purse. Reaching into her pocket she found the twenty-euro note that her mother had given her, which she had been about to put in it. The purse, she now recalled, was on the kitchen table.

Graeme rounded on Sarah, unsure of what direction she was taking. 'She went into medicine because she has an aptitude for it.'

'Yes, Graeme, she does. But a passion for it? I don't think so. Think about it. We never really talked to her about Ben. How when sometimes I was overwhelmed, how we couldn't save him. When I raged about it. I think that she was taking all that in, and yes, she looks up to you. Behind that tough exterior she wanted to please us, to make a difference.'

'Oh, so now you are the expert on the mind. Please enlighten me. What else is going on in our daughter's head that I have been missing all these years? She only has medicine. You've seen what's she like. Well, we are now seeing it. God knows, if she didn't have an aptitude for that, well, she'd be...'

'What would she be, Graeme? Not a talking point at your golf club or a distraction from talking about your son that you also seem to be so disappointed in? I know he brought forward his travels because you just couldn't accept that he didn't meet your expectations. Amazing your sudden interest in Izzy came about when he showed no interest in medicine.'

'Seriously?' he snapped incredulously. 'I have supported my daughter when you weren't there for her. One of us couldn't afford the luxury of disappearing for three months when you decided to leave us.'

'Graeme, don't do this.'

'Not so keen on Izzy's best interests then, were you? Do you remember? Remember what you said?'

Her voice dropped. 'I was ill and you know it.'

'Yes, and it was me that got you through. You have always been weak,' he scorned.

Izzy opened the gate to the apartment block as the downstairs neighbour came out of her apartment. 'You must be Izzy! I recognise you from the photos.'

'Um, yes.'

'I'm Gemma, a friend of your mother's. It's good to finally meet you.'

'Likewise. Mum says you make the most astonishing cakes.'

'That is good to know. I think that when she smells the baking, she actually sees me morphed into a muffin. So, anyway, she says that you are going to be the next William Harvey. Don't be impressed by my knowledge,' she laughed. 'My son is doing the history of medicine. Who knew dissecting cadavers and battlefield gore would be more of a draw than the history of the Corn Laws!' she joked. 'Your parents are very proud, you know.'

'Oh. That might be the next topic of conversation you have with Mum.'

'OK.' She looked confused. 'Anyway, sorry, I have to fly. I have to go and pick up my son from school. It was lovely to meet you, Izzy! If you get a chance, bring your mother down for a coffee.'

'I will. Thank you.'

'She's had a tough time these last few months. With the accident and the operation. A lot of courage, awful what she's come through.'

'Yes, awful.' As she climbed the stairs she considered her neighbour's concern a little overblown for a couple of broken ribs, further confused by the comment about the operation. Her attention was turned to loud voices coming from the apartment. She hesitated outside the kitchen as she heard her mother.

'Jesus, Graeme. Why is it every time we talk about problems in the past, the fault is with my previous issues?'

'Issues and previous? You talk about what is best for Izzy after one afternoon, on a whim,' he exclaimed in disbelief, 'no doubt wanting to come out on top. You think that it will make good for your guilt. Making up for when you decided to abandon her. Months of not knowing if you were even coming back. Do you think that she wasn't taking any of that in? Who had to look after her and Sebastian then?'

'How many times do I have to say that I am sorry? I had to get away, Graeme. I couldn't be in the house. Does that make you feel better every time we go here and I tell you that I still feel the guilt. You have never let me forget it,' she shouted. 'I love my children and I would do anything for them. But I won't push Izzy into something that she doesn't feel is right for her.'

'And you were thinking of her when you left us... And be honest with yourself. You didn't even want her,' he snapped.

'That is a lie. Why would you say that?! But hey, a good excuse to go back to good old Graeme when he saved the day. To go over this again and again,' she repeated as she shouted him down. 'Ad fucking nauseam.' Tears began to fall.

'Look at the state of you. For God's sake, calm down.' He leaned across to close the window. 'Heaven knows how she turned out even vaguely sane with you as a mother. I now see that the apple didn't fall far from the tree. That impulsiveness, lack of ambition. It might have been by the skin of her teeth, but at least I would have got her through medical school. A mediocre doctor is better than a drifter.'

Izzy stood at the door. 'What are you talking about?' her voice confused, sedate.

Sarah rushed to her while Graeme stood his ground and took a deep breath. 'Your mother and I were just having a disagreement. We just want what's best for you.'

'Izzy.' Sarah tried to hug her daughter who pushed her away.

'Wow, Dad. I don't even know where to start. So is it that one of you didn't want me and the other thinks I'm a mediocrity. What is Dad talking about? You didn't want me?'

'That's not exactly true.' Graeme unconvincingly backed Sarah up. 'It was in the heat of the moment.'

'What was your neighbour talking about? You had to have an operation? Why didn't someone tell me about that?'

'Because your father and I, we didn't want you to worry.'

'No. That's bullshit. It is the usual conspiracy of silence. So again, why didn't you want me?'

'Listen to me, darling. It wasn't how it sounded.'

'Dad.'

Graeme said nothing.

'For God's sake, tell her that isn't true.'

'Even so. Maybe she deserves to know what happened. Your mother left you, us. It was for three months. You were too young to remember. She said that she wasn't coming back. I had no idea where she was.'

'That is not how it was,' Sarah cut in sharply. 'You are such a manipulative...'

'I don't understand, Mum, I wish you had told me.' Instead of being angry she hugged her mother. 'It's OK. I know you have always been there for me. I'm sure that you had your reasons.'

'Christ, now your own daughter is looking after you. You don't deserve her.'

'Dad, what can I say? Thank you for making things easier for me. I'm afraid I'm going to disappoint.' Her voice cracked as she left the room, resisting all Sarah's pleas to talk.

Sarah gave her the space by not following her into the bedroom as Graeme left the room, shortly after which she heard him switch on the television. The news headlines sounded loudly as the volume was being turned up. She then heard the sound of Izzy making a phone call, the emotion clear in her voice. She was telling David that she was getting on a plane in the morning.

Sarah felt a surge of rage as she went through to confront Graeme. Before she could even speak, he pre-empted her. 'Is there anything that I said that wasn't true?'

'What?' she responded incredulously.

He repeated calmly, 'Is there anything I said that wasn't true?'

She reached forward and turned the television off. 'You twisted it. Why tell her now?' she implored.

'It would have come out sooner or later. You should be thankful I didn't tell her everything.'

'Don't you dare go there, Graeme. This can only hurt her,' she said in desperation.

'Good job I was a doctor then. Bringing you around.'

'Low. Really low. Fine, you tell her. I get it. She hasn't done things your way. Christ. You are sulking like a bloody child. Is it so bad that she is not going to do medicine? Who knows, you may be right. She might change her mind. What room have you given her now? I've just heard that she is going tomorrow.' Sarah's voice became more desperate. 'Do you want her to leave like this?'

'You were the one who said she needs to make her own decisions.'

'OK.' She tried to regain some composure. 'When Izzy comes out we can talk. We might only get one chance at this. One. God knows what she must be thinking. We have to reassure her.'

'You are so keen on her reaching her own conclusions without help. The same goes here. I'm going to go and finish some paperwork upstairs.'

'Graeme! You need to apologise to her. Sort this out.'

Ignoring her, he left the room as she tried to appeal to him.

The hallway was silent. Izzy had finished her call. In anticipation that she may see the door open, she sat down in the kitchen and waited. Pouring herself a glass of water, her hands shook as she fought the urge to go in. Of the few characteristics that she had gained from her father, sulking wasn't one of them. Every minute that she stayed in her room, Sarah feared that Graeme's words would become entrenched.

For another thirty minutes, Sarah waited in the kitchen. Everything was still, the time passing agonisingly slowly. Waiting for the opportunity to reassure her daughter. Going over an unwanted recollection of that time when she left, but as she did, Graeme's words came as a challenge to nearly every justification. 'Is there anything I said that wasn't true?' She had left Izzy and Seb for three months. No contact except to leave a message on the answerphone to say that she was OK. Her attempts to write a letter and explain were aborted after the first few lines. When faced with her explanation it could only come back to one thing. Her need to get away. It was impossible to explain that she couldn't face the day ahead looking after them. Her fears were too overwhelming. Three months later, in the same impulse that led her to run, came a similar urgency to return. As if it were yesterday she recalled the look on Graeme's face as she walked through the door. Instead of recriminations or fallout, they didn't talk about it for nearly a year. Every time she began to offer an explanation, apology, he responded with a cool acknowledgement that she was back, and that was what had mattered. She acquiesced to a course of antidepressants, and the same routine was re-established. Until she had another decline and he held her to account. Going over again with her the fallout she had caused. If she went away again, if she left them, then she wouldn't be welcome back.

It was another half an hour before she heard Izzy's door

open. She remained in the kitchen as she waited for her to appear.

'So, waiting in here knowing I had to come for hydration at some point was your plan.' Her face pale, her eyes betrayed the fact that she had been crying.

'No, the certainty would have been the drinks cabinet.'

Her attempt to break the ice raised a smile with Izzy. 'Where's Dad?'

'He's gone up to his study to sort a few work emails. Now, come here and sit down. You need to hear what I have to say. I understand why you might be angry. I didn't tell you because I thought that you didn't need to know.'

'It was more of a shock that I didn't know. Why you didn't tell us. Don't take this the wrong way but what must have been going through your mind? It was obviously your illness, wasn't it? You were depressed. I wish you had said something. Do you ever regret coming back?'

'No! Never. You must never think that.' She reached out for her hand. 'It's difficult to explain. I need you to understand that I loved you and Seb more than anything.'

'This is to do with Ben, isn't it?'

Sarah looked at her in surprise. Ben was something else that they barely talked about. 'It wasn't just about him,' she faltered. 'You haven't mentioned him for a while.'

'We never can.'

'Your father, I assume that's what you mean, he took it very hard.'

'I was thinking the other day, about Ben. I often wonder what he would have been like, don't you, Mum? Of course you do,' she chastised herself. 'Ridiculous thing to say. It seems funny to think that you were so young when you met Dad. Only three years older than me when you had Seb. That's just, I don't know, difficult to imagine.'

'What, us being under thirty? You and me both.' She

smiled. 'But it wasn't all about Ben. You and Seb, you were so precious. It became overwhelming. Let me try and explain. OK. Just bear with me. I'm not sure where to start.' She took a deep breath in. 'One day, it hadn't been long since we lost Ben. I had a call from the school, Seb had taken a fall. He had climbed a tree, went out on a branch, and you can imagine the rest.' She rolled her eyes in a moment of levity. 'You know what he is like. God knows how he got up there. Anyway, he was fine, but that afternoon he went to the hospital. Going back again to the same place where Ben… I barely felt able to breathe. I saw your brother sitting up as he was being made a fuss of. I ran over and hugged him, then I started shouting at him. I was barely aware of what I was doing. His face, Izzy. The nurses, they looked at me as if I was unhinged. One of them firmly told me to keep my voice down, another, and I recall this as clear as day, was holding Seb's hand in reassurance. It was then I could see the confusion and angst in his face. This was my son. And I felt like an outsider. Bad for him. Undeserving of him. You had started crying. You were so little, Izzy.' She broke off. 'I'm not trying to get you to feel sorry for me. That isn't it.'

'Don't. I don't think that,' Izzy interrupted. 'I want you to tell me. What happened then?'

'I just became overwhelmed. As I said, after those first waking moments is always the worst. After Ben died, when I saw him in my dreams, when I woke up, I would believe just for a split second he was still alive, then, it was then I realised that he had gone.'

'The photos that we have, of Ben, he looks happy, Mum.'

Sarah suddenly choked out a cry. 'Sorry, I'm fine.' She resisted Izzy's attempt to comfort her. 'Oh, he was. He was also a little so and so, and he was into everything. Like you and Seb.'

Izzy hesitated before she asked the next question. 'Mum, I need to ask. I don't want to upset you.' She gauged her mother's expression. 'But why didn't we talk more about him? I always wondered why we didn't have any photos up in the house.'

Sarah took a moment to compose her thoughts, as she wanted to make sure her answer was accurate, considered. 'Your father really suffered, Izzy. He didn't want them out on display. He couldn't bear it when someone came into our house and asked about Ben, not knowing he was gone. Not long after, he took them all down and that was it. But he was so good with you and Seb, and holding family together. I really don't know how I would have coped without him. He held it all in and didn't want to talk about it. We grieved differently. You shouldn't think less of him for that. He has always been a good father to you.'

'I know, that's just Dad. I understand. It was difficult to talk about him, Mum. You know, Ben. We had these couple of photos and you would tell us the occasional stories but Seb and I, well, we decided that it was too much for you.'

'What?' She wiped away her tears. 'I'm so sorry. I didn't realise. Let me show you something.' She squeezed Izzy's hand, before opening her purse that was lying on the table, pulling out a number of tickets and cards. 'Just give me a second.' From a deep compartment she pulled out a photograph. 'Here. I like to keep this one.' She handed it to Izzy.

'Wow. I haven't seen this one before. How old was he?'

'Three.'

She held the photo up to the light at the window. 'He looks so much like Seb.'

'But he also had your determination. You were just the same at his age. Into everything, exploring everything... doing whatever we told you you shouldn't do...'

Izzy laughed. 'This is good, Mum. I like to hear about him.'

'He was fearless. But anyway, I wanted to show you this.'

'Where was this taken?' She scrutinised the photo. 'That doesn't look like the beach where we went on holiday in Wales.

Where was this? Was it where you went with Granny?'

'No, it was in Wales, just a bit further down the coast.'

'Do you recall how Dad would moan about the signs in Welsh?'

'And the Welsh. You won't remember but he got into an argument one day because someone in a pub refused to speak in English when he tried to complain about the meal. Well, not before he called Wales "a principality with delusions of grandeur and a painfully bad rugby team".'

'He didn't. Oh God, poor you.'

'If it hadn't been for you children I think your father would have never made it out of there,' she laughed.

'So I assume you didn't go back to the other beach because of Ben. Tell me about it. This day, I mean.'

Sarah ran her thumb gently over the photo. 'This was the first time we found this beach. It was the most beautiful place, and on a wonderfully sunny day. We actually found it by accident. Seb had started playing up. My third rendition of "Especially For You" had failed to have the desired effect, and I was being roundly rejected by all the passengers.' She smiled.

'Oh no... I thought "The Loco-Motion" was bad enough.'

'To your father, Kylie Minogue made *Mamma Mia* a comparative operatic triumph. Anyway, usually Seb liked my singing but...' She looked at Izzy who was pulling a light-hearted expression of disbelief. 'No, really, he did, but he suddenly decided that enough was enough. So we pulled over to take in some sea air and have a sandwich. As I went to get the hamper out the back, I saw it, this beautiful golden secluded beach. From the road you wouldn't have had a clue it was there. We discovered an overgrown path down to the bottom and found a place for a picnic.'

'It sounds wonderful.'

'We took a walk down to the water. You see he is wearing a jacket. Oh my goodness it was sunny, but still a chilly day.'

'When you left. You said it was what, for about three months.'

'Izzy, he is telling the truth about me leaving... although it wasn't as it sounded. I don't know if you want to hear all this?'

'Yes, I do.'

The first thing that came into her head was the afternoon that she left. 'I never wanted to leave you.' She thought back to the moment when she packed her bag to make her way to the coast.

'Where did you go?' Graeme had never asked where she had been. He said he didn't want to know. She was back.

'Does it matter?'

'Yes, I want to know. Were you safe? Were you with anyone?' She quickly continued, 'You know, I mean someone in the family or a mate?'

'I didn't want to see anyone. It was because I was ashamed. No, better to say I couldn't face seeing anyone. I read later that children who are separated during the early formative phase... I wondered if that is why you have always been so independent.'

'Read or told? Don't answer that. Wow. Huh. All that guilt piled on a woman. Aaghh, everyone cries! It's against the natural order of things! The universe turned on its head. Women who give up their babies, or women who dare to say that they are not happy. You know my friend Nick from school, well he lived with his dad from the age of two. And he's alright. And you should ask Dad if he would have given up his career to look after us. Cook, clean and be a stay-at-home parent. It's prehistoric crap, Mum.'

'Is that right?' She laughed at her daughter's ability to switch back to her feminist narrative. 'This is where you tell me it is down to the church, and men frightened of losing their domestic grip on women who are dissatisfied.'

'Exactly!' Izzy continued. 'Do you know what Dad said

238

once when I challenged him about all that patriarchal rubbish he doesn't like to admit to believing in. You know, when I was little he would tell me that I was "wilful" because I didn't want to… I can't recall exactly, something or other.' She rolled her eyes. 'Ha! Wilful! Like he would have said that to his son, when he started wanting to strike out on his own! He said that I would have taken charge of Romulus and Remus had I been the third sibling. As with the time…'

'It's alright,' Sarah interrupted her. 'You don't have to joke about it, darling.'

'I'm so sorry. I wish you had told me sooner. I'm not going to judge you. You have always been there for us when we needed you. Do you see? I'm independent mostly because it is who I am, and what you helped me to be. We might not always see things the same, no, we do see the world differently. But you have allowed, no, encouraged me to be who I am. So now that has been dealt with…'

'That's it? You don't want to ask any more.'

'Not unless you want to.'

'You never cease to amaze me.' Sarah was thrown by the conversation they had had. Everything that she had always dreaded her children finding out had come out. 'Don't you have any more questions?'

'You mean do I need reassurance? I know you are telling me the truth. Maybe, there might be, if something comes to mind later.'

'Do you want to know if I regret having you?'

'Do you?'

'No. Never. Your father and I love you very much. It was the best thing that we did. Whatever problems, you children are our greatest happiness.'

'Seeing as we are being honest, there is something else I wanted to ask you. Would you have stayed with Dad, you know, without us?'

'Wow. What a question. Of course. Why would you say that? I know we argue. God knows. He was right about one thing. He was always there for me, for us. We have had so many happy times. But as for you, life is so precious, Izzy. You take every day to fulfil your dreams. Do whatever you want that makes you happy.'

'I will, Mum.' She leaned over to hug her again. 'I'm so glad you told me. But what's this about the accident? Your neighbour said you had an operation. What happened?'

'I had a couple of broken bones. But you can see I am fine now. I was shaken up but it looked worse than it was. If Gemma made it sound worse than it was it is because I laid it on a bit thick to prolong the regular deliveries of muffins. Seriously, if you tasted them...'

'Hmm. I'm sure,' Izzy replied sceptically. 'But you are alright now?'

'Of course.' Sarah got up from the table. 'How about you open a bottle of wine from the rack? It's your last night, I take it.'

'Oh. You heard. Look, I was upset, I can call David back. I can meet up with him next week. No hurry.'

'Go if that is what you want to do. Your father will come around. Understand that he's only ever wanted to be a doctor. His mother said, since he was a boy, like his father. He thought that you might feel the same way. But, as I said, when he has time to adjust he will come around. You never know, we might even visit you.' Sarah began to well up as she stood up from the table. 'I'll be back in a moment. Now, I don't see any reason why we don't open something nice. Just pick out one from the rack. No, in fact I think there is a nice chilled bottle of prosecco.'

Sarah watched her daughter go to the fridge, wondering how the thing she had most dreaded her finding out had passed with so little effect, Izzy's easy acceptance now leaving her with conflicting emotions about the conversation that had just taken place. 'You know that jacket of yours hanging up in the hall? I had one just the same. A Soviet overcoat. In fact I was wearing it when I met your father.'

Izzy quickly turned around. 'No way! You are joking. Are there any photos?'

'Mercifully none. Not that I am aware of anyway.'

'Oh my God, comrade. You are a dark horse. You didn't meet Dad at one of the meetings, I take it?!' She began to laugh. 'Can you imagine Dad in a floppy Mao cap and espadrilles?'

'If only that were true, I would definitely have kept the proof,' she laughed.

At that point they heard Graeme come back from upstairs.

'I will talk to Dad later.' As Izzy left she crossed paths with Graeme as he went into the kitchen.

'I'm glad you're back. We've been talking. Look, I know that this is difficult. But she is going tomorrow. Just listen to what she has to say. Please tell me you didn't call her tutor.'

'This isn't a popularity contest. We shouldn't simply pander to her. She will thank me for it.'

Sarah closed her eyes in resignation.

'It was very cordial. He knows what she is like so I have asked if he will speak to her. He said that she wasn't having any problems with the course. What does that tell you?'

'Why do you never listen?'

'Why are you so jealous of her? Don't you want her to surpass your efforts? To be honest,' he replied coolly, 'I expected you to end up trying to live vicariously through her achievements, not sabotage them.'

'Have you listened to yourself?' She lowered her voice further. 'I'm not doing this now. I want to spend this last evening with our daughter. Her life is going forward. Do you want to be a part of that or not?'

'I have no intention of rolling over. She's worked too hard

to get here. You told me to encourage Seb to get the travelling out of his system before starting work and look how that worked out.'

'I'm sure one day he will elevate himself to providing triumphal anecdotes for the clubhouse.'

'Is that the best you can do?' he scoffed. 'Just to let you know, I've called the office and switched back with Ian who was taking the course next week in Poland.'

Sarah stopped in her tracks. She turned to look at him as he maintained his contemptuous gaze upon her.

'The problem with you is that you are never satisfied. It was a bloody mistake bringing you here. I'm just sick of it. Sick of you. You and Izzy can do what you like. I'll be here when she tires of her silly adventure.'

'And us?' she replied, trying to conceal her anxiety. 'What about us?'

'We need a break from each other.' He looked at her intently for her reaction.

His words cut through her. 'What do you mean?'

'This isn't working. Changes have to be made. Either you start showing an effort or...'

'Or what?' she replied, confused. 'I don't understand? Where did this come from?'

'Well, it isn't as if the children are living with us anymore. You don't seem remotely interested in what I am doing.' He watched her response as he knew she was struggling to contain her emotions.

'You are wrong, Graeme. We need to talk. But Izzy. We have to put her first. Please just be happy for her. She knows that you don't approve but for her sake, just one day, then we can talk. I love you.'

'Don't worry. I'll play along. Play the game for the evening for Izzy's sake. But you need to think what you want. What your priorities are. I have always put you first, supported you.

You seem to have forgotten that. I thought this time would be about us.'

'OK,' she responded softly. 'I understand. I see that now, you know how I've not been there as much.' She looked him in the eyes. 'I mean it. I think we should start afresh. I'm sorry.'

CHAPTER 26

SARAH AWOKE TO the sound of Izzy on the telephone in cheerful voice. Graeme had come to bed at 3 a.m. after disappearing to his office when Izzy called it a night. It was 9.30 on the bedside clock. She quickly scrambled out of bed, hastily wrapping a dressing gown around her. In the hallway she could see her daughter's bag packed, the sight of which gave Sarah a sick feeling in the pit of her stomach.

Hearing that Sarah was up, Izzy came through to meet her. She handed her mother a coffee. 'I have to say, this is a reversal of roles! Oh dear, letting standards drop.'

'I can't believe I slept in that long! Why didn't you wake me up?'

'I thought you could do with the rest. Now, Mum, I don't want you getting upset. I will visit again very soon. It's just I could really do without Dad trying to get me to change my mind. You know it's coming.'

'Where is he?'

'Oh, he left hours ago. He said he would call when he

gets there. He also insisted that you needed the lie-in. We sort of sorted things out after you went to bed. I think he understands. I've told him I'll consider at an outside chance going back to uni. I thought it better to say that until he gets used to the idea.'

'We'll see. But I'm glad at least that you patched things up. Let me go and throw on some clothes and at least make you some breakfast to set you on your way, and no arguments, I am taking you to the airport tonight.'

'About that. I managed to get a flight for the early afternoon. I hope that's OK.'

'I understand. It isn't going to make it any easier delaying it by a couple of hours.'

She hugged Sarah. 'I will be back before you know it.'

'I will hold you to it.'

Going back through to the bedroom, Sarah found a note by the bedside table. It had a simple message. 'I'll call you tonight. I've spoken to Izzy and I have told her that we are here if she needs anything. We will talk when I get back. I'm sorry if you thought I overreacted. We both want what is best. Graeme.' She folded up the note, relieved at his words, placing it in the dressing room table.

An hour later, having finished what turned into a long brunch, Sarah prompted her that they should be getting on the road. 'It feels like you have only just got here,' she sighed in resignation. 'Now, just wait here.' Returning to Izzy she handed her a cheque. 'Now. I want you to have this.'

Looking at the folded cheque she immediately tried to hand it back to Sarah. 'Really, I don't need anything, Mum. I've said this.'

'Please don't start on the "I need to pay my way". You have years to apply that principle, trust me. And you are not exploiting my guilt! I can't say that I am not just a little concerned about this change of direction. This is a big step.

I understand. You should also know that if you do change your mind it won't be a backdown or any such thing. We will support you whatever. Now here, take it!'

Reluctantly Izzy took the cheque from Sarah. 'I really appreciate that. I do, Mum. As for this? OK, I may be able to battle my conscience just this once,' she joked. 'It had better be a good wedge or I might start having flashbacks to repressed memories of a cruel nanny that left me crying in a cot all day.'

'Very funny.'

'Because you know therapists don't come cheap. This had better be good because…' She then opened the cheque which stopped her abruptly. 'No way!' She instantaneously put her hand to her mouth. 'You have to be kidding. £5,000! You can't afford this! No, I don't need it.' She attempted to hand it back to Sarah, who swiftly rebuked her.

'Enough! I will be giving the same to Seb. This time won't come again, Izzy. You make the most of every day. I can afford it. I got a much bigger profit on the shop than I expected. It is just to help you find your feet. Give you some breathing space. You told me about David's car that you drive to these remote sites in, and given what you have said about Turkish drivers, it would make me feel better. You will have more independence this way. This way you can make sure you buy something that is sturdy. At least a chunky four-wheel drive should do.'

'That would be amazing! I will be able to get a really good one for that! Does Dad know about it?'

'Probably best not to mention it. One last piece of advice, my clever girl. Don't spend your life chasing something that you already have. Happiness isn't found in certificates or big salaries, it is what makes you feel good.'

'Definitely don't let Dad hear you say that.'

'Be serious for a moment. Listen, you are an individual, don't let life grind that out of you. Ambition is having the courage to make things happen to that end. You have your life ahead of you. Obligated to nobody, or anything. How marvellous is that! Now, not another word.'

'A sponsor, philosopher and a chauffeur. Are there no ends?'

'I'm just waiting to pull in the favour for an introduction to our namesake, Bettany Hughes, you know that, right?'

'Yeah. When I am confident of which way to hold a trowel.' Izzy hugged her again. 'Thank you, Mum. I love you so much.'

'You are welcome, sweetheart.'

'Seb is going to be pretty made up at his windfall as well.'

'How do you think he is doing out there?' Sarah asked. 'He's not the best at emailing.'

'You know what he's like. I think he is just having a great time. He seems fine. You shouldn't worry. If there was something wrong, you can be sure we'd know about it. Like when he was bitten by a spider he thought was poisonous but just gave him a stinging nettle type rash. You know Seb, he doesn't suffer in silence.'

'You're probably right.'

'He's told you he is off scuba diving next month? Then he's going island hopping or something around Indonesia. Trust me, Mum. He is having the time of his life.'

'Yes, he told me about the scuba diving. So long as he is alright.'

'Yes, now stop fussing. If you want to give him a hard time ask him about a girl that seems to be in at least half of his photos. That will be why he is preoccupied.'

'You don't miss anything, do you? I assume you have already given him a hard time.'

'Within about thirty seconds of him posting them online,' Izzy smiled. 'Oh come on, it isn't like he wouldn't do the same.'

Sarah laughed. 'I'm so going to miss you.' Feeling a well of emotion at Izzy's imminent departure, she made a move to get ready. 'Now, no slacking. I have to stop and get some petrol.'

Later, after a subdued lunch at the airport, she waved Izzy off as she made her way through to the departure lounge. Once she had gone out of sight, the loneliness that had been there before she had arrived at their door returned. A void that she knew would become worse when she got back to the silence of the apartment.

On the way home, driving past the site of the crash, it was as if nothing had happened there. The carnage that had been in her imagined thoughts was difficult to picture on the bright early summer's afternoon. The orderly and smooth passing of vehicles didn't show a mark of the violent flashing recollections of that day, which still pervaded her nightmares. On the verge, a covering of daisies flittered in the breeze. Their bright, pure white petals and golden florets laying a delicate and uninterrupted blanket across the undulations of the verge. As there was a car behind, giving her little time to dwell on the sight, she was thankful of being prevented from what felt like an obligation to take a longer look.

Sarah had had little opportunity to think about Graeme's departure, given the short time that she had left with Izzy. The infectious energy that her daughter provided had dissipated as quickly as it had appeared. She went back to the bedroom to reread Graeme's note and thought of his words from the previous night. She also knew that deep down Izzy would be carrying the disappointment that her father had shown. Then when she would get the call from her tutor, and become aware of his duplicity.

The events of the last couple of days had left her exhausted. Keeping up a front for Izzy, now she thought of how she had been since the accident. Uncomfortable about having to look her daughter and husband in the eye whilst lying felt like the jolt she needed, and now making an immediate commitment to get better and give up the gambling.

Talking to Izzy about the time she left them had brought

the past she had tried to long since bury once again to the fore, especially the memories of the day that she drove to the coast after leaving them. The few times she had talked about it had been with her therapist, Tom, not Graeme. But even then she couldn't fully open up. Not to anyone. Not about what had fully happened that day. The shame she felt had never gone away was sometimes brought rushing back whenever there was something that would remind her. Especially on the occasions when she was at her lowest and she held the same desire to disappear as she had fifteen years before.

On that day when Seb had ended up in hospital, after a month of trying to hold things together after the funeral, her life was triggered into free-fall. Feeling she had lost control and was almost outside of herself, barely able to see herself in the present. She recalled hurrying down the corridor as Izzy was crying, feeling unable to go back to Seb. Repelled by the smell of the ward, the familiar sounds of the place where she lost her son, which was now pulling her back into vivid torment.

Once out in the air she had taken in deep breaths before she could get into the car. Finally feeling steady enough to start the engine she soon left. As Izzy was unable to settle in the back, she had made the decision to drive to Lydia's, who had previously offered to babysit whilst she went to visit Seb. Entering the driveway, Sarah first saw Lydia's cleaner, Vanessa. Then, only confirming if Lydia was in, she handed Izzy to her, hugging her daughter and telling her Mummy wouldn't be long. Responding to Sarah's anxiety, Izzy once again began to cry, reaching out and trying to wrap her arms tightly around her neck, before Sarah hastily told Vanessa that she couldn't wait for Lydia, and she would call later.

As she drove off, she watched Vanessa console her daughter, which made her quickly look away. The guilt burning inside, she wanted to tell her little girl it was alright. But nothing, even for a second, made her hesitate and turn around. As she made her way home, anxious to get inside, she passed the place of the accident with Ben. In a moment, she spontaneously pulled over, sitting in the car watching the traffic pass. Recalling in her mind the same details, seeing the traffic lights perpetually change as they had done when she was pinned into the car. The people who had come to help were almost lost in her memory, as she kept desperately asking the woman to tell her Ben was OK as she kept calling out to him.

As she sat there reliving the accident over and over as the cars passed her, she invited the pain back, going over the same questions and what-ifs that had haunted her since that day. Why hadn't it been her that had taken the impact? If she had pulled away from the junction a split second earlier, if she hadn't hesitated at the lights on the previous crossing, if she had just gone through on the amber as it changed. If she hadn't stopped to get some shopping, that she should have picked up the previous night, or if she had just paused for a moment to say hello to an acquaintance who she had made a point of avoiding, she would have been home. Her last words to Ben were to tell him to stop asking her if they could go for an ice cream.

After a while of sitting there, she decided to drive away. She hadn't slept properly in days, her head fragile to sound. Every noise in the traffic, every moment of the encounter at the hospital played over in her mind.

Turning into her road, she misjudged an oncoming car, which put on its brakes to avoid her. A loud horn sounded as it passed her, the driver angry at her reckless turn across his path, which had left her breathless as she pulled into the driveway.

Opening the door, she could hear the phone was ringing. On the other end was an irate Lydia who said that she had been trying to contact her. Saying that Graeme had called her because the hospital had contacted him to say that Seb was upset after she had left and he wanted to see his daddy. Lydia was angry, telling her to pull herself together, asking why she wasn't still with him at the hospital. Why had Izzy been so upset? What kind of mother was she? And finally, with a parting shot, reminding her that she had two other children to look after.

Pacing the house, she picked up the keys to go back to the hospital, but she couldn't. Before she was able to call Graeme he rang first, echoing his mother's words. She had to pull herself together. What kind of mother leaves their child upset in a hospital?

Not wanting to step back in the car, she continued to pace around. The phone going again, Graeme was somewhat calmer, insisting she get some sleep as she needed to get herself straight for when Seb came home.

Going into Ben's room she curled up on the bed. The quiet of the bedroom left her overwhelmed with her memories, anxious at when she would have to step back into her role. Wrapping herself tighter under the covers she began to cry uncontrollably. Around her everything about Ben that she been hanging onto was slipping further and further away. No photos of him on display, and every day Graeme telling her it was time for the last of his things to go. The time she had been spending resisting change, and her bargaining day after day that she needed a little longer, was coming to an end. He had become insistent.

For just that afternoon, she would have a sleep, for only a few hours. She called Lydia back to apologise, asking her to keep Izzy until Graeme could pick her up that night. When one sleeping tablet didn't work, she took another, then a few more, wanting just enough to be able to shut down, to close her eyes, to not feel anything.

The next thing she knew she was in the bathroom as Graeme was talking to her, forcing her to be sick, most of which she was barely aware of. When he was sure she had stabilised, he helped her through into the bedroom. When she awoke the next morning, he was sitting watching her. As he saw her open her eyes, he moved over to comfort her, encouraging her to drink more water. As she forced it down, he said nothing. Lying back to sleep, she reassured him. Promising him it was an accident, it wouldn't happen again. Closing her eyes as he went downstairs, she could hear the television going. It was one of Izzy's programmes.

When she was fit enough to get up, his tenderness turned to fury. Asking her if it was some pathetic cry for help, raging at her that if she really wanted to do that she needed at least another two bottles. All the while she had been pleading that it was a misjudgment and she wasn't used to the pills yet. Then promising she would get help, this time stick to a course of antidepressants, even though she was already stalling on that by the time the effects of the tablets had worn off.

Being vigilant to Graeme's supervision, she threw herself into going through the motions, until the day she packed a bag and left.

She never disclosed to Graeme, or to Tom, how close she had come to never returning. She drove to the coast where they had taken their holidays with Ben. Parking the car on the blustery cliffs, the place had changed from how she remembered it.

Walking onto the deserted beach, her memories became darkened. Sitting down on the sand in the solitary surrounds, she felt haunted by his absence. She hadn't fought hard enough to save him that day in the car. If just for one moment she could be with him again.

The only sound was of the breaking tide, as she was drawn further into the abyss. Wanting to be away from a life that was joyless, where she had nothing left to give. She slowly stood up and walked down towards the water. As she took her first steps into the sea, she felt the cold embrace of the gentle break of the waves, setting in motion the end that she had been fantasising about since the day they switched off Ben's life support. With each step forward, the soft sands yielded beneath her feet, making her unsteady. Going in deeper up to her chest, the cold suddenly took her breath away, to which she stalled before pushing herself to wade out further. Her coat was quickly becoming weighed with stones she had gathered on the way, knowing with each step that in a couple of minutes it would be over, there would be nothing.

Underneath the chill waters, she lost her footing as the tide was taking her off her feet. The salted water choked her as the current swirled around her, gradually pulling her under. As the enveloping waters began to overwhelm her, taking her into the darkness, their faces, her children who needed her, came into her mind. She couldn't leave them.

Suddenly, every muscle, every bit of energy that she had kept latent as she made her way out there was now given to fight. Her hands began frantically searching for the stones in her pockets that were weighing her down. A coat she couldn't rid herself of held her fight in the balance as she was clawing herself back towards the shore. Fighting for air, and to bring her back from the oblivion she had sought, her struggle finally won through as she dragged herself from the water.

Once making it to the edge she collapsed, every breath an agony as she purged the last of the salt water, until she lay on the beach in exhaustion. Looking to the sky, she felt unworthy of those that brought her back, too frightened to end it, too scared to return. She curled up, closing her eyes as she lay in the sand, blue skies fading against the closing light.

When she was awoken by a dog walker some time

afterwards, she was shaking in the cold. A man was talking frantically on his phone as he took off his coat to give to her. Summoning the energy, she went back to the car as fast as she was able, the man telling her to wait for the ambulance, that it was on its way. Without a purse or a penny to her name, she began driving to a place she knew would give her respite until she was ready to go back, her hands shaking as she started the ignition, as the heater burst through the vents. When she was ready, she left a message for Graeme. She was sorry, so sorry, but she needed time. She would call him.

But one week turned into two and it became harder to return, wondering every day how they were. Every week she would leave him a message. She was alright, she would be home soon.

As in the moment she decided to leave, three months later the day came when she decided to return. When she arrived home, the anticipated post-mortem from her husband on her leaving never came. Graeme called an amnesty, to which her shame was overridden by her relief that she had a home to come back to. The past was the past. He had every faith in her becoming well again. The children had missed having their mum. He said that he would never ask her where she had been and was just glad that she was home.

It was soon after that she found Tom, and between him and Graeme they had kept her together.

When she was ready, on the first day after returning she got out of bed and took a shower, picking out some fresh clothes to put on, and went downstairs to join her family. She thought of how, before she left, when she had been upstairs listening as Graeme had got them ready, she hadn't the energy to help. Now she was able to join them and do the things that she took for granted – getting her children their breakfast, packing up Seb's bag for school. She began to feel, for the first time since she couldn't remember when, despair give way to hope. The talk of a future that she had given lip service to she now began to feel possible.

Her family was sitting around the breakfast table as she drank a cup of coffee, accepting a plate of toast her son had brought her as she listened to him talk about the football game he was going to win that day. Each bite that he saw her take, he excitedly talked more and more of how he was going to score three goals.

Seb smiled at her first comment, that just one goal would be fantastic, joking with his dad about how Mum always said that. Graeme telling him that he should get at least two goals and under no circumstances should he listen to his mother when she said, 'It's just about the taking part.' It was to 'annihilate, obliterate.' Graeme, then stopping at his son's quizzical expression, continued, 'crush them like a louse.' To which came a resounding cheer from Seb as he then proceeded to say how useless the team were he was playing. And his little sister could beat them. All the while Izzy was content to eat her breakfast as Sarah leaned over to kiss her on the head. For the first time since she had got back, Sarah later told Tom, she saw the weight, the strain of the last few months ease from Graeme's shoulders.

Once she was ready, she began what she had committed to, and took each day one at a time. After the tenth session with Tom, just over a month after she returned, they found the house they decided to make their home. She and Graeme sat and talked in the car about how they had to move forward as a family.

After they moved in, every tile put in place, every coat of paint she brushed, she thought of her family. To not drink, to keep to her medication and keep seeing Tom long after she thought that she didn't need him. And when the bad days inevitably returned, she was thankful for it.

She made a promise to herself that she would never

succumb to self-pity again, that when her last breath left her, it would not be at her hand. Everything would be about her family. Never contemplating a day, as with Ben, when another of them would leave her.

CHAPTER 27

A COUPLE OF hours after dropping Izzy at the airport, Sarah picked up a novel and lapsed in and out of the book as she thought about the last couple of days. Half an hour and six pages barely absorbed, she opened her laptop, scanning the news, which failed to engage her. Looking at her watch, she anticipated that it would be a while before Izzy would call to let her know she was OK. She resisted the temptation to telephone Graeme, angry that he had left without speaking to her, knowing the uncertainty would prey on her mind, as he would normally call in when he had landed, or at least message her. The morning flights had left on time so she knew that he would most likely keep her waiting until the evening, as when they had an argument a year ago and he didn't call until she contacted the hotel later that night. Her cheque book sat on the table next to her, and she was thankful that she had given the money to Izzy, the amount visible on the stub. £5,000. She thought about her daughter, feeling guilty and ashamed that she had lied to her about the money.

It was nearly 10 p.m. when a message came through from Izzy that evening to say that she was back in Turkey. Not long after that, Graeme called. They spent the first couple of minutes talking about the delay that he had had at the airport and how the driver had been late. The pause after that opened a void for one of them to talk about the previous night. It was Sarah that began first by telling him again they should put the last couple of days behind them. In fleeting agreement they left it at that, as Graeme returned to the topic of his schedule. He promised to call every evening after he returned to his room. The conference was on the outskirts of Krakow, and with the travelling to and from there and, what he would say with exacerbation, the long evening meals for those attending the symposium, it would leave him little time to call. At that time it suited her. She had been considering a dozen ways to talk to him about the gambling, but wanted him to see that she was committed to sorting it out. All the while she vacillated between the timing of her disclosure and perhaps getting their relationship back on track before she told him. Uppermost in her mind were the last words that they had spoken on the night before he left.

Her affirmation to get better after Izzy's visit was put into action the following morning. The first thing she did was go to the cabinet to begin taking the antidepressants that Graeme had given her. Then, later that evening, taking a double dose of her sedatives she went to bed early. After staying on just decaf coffee that evening, she left the computer switched off, having earlier placed it in a high cupboard in the kitchen. Even though the internet was accessible on her mobile, she turned the facility off, as she had to keep the phone in the room, should Graeme or the children need to call her.

Up early the following morning, she felt reasonably rested, despite having taken an hour to get to sleep. Although she decided to get up twice during that time, so as not to let the darkness be a place for her conscious anxieties to take control, in due course the medication had taken effect.

In what was a comparatively early start, she got out of bed at around 8.30. The morning news began talking of the sensational win for Serena Williams the previous night. She turned off the radio as the missed opportunities for wagers ran through her head.

From the window the thoroughfare was quiet. The school runs had finished and most people were at work. Opening the window, little could be heard apart from a couple of passing women with pushchairs in sedate conversation. Once they had gone, the place fell silent, the click of the kettle breaking her distraction. The concealed presence of the computer began to nag at her. Making no physical move to retrieve it, the day's impending sporting events came to her.

The empty flat once again became a void that could be filled with the roar from the crowds, the delirium of the victor, the sight of the accumulation of the funds she would accrue. Chelsea were playing in the cup in just a few hours. Injuries aside, she had a feeling at the start of their cup run they would win. Then she forced herself to remember the last-minute goal that saw her day's winning evaporate and all the bad times, when she sustained the big losses. Her anger as the basketball bounced off the rim, which, if it had gone in, would have set her up for the day, or the quarterback taking the knee to run down the clock to finish the game when they could have run it in from ten yards. She had ignored the increasing increments of deposits that were made as she fought to recover lost ground. The sickness in the pit of her stomach as Graeme talked about the calculations of savings he had made on a purchase, which had been a fraction of what she had lost on a single game.

Staring up at the cupboard, she felt restless at the thought that she would open up the website after a couple of glasses of wine. If her anxiety grew about what she was facing when Graeme returned, or when she was lying awake in the quiet, and most of all when her nightmares roused her from her sleep, when nothing else could break through the blackness, she knew all the while that there was a way of blanking it out just metres away.

It came to her that if the internet in the house wasn't on, the laptop would not be of concern. An essay not due for a while, there was no pressing need to have it. With that in mind, she packed up the router into a fireproof box, the only secure container to hand, making up some story with her neighbour Gemma in asking her to look after it for her, saying it was a present for Graeme that she didn't want him to find. It sounded flimsy as the words came out of her mouth, and, looking a little perplexed, Gemma duly took the box and said she would keep it. In a bid to be more convincing, she said that he was notorious in looking for his presents as the day approached. As she noticed the further subtle scepticism on Gemma's face, she made her excuses and left.

She made a plan to fill every hour, spending all the time she could outside the apartment. Beginning Monday afternoon, she decided to switch from aerobics, which she hadn't been able to do since the accident, to yoga. Early in the morning she loaned a book from the library to read up in detail on the philosophy, the history and the benefits, and took it to a café in Celle where she sat for an hour having a coffee, in a place across the square from where Izzy had told her of her plans.

On Tuesday she took a drive to Huttenseepark where she spent the afternoon walking, having offered to take Larry for the day when Katerin had a meeting in Hanover to go to. A less welcome distraction was when Larry caught sight of a grazing deer and chased it the full length of the park, which led to a few extra miles which she hadn't accounted for, finally finding him as the light was failing, in a state of exhaustion after his long fruitless pursuit. Half an hour back through the darkening paths he trotted along sheepishly next to her, as she explained in a firm tone that this naughty behaviour wouldn't wash with her, and the usual post-outing treat had been revoked. In the car when they were halfway home she began feeling guilt-ridden as she saw in the interior mirror his gloomy face fixed on her. It was only a couple of miles down the road that she caved in, pulling over. In the dim light a search began in the back for a bag, all the while accompanied by an impatient fluffy tail beating a quick tempo until it was mission accomplished, and the bacon treat was duly presented.

Back at camp she returned him to an apologetic and grateful Katerin, who told Sarah that if the deer had only stopped and turned around, he would have bolted back to her as apparently was the case with rabbits, squirrels and anything above the food chain of a field mouse. Larry watched their exchanges as if at a tennis match to see what, if any, repercussions there might be for his impromptu excursion. However, Katerin just scooped him up to cuddle him – 'Oh, my poor pickle' – then proceeded to cover his ears. 'Unfortunately, he is also not very lightning quick between these.' Larry, with certain confirmation there would be no further punitive measures, began licking Katerin's face. Sarah, just relieved to have delivered him back in one piece, left with the longed-for prospect of a long bath and something to eat in mind, at which point she picked up a consoling takeaway on the way home. The toll of the day, albeit not in the fashion that she would have wanted, ensured a quicker path to sleep that night.

As was usual, on Wednesday she went to the coffee morning, further taking up the invitation to go to the garden centre with Katerin in the afternoon. On the Thursday she went to her tennis club, which she hadn't been to since before the accident. A gentle reintroduction and post-match drinks left her with a free afternoon, a time she filled by going to a large supermarket a good distance of twelve miles away, to get in supplies for when Graeme was back.

After returning home, having stacked the shopping away, her thoughts turned to his return. Feeling restless in the house she took a long walk through the camp. When passing the sports centre she saw the garrison's cinema advertising *War Horse*. Not one likely to lift her mood, but nevertheless, it would keep her out of the house. When she bought some wine, she thought of how a few days of sobriety had given her clarity. No heavy mornings, and less interruption in her sleep. Not wanting to tempt fate, but two out of the previous three nights had been absent of nightmares. She had been sticking habitually to the medication, taking every day at a time.

CHAPTER 28

On the Saturday, three days before Graeme was due back, Sarah returned to Celle as it was market day. Having prepared a list of goods that she would buy, she thought she would then take lunch in the square, and then a visit to the baker, the greengrocer's stall and the cheesemonger's would take her up to 3 p.m. at least.

As she finished lunch and prepared for the market, Sarah saw one of the ladies from the coffee morning approaching. Chrissie was a passing acquaintance she had seen at two of the book club meetings and they had had a couple of chats at the coffee mornings. Their mutual appreciation of food, especially the local market produce, had mostly been the topic on the few times they had spoken.

'Hey, Sarah! How are you?'

'Hi, Chrissie. I'm good, thank you. Just getting in a few supplies.' She effected being weighed down by the bags. 'So, I know how much you love your cheese. To let you know the cheesemonger on the square just started selling a new variety from the South. Delicious. And he says there is another new one coming in next week.'

'Thanks. Will do. We live life in the fast lane, eh?' Chrissie laughed. 'Well, if you want to take it to the edge they are offering wine tasting in that shop. You can push it for three samples if you hold your nerve.'

'Hmm. We're nothing if not Hellraisers.' Sarah rolled her eyes. 'Do you know, I'm not sure when middle age hit, but I think it started when I began to realise that the volume on my TV had increased by an average of three or four notches in the last year. If it wasn't for catching Graeme reading a label on the Horlicks jar with a magnifier, I might be more self-conscious.'

'I can do one better and raise you, by the fact I now set a timer for *Countryfile*.'

'OK, that isn't something I would admit to, but speaking of feet up and slippers, how are you getting on with the latest book?'

'I've read better. But, with it being Tessa's choice, we had better plough through to the end or we won't hear the last of it.'

'True,' Sarah laughed.

'Now, while I remember. I know these are early plans, but I take it you are coming with us to Berlin for Oktoberfest. Katerin said she spoke to you. We are going to be staying at her parents' estate while they are away.'

'I wouldn't miss it. She has promised a tour of the gardens by their gardener. So, no, I won't be missing that. I'm hoping to pick up a few ideas for when we go back. The place sounds incredible,' Sarah enthused.

'I'm getting the impression it won't be a squeeze. As for the gardens, I can't wait. Anyway I'm just off to meet a couple of others for lunch. Would you like to join us?'

'That's kind but I had better get back. But, hey it was good to see you.' Her mention of Graeme led once again to a feeling an unpredictability of what may or may not happen upon his return. It was best to avoid a lunch where she would get an inevitable inquiry about how he was doing and what she was up to. 'Enjoy your lunch.'

Walking back to the car she felt buoyed by the trip to Berlin ahead, to be out of the camp for at least three days. A busy Oktoberfest and a few days that would be another welcome distraction, as when they were not enjoying the hospitality of Katerin's family's *schloss*, they were going to be swinging around large steins of strong beer to the backdrop of booming Teutonic song.

As she continued along the pavement, she smiled to herself as she imagined the sight of Katerin, with her elegant poise, hoisting aloft a couple of litres of Pils. She suddenly stopped in her tracks. In front of her, a group of young women were about to take a seat at a table at one of the outdoor cafés. She recognised one of them straight away. She was from the photo with Andreas. The woman took her seat with her friends, who were all engaged in cheerful conversation. Instinctively she looked away. Her heart pounding, she began to walk away, before stopping and being drawn back. With no idea what she would say, if she was going to say anything at all, she passed their table twice. On the second occasion she realised that she had caught her eye.

'I had to come over. Sorry, I don't know, do you speak English?' She faltered. '*Sprechen Sie Englisch?*'

The young woman looked at her quizzically. 'Yes, of course. Can I help you?'

'I'm not sure how to say this,' she stammered. 'I saw you and I wanted to say again that I was sorry.' She could feel herself go red and lightheaded as she failed to find the words facing an unpredictable response. Unsure if she would be able to effectively communicate her feelings with the right words that still eluded her.

One of the young woman's friends at the table said something in German, which made Sarah realise that she was on the end of a joke. 'I'm not sure what you are talking of. I have no idea who you are. I think you have me confused.'

'My name is Sarah Hughes. I'm not sure how I should start. I am so sorry… it's about the accident… I can't tell you how much…'

The woman's face changed as she recognised her name. Her sudden altered expression prompted concern from her friends. 'You need to leave now. I have nothing to say to you. Please leave.' She became insistent.

Unnerved, Sarah was unsure how to continue. 'You can't have got the letter. I sent one to Andreas's parents. I understand that you might not…'

'Andreas?' The woman looked at her incredulously. 'Andreas? What do you know about him?'

'I didn't mean to upset you.'

The other women were beginning to realise who Sarah was and she became subject to a mixture of curiosity and contempt for the anxiety she was causing their friend. 'I didn't, of course. Know him. You're right. I should have left you alone.'

The woman stood up. 'No. You stop now. Do you honestly think that you can just walk up and make yourself feel better? You want to know, I will tell you. Andreas and I had our lives ahead of us. Who do you think you are? Telling us of your loss. You. Why do you think this is of interest to us?'

Sarah began to well up. 'I'm sorry.' She turned away as the woman stood up and took her by the wrist. 'Don't think we have any interest in you. You should have seen him coming.'

'If I could go back. I think of him every day. You should know this. I didn't see him.'

'You are a liar. The woman in the other car. She says you were not paying attention.'

'That's not…'

266

'That night at the hospital,' she angrily interrupted, 'they operated for six hours. Do you know how that time passes? But we had been told that he had been in water for too long when he was pulled out. Four men pulled your car off him. The doctor said he would have probably brain damage, even if he wakes up. We waited. Because we told each other, he could come through.'

'Please don't.' She became more desperate. 'I shouldn't have...'

'No! You wanted to know. His father had a heart attack, he doesn't speak of him now.' She lifted a silver pendant out from under her blouse. Sarah instantly recognised it from the photo. 'This is all I have left.' The silver necklace glistened on the sunlight. The first real and tangible connection that she had to him. His life and his absence was now in front of her.

Sarah broke from her grip. 'I have to go.'

'About your son. I'm glad you still suffer. It should never leave you.'

Sarah ran back to the car. Quickly closing the door she leaned against the wheel and began to sob, gasping for air, trying to come to terms with what had happened. She pulled out of her wallet the photo of Ben. She found no sanctuary in the bright crystal waters or his joy. She just remembered the day he slipped away. The shabby hospital ward on the last night, where the darkness penetrated and had come to rest. Leaving the town her thoughts raced with the young woman's words.

The image of Andreas was reimagined in her head, the idea of him being under the car. The desperate cries that she heard in her dreams were real. She knew they were real. If only she had seen him a split second earlier, avoiding the car that took her off the road. His life squeezed away and he knew, he must have known, that he wouldn't see his family again. His final moments, aware that he was going to die. She grabbed a glass from the cupboard and took the closest thing to hand, which was a bottle of vodka. She poured a half glass and took it down. Then another. She paced the kitchen not knowing where to go or what to do. Her hands shook as she picked up the telephone to call Graeme. The phone rang but there was no answer. The vodka was now coursing through her body. She called again, when there was no answer she placed the phone back down. The alcohol was failing in its task. In a moment she went down the stairs to see Gemma.

Drawing on every reserve, she composed herself before she knocked on the door, after which she heard Gemma approaching.

'Hi, Gemma. Sorry to disturb but I was wondering if I could have the fireproof box.'

'Are you OK?' she responded with immediate concern. 'You don't look that well.'

'No,' she replied sharply. 'I'm fine, I just need the box.'

'I've made a fresh set of scones if you want to come in. Has something happened?'

'No! Absolutely not!' The last thing she needed was this intrusion.

'You seem a little upset.'

'I'm fine, really. But would you believe I have just had an email from my tutor. It was my submission. I put a disk, my backup, in there with Graeme's present. I'm just a little anxious in case that copy hasn't taken.' The lie came easily, surprising even her. 'There was a corruption on the file. I have the backup in the box. If I don't get it in, ugh. A host of problems.' She ignored Gemma's look of scepticism.

'OK, I'll get it for you.' Gemma reached into the base of the hall cupboard and retrieved the box. 'But if you change your mind after you have sent it you know where I am.'

Sarah sighed in relief. 'The scones. I would love to, absolutely. They smell delicious, but I feel a damned headache coming on just from the stress of it all. Not to mention Izzy is calling later.' She took the box. 'Thank you so much.' Having the router back in hand was a relief to her. 'You are a star. I appreciate it. Perhaps one of those scones tomorrow.'

Once back at the apartment she plugged in the computer and waited for it to start up, impatient as the router slowly flickered into life. The doorbell went again. It was Gemma.

'I thought you might like these anyway.' Trying not to look ungrateful or resentful at the intrusion she took the scones. 'I appreciate that. I would invite you in but...'

'No, not a problem. I'll speak to you later, then.'

'Absolutely.'

Fearing further intrusion, she picked up the laptop and the keys to Graeme's office, along with the vodka which she tucked under her arm, and made her way to the loft.

In the couple of minutes it took the screen to appear she poured a glass of vodka. There was the familiar flurry of activity – matches, games, roulette, blackjack. Quickly signing in, her account came up. £286. A win that she hadn't waited up to see cashed from the night before Izzy arrived was now showing on the balance. In a flash she placed £100 on a football match that was in its thirty-fifth minute. She took a drink of the vodka. The time clicked slowly past. Nothing happening. Ten minutes in, little change. Two yellow cards. A shot wide. The young woman's voice came back to her. His last hours. On the side of the page the roulette wheel attracted her attention once again. She clicked onto the casino page, quickly depositing another £100.

Without any thought she went straight to six black, five red, then evens. As the ball came to rest, the next stakes were being readied. Then a succession of chips placed on impulse, reactive to perceived patterns or a gut feeling. The wagers were staked and the wheel barely rested. In her mind, frenetic calculations at the conclusion of the turn. An hour in, the balance failed to purchase another set of chips. Inputting three digits from her card to replenish, the chips were once again stacked. Eyes fixed to the screen, she sat back into the chair and sipped on her vodka.

After losing consciousness, Sarah awoke a few hours later to the bright light that shone in through the window. She orientated herself from being slumped over Graeme's desk. The clock above displayed 6.46 a.m. Lifting up her head, her stiff neck made her slow to move. She saw the vodka bottle near-drained next to her and stood up to avoid the harsh early morning light. Inadvertently, she brushed the mouse pad, causing the screen to light up. The memory of the night was coming back to her in patches. She was faced with a message telling her that the session had expired. She quickly logged in. The balance in the corner displayed £34.23.

In desperate need of hydration, she poured herself some water, the balance not matching her gut feeling that the night had been worse. She couldn't recall what her last bet had been. The visceral feeling of underlying dread began to find clarity. She urgently clicked onto her account. A list appeared displaying a succession of deposits. £100, £200, £1,000, £5,000. The sight of the last amount took her breath away, incredulous that it held no memory for her. She had taken the money that she had set aside for Seb, and by rough calculation there was only £3,200 left, not taking into account that Izzy hadn't cashed her cheque. The realisation made her burn with shame and incomprehension. Instantaneously she closed the page, her attention then drawn to the photograph of the family. How hard-gained that money had been, gone in the space of hours. Her thoughts raced as to what she should do. With nearly £7,000 to make up, the shortfall of Izzy's pending cheque was the most pressing. Her hand hovered over the keyboard before quickly opening the site once again.

Once on the page, without the slightest hesitation she

signed in. Clicking on the casino the familiar wheel spun. Now she was sober and could pay proper attention, this nightmare could be over in the space of minutes. The wheel continued to turn in anticipation of her re-engagement. A few of the numbers seemed to hold in her gaze. In a few short minutes if she held her nerve, this would be reversed. There was no choice. The router could go back to Gemma. She quickly deposited £3,000. Her palms sweated. Two bets. Two spins of the wheel. It would be over. Red/Black. It came to her that would be the order. To stick to it. No hesitation. To be positive that this would win. The combination sounded again in her head. She focused on the wheel. Red 23 stood out. Her eyes fixed as she watched the wheel in full rotation. In a moment she placed the full amount on red. Her wager accepted. It would need two spins. Once this was in, then it would be black. The call for no more bets echoed as her committed stake. She looked away, then looked back as she heard the sound effect of the metal ball about to come to rest. It sat there. Red 18. She shouted in delight. That easy. Just over £6,000 sat in her account. Betting £4,000 of that and it was over. But then if she were to make it £5,000... The extra £1,000 she would put towards the holiday with Graeme. No, she would give £500 to charity. Something good to come out of this. But putting it all on. £12,000. What she could do with that. She could surprise Graeme, fly out to see Seb. Get away from this. She placed the full amount on black. Before spinning the wheel she took a moment's hesitation. At the top of the screen she saw the previous number posted. Red 18. The colour seemed to burn brightly. More so than she remembered. A quick glance back to the wheel she focused on red 23. But her original conviction was black. She must stick to it. Red 23 once again caught her eye. In an instant she moved the stake to red and pushed the button. The stake accepted. The wheel was in motion. The ball bounced.

Trying to judge the momentum against the slots, her heart raced as she agonised over each leap of the ball. Green zero approached as the wheel began to ease down. The ball clipped over the green, kicking up, her anticipation spiked as red 3 looked primed to receive the ball that seemed too strong for the black the other side. She had made the right choice. Kicking the rim of zero, its momentum took it past. The ball's final impact made by the outside rim of black 26, sending it straight upwards, red 3 positioned for the taking. The ball dropped. The number flashed on the side of the screen. Black 26. She let out an anguished scream. Why had she changed her mind? Angrily she watched as the wheel came to rest. Her head rushed with guilty regret. Why hadn't she just stuck to the original choice? What had she done? How could she have been so stupid? These things had to be fixed.

Leaning across the desk she ripped out the router. She left the office to make her way downstairs. The stifling, stale atmosphere exacerbated her nausea. Discarding her clothes on the bathroom floor she stood in the shower contemplating what to do.

Wrapping herself in a towel, feeling lightheaded, she sat on the side of the bath. Her hands shook as the scale of her loss began to set in. Lifting up the toilet lid she held back her hair as she vomited. Sinking to the floor, she leaned against the rim before she was sick once again.

The next most pressing issue was that the router had to go back downstairs before she changed her mind. Since she had left the screen the figure of £200 had burned in temptation. To give it another chance this time, gradual and split amounts. To even salvage half, to try again tomorrow. But she resolved to get rid of any temptation. If she could hear Graeme's voice, not to tell him about the money but to know that he would be soon coming back, that things could once again be right between them. To remind him that they had been happy before. To put aside her resentment for the place they had come to. In twelve months' time, once they were back in England they could go back to their lives. To go back to work. The thought of the losses blanked in her mind by the ideal of what could be. The only person who knew the money wasn't there was her, and Izzy she could speak to. If she spoke to Graeme, this would be her first step. To get a grip, to escape her own disgust at the previous night.

She packed away the router, locking it in the box. Before gathering the glass and bottle, she opened up the windows to let in the fresh air. She tidied what had been displaced. She picked up her phone from the desk and decided to try once more. At just before eight o'clock there was a chance that he was in breakfast.

She dialled the number. After a short break a telephone began to ring on the desk. In front of her there was a newspaper that appeared to be half concealing its sound. It was Graeme's. It occurred to her that he must have been calling on the landline and she wondered why he hadn't told her he had left it at home, a thought soon followed by the expectation that he had been too proud to admit that he had left it behind. Because they had argued. Like the time he went away two years previously and forgot his suit for a meeting. Only later did she discover he had bought a new one. It was a source of amusement to the family, who laughed at the fact he could only purchase one that was a couple of inches too big around the shoulders. But in a burst of vitriol aimed at her, he suggested that she had probably done it in some unconscious act of retribution at the fact he was going away again. If she went to his work they would have a contact number for him.

The usual clerk was on the desk when she arrived at the medical centre.

'Hello, Sergeant, how are you?' She approached the desk as he was in the process of binding a folder. 'Keeping busy, I see.'

'Hello, ma'am. Yes, you could say that. A new battalion arrived yesterday and all have to be processed. There are better days to be had.' He smiled. 'Anyway, how can I help you?'

'I was just looking for a contact number for my husband. I seem to have misplaced it. I would be immensely grateful if you could give it to me.'

'Aye, ma'am. No problem. Just give me a minute, it will be on the system.'

'So a battalion? How many is that? Three hundred?'

'Wishful thinking today,' he joked. 'No, it's closer to 800.' He tapped away on the keyboard. 'And there are the families. It might help if they brought the computer systems up to accepting more than five files at a time.'

'I hear that no expense is spared,' she joked as she tried not to look impatient for the number, her head sensitive as he bellowed at one of the corporals going out of the door to pick him up a sandwich at the NAAFI.

'State of the art. Well, they were when the Berlin Wall was still up,' he replied dryly. He then scribbled on a piece of paper, smartly folding it and handing it over.

'I know he's in Poland, out there somewhere in the *oo loos*. I don't envy him that.' Sarah felt relief at having his phone number in her hand.

The clerk's expression changed as he looked at the note again in her hand. 'Yes, Poland, but we do sometimes get sent from place to place. You can start in one area, country even, but you can be called to anywhere.'

'Indeed. Well, good luck with the paperwork.' She wasn't sure what to make of the last comments. His expression seemed slightly ashen as he returned to his work.

She unfolded the paper with the contact number. It began

0044, the code for the UK. Unable to wait until she got home she quickly dialled the number once out of sight of his work. The wind blowing against the handset, she could barely hear when a voice came on the other end of the phone.

A young man answered the call. 'Hello. Swan Hotel. How can I help you?'

'Yes, hello. Can I speak to Graeme Hughes, please. It's his wife.'

The receptionist patched her through. The phone seemed to ring for an eternity before he came back to confirm he wasn't there. Sarah declined to leave a message and said she would call later. Her heart racing, she picked up the phone and immediately redialled, asking the receptionist to pass on the message that she would need to speak to him right away, her frustration not only because of his absence, but because she was struggling to hear the receptionist at the other end, who appeared almost apathetic to her request, and was evidently irritated that Sarah asked to repeat that he had the right room. Ending the call, Sarah regretted her haste, wishing she had waited to catch Graeme before he had a chance to prepare a story.

At home she ticked away the time. As the UK was an hour behind, the time seemed to go even more slowly. She resisted the urge to open a bottle and was thankful that the router was once again downstairs.

Finally, after a couple of hours the telephone rang.

'Sarah.' Gone was his distant tone of the phone calls that week. Instead she could hear the unease in his voice. A familiar one if he was breaking any news to her that he knew she wouldn't like. 'I know this looks bad.'

'Do you think?' she snapped at him incredulously.

'Let me finish. It is not as it seems. It was one of my patients from Cheltenham, she is being looked after by her son in London which is why I came here. I didn't tell you because you would read something into it. She is a woman. Of course you would have got the wrong end of the stick. I had to have her absolute trust. I've kept things strictly separate. If you knew the circumstances, you would see. I didn't really have a choice.'

'Of course you had a choice! There are other people, Graeme. What about the others, Jane or Piers?'

'OK, I did initially, then anyway, long story. I had to sort it out myself. She hadn't long been a patient. She took an overdose. An awful situation.'

Sarah held on the line in silence.

'Think about it. Why would I leave my phone number at work? I knew that you could contact me at any time if you asked for it, Sarah. You know when you are not feeling well these things can be blown out of proportion. How are you? I'm sorry that we left things how they are. I've been thinking about us. I should have taken better care of you after what happened when you came back. You...'

'What's her name?'

'Sorry, what?'

'Her name. The patient.'

'I can't do that.'

'OK. Her first name.'

He sighed in frustration. 'If it makes any difference. Alright it's Lucy. Something else you should know. She is in her late sixties struggling with grief and her son is in the house when I am there. You would understand if you saw her. No lines have been crossed. If I could I would introduce you.'

'I don't get why you wouldn't tell me? That doesn't make any sense.'

'Because we argued, I knew you would jump to the wrong conclusion. You have been really distant since the accident. I was worried that it would trigger another spiral for you.'

'Don't put that on me. You can see what I am thinking,

Graeme, surely. We argue and now I find out you have gone to a hotel in London. What would you think if you were in my shoes?'

'It was sheer coincidence. Two months ago, her son called to say that she was suicidal. I didn't think that she would attempt to go through with it. I had pushed her case onto Piers. What I was thinking I don't know. But, you can see what I mean now. I was abrupt with her when I left for this job. Head up my own backside about the move. But you know how clingy some patients are, and the parting wasn't a smooth one with the practice. So, when her son called me after it happened, I felt responsible. Look, you are getting the idea. You know better than anyone, your mother…'

Sarah cut him off. 'But why is it taking over a week?'

'Yes, I'm sorry. I did only need a couple of days, but I was angry and I just thought we could do with some space. Any other time I would have told you. I promise. I was trying to protect you. What with the crash. But as it turns out I did need the extra time for her. It's been tough, but I have things sorted out now.' He hesitated before continuing. 'I know you understand where I am coming from. You know what it is like to be in that place. The new doctor I have set her up with has been delayed in coming. But anyway, that's by the by, it's all in place and I will be back as scheduled.'

'How is she? Now that she has seen you.'

'She's stable. I've lined up with an old colleague here in London, Michael West, who they have agreed to in principle. Coincidentally, we were at UCL together. He is a brilliant guy and I know he will give her the best care. To be honest it had been troubling me that I left her that way. Piers was bloody useless, she needed extra monitoring.'

'I don't know what to think, Graeme. You lied. For whatever reason. You lied.'

'I know and I am truly sorry. If it makes you feel better you

277

could fly here. We could spend a couple of days, well, evenings, back in England.'

'Yes, I would like that. To spend some time away.' She held back the desperation and anxiety of the past few hours that had rushed to the fore in her mind. 'We need to talk. But please stop treating me sometimes as if I am made of glass, Graeme. I would have wanted to support you on this.'

'I will, I promise. But about coming over, perhaps on second thoughts that's not a great idea, dragging you here. The weather is pretty awful. I was soaked through today trying to get a taxi. Look, I am only here for another couple of days. Fresh start, make plans to get away. Just us.'

'If you think so. And this is where you tell me you love me and it will all be alright.'

'It will. Why did you call me anyway? I'm not trying in any way to turn this on you, of course. But sometimes when you are like this… You know what you are like under pressure. When you hold things back. Is everything OK?'

'Yes, of course.' She faltered as the conversation turned to her. 'I just wanted to talk, I was trying to get hold of you. I heard your phone in your office upstairs.'

'All the way up there? OK,' he replied, failing to conceal his irritation.

'I was only in there briefly. I won't make a habit of it,' she responded defensively. 'It is your space. I understand.'

'You seem to believe I have something to hide. Feel free to have a look around if you don't trust me. Go ahead. But if you let this paranoia fester… For goodness' sake. When have I ever let you down? Ever. All these years of marriage. Think about it, Sarah.'

'We should talk when you get back rather than over the phone.'

'I think that we have to. Now get some rest. I will be home before you know it. It has been a wake-up call, you know, being away, after how we left things. I've missed you. We'll speak tomorrow. I'm having dinner with Michael and will be tying up some loose ends. You have no idea how happy I will be to get back home.'

'Let's just see how it goes. You too. It's good to hear your voice.'

'I love you. I always have,' he said tenderly. 'From the minute we met. You know that in your heart. I will make this right.'

At the conclusion of the call she tucked herself up into the chair, feeling a million miles away from him, wishing that he was there now. Going over when he said he had not been able to tell her, then thinking over the times she had left their bed for him to wake up alone. Something that she had given no thought to. She trawled her memory for passing comments about patients before they left. The move had been such a blur. Graeme's work issues had been something that she had paid little attention to.

Although it had occurred to her to tell him about the money, she was relieved that she didn't. She would get everything ready for him to come home to. Give them space to talk. A fresh start, no need to hide. Switching on the television, she flicked through the channels, their conversation going over in her head. The morning news was coming to an end and a map of the UK came up behind a weather forecaster showing a picture of a line of ducks making their way across a puddle-filled street in Stirling. It was the same weather forecaster who she would often catch after returning home from work in Cheltenham, when they would make plans for the weekend and decide the best parts of the week for her to work on the garden. Home seemed a long way away. Grey squalls of a cold front making its way through Scotland were bypassing most of the UK, which was experiencing something of a hot spell. As they panned to the news desk, this forecast prompted a comment from the Scottish news anchor about being thankful of his current move to the South. What had once been welcome reports from back home now reinforced her distance from it.

Glancing outside she could see the clouds opening up for a bright day, a sight that moved her to think of taking a walk in the park. It was usually quiet before lunchtime and would give her a chance to get some fresh air. An opportunity to gain some perspective away from the stifling confines of the apartment. She felt too distracted to take a book. With Graeme's return she had to think of a way to talk to him. To do it from a position of strength, so he wouldn't just take over. Opening up the windows the cool air breathed fresh life into the bedroom. Stripping the bed she gathered a load for the washing machine before leaving. She took stock of any last-minute shopping she might need. Flicking the radio on in the kitchen she cleared away the remnants of the previous night. A few cups left on the side had gathered over the last day. In the sink lay abandoned a few plates and some cutlery, which she rinsed before putting them in the dishwasher.

The radio DJ was rounding up his morning session, finishing with a dedication from one of the soldiers currently away for six months in Afghanistan, who had made the request for his wife. Al Jarreau's 'Let's Stay Together' began to play. She imagined the soldier stuck in a sandy tent, missing his family. At that moment she wondered why he had chosen that song. Maybe this was a crisis for them, or the distance had given them an appreciation for each other or it was a follow-up to a call as they endured the usual relentless strain of being separated.

Sarah groaned at the radio presenter's trite 'Thought for the Day' which he offered preceding the request. 'If life gives you lemons make lemonade.' She wondered if they could get any worse, suspecting that everyone else who tuned in was probably feeling the same. Not least the soldier who was picturing his wife's reaction as the music played.

As the name Michael West went round in her head, she couldn't recall any previous mention of him. After clearing the kitchen she took a coffee through to the sitting room to catch the news. The usual weather report was backed by a photo of Hyde Park in the early morning sunshine, then she remembered Graeme saying that it had been raining heavily. The weather presenter concluded that we should make the most of this enduring hot spell. Turning off the television she thought again about his colleague, Michael West. She remembered a few of the others, but not him.

To put it to rest she went to his office. A volume of his alumni rested on the top shelf. Without hesitation she took it down, flipping quickly to the back. There he was. The same intake as Graeme. Feeling foolish, and without needing further investigation, she snapped the book shut, feeling guilty for doubting him. Carefully sliding his book back into place, she looked at his collection. The first editions he was so proud of, obtained by scouring the internet or picking them up during their trips to Hay-on-Wye. She wished they were now there, having a pint in one of the pubs, watching him delight over the bargain he had picked up. Volumes of medical books from the eighteenth century. He would read out some of the gorier experimental surgeries in a joking attempt to put her off her pub lunch, her abandoned steak and liver pie that he finished after one recitation sticking long in her memory. As she secured the book back in place she caught sight of a copy of a gallery brochure, one that she recalled from an exhibition of a young up-and-coming artist based in Cheltenham. They had bought a small statuette that she remembered talking Graeme into purchasing with relative ease, joking with him that he had secretly liked it, which was why he had come back to it twice. She had forgotten about it until then, but now remembered it had been placed with the other things in storage after finding a concealed flaw at the base, that she hadn't noticed even in the focused lighting of the gallery. She was going to return it. Even more to her surprise Graeme, having paid a reasonable sum for it, was relatively unfussed when she told him, saying there was no point trying to get a refund, as they had no proof that it wasn't them. The memory and her regret at not having it out with the gallery still irked her. It was something like £500, or was it even £700? She reached up to the catalogue. As she took it down, a sheet of paper fell out of the cover. Then another few as she leaned down to pick them up. As she unfolded the first, she could see they were letters.

Friday
Darling G,

6 days and I miss you. 6 days and it seems like an eternity since I saw you. I know that you are busy but all I ask is that you just let me know you are OK. I know, patience, how sick I am of hearing that. Do you have any idea what it is like to not be able to see you, to speak to you? I often think I should just call you at home. Don't worry, I won't. Oh I can just imagine what your face was like when you just read that.

Trying to make sense of them, Sarah flipped through to another letter.

Did you think that I wasn't serious when I said that I love you? We can have a future. No one needs to know our past. The place I told you about, I have been told I am going to be offered some work there, you know that apartment I showed you, so anyway that's the surprise. Can you imagine? I'm not telling you more until you call. But I won't need your money, I have a job now because of you. You said I could do it. What a feeling, how far I have come. This is all you, remember when I walked into your office? We both knew it. I think of you every minute of every day. Christ, why should we wait so long? Is it her?

Darling G

I've been so patient with you G and now you are telling me it will be longer. What are you waiting for? I should come out and see you. I know this is her. What do you see in her? You are worth so much more. God, I don't know how you stand this suffocating suburban prison shit. She will have to find out sometime anyway. You know when you are with me it's right. How you feel when you are with me. You shouldn't feel that you have to stay with her. Seb and Izzy have gone. A fresh start, remember. You know everything has changed, there's no going back now.

The mention of Seb and Izzy made Sarah flush with anger, feeling the frustration as she looked in vain for a name, not knowing who the letters were from. Not a single date on any of them.

I had to write after our call. Why don't you fully trust me? I know we can be happy if you just let go. We need to speak face to face, I can't wait another month. Last night I was standing in the street and I couldn't breathe. I need you so much. I am going to get ill again, Graeme, I know it. This medication isn't working and I am going to stop taking it. You said that you would look after me.

Sarah came to the last letter.

I'm sorry I shouldn't have got angry. It is this shitty distance. Do you know how difficult it is to wait? It can't be a bad thing that I love you. Of course I won't come to Germany. I wouldn't do that. I was just angry. I've just missed you so much. To hear your voice. We can't go back now. I know you don't like surprises, but I've booked a weekend at that place I told you about. Can you imagine, a whole weekend. It won't be difficult to get away. You're the boss right? Leave her baking cakes or whatever hausfrau shit she likes to do, pity the garden has gone... Sorry, couldn't resist. Call me. I love you.

Sarah placed the letters on the side. For a few moments she blocked them out, overwhelmed as she was unsure where to begin to make sense of what she had read. The words muddled in her head. She picked up the first one to reread it. Starting from the first, she began to digest the words as she continued through the pile. 'I love you' and 'future', the familiarity shown in the mention of her, Seb and Izzy. He had to be there with her now. She pulled back the books to see if there were any further letters. Then flipped through them. As the empty texts proved fruitless, she began dropping them on the floor. She searched under the desk drawers, on the tops of the shelves. There were no more to be found.

She ran downstairs, scrambling for her passport, her purse and then grabbed a case down from the wardrobe. There would be a flight there that night. Her anger raged as she thought of him there in the hotel. His lies.

After calling a cab she stopped by the cash machine as she headed for the airport. Tessa was coming out of the NAAFI with a couple of what she briefly announced were two new recruits to book club, the introductions cut short by the sight of the waiting taxi. Sarah fully expected an inquiry by means of Tessa offering her a lift to 'wherever she was going' if she needed it, 'wherever it was' and was it 'anywhere nice'. Sarah's anticipation of her inquisition was confirmed at Tessa's subtle disappointment that her destination had not been disclosed, although if she had seen a case in the boot Sarah doubted she would be able to contain herself. Booking a flight for Heathrow she arrived three hours before it was due to take off.

CHAPTER 29

HER FLURRY OF activity came to a sudden halt once she had checked in. A soldier's family, who she vaguely recognised by the wife from the coffee mornings, were sitting across the row. She offered a brief smile, which was reciprocated. It was the first time that Sarah had been relieved at the separation of ranks between their husbands, as she was unlikely to wander over for a chat.

The letters that she had read earlier once again came to the fore. Folded into her bag she would face him down with the evidence. 'Evidence' – the word brought about all the unexpected doubts she had never had about him. He couldn't possibly have had an affair. Why would he do that? They had always committed to saying if one became unhappy. It had been his insistence all those years ago. No deceit. How many miserable patients he had seen hold it together, for what would inevitably fall apart. Had there been anything in the letters from him? There could just be a rational explanation. He had a handful of cases where the patients had been too attached. It was an occupational hazard. Perhaps there was a good reason, but she needed to see his face when he told her. The flight board announced that there would be a forty-five-minute delay. But why had he kept the letters? Sarah got up to go to the bar.

A double shot of vodka followed another before she took stock and ordered a glass of water to go with that. The sniffy look from the barman was one she interpreted as 'another Brit knocking it back before the flight'. Another tip from Graeme – for those patients who needed some Dutch courage to get through the sessions, vodka was their drink of choice, mostly undetectable on the breath. Something that, unbeknown to Graeme, she had done more than a few times with Tom at her worst when she couldn't face divulging anything further but just needed the reassurance of being there. Now, this would take the edge off, and was unlikely to cause any potential problems with acquiring a few more on the flight, or later the outside possibility of an overworked and fractious passport official causing her to be held up. She looked at her watch. What was he doing now? It was now 6 p.m. Would she catch him at the hotel, as she would be there about midnight? Then she would know.

The clock in the bar ticked past slowly. A surge of tracksuited football players came into the lounge. The young men jostled for position at the bar to place their order.

A couple of the footballers then passed her table, pints and spirits in hand, laden with assorted snacks. As they took their place behind her, one teased his friend. 'I hope you haven't spent all your money, your missus is going to kill you.' The words from the letter came into her mind. 'I won't need your money.' If he had been giving her money she would have known about it. She did the accounts. This was fantasy. There was nothing. The army gave him one income, and they had their long-term investments and the money from his practice.

In a moment she thought back to the argument with Jane at his leaving party. The frustration in her grew once again.

Avoiding the scrum at the bar to purchase another drink, she opened up her phone, then accessed the internet. The familiar bright screen flashed up, but there was little left in the account. She thought of the money in one of the savings accounts that was about to mature the following year. £20,000. The discipline that they had shown not to touch it because of the penalties they faced. Their financial projections were something that she hadn't wanted to bring up in the last few months. Then there was their current account, which, as she noted the previous day, had at least £3,000 left, give or take. She had to put all possible variables out of her mind until she confronted Graeme, when she would know everything.

In a moment, she transferred £2,000 of it into her account. It was the start in making up the money to cover Izzy's cheque. She knew that she had a couple of days for that. Finally, the crowd in the bar died down as they were all served their drinks. It gave her the opportunity to order another double. The first wager, the 5.15 at Newmarket. Sinking back into the chair, she waited for the flash of silks to burst from the stalls.

An announcement came for boarding two hours later. The last wager she placed was at the start of a night cricket game that was coming to the end of the first innings. The queue for the aircraft was backed up in the walkway. Further down the line she could see the woman she recognised earlier. She was engrossed in conversation with her husband, until their young toddler began pulling at her father's glasses as a means to get their attention. The woman took out a fluffy rabbit from her handbag, which exacted a joyous response from the child. They teased her with it before handing it to her outstretched hands. In a brief moment Sarah noticed the husband squeeze his wife's hand as they edged slowly towards the door. She then looked impatiently to see what the time was. The loud sound of a crowd roar came from her phone. Those immediately around her turned to see where it had come from, including the family from the camp. She quickly switched off the volume and pushed the handset into her bag, not before confirming that a wicket had fallen and her team were now down the last effective batsman.

The plane was hot and stuffy from the delayed turnaround after its last flight. The hastily executed clearing exercise had missed the squashed sandwich packet shoved into the front pocket. A man next to her with pungent cologne and sour breath leaned over to grumble about the state of the plane. He began a monologue about the decline of service, before producing his antidote, three small bottles of wine and two pains au chocolat, one of which he began tucking into. She declined his offer of one of the wines, which he seemed relieved at. One of the air hostesses passed as he shoved the last of the pastry into his mouth. He swiftly brushed the flaky remnants off his shirt into the footwell below his feet. Sarah noticed the hostess glance at the bottles that protruded from the pocket but swept past on a mission to placate two people a few rows back that could be heard arguing over space in the overhead locker. A further announcement came. The captain apologetically informed passengers that they were fifth in line to taxi, which would mean a further delay. He ended by praising the passengers for their patience. The statement brought a mixture of groans and frustration. The man who had clearly lost the battle of the overhead luggage space shouted it was a 'damned disgrace'. Others tutted and several pejorative epithets aimed at the airline abounded amongst a general grumbling consensus of agreement.

The man next to her asked for a cup of water, his excuse being to take medication, but the intention was to acquire a cup to facilitate the cheap Côtes du Rhone secreted in the seat pocket. Glancing at her watch it was another half an hour before they were due to take off. She calculated that it would now be at least past midnight when she would reach the hotel. The captain came over the tannoy, prompted by the reports of irritation from the crew informing them they were not that far away from being at the head of the queue, and then, as if in consolation, saying the weather was warm in London that week. The man muttered something under his breath before taking a large sip of his wine. The plane crawled forward as it waited its turn. Whilst he was already looking to open his second bottle she took the opportunity to check the scores in the match. Her team were in a fierce battle with the opposition. There was a chance she would be £2,400 better off by the time the plane landed. It would be a start in recovering her losses to secure the money into her account that she needed. She clicked off the phone as they inched forward. Her thoughts came back to the letters as she impatiently waited for take-off. Taking the book from her bag into which they were secreted, she went over them again, shielding their contents from her inquisitive fellow passenger. Re-going over the words in her head. Seething at the betrayal, she was deep in thoughts of her impending confrontation with Graeme, unaware that one of the stewardesses had asked her twice if she wanted any refreshments. Breaking away she noticed the man next to her was taking the opportunity to take a peek. In a rush she folded them back into the book before stuffing it into the pocket in front of her.

By the time they landed she had consumed two small bottles of Chablis, which brought an unwanted nod of approval from the man next to her. Fractious and tired passengers were taking down their bags to leave. The man and woman who had been arguing over the overhead locker had clearly settled their differences, as he was putting her number into his phone and suggesting they meet up the next week for lunch. Sarah's impatience grew as she waited to move. It was a welcome sound to hear the outer doors finally open.

Two options faced her once she was through customs: taking the train or a taxi. With little desire to get sucked into even a ten-minute conversation about what brings you to London with a cabbie who was most likely to be understimulated on the night shift, she opted for the train to Victoria, a forty-minute journey that passed relatively quickly once she had placed herself in the corner, separated from others by firmly placed earphones.

CHAPTER 30

Arriving at the hotel, it was not what she expected – a small boutique hotel tucked away in the quiet streets of Belgravia. Matching the uniformity of the Georgian townhouses, it was only a small plaque next to the door that marked it apart. Making her way through into the dimly lit hallway she was greeted by a young receptionist, who failed to disguise his mild irritation at being disturbed from his book, into which he placed a marker before standing up straight.

'How can I help you, madam?'

'Yes, thank you. So I know this is a late hour, but I'm looking for, I mean I'm here to see Graeme Hughes. I'm his wife,' she said impatiently, still keeping her case in hand. 'I called earlier.' Her arrival into this sedate empty hallway emphasised her anxiety as a result of the whirlwind journey, which had left her exhausted and perspiring.

'OK. Let me just call up and see if he is in.'

'As I said. I'm his wife.'

'Just give me a moment.' He opened up a book under the

counter then began calling. He smiled awkwardly at Sarah as there was no answer, his expression betraying the fact that he was already going through a contingency plan should she decide to stay put.

After a time when he was content that the room was empty, he placed down the phone. 'I'm sorry but...'

'Please just give me his room number. To save us all time, because if you don't I will knock on every door until he answers. If he isn't there, I will leave.' She started towards the staircase.

'OK. Alright. Room number 4.' He picked his book back up. 'First floor. Please remember we have other guests.'

'Thank you. Look, I'm sorry to have disturbed you.' She hurried up to the room, and after a third knock Graeme opened the door.

'Sarah?! What on earth are you doing here?'

'Why didn't you answer the phone? No, that doesn't matter. We need to talk.' She pushed past him into the room.

'Sorry? What is this about? Are you alright? Has something happened?'

The first words didn't come easily. The plan of getting him to incriminate himself was abandoned. She just wanted him to feel the uncertainty that she had been enduring over the last twenty-four hours. She went over to the minibar. 'Not much choice is there.' She rattled through the fridge, before producing a bottle of wine. She cracked open the top before shakily pouring the contents into a glass. 'Never really quite sure about the hygiene of these things, are you. Who knows what...'

'Sarah!' he angrily interrupted. 'What the hell is going on?'

His anger was met with equal measure. 'You, Graeme... I found them. You were always a smart arse. "Hide things in plain sight." You remember telling that to Seb? Always taking other people for idiots.' She looked at his confused expression. 'No, I see that you're still not picking up on this.'

She reached into her bag for the letters. Unable to immediately put her hand to them she urgently searched deeper into her bag. 'Oh no.' The sudden recollection of the magazine pocket came to mind.

'What on earth are you doing? Why don't you just tell me?'

'The letters, Graeme. I found them. Lucy. Your supposed little old lady,' she snapped.

His expression remained fixed, without a flicker of emotion. 'Oh.' He hesitated. 'What were you doing in my office?'

'What? Is that your response?' Sarah replied incredulously. 'So where is she?'

'I was hoping I would have this dealt with without you needing to know. Lucy is nothing more than a patient. If you sit down I can tell you.'

'Let's hear what you have prepared.' She was certain that when he said her name she detected affection.

'Before I go any further I want you to know that there is absolutely nothing going on between us. Yes, she is a patient. I'm sorry I didn't tell you the truth about her age. Just sit down first.'

'Don't tell me what to do, Graeme.'

'As I said to you before, it is now all under control. I know I should have told you but I didn't want to worry you, for you to misinterpret and well, I am bound…'

'By confidentiality?' she sharply interrupted. 'Yes, I know. No way are you hiding behind that now. Things have gone too far. I want to know everything about your relationship with her. From the start, Graeme. You can do that without breaching your sacred codes.'

'If that is what you need. Alright. But this stays between us. Why don't we go for a coffee? Talk things through. I'm not drinking that screen-wash and I could do with some air. It'll take me five minutes to throw something on.' He leaned forward to kiss her on the head from which she flinched. 'Trust me, when you hear this you are going to wish you had saved yourself the journey.'

They barely exchanged words as he took out some clothes and began to get dressed. His laboured preparations made her frustrated in her impatient quest to find answers to all the questions.

A couple of streets away there was an all-night bar. With all the life of Hopper's *Nighthawks*, it was the perfect place to find a corner booth to settle in. Sarah took a seat at the table as he went up to order the coffees.

She watched as he ordered the drinks, having a light-hearted exchange with the barman, as if they were on any other night out. 'He says he'll bring them over in a minute. I've ordered us a bottle of red.'

'So what happened to coffee?'

'I have a late start tomorrow. You… well, that is up to you. But a couple of days in the city might not be a bad thing.'

She watched him incredulously. 'Am I in some sort of parallel world? I found the letters, Graeme. There can be no good answer to this. You are unbelievable. You have lied for so long.' Her voice elevated with angst. 'You could have told me in Cheltenham if it was so innocent.'

He could see the barman coming over with their order, their conversation suspended as he placed the glasses on the table. Graeme accepted the bottle and the invitation to taste the wine. Before he could pick it up she reached out and took the glass.

Gently swirling the wine she took a sip from the glass. 'Do you know, this isn't my taste.' She turned to the waiter as she made a quick perusal of the wine list. 'Can we have a bottle of Volnay? We will of course pay for this bottle. I'm sorry about the change.' She looked across at Graeme. 'You can have a beer if you prefer, darling. He's not very good with wines, you know.'

She handed the uncomfortable-looking waiter the wine list who then addressed Graeme. 'Is there anything else I can get you, sir?'

'No, that will be fine. Thank you.'

'Yes, wait for the man to give the go ahead,' she called out to the waiter who continued walking to the bar.

'Don't make a fool of yourself, Sarah. Just calm down. Give me the letters and I will show you how you have misread them.'

'I don't have them. I left them on the plane,' she answered in frustration. 'But, trust me, they are indelible in my mind. Christ. I feel sick.'

His expression changed. 'You lost them?' He held his composure. 'OK. But I could have answered everything you needed to know. So, you left them in the plane?'

'It's not a problem, they don't have any way of being linked to you. All very clandestine. Was that your thrill?'

'Sarah, now, I want you to listen,' he said firmly. 'I will tell you from the start. How this came about. Lucy,' he fixed eye contact with her, 'is a patient from Cheltenham, as you may have gathered. She became my patient.' Sarah gave him a contemptuous look of disbelief. 'Listen to me, she became my patient two years ago. As, I told you, I handed her over to Piers when I left. I thought that she was OK during the transition, but I got it wrong. She has become too attached.'

'This started a while before you left Cheltenham.'

'And I feel badly about it. There was a time not long after I became her doctor that she began to develop feelings for me. I should have immediately referred her but I didn't. She was vulnerable, fragile and I just thought we could work it through. I made things worse by involving myself further, helping her get a job. You know this happens, transference.'

'You were giving her therapy? You said that you had given most of that up. Why her? Perhaps I will have that easily answered when I see her. Otherwise why would you say she was old?'

'I don't want you to overreact. Please, Sarah, I mean it. Let me explain. If you knew how much sleep I had lost over this. The effect this has now had on you. I want to say...' She could see him deliberate over his choice of words.

'Oh for fuck's sake, Graeme. Just spit it out. You have been having an affair. What's complicated about it?'

'No! No, you have that wrong. Not an affair. I was flattered for a fleeting moment. Pathetic. Without question. But, we were going through a rough patch. I was spending more time at work, we both were. No. I'm not saying that as an excuse. In answer to your question, yes she is a bit younger and, pretty, I suppose. But it was just flirting, vanity.'

The words cut her to the core. She wanted to come back with something along the lines of appreciating his honesty, to encourage him to disclose more. The anger welled inside her and the humiliation at suddenly feeling so adrift, older. She was frightened to open her mouth to form the words, to allow him to see it.

'If you had kept the letters I could talk you through them. You would see how... Also, think about it, Sarah. Who writes letters these days? Does that sound like someone having an affair? I told her it was OK to write. She wasn't ready for the complete break. Naively I thought that she would lose interest, the infatuation would fade through the distance.'

The sight of the waiter coming over made her gain greater control over her feelings. The awkward exchange occurred as she tasted the wine he poured for her, her hands trembling as she put the glass to her lips. The liquid she was struggling to swallow in her anxiety, she momentarily held in her mouth as she smiled in acceptance.

As soon as the waiter left he continued, 'You had so much to deal with. The accident. I thought that it would be better if you didn't know. You would have blown this up into something that it wasn't, which, don't jump on me, but you see that you have. I wanted to protect you.'

'Is this why you and Jane parted ways? Yes, of course, the argument in the office. How could I have been so stupid? Perhaps I should speak to her.'

'The reason why we parted is completely unrelated. It was over the circus she had turned it into and yes, the argument over the money. But you know that I decided to leave over a year ago because we had two very different visions. You remember what it was like, fluffy upholstery, inspirational platitudes on the wall. Bloody insufferable. But you know Jane. Everything to the letter. As if she would have gone along with that? Don't forget she was all about her brand, the caring, sharing team. And why would I have left if I was having an affair? If I was continuing an affair? When am I ever away aside from assignments?'

'You lied about this being an assignment.'

'Just this once. I was worried she was suicidal. I didn't want that on my conscience. As for going away. What was the last time? Scotland. I even brought you back a souvenir.'

'Yes, St Andrews. The type of tourist crap that they sell at every airport.'

'Yes, or I could have bought it online if you go with that logic. But I simply didn't. This comes down to trust. Show me just one thing, one piece of proof. You can't because it doesn't exist. You said it yourself. We live in a goldfish bowl in Germany. And I don't question you.'

'What is that supposed to mean?'

'I overlook things you do.'

'Sorry, I'm confused? What are you talking about?'

'Sarah, your spending?'

Her expression was ashen. 'What exactly? I don't know what you mean.'

'The trip to Berlin. Do you think that I am a complete idiot? The bag, the dresses, the shoes. They will have cost a lot of money. I didn't question you when you said that it was from the sale of the shop. How do I know that on your weekend away you didn't see someone behind my back? Or that when you go out of camp that you aren't seeing someone?'

'You are being ridiculous. You know that I wouldn't do that. Have an affair.'

'No. I know you wouldn't. Because I trust you. If it makes you feel better, do it. Call Jane. But if you do, then she will know I have been in contact with a former patient being treated at her practice. I will be compromised.'

'Couldn't you see it coming? What was her condition?'

'You know I can't tell you much about her illness.'

'This is our marriage, Graeme. You choose what's important.'

'All I will say is that in layman's terms, sparing you the jargon, she had an attachment disorder, along with depression.'

'No, I still don't understand why you would take her on as a therapy patient.'

'When she came to the practice Jane thought I would be best placed to treat her, and suggested I give her therapy. She caught me on a good day. I was just leaving the office, we were just off on holiday for a couple of weeks. She had been banging on for weeks about her latest drive on having a closer working relationship with the psychologists, for best practice. You remember what she was like, how irritatingly pushy she could be. I thought that taking on this one case would placate her. I didn't have to do it of course and it was against my better judgment. So anyway, I see now...'

'Why did you keep all the letters?' Sarah interrupted. 'Why was she going on about you having an apartment together?'

'Pure fantasy. I didn't indulge her for a moment. You will have seen that from the letters. I didn't write any letters to her, not once. This was all her. Why I kept the letters, I don't know, I should have destroyed them.'

'OK. What about the money she wrote about?'

'I gave her money once. To help her out one night, she was stranded in the middle of nowhere. That was it. I was nowhere near. I couldn't possibly have been there. It was while we were in Germany, so you see it was impossible. How would it be remotely possible for me to give her significant money without you knowing? Think about it. Please. Everything we have is for us, right? Our future.'

The mention of money unsettled her as the gambling losses that had been at the back of her mind since she found the letters came to the fore.

In her hesitation he continued, 'Do you see that it all makes sense now? She found out details about my private life. You will have read that she talked of Seb and Izzy. I think that was in there. I don't remember too well every detail. How many did you read?'

'All of them. If indeed I found all of them.'

'In the gallery catalogue. That is it. Do you remember her saying that I told her not to come to Germany? If I was seeing her surely I would have arranged to see her when you were laid up in the apartment. You can search the rest of my office if you like. I agreed to help her because she left the practice and was threatening to hurt herself. I couldn't have that on my conscience. I knew you wouldn't approve if I had told you.'

'Why didn't you?'

'Because, I didn't want your imagination to get the better of you as you know it has done before. You know how that can affect your state of mind. I wanted to protect you. Look at yourself.' She watched him as he picked up his glass, vigilant to a flicker of affectation or faltering of his voice, reassured when he wouldn't break eye contact. He reached across to take her hand. 'I am telling you the truth. Do you see it wouldn't make sense? To throw our marriage away for some neurotic mess?'

'Neurotic mess? Jesus, Graeme, she sounds like she needs serious help. You idiot. How is she? More to the point, where is she?'

'The part about arranging another doctor, you know when I said, pretended it was someone else? That is true. I have it all set up. I will deal with that and we can fly back tomorrow night if you prefer. This has been the wake-up call. I will leave her in good care.'

'I don't know, Graeme, this hasn't really sunk in yet. I need to ask you more questions. Do you have any feelings for her? I need to know.'

He squeezed her hand. 'God, no. Christ. Pretty, yes, but no, I wouldn't touch her with a bargepole. She's an ex-junkie. You should see where she is from, you would laugh if you saw her.'

'I doubt that.' She pulled her hand away. 'But enough for you to be flattered by her.'

'Trust me. It was fleeting. As I said, the only reason I didn't just walk away was because I felt I had failed her. If something had happened, I couldn't have squared it with my conscience.'

'It still doesn't add up. You are always so straight down the line. In the past you had no qualms in handing them over, even the pretty ones,' she replied sarcastically.

'Am I not allowed one slip-up in all these years? I said, we were having a tough time with Seb and Izzy flying the nest, I was too cavalier, I missed it. I feel pathetic. Truly.'

'Well, that is the first time tonight we have found the same perspective. Can I meet her?' She then quickly followed up with, 'No. Of course I can't.'

'You mustn't make more of this than it is. I know this is frustrating.'

'You know, do you, Graeme? Do you really?'

'We can talk about everything when we get home. Tomorrow I will sort this out. I will take some leave.'

She didn't respond, taking another sip of her wine.

'I understand this is about trust. I will do whatever it takes. You can search everything. If that is what makes you feel better. It is so frustrating. I wish you could meet her then you wouldn't have a moment's hesitation. If only you hadn't lost those letters. I'm so sorry that you have been through this. I love you so much. I hope something good can come of this mess and I'm sorry for everything that happened with Izzy. I will speak to her. Make it right. From now on this is all about you. We've just lost our way. That's all.'

She lay awake that night going over the last few hours, contemplating what he said, the anger at him for his deceit still there. Where to go from here and how was she going to tell him about the gambling? The shame burned in her, thinking how this temporary clearing of air and stability would be rocked again.

Graeme was already dressing by the time she woke up. 'Hey. Morning.' He opened the wardrobe as she sat up in bed, adjusting to the light. He took a hanger out with his suit on. 'You see. Would I really have brought this otherwise?'

'Alright. I believe you. We have a long way to go, but OK. I believe you. But we will talk later. Listen, I'm going into Knightsbridge to pick up a few things. You know how much Gemma raves about Fortnum's tea. Remember what I said, Graeme. I'm not making any promises.'

He straightened his tie. 'I know. Absolutely. After this meeting I will be finished. We can go back to Germany and get on with the rest of our lives.' He braced his tie as he leaned forward to kiss her, from which she pulled away. 'I understand. Try and get some more sleep. I have paid up for the room, so just meet me at Fortnum's. I will see you there about 4ish. I've managed to get us together on the flight. I sacked mine and booked us in business class. I thought you deserved it.'

'You didn't need to,' she replied flatly. 'What time does breakfast stop being served?'

'Um, 9.30, I think. But I wouldn't do that,' he promptly responded. 'I've been giving it a swerve after one look. The cereal is stale and they are only serving tinned fruit and cheap bangers. If you go around the corner there is a beautiful coffee shop. About eight different blends and the muffins are something else, but have a lie-in first. I'm sure you need it. You have eight hours to kill before I see you. If you need me, ring me, and thanks for bringing my phone over, by the way, but only call if you have to. This is going to be a difficult one.'

'I'll be fine. Just make sure that this is the end of it, Graeme.'

CHAPTER 31

AFTER TEN MINUTES of trying to sleep, her restlessness forced
her to get up. Within thirty minutes she had showered and
packed her bag. The quiet and remote room was one she wished
never to see again. The large wooden door echoing shut behind
her, she carried her bag down the stairs. The smell of bacon
greeted her as she reached reception. As she put her head around
the door, a couple were just taking their places at a table whilst
placing their order of coffee. A sign on the door reminded guests
that breakfast was between 7.30 and 10.30. The food was more
or less as Graeme said. A meagre selection of pale cereal flakes
and an assortment of tinned apricots and pineapple.

Sarah approached the reception desk sheepishly as the
same young man was still on the night shift. 'Hello again.'

'Good morning.' The bacon sandwich, it appeared, was his.
He quickly swallowed his mouthful before secreting his plate
under the desk. 'Sorry, excuse me.' Their minor altercation
clearly put aside, she considered that he was down to his very
last reserves of energy. 'Now, how can I help you?'

'Just checking out of room number 4. My husband said he has settled up but I thought I should double check. To confirm, there was one bottle of white from the minibar. And I'm sorry about last night, it had been a bit of a long journey.'

'No problem.' He began flipping through the pages of the log. 'Trust me I've had far worse.' He stopped at a page, running his finger to a point. 'Ugh. This handwriting of my colleague. When did he check in again?'

'Last Saturday.' She thought not to make comment on the fact that it was possibly ten years since she had seen a business without a computer.

'So that's no meals and eight breakfasts each.'

'Eight each? Sorry what. No. That has to be an error. I only joined my husband last night.' Her face became flush. 'Please check it again.'

The young man was taken aback by her abruptness. 'OK, let me see. Dr Hughes.' He ran his finger once again along the page. 'Oh! You are right. Sorry about that. I was getting you confused with the Boardmans next door.' Oblivious to her exasperation he continued, 'Between you and me I can't imagine why you would eat here when there is a delightful coffee shop around the corner.' He tapped his pencil on the book. 'I don't think that the owners have changed a thing in forty years. It is in keeping with its traditional character apparently.' He rolled his eyes.

She placed the key on the counter. 'So, nothing to pay.'

'Well, so long as you haven't laced into the rest of the minibar this morning,' he teased. 'Seriously, you would be surprised.' He then lowered his voice. 'The Browns aren't shy. They are the elderly couple in there.' He leaned over to point through the door. 'Creatures of habit. Two eggs, three sausages and always a second helping of beans.' He subsequently winced and shuddered at listing the completion of their requests. 'Eggy bread. Ugh. Daisy, that's our cleaner, she filled in the dots when she told us that she has to restock the minibar every morning. Not to mention a couple of bottles of supermarket plonk in the wastebasket. Who says life stops at seventy, or indeed eighty apparently. God knows how they even make breakfast. I've told the owners...' he then raised his hands with exaggerated affectation, '... with no lift, and these steep threadbare stairs, it's only a matter of time before one of the geriatrics does the helter-skelter.'

She couldn't help but smile. 'Are you sure that you want to work here?'

'God, no. It's that or serving flat burgers and sticks of saturated fats to hordes of hormonal teenagers. It's the lesser of two evils, and means that I can get through art school. There are worse gigs.'

'I suppose you're right. Well,' she gathered up her bag, 'good luck with art school.'

'Thank you and remember us next time you are here in London!'

Sarah closed the door behind her as she spotted the coffee shop on the corner. She had barely noticed it as she passed it last night – a dark façade with little to mark it out against the street. In daylight the full character of the traditional Georgian establishment came to the fore, set into the corner of the grand terraces, the name 'Breton's' immaculately scribed above the front window, in a dull gold against a racing green gloss. Now, its pavement hosted a vibrant scene as outdoor tables were filled with customers basking in the morning sunshine. Freshly squeezed orange juice, cappuccinos, and most enticing assorted pastries and the fabled muffins. In contrast to the smell of bacon she had met within the hotel, she was greeted with the aromas of freshly ground coffee as she walked through the door. A duo of neatly aproned baristas worked the orders of the people in front of her. A couple of smartly suited gentlemen talked of the latest trading on the Nikkei, which seemed a source of concern. In front of them, a young woman waited patiently, a Chanel handbag neatly resting in the crook of her arm. Sarah perused the deliciously laden display cabinet. Arranged neatly in trays were golden baked croissants, pains au chocolat, Danish pastries, then, at the end, an assortment of fruit muffins, a difficult selection from which she had to quickly decide upon due to the fast efficiency of the staff, who had almost finished serving the people in front. She settled on the third choice of coffee chalked into the boards displayed behind the counters. Then, on an impulse, feeling the pressure of a sudden glut of new customers behind her, she made a quick addition of a croissant and an orange juice.

Outside a table opened up as a couple got up to leave. Passing through the door, Sarah placed a copy of one of the broadsheets under her arm as she set a pace to take the slim window of opportunity for the vacancy that was already being eyed up by a couple just behind her. Relaxing back, she took out her sunglasses and embraced the warm sunshine. From nowhere, a third employee appeared, cheerfully wiped down the table and left with the used crockery. A gentle breeze cut across the tables, the quiet Belgravia road a world away from the melee at the airport the previous day. Her first chance to digest the last twenty-four hours. The thought of Graeme meeting this patient was unsettling, and how she couldn't shake the familiarity in her letters. The desperation, the intensity. The anger returned when she thought of the intrusion into their lives and when she talked of her, Izzy and Seb. She had an overwhelming wish to meet her. Perhaps she could understand more, to put her mind at rest. She rejected his offer of the address he was going to, because, despite his screw-up, he would be apoplectic at her turning up. If the woman was desperate, she wasn't acting out just to get Graeme's attention. What might the further consequences of her instability be? Sarah thought back to her first time in therapy, that feeling of vulnerability, the desperation to escape the depths of hell and to have someone to reach out to. It was something that she had always envied about Graeme, that ability to save lives, transform lives, to be able to bear the burden of losing those that couldn't be helped. Remembering vividly the day he came home after finding out a patient had killed themselves. He had left his mobile at home and waited until the afternoon before he went home to get it. The next day the young boy's parents came in, raging at him for not taking their son's calls.

It was over twenty years since she had first met Graeme, when he had known how to save her. When they met on the steps of the charity shop. When she could barely put one foot in front of the other. He had got her through every rough time, and somehow through losing Ben. How different her life would have been. She looked at her watch. He would be there by now. It would be another six hours before they could leave, get back to Germany where they could have some time to talk.

The opportunity to stay and have another cappuccino was too tempting. The breakfast rush had subsided and most of the tables were empty. With several hours to go, it would save the inevitable spending if she were to indulge in Knightsbridge. Reaching into her bag to take out her purse, she resisted looking at her phone, which would lead to her checking her bank account. The £2,000 withdrawn would be there in black and white. Even if she wanted to there was no hiding it from him now. If he hadn't looked already, he would know soon. With everything that had happened the previous night, she hadn't seen if her wager had won. For a fleeting moment, she could put one more bet on. A large win would soften the blow. But if she resisted the urge, he might go some way to believing her commitment to stop. In the back pages of the paper that she had avoided reading would be the result of the match. In just a couple of moments she could find out. She stood up, taking the paper with her, placing it back into the rack on the way to the counter.

'Hello again. That cappuccino was just too good not to have another cup.'

The assistant smiled at her. 'We can't tempt you with one of our muffins?'

'You could. Easily.' She smiled as he began preparing her drink.

How she had missed her shop since moving to Germany, more than she thought she would. The frustrations of difficult customers, or maintaining cash flow in lean times, all put in perspective, countering anything Graeme would say about rose-tinted glasses.

The time left in Germany was just over eighteen months. She could manage that. Then Graeme would have to apply for a UK posting. If she decided not to go back into business with Chloe then she would find something else. But, something full-time. No more hours than necessary enclosed in the four walls waiting for Graeme to get home. She had to get back to something she was good at.

'Here we are.' The barista presented her with a coffee. 'One cappuccino, and here, try one of these.' He offered over a plate of neatly wrapped chocolates. 'They are a new line we are trying. Made from the best cacao beans of Venezuela. To die for.' The other assistant leaned over, taking one from the plate, closing his eyes as he placed the square in his mouth.

'Please, take one.'

She then followed suit. 'Oh wow. That is good. Wow.' She looked at the promotional box on the counter. £15.99. 'That is why they are so good.'

The assistant held out the plate for another. 'You know you want to.'

'It's OK, your work is done,' she joked. 'One box, please.

309

Dark chocolate is my husband's favourite. Not that he will see any of them.'

'Your secret is safe.' He placed one of the boxes into a bag.

Sarah opened her purse. 'It will have to be a card, I'm afraid.'

The assistant placed the plastic into the machine. The first attempt didn't take and it reminded her that the worn strip had been on the brink of out-and-out failure for the last two transactions.

'If you could try just once more.'

His expression suddenly changed to one of scrutiny. He pushed a button and the paper began printing through the other side.

'Sorry, madam. Would you mind waiting a moment.' He then smiled, responding to her sudden concern. She tried to lean forward to see if the payment had processed. 'Oh. It's not a problem, I'll just be a minute.' He returned after a brief discussion with the manager who had handed him something from the drawer. 'Sorry about that. I just needed to check something.'

'Is there an issue with my card?' Her stomach turned as she thought of the current account and the gambling, whether she had miscalculated after the double vodkas. Her anxiety intensified, as she couldn't be 100% sure exactly what the numbers were.

'We noticed that this is the same card for the account of both you and a Dr Hughes. I have a bill here from yesterday.' He handed over a slip of paper. 'Yesterday morning, he took the payment slip, not the receipt with him. Our fault. I handed him the wrong one. But I wondered if you wouldn't mind settling up. It's just it will come out of my wages. You don't have to, of course. But we, I, would be really grateful. Please use our phone if you want to call him.'

'Oh!' The relief washed over her body. 'No problem at all.'

She opened the piece of paper. 'Anyway', she continued dryly, 'I can't imagine that you are running a fraudulent heist behind the cover of muffins.' She then closely inspected the receipt. The same mistake had happened to her twice when she first worked at the shop. Except she didn't have the good fortune of the customer returning the £155 dress and matching shoes. 'It happens to the best of us. If you give me a pen I will sign it for you.'

The amount came to £28.50, although with no itemisation. She duly signed the bottom. 'I suspect he was lured in by those chocolates. And no, I won't be anticipating seeing any of them.'

'No, I can say that he did resist.' He did a once-over of the receipt before opening the till. 'Although, your daughter was a different matter.'

'Daughter?'

'A very pretty girl. Not that I'm sure she looks as if she eats an ounce. Fabulous figure.' Noticing her sudden change in expression, he then quickly corrected himself. 'Sorry, inappropriate. I didn't mean to cause offence.' He urgently continued to try and backtrack.

'No, sorry, you must be confused.' She gathered her handbag and turned to quickly make her way out of the shop. At the first opportunity away from the street, she then opened up her phone, her heart pounding. She thought about calling Izzy, but as she had her father's instincts for any kind of distress or dubious pretexts, she then messaged her. Sarah knew what the answer would be, but typed it anyway.

'Hi darling…' She tapped her fingers against the side of the phone trying to come up with something plausible to be texting her in the middle of the day, all the time her head spinning with the words from the barista. 'Saw a documentary last night from your neck of the woods, just reminded me to say I hope all is well and was thinking of you!'

She waited a minute before a reply. 'Hey Mum! Up to my

eyes in dusty soil. I hope you recorded it! Will call next week when I get a chance. Love you xxxx (PS Still waiting on a sight of Bettany.)'

With confirmation of what she already knew, a chill ran through her body as she began to sweat. Why hadn't she asked for the address when Graeme had offered it? What do liars do? Another tip from a condescending shrink: they keep things as close to the truth as possible. Had he mentioned anywhere? Her mind drew a blank. She then thought to sit down and regroup and think how to move forward. There was no sight of another café nearby. In her search, two streets away she soon came across a pub. The Duke of Marlborough, a small inn discreetly set into a corner of the street.

Once inside, she ordered a glass of Merlot from the friendly landlord who was chalking up the list of lunchtime specials. She barely listened as he suggested that it would go a treat with the game pie they would later be serving. As she was waiting for him to pour her wine, she considered where she should start looking for Graeme. Taking her drink to the table, she thought that even if she waited until they met later, there would be an explanation. A meeting in the café was all she had. The limbo of uncertainty raced in her head. But she also knew that if she gave him a chance to explain, she would never know.

Next to her table, a man playing a fruit machine cheered as it dispensed a sizeable amount of coins, which rattled into the scoop below. As the lights flashed around the façade, the landlord disingenuously congratulated the customer from across the bar. As he took the victorious man's order, he smiled wryly as he pulled the pump. The customer turned back to the machine to reinsert the first of the coins. Another man bumped into her chair as he went to see how much his friend had won, the impact thudding into her back. Two tables in front, an older gentleman, who was watching a rerun of the previous night's football game on the TV, threw a disapproving look, then countered the noise by cranking up the volume. Just after that two young women came through the door, who, at the sight of a group of friends, emitted a loud squeal of delight then feigned shock at the sight of a large collection of shopping bags squeezed into the booths. They had allowed the door to bang loudly behind, to which the man watching the television muttered something under his breath, before cranking up the volume even further. Barely able to hear herself think, she picked up her bag and made her way into the back garden, taking a seat at one of the tables.

The urge to call Graeme was becoming overwhelming. She brought up his number, but then moved promptly away and straight to her contact list. She scrolled down to his old office number. If there was one way of finding out the truth, it was through Jane.

Once the contact number was in front of her, Sarah hesitated over the immediate prospect of how to approach this. She sat for another ten minutes before she was able to make the call, after making two abortive attempts, doubting herself. If Jane was in on this, she would ring Graeme. Because if there was a patient involved, that would be her priority, or rather it was her livelihood. But, with no other ideas of what to do, she decided to go through with the call.

Jane's receptionist, Franny, responded to Sarah's voice with a burst of enthusiasm. In her usual gregarious manner, she began asking Sarah how she was doing, what was Germany like, had she donned any *lederhosen* yet, or any plans for the upcoming Oktoberfest? She used the enquiry as an opportunity to relive a holiday in Bavaria where she and her husband had been five years before. Sarah tried not to betray the anxiety in her voice as she hinted once again at the wish to speak to Jane. A hint responded to by finally revealing that Jane was in with a patient, then another scheduled following that. She would be busy for at least the next hour. Sarah's frustration simmered as Franny continued with an anecdotal account of a near avalanche that they were close to, in a village eight miles away. Sarah answered her questions about Celle, the apartment, omitting the history, for fear of another lengthy tangent. All the time she kept looking at her watch. Having to wait another hour with no guarantee of Jane fitting in her call became her main concern, her other wish being that another line would ring demanding Franny's attention. An event that prompted the end of the call came in the form of a patient arriving for an appointment with one of the new therapists. She quickly assured Sarah that she would get Jane to call her when she was free, but she couldn't make any promises.

With still fifty minutes to go she tried to pace herself with her glass of wine, wanting above all clarity when she spoke to Jane. Half an hour later the other barman came out to collect some glasses. His suggestion of another one was difficult to turn down as she had nearly finished hers. The last thing she needed was the landlord coming out midway through the conversation to Jane to hint that it wasn't a communal park. It occurred to her that during the entire fifteen-minute conversation, Franny hadn't asked about Graeme once. Her thoughts were broken up by the arrival of the barman with a substantial glass of red, with which he placed down a dish of unappetising-looking assorted nuts. As she thanked him for bringing them out he half jokingly, half frantically lamented the more hectic than usual day in the bar, and, as if on cue, he was drawn back in by the sound of dropped crockery.

The time passed slowly, the hour ticked around, then another. An hour and a half later and still no call, she had finished her second, then decided to make her way in for a third.

Over two hours after she first called, the phone rang. Taking a large sip she looked at Jane's name, or rather the name of the practice. There was no going back.

'Hello, Sarah. It's Jane.' Her voice sounded quizzical and cautious. The last time they had spoken it was at the farewell at the office. Her clarity made Sarah focus on the careful deliberation of what she was going to ask.

'Hi. Thanks for getting back to me.' She hesitated as all the preparation that she had made for the call had suddenly abandoned her. 'Wow. I thought I would know what to say. I need to ask you something, Jane,' she firmly asserted. Her courage lapsed as she tried once again. 'I don't know where to start.'

'Sarah,' she interrupted her, 'obviously there is something wrong. Just start at the beginning.' Her formality reminded Sarah that she was talking to a shrink, one that she hadn't really known, not as a friend, her voice now showing concern. 'First of all, where are you?'

'I'm in London. On a visit. I'm fine, really.' She fought the urge to offload, tell her everything. 'I need to ask you something. Something you need to tell me, about Graeme.'

'Graeme? I'm not sure I can help. But what is it?'

'When you split from the business,' she sensed Jane was about to interrupt her, 'I need to know if this was all about a patient.'

The line was momentarily silent. 'I'm not sure what you mean?'

'OK. Well, I think you do.' Sarah's reticence turned to irritation as she could hear the anxiety and disingenuous tone in her voice. 'Because don't tell me the break-up of the partnership was about fluffy cushions or bloody platitudes on the walls.'

'I can't discuss patients, you know this. We had a different approach to treatment, that was it. It just came to a head, that was all. The final straw that broke the camel's back. Has he said something?'

'Different approach? That I believe. You don't strike me as

315

the sort of doctor who sleeps with their patients. You just turn a blind eye, is that it?'

The line was once again silent, quickly preceded by a sound of footsteps and the closing of a door. 'Sarah, you have the wrong end of the stick. Here. I think you should speak to Graeme about this.'

'I'm talking to you, Jane. If you don't tell me right now I will come to Cheltenham and we will continue it there.'

Jane immediately shut her down. 'He had a problem with a patient. He became too involved with the case. It came to a point that we decided we couldn't work together. Graeme convinced me you were at maximum strain. He said he had dealt with it and there was no need for you to know. Given that, well, to be straightforward with you, he said that it would upset you. It was near to the anniversary of Ben's death.'

'What? Ben? What has he got to do with this? Don't you dare use him to cover up whatever this is!'

'I'm sorry. But it is history now, nothing can be achieved by opening up that old wound. You also have to understand,' she abandoned her reticence for annoyance, 'this is my practice, you know better than anyone that I have invested a small fortune. Look, it was agreed he would go. I have done everything to try and help her. I have offered her free treatment to help her through this.'

'How noble of you.'

'Your husband is to blame, not me or the other partners. Over a year ago, she took an overdose. The last contact I had with her was months ago and she dropped out of college.'

'College?' Sarah's anger came to a sudden halt, not being able to make immediate sense of this revelation.

'She's only twenty, Sarah, and vulnerable. Have you seen her?'

'No, I haven't.' She felt revulsion at the realisation she was not much more than Izzy's age. 'I don't know where she is.

Really, I have no idea. I wouldn't know her if I passed her in the street. Who is she? I mean it, Jane, I want to know everything. I mean it, I will come to your office and create a shit storm.'

'Alright. Just calm down. It seems I have little choice. Do you remember the young girl who turned up drunk at Graeme's leaving drinks, who I took through to my office? Christ. Your husband shouldn't even be practising,' she snapped. 'I found out not long after her overdose that he had been seeing her outside of his office. But he said he could deal with it. I'm sorry to have to tell you that, but for heaven's sake, Sarah. I implore you to keep it to yourself.'

'When was the overdose?'

'It was the end of last January.'

'But if you found out, why was she still coming to the practice? Was she still his patient? If you knew, how could you let him still treat her? What is wrong with you? Of course, yes, what am I thinking, you thought he was the best way of containing it. Well, great fucking job, Jane.'

'I made a bad judgment. One I regret deeply.'

She didn't reply. As she processed Jane's words, the pieces were falling into place. The memory came to her, the end of January. It must have been when they were in France and he had been called back, only to return four days later. They had argued because she told him he was sullen, as if he didn't want to be there.

'Sarah? I need to know that you are not going to take this further. I understand how you must be feeling but that isn't the solution.' With still no response she desperately added, 'You wouldn't want yourself dragged into this, unfair as it is, your condition, well, it will be a factor in people believing you. You should also know that she won't have a word said against him. Focus on yourself, this will make you ill again. If you need any help I can...'

Sarah ended the call. Her head began to flood with images

of the night of Graeme's drinks at the practice. He had barely flinched.

She telephoned Graeme. His phone went and a few rings later it went to voicemail. She urgently called again, this time an instant cut-off. A third, then she sent a message. 'Call me now. I need to speak to you.' She left the pub, gaining pace as she rushed down the road. Not sure where she was going, she kept walking, holding on tightly to the phone in her pocket. Her mind raced with everything that Jane had told her, desperately trying to flesh out the details. The time he came back to France. How he was with her. How oblivious she was to what was going on. As she crossed the road, the girl's face was vivid in her mind. Mostly oblivious to the traffic, Sarah walked in front of a cyclist, who swore at her as he was forced wide into the road. Apologising, she continued at a pace, causing a taxi to slam on its brakes, the driver emulating the flash of anger of the cyclist. She halted on the island between the roads, leaning up against the lights, as she gave way to an outburst of tears. The red traffic light prompted a surge of crossing pedestrians, many curious at her condition. A couple of girls giggled, one uttering the word loony as they passed. But most, having satisfied their curiosity, rushed past, continuing their own journey.

Only one young man stopped to ask if she were OK. The look of pity made her straighten up and give him the grateful reassurance that made him walk on. He reminded her a little of Seb. Now, she thought of her son. He never asked about his father. Had he known? She filled up with dread at the possibility. Izzy would have told her, of that she had no doubt, but could she be sure of Seb? He would think he was protecting her. Was it why Graeme had surprisingly shown so little opposition to him going travelling? Checking her phone, in case it hadn't been audible over the busy traffic, her mind began to look for reasons why Graeme hadn't called back. Perhaps Jane had called him. No less than a few seconds after placing her phone back in her bag, it rang. Her stomach churned as she faced the imminent reality. She listened as she waited for him to set the tone.

'Hello, darling. You telephoned. Sorry I couldn't answer. Things are pretty busy. Is it important?'

His manner made her unable to contain her contempt. 'Yes, Graeme, it's important. I wanted to know, are you still seeing her or is it now about damage limitation?'

'What's wrong? Are you OK?'

'You do worry about me, don't you, Graeme. How lucky am I? If I didn't feel so sick, you disgust me.'

'Just calm down. What are you talking about?'

'At the coffee shop yesterday. I know you were with her.'

'The coffee shop?' He took a moment of brief hesitation. 'Oh. I see. Is that it?' he laughed. 'She came to the hotel. Everything was above board. That's why we ate there, not at the hotel.'

'I can't believe that I have fallen for this bullshit. You can't talk your way out of this one.'

'Christ. Enough! This is all in your head. When I see you later we will talk. We agreed. Look, I'm not angry with you. I will answer any questions that you have. But, now I have to do what is best for this young woman. It is the right thing to do.'

'The right thing to do? I spoke to Jane. Just give it up, Graeme. Aren't you just exhausted lying all the time?'

It was his turn to be silent.

'No answer to that. What, Jane isn't telling the truth?'

'She probably didn't tell you how disturbed this woman is. It is an unrequited infatuation that spiralled out of control. The stupid thing was agreeing to meet her out of the office. But, now, if I don't fix this my career is over. The things we enjoy, our lifestyle. It's over. For nothing, a stupid infatuation.'

'The things we enjoy? Our life?'

319

'What about our children? What effect do you think that this will have on them if this gets out?'

'Now you think of them? I have to ask, not that I am expecting an honest answer, but did Seb know what was happening?'

He hesitated once again. 'Yes. He saw me out with her once.'

'Wow.' She choked.

'He wanted to protect you. It was the right thing not to tell you.'

'Right for you, you mean.'

'Do what you need to, Sarah. Take it out on me, whatever you say goes. But as I said, think what effect and fallout this will have.'

'And what about this Lucy?'

The sound of Sarah saying her name made him falter. 'This is about us. Let me sort this out. Look, this is ridiculous trying to talk like this. I need you to give me a chance to explain. Face to face. Everything else I said is true. I just need another hour here,' he implored. 'You know the army would kick me out for this. All I did was meet her outside the office where I thought I could deal with the situation better. I shouldn't have done. I got out of my depth and didn't want to admit it. And Jane? She just wanted to shut it down without listening to anything I had to say. Really, Sarah, if you knew what I have been put through over the last year.'

'And still you make this all about you. An hour? You mean you need time to put together a plausible and convincing performance for me. I'm not interested, Graeme.'

'If you didn't want to work out a future for us you wouldn't have called. I understand this is painful but you know that I love you, and we will get through this.'

'I just want answers. Is there even a doctor taking her on? Is that even true?'

'Oh yes, absolutely. I promise you that.'

'Of all the things,' she continued, desperately trying to keep on top of her emotions, 'I just didn't see this coming. That is what is the most difficult part. Were there others? Has this happened before?'

'No. Sarah, this was an aberration.' He softened his voice. 'We can talk. Give me an hour tops, no, better make that two. To make sure everything is tied up with Michael. I'll come to you. Where are you?'

'I will listen, that's all. I need answers but we are over.'

'Whatever you need to do, Sarah. You are in control. Whatever you decide to do after that I will understand. Give me one chance.'

'I told you, Graeme, I only want answers, OK? Where to meet? Hyde Park seems as good a place as any. I'll meet you by the old bandstand, you know where that is. We sat there one afternoon when we came here for our anniversary,' she said cuttingly. 'You have two hours. I want to know everything.'

'I will be there. Remember what I said. I love you, Sarah.' She heard the line go dead. Another look at her watch. Two hours to go.

Entering the park, she took a space on one of the empty benches. A languid branch of a willow provided shade overhead as she wished she had insisted he came sooner. Largely unnoticed by her, a steady but thinly drawn-out succession of people passed by.

A young woman came and sat on the bench next to her without saying anything, just a brief smile to acknowledge Sarah's presence there. Loud thrashing music emanated from her headphones, which to Sarah was unrecognisable, played loudly enough to interrupt her thoughts. The woman carefully took out a tobacco tin from her bag. Shielding the flakes from the breeze, she hunched over to roll a cigarette.

As she lit the end, it burned brightly, sending a large billow of smoke into the air, as she took in the first satisfying draw. When she saw Sarah move to avoid the smoke she made a gesture with her other hand, to attempt to waft the remains downwind from Sarah. It was merely a gesture as the breeze gently interchanged around them. Sarah acknowledged the courtesy, as the woman turned up her headphones, relaxing back into the seat. Taking out her phone, she began a flurry of activity on the small screen, making it seem implausible to Sarah that she should be forming coherent words.

Sarah took out her phone. There was still another hour and a half until he would get there. She brought up the gambling website, then closed it down. Instead, she began flicking through other websites, one after the other, hesitating for the briefest of moments.

However, she was inevitably distracted by subconsciously trying to make sense of her conflicting emotions. She snapped her phone shut, knowing that she had to face whatever was ahead, and prepare herself. Instead of Graeme's words, the first irrepressible thoughts were the memory of the night of his leaving drinks. The fallout with Jane, and then of course the image of the girl. The memory sent her thoughts racing. How she had given so very little thought to it. Instead, thinking of the money, the move, she had been missing something that was right in front of her. When the young woman had given her a look of familiarity, it hadn't occurred to her for one second there was anything behind it.

Feeling her isolation, she thought about how everything that she had been certain of about her life had disintegrated. Forty-eight hours ago he was on a work trip. Their apartment now seemed another lifetime away, one that no longer held meaning. A life in Germany that had never felt it should be hers. She felt a sudden realisation of vulnerability, nowhere to go. A life built together to be pulled apart and left behind. Since her initial rage had subsided she thought of the argument in Germany when Izzy had been there.

He had been right on one thing: she had shut him out and for the past few months she had been lying to him. For a moment, she thought that there may be the slightest possibility that this had been a one-sided infatuation and, despite his betrayal, he had stayed faithful to her. If they returned home, she could go back to work. They had been happy for over twenty years – she thought so, had thought so. After briefly entertaining the idea of a life back with him, she felt contemptuous of herself for wishing just for a moment she had never found out.

Suddenly, a waft of smoke hit her as the wind took a rapid change of direction. Sarah instinctively coughed against the unexpected inhalation.

The woman quickly dropped an earphone out. 'Oh shit, sorry. Bad habit.'

The previously cool exterior of the woman was abandoned as she made her apologies, which to Sarah felt as if the young woman was talking to her grandmother. The moment of being perceived by the girl as almost elderly gave her a moment of levity.

'No problem.'

'Are you alright? I don't mean to be funny or anything, but you don't look that well. Here, would you like a drink of this?' The girl offered her a drink from a half-empty bottle of water.

This casual informality Sarah hadn't in the least anticipated. 'No, thank you, that's kind of you though.'

'My mum keeps saying that I should give up. You know, smoking. Apparently, no one my age smokes anymore.'

'Mums, they worry.'

'She should try living with five housemates in a pokey terrace who all smoke like trains. She's lucky,' she began, genuinely indignant. 'If she knew what the others have as a side order, she would be thanking me.' She stubbed out the cigarette under her motorcycle boots before putting it into another tin. 'It wouldn't be as bad if she hadn't smoked like a train in her teens. Anyway, she totally doesn't get the point. It isn't as if twenty years down the line it is now easier to give up.' She rolled her eyes. 'Everything was harder then. But also, I am teetotal, does that count for anything? Of course not. Sorry, no offence.'

'None taken.' She wondered for a second if this was a generational observation or that the effects of the wine, now leaving her system, were evident. 'So what is it you are studying?'

'Chemistry.'

'Oh. So the next Marie Curie?'

She looked at Sarah, smiling. 'Rosalind Franklin more like!' Before Sarah had time to respond the young woman continued enthusiastically, 'She was completely amazing! So, she was critical to the discovery of DNA! OK, long story short. In the fifties and sixties she and three other scientists, they conducted research into DNA to end up discovering the double helix. Etc. Etc. Unprecedented, groundbreaking progress in the field of physiology. But does she get the recognition? Of course not! The men get the sodding Nobel Prize, and, surprise, surprise, she didn't. Misogynist twats.'

Sarah burst out laughing. 'I heard that one from my daughter. Crick, Wilkins...'

'... and Watson,' the girl keenly interrupted.

'Watson. That was it.' She remembered Izzy coming back from a class one day and having a similar indignant outburst. Calling them a comparable epithet before she was told the rest of the story. 'So I might be in the presence of a future pioneer.'

'You might be.' The girl beamed at the flattery. 'Look, I don't mean to be intrusive, but are you sure you are OK?'

'Thank you but I'm fine.' The directness of her enquiry took her straight back to the present reality.

'Do you know, my boyfriend was supposed to be here ten minutes ago. He is absolutely hopeless. If the truth be known, I told him to be here half an hour earlier than I wanted, which usually makes him bang on time.'

'What if he had turned up twenty minutes ago?'

'Not a chance. Creature of habit. When he is ninety he will still be the same. Perpetually distracted and no sense of direction. No matter how much I try. Let me see.' She opened up her phone. 'Last night I put this app on his phone. I told him if he were to get lost, he could find me on this.' She rapidly brought up a map with a dot. 'He got lost for twenty minutes when we arranged to last meet in the park. He's pretty but not much going on upstairs,' she joked as she took a drink from her bottle. 'Yep. Here he is, on the corner.' She showed Sarah the screen. 'Hopeless.'

The map looked familiar. 'Sorry to be nosey, but what is that?' Sarah sat up, enquiring. 'I recognise it.'

Initially not paying too much attention away from the screen the woman continued, 'Hmm. Not moving, just about where they have opened up that new vinyl store. I think I better call his phone.'

'That map,' she insisted, 'or app, is it an app? How did you get that?'

'Um. You get it from the app store. It's not stalkerish or anything, although I have my doubts with its potential abuse of civil liberties if it...'

Sarah wasn't listening as she reopened her phone. 'I think I have that. I can't find it.' She then began to wonder if she had imagined it or, at the mention of civil liberties, if it had come from an example of Izzy's causes. She flicked backwards and forwards on the phone. 'Can you show me what the box looks like?'

'The app? Here.' She confidently took Sarah's phone. 'Let me see. You read *The Telegraph*? I'm not sure if I should be helping you,' she joked but Sarah wasn't listening as she was leaning in.

'Here. You had it in social. Do you want any help?'

'If you could remind me.'

'You didn't know it was on there? That can't be good.'

'Please.'

The app opened. 'You have a request from Dr Graeme Hughes. If you want to accept him.'

'That doesn't make any sense. No, hang on! It does!' She took the phone back. 'I have no sense of direction either.' She recalled him telling her something about it after she came home flustered after not finding a restaurant she was supposed to meet him in for lunch in town and got lost in the back streets. After her phone broke in Berlin, she had forgotten he mentioned that he put some navigational tool on her new phone. Until now, she had mostly remembered the subsequent argument as he told her that he only had twenty minutes for lunch. Pressing the accept button she waited as the screen told her she was locating him. The location was Trafalgar Square.

'Thank you so much.' Sarah quickly gathered up her things.

The young woman looked confused. 'Um. You're welcome.'

'And don't be too hard on him when he arrives.'

Sarah ran to the edge of the park, flagging down a taxi that had just left the Hilton. Her heart raced as she thought of what she would find once she got there.

The journey seemed like an eternity. Every light, every queue. The closer they got, the more she was tempted to jump out to make faster time, her lack of familiarity with the city being the only thing preventing her from doing so. Sensing her frustration as she leaned forward to survey the traffic ahead, the cabbie saw it as a cue to lament the apparent three banes of his existence: road works, cyclists and the flood of freelance drivers undercutting them. The monologue bypassed her as she checked on her phone that he was still there. A few minutes later, they turned onto Pall Mall where they hit another traffic hold-up. A builder's truck had broken down, causing a delay as frustrated drivers queued up behind. The square was close as she asked the driver to pull over. Compensating him for the early termination of the fare she thrust a £20 note through the divide, from the diminished amount of cash she had left, before making a hasty exit. As she rushed down the road, she tried to prepare herself for what she was going to see. To control her emotions. Whatever it was. Whatever was waiting for her.

The square was busy as she ran up to the balustrade in front of the National Gallery overlooking the area. The sunshine that the morning breakfasters had been basking in earlier at the café had endured. Groups of tourists and city workers, who were taking full advantage of the weather, sat with their coffees or lunches, or just taking in the sights. Scouring the square she was unable to see Graeme. The blue suit that he had gone out in hardly set him apart. There were a couple of false alarms, mistaking two others in similar attire that had made their way up the steps towards her. She checked her phone once again. He was close. She walked down the steps. Her attention to orientating herself caused her to push into a couple taking a selfie in front of the gallery. Their staged exultant pouting pose dropped momentarily as she mumbled a fleeting apology in response to their complaint as she continued down the steps. The woman's call of 'stupid bloody woman' was countered by her dismissively calling them 'vain imbeciles', adding they might want to detach their nose from their screens and actually try going inside.

'Oi! What did you say?' The young woman moved belligerently towards Sarah as she was about to confront her.

Sarah stopped suddenly on the steps to head off any further engagement. Her already fractious state escalated to one of anger. 'Just one fucking word, Barbie. Really. One more fucking word.'

Sarah's sudden flash of rage took the woman aback, the man telling her not to waste her time on some sad old bat.

On the edge of a fountain just in front she saw Graeme. The sight of him halted her in her tracks. He was talking to a man more casually dressed. It was then that she saw Lucy, who was seated by the edge of the water. Every part of her wanted to go over to speak to them. One sentence, one exchange with Lucy would be telling.

Lucy's manner was easy as she consumed an ice cream, as the two psychiatrists appeared to be mapping out her treatment. She was sitting next to a woman on the fountain's edge that was filled with sightseers. There was a pram squeezed next to her, as the woman attentively picked up a toy that had fallen out onto the pavement. Sarah noticed the woman politely acknowledge Lucy with a smile, after Lucy had begun pulling comical poses at the baby. Her demeanour reminded Sarah how young she was. Dressed in a loose summer dress and a denim jacket, she paid little attention to what Graeme, and what had to be Michael, were saying. She was certain that this was all part of the backtracking he was trying to do, now distancing himself from his mess, whilst leaving Lucy waiting on his instruction. The anger and contempt for what she could see now was a young vulnerable girl at least had dissipated to a degree. When confronted with the sight of the two of them together, she was beginning to see that the idea of them being a couple was ludicrous. Sarah knew there would come a day when Lucy would wake up and see him for what he was, and the scales would fall from her eyes. Had he not held her a lifeline out of the darkness, her attraction, her infatuation with a vain, middle-aged man, who under different circumstances she wouldn't have given the time of day to, wouldn't have happened. As Sarah looked at him, she felt a kind of pleasure in the fact that most of all he knew it too.

But if he was finally helping Lucy, releasing her from her

attachment, then she felt that was something. If nothing had actually happened between them, if he had just got out of his depth, then that was something that she should perhaps try to understand. There was resonance in his plea that things can escalate quickly, despite fooling yourself you are in control. Perhaps she should have given him the space to talk, not assumed he could deal with everything, always having to be mindful of her lows, feeling he needed to protect her.

As Graeme continued in conversation with the man, Sarah watched Lucy as she dipped her hand in the water. The intensity of this girl's desperate, vitriolic words in the letters didn't seem to fit the happy-go-lucky girl that now sat awkwardly on the edge of the fountain, watching the world go by.

Her thoughts broke off as she could see the man open up a map, then appear to cross-reference with Graeme who was pointing some directions. The man was then joined by a woman, who folded the map away in her bag as they walked away.

Graeme then sat down next to Lucy. In a quick gesture the young girl leaned over, kissing him on the cheek. A display of intimacy he played down. Sarah felt unable to breathe, as if she had had a punch to her guts. Lucy's response was to tease him, putting her hand up to caress his face. Openly mocking him. Her persistence made him yield as he placated her by kissing her on the lips.

With her hands trembling, Sarah took her telephone out of her pocket. She rang Graeme's number. She watched as he took his mobile out of his inner jacket pocket. As he looked at it his immediate response was to reject the call. Lucy attempted to take the phone from him. He withheld it, rebuking her demands. As she got up to walk away he took her hand. She quickly snatched it from him. In a moment she rapidly typed something before handing it back, affecting a remorseful look before laughing at Graeme's sudden anxiety. A message notification came up on her phone.

'Hello Darling. Won't be long. An hour tops, just finishing up. Love you love you.'

He snapped in irritation at Lucy, his rebuke making her come to a sudden stop. Her immediate reaction was to sulkily pull away, but was prevented from doing so by him giving her an affectionate embrace then playfully picking up her hand and kissing the back of it. Even in her state of shock, Sarah could see they were oblivious to the fact that the woman with the pram, who was now forced to make room for them, was looking in thinly veiled disgust.

Sarah rushed towards them. A multitude of ways to respond came to her head. Anger, threats, each came and in turn were disregarded as she watched them. Before she got halfway she stopped. This was hers to control. No chance for him to come back. For him to not know what was coming next. If there was one thing he hated it was that.

She walked back up to the top of the steps, trying to organise her thoughts. Once at the top, seeing they were still in sight, she calmly began to type. She deleted her first efforts, the seething retribution that she wanted to hurt him with. She loathed him. No weak passive-aggressive, so he might think there was any coming back from this. She also discarded the obscenities, the self-pity. She took a deep breath in and began to type her finalised message.

'Careful that you don't get ice cream on that suit. You'll need it for court.'

She pushed send and waited for his reaction.

She had a perverse feeling of satisfaction as his demeanour transformed, looking around in frantic expression. Not something she had seen before, watching him dismantle, his façade spontaneously evaporating. She stood for a moment surprised that, through her anger and satisfaction, she felt a fleeting moment of regret at putting him into this pitiable state. Seeing him like that. Her world crashing in tandem. Her worst fears of him realised. She turned away, not looking back.

Her phone began ringing in her pocket. Every thought rushing through her head, including going back to confront him. The ringing unceasing, she took it out to switch it off. Before she reached for the button, she stared at his name on the screen, now having changed in all meaning. So often he had told her he loved her, missed her when he was away. On the days when she knew he would be coming back from a trip, the sight of his name, feeling the anticipation that he would soon be back. Calls from airports saying how much he had missed her. The memories now hollow.

In the crowded street, nowhere to go. Again, she hated herself for having been so desperate for looking for every reason to believe him. She came to a stop, leaning against some railings. She reran the image of him with the young girl in her head.

A stream of people continued to pass. More groups, more selfies, more couples. The phone continued to ring. Then in the corner of her eye she saw him at the end of the road, turning her phone off as she watched him. He was looking frantic as Lucy tried to get his attention. Sarah felt contemptuous of his desperate balancing act at trying to placate the increasingly agitated Lucy, whilst scanning for any sign of her. If anything he looked as lost as her. She could see it in him. But there was no pity, just anger. Then in a moment he saw her. He looked at her with regret, desperation. They exchanged a look of intimate familiarity, and in a fleeting gesture he repelled Lucy's attempt to take his hand. He turned to say something that stopped her in her tracks.

The young woman looked at Sarah, desperate, her previous flirtations now reduced to an almost childlike abandonment. He didn't look back as she watched him coming over, imagining what he was going to say. As he came closer, she hailed a passing cab, hesitating until he was almost within reach so that she could retain every memory that she knew would sustain her for whatever was next. Getting into the taxi, she thought of the first place just to initially put some distance between them, she then told the driver to head towards Piccadilly.

When she had been sitting on the park bench she had been preoccupied with thoughts of his infidelity, but now it was a reality. Seeing it was something that, even knowing it with prior certainty, would still not have prepared her for. The image of him kissing her burned into her mind, and most of all, seeing him embracing her in a way that made her realise how things had changed between them over the years. Knowing they had been apart a long time before now.

She suddenly leaned forward towards the front of the cab. 'Excuse me.'

The cabbie was engrossed in listening to a radio debate. He hesitated for a moment as he waited for the final words by the resident polemicist. Rounding off in controversial form, to keep the audience ticking, he introduced the next host.

The driver then turned down the sound. 'Yes, love.'

'Can you tell me where there is a hotel with a casino?'

'A casino? Well, there are a few. A range, I mean.' He broke with his thoughts momentarily to pip the car in front which hadn't noticed the change of the lights. 'So, a casino?'

'A good one.' She quickly followed up with, 'A nice hotel. No, a very good one. In fact, one of the best you can think of.'

'Well, we have several. Mayfair, Piccadilly. Taking the private clubs aside. I think I know.' He swung the cab around. 'I know just the one. It's in Knightsbridge.' His eyes glanced up to the mirror to engage with her. 'Pricey though.'

'Not a problem. What's life if you can't spoil yourself.' The case she had was modest, with nothing to wear that would do, and Knightsbridge was the perfect place to pick up a dress.

They pulled up at the hotel, where the cabbie wished her luck.

Whilst checking into the hotel, the receptionist's request for her address left her feeling exposed in her remoteness, the reality of her situation sinking in. She couldn't contemplate going back to Germany, nor go to friends or family and face the inquisition that would follow. Knowing them as she did, she would be swept away on a rollercoaster of how to punish Graeme, or what she should do next. The pity, the outrage, none of which she knew would compensate for the humiliation, the betrayal. Worse, the pity. He wouldn't be calling anyone, she was certain.

Sarah's impatience at curtly requesting that the receptionist please just hand her the key prompted her to cut short her rundown of the luxuries and facilities they had to offer. After which, Sarah took the elevator to one of the upper floors. Discarding her bag, she took a bottle of water from the minibar, quickly downing its contents.

Her attention then turned to finding something suitable to wear. Instead of what would usually be a longer shopping trip, and taking her time to enjoy the experience, Sarah just went into the closest shop. She sized up the first dress she saw, not bothering to try it on, then told the shop assistant she would take it, along with a pair of shoes she thought suitable.

As she passed back through the doors of the hotel, she mistakenly thought she caught a glimpse of Graeme. She relived the moment she saw him with Lucy. She had looked even younger than Izzy. God, Izzy. What would they say to her and Seb?

CHAPTER 32

AT FIVE O'CLOCK she prepared herself to go up to the casino. Upon arrival, she made her exchange of money for chips, and took her place at the table. She politely acknowledged a businessman as he was about to engage in conversation, but immediately she focused her eyes on the chips, running a small stack through her hands as she sought out her choices. Her usual numbers ignored, her eyes fixed on the wheel as she calculated her selections. Another man joined the table. The two men, it became clear, had been at the same meeting. The details of which she didn't take in as she waited on each spin.

The first drink arrived, a glass of Veuve Clicquot which she had previously ordered. The two men seemed more animated about the day's meeting than the speculations they were casually placing on the table. Until one of their numbers came in and there was a brief pause for celebration. The room gradually filled over the next few hours. She continued spin after spin, the chips moving back and forth, the only engagement being with the croupier, to whom she intermittently passed on a tip from her winnings. Each win or loss met with little contemplation.

Her anger festered at the thought of Seb knowing, making her feel sick to her stomach. How much did he know? But it was better to be left for now and for the moment she knew she couldn't call him. With no plan as to what to do next, telling him everything would only make him worry, as it would Izzy. For now, for them, it had to wait until she was ready with reassurance.

A couple sat next to her. They soon lost their chips as the man sought to keep pace with Sarah. The more he lost, the more he bet the opposite of Sarah's stakes. They left after their last turn of the wheel, deflated by their swift depletion of funds. The man was further admonished by the woman he was with, reminding him that it was two hours of her gains at blackjack that he had just blown. They saw the timing of Sarah's request for another glass of champagne as a dig. Their disapproving expressions didn't register as she doubled her previous stakes.

At the latest change of croupier, she looked to see the time. Her winnings stood at £4,650 as she realised it was now five hours since she had taken her seat. She needed a break, taking account of the dehydration that she was now feeling from the hot lights and having finished the latest of the glasses of champagne that she had lost count of. The last half an hour had seen her on a winning streak. A man across the table who had been matching many of her bets betrayed his disappointment at her departure, as he then considered a new strategy.

In the bathroom there were a couple of women attending to their appearance in the mirrors, as they prepared to go back into the hall. One of them, not far off Sarah's age, standing next to her at the sinks was reapplying her lipstick.

As Sarah was preparing to leave, a group of girls then walked in, full of excitement about their fortunes on the tables. A twenty-first birthday party that was riding high off the good luck of one of the particularly lucky members. Three times she relived the turning of an ace that had earned her a month's rent. The girl whose birthday it was had gained the number of a particularly 'fit bloke' who had been sitting across from her. The lady, placing her lipstick in her bag, gave them a look of irritation as they delighted in raucous crescendo. Her parting inaudible comment muttered in disapproval was noticed by a couple of the girls. One of them laughed, offering a mocking conclusion that she was a bitter old bird who was probably jealous and should lay off the slap, a comment that was rebuked by one of the others, who had seen Sarah, remarking how would they feel if that was their mum. The reply from the girl was that should she look like that in thirty years, they should put her out of her misery.

They then dispersed as two disappeared into the cubicles. The rest took their place at the mirror, one initially jostling against Sarah at the end, who, with one withering look, made the girl edge back towards her friend. Sarah anticipated that the comment now ruminating in the young woman's mind would be given air the minute she left the room.

The birthday girl once again began gloating to the others about her triumph at having acquired the phone number. Her friend, half listening next to her, was adjusting her hair as she examined her appearance with detail, swearing that she was developing bags, worse, laughter lines. The others collectively empathised, saying that it was the lights, as they critiqued themselves closely in the mirror. One of them then took the phone out to send a collective selfie to post. Upon inspection it was decided that the one by the entrance would suffice.

Returning to the table, she was relieved to be away from the noisy chorus of the girls. The man who had previously been matching her fortunes, and had taken somewhat of a hit since, smiled warmly as she took her seat.

A further two hours down the line and another change of croupier, the other man at the table had long since gone. Three of the girls from the bathroom had joined them. Placing their bets, one of them recognised Sarah, nudging the other when she saw the stakes that she was placing. A newfound respect for the middle-aged woman who had suddenly gained visibility. Initially, the rapid calculations and spreading of chips overrode all, but then an older man came and sat next to the girls. He placed down a glass of whisky and neatly lined up his chips on the table, making sure that everyone had the opportunity to survey his stakes. He leaned over to one of the girls, suggesting that she pick a number for him. He took a £50 chip and slid it over to her. Frowning, she politely pushed it back. She moved a little closer to her friend.

He then took another chip from the bottom, this time a £100 stake. The girl gave a wry smile. 'Make it a £200,' she joked.

He slid over the requested amount.

'Sorry, mate. I was joking. I really couldn't.' She suggested to her friend that they leave, thanking the croupier who was keeping a subtle eye on the situation.

He made a final pitch. 'I will send for a bottle of Cristal in my suite.' One of the girls hesitated to hear what he had to say. 'Then my driver can take us to see first light over the city. Lunch at The Ivy.'

Sarah placed her counters on the table, assigning them to different numbers. 'Why don't you give it up? Let me guess, you are counting on them being drunk and gullible. Pathetic. Cristal in your suite? I'm guessing prosecco and a standard double room.'

They looked over at Sarah. The girl who had paused to hear him out, seemingly more for sport, now conceded to her friends' encouragement to leave, and they took the opportunity to slip away to join another couple of their friends at the next table. He then turned on Sarah in frustration, showing more restraint than he wanted to under the gaze of the croupier. 'What business is it of yours?'

The croupier called the latest number as she gathered in her winnings from the latest spin. 'Let me guess, married, your wife doesn't understand you. No, I've got it, it's your last chance to grasp at your youth.'

He gathered up his chips and finished the last of his whisky. He flipped a £50 chip towards the croupier. Glancing once again at Sarah's chips, he tossed him another. He walked past her. Whisky-breathed he leaned towards her. 'A wife? Heaven forbid.' He looked her up and down disdainfully as if rejecting her for the role. 'But coming from a woman who is sitting on their own at 3 a.m... Who's the sad one?'

'I think we both know the answer to that,' she replied casually, as she placed her stakes, considering whether or not to change this time to odds instead of evens. 'Well, I shall attempt to contain my infinite despair at your departure.' She looked him up and down. 'So, if you don't mind.'

Turning her attention back to the table, she waited with anticipation for the wheel to be set in motion. Behind her the man took a place at another table, where he secured a seat next to another woman, not much older than the last one. They were striking up a conversation as he slid one of his chips to her – a well-received gesture as she excitedly placed her stake. A spin of the wheel resulted in success and he encouraged her again. He clicked his fingers towards a passing waitress, who was trying not to look fatigued as she serviced the thinning crowd. He then placed an order that appeared to impress the young woman.

Everyone from Sarah's table had gone, leaving her alone. A further two spins she decided to cash out. The tiring croupier congratulated her on her luck as she exchanged the smaller chips for several larger ones. In total, £5,850, which she duly cashed in. The hallway was silent. A couple walked up behind, stopping at their room.

Closing the door behind her, she opened up the balcony door, the sharp evening air effecting a sobering embrace. In the adjacent room, she faintly heard the couple laughing.

She called up for a bottle of single malt. Room service arrived, placing down the bottle with a polite enquiry as to whether she needed anything else. Placing the 'do not disturb' sign on the door, should she forget later that night, she poured herself a glass. Taking it to the window she watched the city below, barely allowing herself to think where he was. She went to retrieve her phone from the safe. She turned it on. Twelve missed calls. A series of text messages. He was in the hotel in Belgravia. She should go there and he would wait, whatever it took. It was a stupid mistake. She turned off the phone.

CHAPTER 33

SHE AWOKE IN a sudden rush with the feeling that she had to be somewhere. Her anxiety abated when she saw the time. 8.15. She shivered at the cold air that breezed through the open shutters that she had failed to close before she fell asleep. Half-dressed she rose stiffly from the bed to close the window. A relentless surge of commuters urgently made their way around the streets below. Office workers marking a quick pace; a bus below released a spill of passengers, which dispersed in different directions. A woman with a pushchair, who was negotiating the step down to the pavement, remonstrated with a man on a telephone who barely broke his pace to acknowledge the fact that he knocked a shopping bag from one of the buggy handles. Dozens in isolated purpose barely paid attention to their surroundings as they passed through, some drinking coffees, others making calls, many with thumbs pressed to small screens relying on peripheral sense to guide their path along the pavement, sweeping past slower people who were steadily making their way down the centre of the thoroughfare.

Despite the cold, her skin was clammy. The taste of stale whisky made her nauseous as she put the bottle into the bedside cupboard and out of sight. From the table she picked up her phone to find four more missed calls. All accompanied with messages. Yielding to temptation, she began to play them. As she expected, he offered varying degrees of denial then finally contrition. The last message saying he loved her. They could start again.

As she was placing the phone back, it vibrated again. Watching his name on the screen, she wavered between answering and leaving it. Before the voicemail could kick in again, she pushed to accept.

'Sarah, thank God. Are you alright?'

She rested the phone on her lap.

'Sarah, please. We need to talk. A day at a time. I understand. I can't believe I was so stupid. I love you so much. I will do whatever it takes. Twenty-two years of marriage. We can't throw this away. I will…'

She lifted the phone closer to her mouth. 'We?'

He sighed in relief at the sound of her voice. 'Me. I know this is all on me. I wish I'd never met her.'

'Yes, Graeme,' she whispered. 'If only she hadn't come into your life. How were you supposed to resist? I don't know why I should ask because I will never really know. But were there others? Was she…'

'No!' he quickly interrupted. 'No others. I swear.'

'I don't really know. I don't recognise you anymore. This can't be fixed. The worst thing is that I thought that we were happy.'

'I screwed up royally. But, I have always wanted to make you happy. Everything was about you and the children.'

'What, you think that this, whatever it is, your mid-life crisis, gave you a free pass to redress the balance?'

'What I did was a stupid mistake. One I will always regret,

but think about it. From the minute you told me you were pregnant with Seb, I never wavered, not once. You owe me the chance... I forgave you. I was the one who pulled you through.'

The reminder of that day came back to her vividly. The shame returning as it had so often. 'I can't do this. Leave me alone, Graeme. I need time to think.'

'I love you. I've only ever wanted to look after you. Our family. It is everything.'

'So you keep saying. Just give me some space.' She ended the call, and lay back on the bed.

CHAPTER 34

THE NEXT MORNING, once again exhausted from a night of broken sleep, she awoke to the sound of her alarm. Taking a long drink of water from the half-empty bottle on the side, she picked out some roughly coordinating clothes from the wardrobe. Before gathering up her hotel key she prepared to go downstairs. Hearing the cleaners hovering in the hallway she opened her purse, placing a £10 note on the bed – some compensation for the carnage strewn across the surfaces. A quick scan of the room, she saw her pack of tablets on the floor by the bed. A knock came at the door, along with the pre-announcement of room service. Sarah quickly placed her pills into the safe on the way out, before letting the maid into the room, mostly avoiding eye contact as the contrast of the immaculate hallway held a light up to the musty atmosphere that she had left behind her.

The casino was near empty. A room transformed by the more revealing daylight. The mirrored backlit bar, from where the drinks had amply flowed only a few hours before, offered a dull reflection of the shelved spirits. Two of the bar staff she recognised from the night shift were replenishing supplies for the day ahead. The air was heavy with the smell of fresh polish. A garish swirling carpet design stretched across the entire suite, whose purpose was to efficiently conceal the multitude remnants of spills and the wear from the perpetual flow of customers. After choosing a table, she then took her seat. The previous anonymity of being in a busy anonymous room a few hours before now left her feeling more exposed as the solitary player. On a nearby poker table, a couple of young American tourists mulled over their dealt hands.

As the croupier pushed over her chips, she began to calculate her bets. Instead of being able to lose herself at the table, Graeme's words kept pulling her back. Every time there was a break between spins, her frustration simmered in what she understood as avoiding putting off the inevitable. An inescapable need to get ahead of this, to decide what was the best way to go forward.

Taking her phone out of her pocket as she left the table, she typed in a message telling him to meet her at Shaftesbury's Café.

Arriving at the café, Sarah looked through the window. Graeme sat at a table, tapping his fingers against a half-drunk coffee. She looked at her watch. Half an hour had passed after the time that they agreed to meet.

A busker near the entrance was coming to the end of his song, the final bars strummed out to the applause of a couple, saying that it was their song. Before they moved off, arm in arm, the woman reached forward and tossed a couple of coins into his guitar case.

The busker nodded in acknowledgment, as he then turned his attention to Sarah who was unaware that he had noticed her. 'I don't think they know that song is about drug addiction,' he joked.

Sarah broke her attention away from looking at Graeme.

'Sorry, what?' His words then caught up with her. 'Oh, yes, I see, but no, I didn't know that.'

'A few years down the line they will be giving a different reason to their new partners why their mind wanders when it comes on the radio,' he laughed.

'A real romantic, aren't you.'

'I've seen it all. But I can do romance. I will do my Ed Sheeran, drawing the line at James Blunt, what with the greengrocers over there and the offer on the tomatoes that aren't shifting...' he stopped mid-sentence as he noticed that her focus was drawn back to looking at Graeme, '... and Dolly and Kenny are walking over to do a duet...'

'Oh, yes, rotten tomatoes.'

'So, are you going to go in?' He then began flipping through a songbook on his music stand.

'Yes, I am going to do that right now.' As Graeme caught her eye, she prepared to enter the café. A look they exchanged cut through everything that had been said or she had found out in the few days.

'Is there anything you want me to sing? You know, "play you in" so to speak,' he joked. 'It's obviously important.'

'I've been married for over twenty years. I've loved that man since the minute I met him, well, perhaps not exactly the first minute, but, sorry, I shouldn't embarrass you. I can't believe I'm telling you this,' she joked. 'Anyway, you couldn't guess the song that my husband proposed to. It was "Should I Stay or Should I Go". Before you say anything, he did learn how to be a lot more romantic.'

'I should hope so. The Clash? Well, points for originality.'

'Right now, if it wasn't so sad it would be funny. Sorry, if you don't mind, can I ask your name?'

'Sure, it's Ryan.'

'Ryan, why does life just have a habit of going tits up when you think you have things just about sussed?'

He laughed. 'I try not to knock it, it keeps me in business.'

'Doesn't it just. I'll leave you to it. The song. It looks like there's another couple heading your way. OK. So here I go.'

He began to lead into the next song. The couple smiled at each other and headed slowly in his direction. 'Good luck.' He winked at Sarah.

'Thanks. You too.' She took a deep breath before preparing to go in. 'Oh, and lastly, when we come out, he, my husband, will be making a grand gesture. If you could grant his request, it would be great, but just make sure that you make it very expensive for him.'

'OK, I think I can manage that.'

As she approached him at the table, he failed to disguise his anxiety. Once he was certain that she was coming through the door, he hastily went to the counter to order her a coffee. As the barista took his order he kept half an eye on her as she took her seat. Taking off her scarf she neatly placed it on the back of the chair.

'I ordered you a latte,' he began.

'That's fine,' she responded curtly as she waited for his cue to resume their conversation they had had on the phone.

'Sorry, I know you want answers. But Christ I have been worried about you.'

'No doubt.' She looked at him. His exhaustion was evident, the same as he looked after a long call-out without any sleep. She was happy he hadn't slept. He refrained from his usual comments when he knew she had been drinking into the late hours, or stayed up through the night.

'Where do you want me to start? I got into a situation I couldn't handle. You know everything. There has never, will never, be anyone else. When you didn't answer my calls, I thought…' He stopped abruptly before taking hold of her hand. 'Listen to me. I couldn't bear it if anything happened to you. This sounds rather trite but you know they say you don't know what you've got until it's gone.' He reached out to take her hand.

She pulled her hand away forcefully. A woman on the table behind pretended not to notice but appeared vigilant to further developments. Sarah leaned in. 'Seriously? Bumper sticker platitudes. You have just destroyed everything. For what? Was this some mid-life crisis? A cry for help?'

'I told you. I was arrogant, it got out of control. I underestimated the situation.'

'Do you think?' she responded sarcastically. 'She was, is, barely an adult, for God's sake. A patient.'

'I know. It was indefensible.' He paused as a waitress brought over her coffee. Sarah thanked her as Graeme waited impatiently for her to leave. 'I am going to say this to you. I will make this right. I have telephoned my boss in Germany and my corps over here. I have told them I am leaving the army. Within a few months I will be out. They are processing a transfer back to the UK for the last part of my work.'

'Oh, please. There is no way you would do that. What you mean is an extended period of leave.'

He reached into his pocket to take out his phone. 'If you want to check. You know I wouldn't lie about something like this. No more hiding things.'

'You've wasted your time. I just want to know why. No, perhaps I don't, but I need to hear it for my sake and then I'm leaving. Do you understand? I'm not coming back with you, Graeme.'

'It has to be worth giving it another try. Everything will change. No more army, I can take a break from work for as long as we need. We have earned the money. Why don't we travel for a year, whatever we want to do? We can go and see Seb, Izzy, how much would that mean if we were to go and see her? You were right. Everything has been about me. You have, we have, always wanted to go to India. We could travel along the Ganges, see the Taj Mahal, lie on the beaches of Goa. Nothing will be the same. I agree. I feel this could be a second chance for us.'

She took a sip of her coffee. 'That easy.'

'Of course not. But I am going to fight for this marriage. I will do whatever it takes. Just one chance. A year of getting away from it all, everywhere you always wanted to go. Your choice. Your agenda.'

'It's nice here, isn't it?'

'Sorry, what?'

'Here. Look at us. Imagine that this had never happened. Say if we were having lunch now and I didn't know about what you had done. Do you remember the first coffee that we had? Not long after we started seeing each other? No, I'm not quizzing you. I know you do. The café. How did you feel?'

'Well, the coffee was awful.' He smiled, seemingly pleased that she wanted to take them back to that.

'Yes, OK that was pretty awful, but what about us? How were we?'

'You were beautiful. A wreck, yes, but beautiful.'

'Oh spare me, Graeme. Think. What else?'

'Tell me where this is going?'

'Never let yourself open to just say what you feel.' She picked up her cup. 'This coffee. No lattes then. It was a cheap instant, I was wearing an old coat and didn't know which way was up. We would meet up there. You know that I waited for you to come through that door. I would pretend to be cool about whether you turned up or not. But there was nothing else I could think of, until I saw you again.'

'I know. This is what I mean, what I am trying to get you to see. We were always right for each other.'

'I had nothing then.' She looked at her rings. 'This one. What, £5,000. I can't remember. And this one... Look at the things, all the things. Clothes, cars, jewellery. When were you really last happy? I mean really happy.'

'You're right, perhaps, in part… but…'

'I wear £300 shoes, when I was happier to walk in something a fraction of the price. A long time ago, of course, but it was where I was going that I sought to find happiness. And please don't say what I think you are going to. Think as a husband, about you and me. Not as a shrink.'

'I understand.'

'No, I really don't think you do. I think that you have just spent the last minute suppressing some smart-arse send-up, or formulating a new line in how to placate me. What you always do with people, me most of all, tapping into what will hit the right note. To get what you want.'

'That's hardly fair.' He sat back in his seat.

'How long is it since we looked forward to weekends where we just packed a bag and went away? When it was just us, away from everything. One of the best times was the cottage we rented in the Lakes. No heating and more often than not getting soaked in a downpour on the way back from the pub, getting basic food supplies from the local store and drinking that terrible wine at night.'

'Of course I remember. The first time in that cottage, we barely left it. This is what I mean. We can go back to that. A fresh start.'

'But that's just it. I don't think you changed, you have just reverted back to who you wanted to be all along. And I'm not saying I wasn't content to drive around in a Mercedes or wear the best things, accept your gifts. You don't need to remind me. I was wrong. I thought those things helped make me fulfilled.'

'But, leaving us aside, I think I have been a good father. I don't see how being successful and providing for my family is a bad thing? I have always tried to show you I love you.'

'To show me? Yes, there's been plenty of demonstrations, gestures. But I really don't think that you have been honest with yourself. About me. Not really. Of course you were a good father to them growing up. But don't you see what I am saying? Look, we always supported you, Graeme, as a family.'

'I know. I've been selfish.'

'Let me finish. We would never ask you to compromise on the things you wanted to do, months away at a time with the army, weekends away for golf. You didn't even like me staying an extra hour at the shop.'

He was about to interrupt before she continued.

'You have always seen my lows coming, and you had to pick up the pieces. But did you never think just for one moment whether I was happy, you know, content, fulfilled? There is quite an irony to that, don't you think? I don't want to go backwards, Graeme. I'm not saying these things to provoke you or punish you. I want you to understand. Think about it. The holidays, the extravagant gifts were your way of trying to make things up to us. I get it. But then things gradually got back to how they were. You spent more time at work, and then a promotion. In celebration you had bought yourself a new Jaguar. You brought it back with expensive gifts for us in the back, and it was only halfway through our celebrations that night you said about the promotion came with a commitment to spend more time away.'

'I'm sorry. I mean it. I didn't realise and I see that now. I took you for granted. I have just tried to protect you.'

'You didn't see it? We all believe what we want to, Graeme. Since we got together, I never considered making a life beyond you. Not once. When I was ill you held it together. You took over and I half loved you and half resented you for it. We couldn't talk then either. Not about us, not really. More things were bought, this time better holidays, better presents. We just created our own way of coping. Money, things. The person I have become because I have been scared for so many years, I don't even like myself anymore, Graeme.'

'Are you saying that is down to me?'

'What do you want me to say? Partly, yes, but I kept myself there, with you, I didn't take responsibility, and now I am paying for it. Now I see it, and I don't know how I should feel.'

'We should talk properly, I don't know where this has come from.'

'Of course you do, Graeme. But this, I won't even call it an affair. This I didn't expect. Lucy...' she hesitated, 'Lucy. Someone I have never met but now means everything. What you did...' she took off her wedding ring, slowly followed by her engagement ring, placing them on the table, '... I can't forgive you.'

'Sarah, stop.'

'Give me your phone. Your only phone, I take it?'

'Of course.' He took out his mobile from his pocket. 'I haven't called her since I saw you. I promise.' He presented the phone. 'Here check it. The code is our anniversary.'

She began inputting the number. Before looking at the log, she glanced up at him. 'Why is it that I just ignored every time I knew deep down that you weren't telling the truth? But I never pushed it.'

Bringing up the phone records, she saw that there had been no other calls since yesterday, apart from to her, one to a German military number and the unanswered ones from Lucy.

'You see. Everything I am saying is true. If I wanted her I wouldn't be here, would I?'

'So a fresh start is as easy as that.'

'You know I am not saying it will be. But in a few months I will be finished. The CO says that he will get me back to the UK as soon as possible. It will probably be Gloucestershire. The corps also seemed to be happy in principle. We can take it from there.'

She handed back the phone. 'So when did you speak to your boss?'

'This morning. You saw. He's not happy, but I gave him enough information to understand. Perhaps a little embellishment. Anyway, it doesn't matter. I will be back in the UK in a few weeks. Why don't we finish here, go and get some lunch?'

'Somewhere nice. Expensive.'

He looked at her, perplexed.

'You said you spoke to your corps afterwards. That's Glasgow. You have one call. It's to Germany. None to the UK.'

His expression changed. 'Just listen.'

'For fuck's sake! There was no call, Graeme. And what was the one to Germany about? No, I am not even going to bother to ask.'

'Look, they will agree. I couldn't just spring it on them by telephone. There will have to be a formal interview. And this way was the best to…'

Sarah didn't take any of his latest attempts as an explanation. She just watched his expression. He struggled to conceal his resignation as he went through the same repetition. She picked up her rings, holding them tight in her hand. Without saying another word she stood up. He stopped in anticipation, hoping for any reaction, waiting on her next words, anger, anything to keep her there, his confidence leaving him with every passing moment.

Now, as she prepared to leave, she noticed those on the surrounding tables were paying close attention to everything unfolding. A man being kicked by his female companion as he made no attempt to hide his amusement at the attempts to suppress their confrontation.

She composed herself, her voice breaking as she sought the right final words and the strength to go. A number of words came to mind but she couldn't commit to any of them. 'I'll be in touch, when I'm ready.'

'I did everything for you,' he seethed. 'One mistake and you tell me you are leaving me. You would have lost the children, you would have nothing. I am the one who has held it together when it was needed. Don't you think I could have left you, taken the children? If I hadn't been who I was they would have sectioned you.'

'Goodbye, Graeme.' Sarah turned away from him, calmly walking out of the café. He then got up in pursuit as he hastily, after searching for his wallet in his jacket, put some money on the table.

Seeing him following she waited until he was on the street. From her hands she dropped the rings into the busker's case. 'As I said, Ryan, make it expensive.' She then set off quickly down the pavement before turning to see what she expected: Graeme remonstrating with the busker, offering increasing amounts of notes in exchange for the return of the rings, all the time keeping half an eye on her. By the time the busker handed them over she was out of sight.

A spontaneous urge to throw her phone into a passing bin was, at the last moment, resisted as she thought of Izzy and Seb. Approaching the hotel she took a turn at the last moment down a side street. She continued to walk, giving no thought to where she was going, recalling as if for her own torment everything from their conversation. Having to finally accept the reality of what was irreparable. That now, every waking moment would be different. But also, knowing that when Graeme saw past his pride, his fear of exposure, he would see things the same way. The resignation, as if neither could be bothered to keep the plates spinning in the air and acknowledge the joyless times when they didn't have the energy to confront what they had. After her last glance back at him as he secured the rings, she wondered if, when she had left his sight, he felt relief.

From the initial instinct to get away, she began to take stock, trying to think logically of the next step, with a few possibilities conflicting in her head. There seemed nowhere obvious to go. Friends such as Ellie, who showed restraint about her feelings about Graeme – Sarah had often headed off her criticism – would fail to fully conceal their relief at this and how she was better off on her own. She would struggle to explain, without having to face her own disgust, her anger. Offers to stay in their spare room whilst all the time knowing that they were secretly saying that thank God it wasn't them, or whispering to their partners about how they would never do that to the other.

She recalled the night that Ellie was infuriated by her brother-in-law who, after thirty years of marriage, had just left her sister for a young receptionist at his work. She had been furious at her sister for not seeing something that they had all suspected, after the late nights and sudden increase in conferences and time spent away. The thought suddenly occurred to her that there were those that did see or suspected. Perhaps why some of her friends had been cool with him in the last few years.

Most importantly, there would be the problem of how to tell Izzy and Seb their separation. They would take her side, without the thought that she didn't want their sympathy, or anger. Nor did she want to hear the host of names that would be levelled at their father, and all the pitying sentiments that her friends had the maturity or the detachment to withhold. Graeme would leave it to her to tell them, of that she was sure. But she would only tell when she could give them answers they would inevitably ask for. It would all have to wait – talking to the children, family, everything, anything that took her back to her old life. She wasn't ready for any of it.

By the time she got back to the hotel she was still trembling. Hurrying upstairs she quickly changed and made her way down to the casino.

Once seated she hastily placed her first bet, a large

one, £500 to start the evening. Her sudden arrival and the immediate statement of intent attracted the attention of the few others on the table, who were vigilant to see where this was going. It was the familiar look of what she had picked out as the novelty gamblers looking to have that lucky night, maybe to indulge themselves or to clear a debt, or those that were there to reap the luck their life of dutiful routine surely owed them. To be close to a winner, jump on the coat tails, have a glimpse to register the emotion of the gambler as they rode the highs, but most of all the losses. Amounts of money that would be to them serious, reckless and sickening sums to lose on the turn of a card or spin of a wheel. How she would have felt six months before.

Four varying stacks of chips remained under Sarah's gaze. Instead of her usual precise counting of her gains and losses, her exact awareness of her money, she had stopped taking stock. Her wagers moving back and forth for the last several hours had kept her solvent. Twice going down to a few chips, she had managed to work her way back up.

She hadn't left her chair in over six hours. Her eyes heavy, the effects of the last few poured doubles had numbed her senses. The people who had come and gone from the tables went unnoticed. It was only at the changes of croupier that she was dragged back to the reality of that day, her intolerance growing for a cheery couple that, not for the first time, had tried to engage with her as they sat silently waiting for the roulette to resume. She thought of Graeme's face the moment he had been laid bare. Rotating the chips in her perspiring palms, she hadn't noticed the exchange of words between the croupiers. Impatiently she waited for the game to recommence.

One of the waitresses brought the croupier a glass of water. A man next to her joked with him that he should be ready for a long night, before he glanced over at Sarah.

'Please,' Sarah curtly urged the croupier impatiently. 'If you don't mind.'

'Of course, madam.' He began the routine. In her mind, she was sure that he was going slower than the last one, having already pushed her chips onto the numbers with quick certainty.

For half an hour her irritation grew with the previously cheery couple, now seemingly subdued, after having a run of bad luck, as they deliberated over their stakes. They went back and forth, each citing anniversaries or birthdays. At each loss they bemoaned the people for not being lucky or not choosing other ones. When her mother's birthday came in, he let out an expression of affection for his favourite mother-in-law. After that failed to come up after another ten spins, they soon changed the number back once again to their anniversary. The repeated lack of success was quietly passed off without comment, their enthusiasm briefly renewed when they switched to his favourite footballer's number, who had scored the winning goal in the cup. This elation was overshadowed when the mother-in-law's birthday came in two spins later. Another few turns after they chased the missed opportunity, they lost half of their remaining money on the number that once again became illusive. This subsequent run of failure led to them becoming slightly fractious. However, when they became aware that their frustration was being noticeable to the others on the table, the woman then affected a laugh and offered a couple of fatalistic platitudes.

Sarah tried to block them out but, as with them, her luck began to falter, in her mind the couple's voices getting louder and breaking her focus.

With their last few chips the couple made an unsuccessful request to gain the birthday of the croupier, who politely declined. They then began a restrained debate about what they should go on next. They noticed Sarah placing a large bet on black, and the woman quickly followed suit with half their chips, a move defying her husband who had instructed her to go on red. Sarah had placed heavily on black. As the ball settled on red he quietly groaned at the sight. Deflecting from the situation the woman quickly started to mull over where to go next.

The woman tried to encourage him. 'Black, no I think we should go with red. Split the rest over two numbers. We should stick to 13 and 34. Our first houses. No, wait, put one on zero. I have a feeling. It is due to come up,' she continued desperately as if she were compelling the number to comply. 'Yes, zero is going to come good for us.'

'So, love,' he sighed wearily, 'are we going with numbers and red or just zero, and do you mean red as well? I'm not sure about red.' He hesitated as he withdrew his hand containing the chips. 'I think perhaps...'

'Oh for the love of God,' Sarah said under her breath as she decisively placed her chips.

'Excuse me? What did you say?' The woman broke away to respond to her.

'It's ten quid. Please, for the sake of everyone's sanity, will you just make a bloody decision. I can't bear it. Half an hour you have sat here wittering on. Because if I have to hear one more account of your life stories by number... try funerals, that might seem more apt.'

'Please, ladies,' the croupier intervened. 'We are here to enjoy our evening. Now, if you would like to place your bets.'

As the wheel began to spin, the husband restrained his wife from putting them all in. Instead she put two chips on red.

Sarah lost all of her split stakes, including a wager on black. Annoyed, she reassessed her chips.

'Ha,' the woman sneered at Sarah as she coveted her winnings.

'Yes, well done, you can buy yourself a bottle of cava and a packet of crisps,' Sarah retorted. 'All in and you can go crazy with another.' She flicked a chip over to them. 'Get a decent bottle on me.'

The man appealed to the croupier. 'Are you going to allow this woman to behave like this?'

'Thank you, sir, if you don't mind, madam, I'm sorry but I think that perhaps you might want to take a break.'

'No, I'm fine. If you could just do your job.' She then turned to the couple. 'Why don't you go over to the slot machines? You can't do any worse.'

The croupier signalled to the manager who began to make his way over.

'Is there a problem?'

Sarah pre-empted the croupier's response. 'No, there's no problem apart from these two.'

'You are welcome, madam, but perhaps it has been a long day. Can I ask if you are staying in our hotel?'

'So now I am being watched.' She then picked up an empty glass. 'A shame the waiters aren't as prompt. Would it be too much to ask for another drink? It isn't as if I am disappointing the house.'

A third staff member joined them. 'How are we this evening?' He looked to the serious-faced manager who joined in with the concerted enquiry.

'Save your breath.' She slid off her stool in resignation, her legs stiffly readjusting to standing. In front of her a pool of chips that she had no account of. She pushed them across the baize towards the croupier. 'Here. I doubt they pay you enough.' The croupier, nearly successful in suppressing his delight, quietly thanked her as he was taking his cue from the manager.

The walk up to her room failed to give her any inclination towards sobriety. Kicking off her shoes she lay back on the bed. The quiet gave an open forum to the flooding-back of memory. Looking out into the overhead dark skies she yearned for morning, for daylight. To leave this place. No patience to wait for room service she took a bottle of wine from the fridge to wash down what would make her sleep until morning. When it didn't have the immediate effect, she drank a further bottle until she passed out.

CHAPTER 35

SARAH AWOKE AT the disturbance of a loud party making their way along the corridor. Her throat dry, she reached out for the glass of water that she was sure she had put there. The realisation that she was about to vomit came soon after sitting up. Stumbling from the bed she staggered to the bathroom as quickly as she was able. Guiding herself by the little light from the city light that faintly glowed through the distorted bathroom glass, and making it to the toilet just in time, she repeatedly convulsed. Time after time her body continued to violently purge itself, until there was nothing left.

Gathering herself up to the sink, she turned on the tap to rinse her mouth, after which she turned to go back to the bedroom. This last conscious move was something that she had a vague recollection of when she awoke the next morning on the floor.

Gradually coming around, she steadily got up, only just able to see the room by the morning light breaking through the peripheral gaps in the curtains. A splitting pain held her head in what felt a tightening vice-like grip, her body aching from the hours on the hard floor. Unable to find her watch, she turned on the television to see the time. Instead of the usual breakfast news, a panel of commentators were discussing the Prime Minister's Questions from Parliament that lunchtime. She quickly turned the bright screen off, before taking a cold water from the minibar.

The chilled liquid made her wince as it passed down her raw throat, the quick consumption of which she anticipated she would struggle to keep down. Exhausted she recalled the previous night. The perpetual flow of money that had ceaselessly changed hands pervaded her dreams, leaving her unsure of what was reality and imaginings. What had been won or lost or even how she got back to the room. The smell of alcohol and vomit reeked through every pore and breath.

Sarah avoided the mirror as she went for her shower, the flow of water over her aching body failing to make her feel cleansed. She felt a sharp pain as the pressure struck her face. Lifting her hand to her forehead she could feel a lump had formed. Her reluctance to go to the mirror now had to be faced. The bruise that was beginning to come through sat below her hairline. Her hands shook as she brushed down her hair in an attempt to conceal it. Unavoidable, even in the soft lighting, her watery eyes were fused with red, her face ragged. She turned her attention to finding some painkillers in her wash bag. With great relief she found a couple left.

After her shower, she felt a greater need to escape the suffocation of the room. In the wardrobe she took each of her unworn best items purchased on the first day. In careful deliberation she carried out her usual methodical make-up routine, giving careful and particular attention to the part of the bruise that was showing.

She packed up all of her belongings into her case and two carrier bags then put them onto the bed. A hazy telephone call through to her bank gave her the sobering knowledge that once the hotel bill had been paid, and after Izzy's cheque had cleared that morning, there was less than £400 left. The numbers, as they came into her head, provoked an urge to have one more go in the casino. The temptation was close to overwhelming to go downstairs and to know that by early evening she could set herself up for the next few weeks.

There was one number in her phone. There was one place that she remembered she could go to stay if 'ever she needed a bolthole'. If it had been a genuine offer she was about to find out – Graeme's cousin Hannah, who she had only visited twice in the last five years.

As Sarah prepared to leave the hotel room, she resigned herself to the notion that it would be fate if Hannah was in. And if there would be a room or there would not. If not, then plan B. Plan B to be determined in the face of no response from Hannah.

Settling up the hotel bill, that was more expensive than she thought, had left her much lighter than she had anticipated. Checking the itemisation on the bill on the way out, it read as an exhaustive list that even the receptionist had given a double glance to as she checked the computer for any last-minute additions. Sarah's sudden recollection of taking a chocolate bar raised a smile from the receptionist as she printed out the long receipt, telling Sarah that in the circumstances they were content to make it complimentary. Passing the casino on her way out, she anguished at the thought of the chips she had petulantly given away the previous night. Probably somewhere close to tenfold her remaining funds.

Outside on the pavement, the air was dank and it started to rain. The crisp atmosphere provided relief from the flushing embarrassment of the scrutiny at checkout, exacerbated by the overly warm reception area. Her anxiety at facing the uncertainty of what the day held increased the intensity of her dehydration.

The painkillers having hardly taken effect as she determined her direction, it was a welcome move to be leaving the hotel.

Overnight the temperature had dropped significantly enough for her to wrap herself tighter in her jacket. Pulling up her collar, she sought out a passing taxi, regretting that in her haste to get away from the hotel she hadn't taken them up on the offer to call her one. The apartment lay over the river. As they crossed over the bridge, she took out her phone as the cab made good time through. She quickly texted, 'Hi Hannah. I'm in London. Would it be OK to pop in for a coffee?'

As she neared Hannah's road, the taxi driver reaffirmed the address. Anxiously, and to buy her more time, she told him that the top of the road would be fine. On disembarking, she dropped her bags onto the pavement. The idea was now stupid. She hadn't seen or spoken to her in a while, after not making good on a promise to drop her a line from Germany, and yet she felt unwilling, almost unable, to contemplate where to go next. Five minutes later her phone went.

'Hey Sarah! Would love to. In all day.'

She felt a wave of relief. Hastily gathering up her belongings, she quickly arrived at Hannah's front door. Pushing the buzzer, still apprehensive, she looked towards the camera as she heard the door click.

'You know your way up!' Hannah peered over the banister, her hair up in a towel, the sight of which increased Sarah's unease as she knew she was just gatecrashing out of the blue.

Hannah greeted Sarah at the door where she wrapped her arms around her. 'This is a surprise! Did you send that text in my garden?' she laughed.

Sarah burst into tears, hugging her tightly. 'It's so good to see you.'

'Wow. You too. What's happened?' Sarah's embrace momentarily took her aback. She picked up Sarah's bags. 'Are you alright? No, of course not, stupid question.'

'I'm not sure.'

'OK. That sounds rather ominous. Come through. Let me get dressed and you can tell me all about it. It's that prat of a husband, I take it.'

'Hmm. I forgot how close you two are.'

She placed Sarah's bags down. 'This isn't a short visit to London, then?'

'I have no idea, but I'm not here to plant myself, don't worry. If you are busy, I can get a hotel, because...'

'Relax. It's good to see you. It could be good timing. Now, come through and we can catch up. Izzy and Seb are fine, aren't they?'

'Oh, absolutely. They are doing really well.'

In the sitting room, the last ember of an incense stick was burning on a coffee table, with an exercise mat sprawled in the middle. 'Oh.' Sarah took a step back as she was hit by the pungent aromas of the incense. 'Very atmospheric! You are still doing the yoga, then?'

'It keeps me balanced and able to retain a base level of sanity. Atmospheric? This is a new brand of incense I'm trying. Yes, a bit full-on.' She affected a grimace as she opened up a window. 'I'm not certain they even passed any kind of safety standard. They say "export quality" on them, but I'm not sure if that is supposed to be a reassurance to us, or a warning to the locals of Bengaluru who find them on the market stalls. But I'm confident they must at least repel a whole host of bad karma.'

Sarah smiled. 'I'm glad I called you, Hannah. Thanks.'

'Me too. Now, make yourself at home. I'll be five minutes. Or you can put the kettle on if you like.'

'Sure. That would be great.' Sarah deliberated over what she was going to say to her. The relief at seeing her and finding a safe place now abated the urge to reveal much more. But she felt she owed it to Hannah to tell her the basics, without getting drawn into the details. She would tell her that they were separating. It had been a mutual decision. And she knew Hannah wouldn't push her for more.

Sarah took some cups from the cupboard then selected a couple of choices of green tea from an array of boxes. Waiting for the kettle to boil, she wondered where Graeme was, if he had gone back to see Lucy. Her thoughts were then interrupted by Hannah's return. 'Green tea? I think that is a good idea, but there are a couple of bottles of wine if you want one later. Top cupboard. It's a gift, a vegan merlot from one of my friends.'

'Thanks but I'll pass for the moment. No offence meant. I would pass on any wine right now.'

'Probably best. It looks like you've had a heavy few days.'

Her remark made Sarah once again more acutely aware of her state. 'I'm not a great sight at the moment.' The only food that she had had that day was the sugar fix from the chocolate bar.

As Sarah poured the hot water into the pot, Hannah noticed her bruise against the light of the kitchen window, then leaned in to give her a closer examination. 'Ouch. That doesn't look good. Are you going to tell me what happened?' Hannah lifted her hair. 'Is this him?' she enquired attentively.

'Oh God no. He hasn't, no. I promise. I fell in the bathroom. No really, I did. This is down to my stupidity, trust me. Of the many things Graeme has done, that isn't one of them.'

'Many things? Look, I know you have a strong loyalty, but this would stay with me. If you want to talk.'

'It's a mess. Without going into detail…' She continued, 'And I have no idea where to go, where to start.' She burst into tears. 'Sorry, I have just landed this on you. This all feels a bit surreal. How did I not see this coming? See the signs. I have been such an idiot, not just him, but do you mind if I don't talk about it. I'm just exhausted. How about you? Tell me about how you are.' Her nervous energy now began to take over.

'Yes, let's talk about how you are. That would be good. How's Marcus? I want to know more about this man you haven't yet introduced to any of us. Last time we spoke you were off somewhere.'

'Listen,' Hannah took the cup off her, 'I think that you need to get some sleep. Why don't you go and soak in a bath, have a couple of hours' rest. Don't worry about making any decisions right now. Give me five minutes and I will make up a bed. We can talk when you are a little more rested.'

'But I've just got here. I really don't think I can sleep.'

'Trust me, I think once your head hits the pillow... I will go out and pick something up for dinner and we can talk then.'

After two further protestations that she was OK, Sarah relented and, as Hannah predicted, the effects of the hot bath and lying on the soft sheets had the desired outcome. It was nearly dark outside when she finally awoke, spicy cooking aromas from a soup that Hannah was making motivating her to get up. The exhaustion still with her, she threw on some clothes to go through.

'That smells wonderful.'

'Can't go wrong with soup. I've also picked up some nice fresh rolls from the baker's. Come here and taste it.' She handed Sarah a spoon from the drawer.

'Oh, that is so good.' She leaned over for a closer look. 'What's this?'

'Ezogelin. It's Turkish. Red lentils, onions, paprika, mint...'

As Hannah continued, the mention of Turkey brought her round again to thinking of Izzy and Seb.

'And I forgot to mention that you put the bulgur in ten minutes from the end along with the mint.' She turned to see Sarah deep in thought. 'Listen, you know that you don't have to tell me anything. But, I think that it might help.'

'I wouldn't know where to start. It isn't all his fault.'

'You've said that twice now. I'm not going to judge. Just

say it as it comes,' Hannah responded in a quietly attentive manner, as Sarah's reticence made her struggle to be coherent.

Sarah began to busy herself with getting out the placemats and cutlery. 'Everything that has happened is because... You should know, really, I have done some stupid things.'

'Tell me what happened. But no self-pity. Don't worry about what I think, or feel guilty about Graeme.'

Her directness focused Sarah. 'I haven't seen him for days. He was here in London. Actually, I wondered if he might call you.'

'He did. He Skyped. He said that he was planning a family something or other for your next birthday and wondered what I thought of the idea and if I would go. Asking my opinion.' She rolled her eyes. 'I thought it was strange.'

'Now you know he was just seeing if I was here.'

'Why can't he ever just be upfront?' Hannah asked.

'Most likely he thought if I was in another room he would see it on your face. He is always saying that he spots micro-aggressions and such like. Apparently years of watching patients withholding disclosure.'

'Is he really that bad? Bloody hell, I thought he was a bit intense.'

Sarah hesitated before answering. 'Did you see him much, you know, when you were growing up?'

'No, well not too much, as I was quite a few years younger. But I remember when his father died he became very serious, almost overnight. Resentful even. He found it difficult with his mother. The more he tried to help, the more she pushed him away. But listen. He is a grown man. Whatever he has done, that is on him.'

'He doesn't really talk about his father, even to me. I only really know what I do from Lydia. An impressive man, your uncle. Mentioned in despatches for a rescue in his time in the military and a highly rated surgeon.'

367

'Yes, he was a wonderful man, he was kind and generous. It was awful, he died of lung cancer. I was only young when it happened. But you know he and Graeme didn't get on that well.'

'I sort of got that impression but he just said his father was a very quiet, reserved man. But nothing else to my mind was significant.'

'No, so he won't have told you. What is it with my family and secrets? So, the last time Graeme saw him alive was about a week before he passed away. Graeme was only about sixteen, no, of course he must have been about seventeen.'

'He was seventeen. Sorry, carry on.'

'He was leaving the house to go back to boarding school. I don't know what words transpired between them, they had obviously had a bad argument, but his last words to Graeme, apparently, were that he told him was glad to not have to see him grow up. He shouldn't consider medicine, he wasn't fit to practise. Well, words to that effect, you have to bear with me, it was a long time ago since I heard it.'

'Wow. That's terrible! I didn't know that. Why on earth would he say that?'

'Sarah, as I said, I was young when this all happened and wasn't told very much at the time.' She continued as she sighed in frustration, 'I thought with you being his wife he would have said something. But you know our family. If we don't want to acknowledge something, it doesn't exist. I only found out the real version when I heard Aunt Lydia and my mother talking a few years later, and when I asked my mother later, but she wouldn't be pressed too hard on what happened.'

'Please, just whatever you know.'

'It isn't very much but I will tell you as much as I was told. There had been a party. Graeme's sister, who had tagged along, wanted to leave, she was only fifteen. Everyone was drunk or high and the party had got out of hand. When she wanted to go, he refused to take her home, as he wanted to stay. However, when it came to an official inquest, he testified that she must have taken something after he left the party, saying she was OK at the time he left. Everyone involved said they didn't remember anything. One of his friends also testified she had got the drugs from a dealer from the city, who, surprise, surprise, they couldn't track down.'

'Oh my God. What happened after that?'

'It all came out, as Graeme's father knew the father of another boy who was involved. It had been Graeme that had brought the drugs and given them to her. Who knows why, perhaps because she was annoying him. I don't know what happened after that but they found her dead in one of the bedrooms the following morning. Choked on her own vomit.'

'Christ, that is horrible.'

'Anyway, his father confronted Graeme and he crumbled. It was all brushed under the carpet. That's what money and connections do for you. We were told the inquest version and nobody really talked about her. You can imagine how devastating it was for his parents. But, I don't think we will ever hear the full story.'

'I can't believe this. That's horrific, what a tragedy. She was only fifteen.' She sat down at the table. 'What was going through his mind? But I don't understand why he wouldn't tell me...'

'Do you think you would get an honest answer if you asked him? But then again, it's hard to imagine what the guilt of carrying something around like that would do to a person. He was very close to her, by all accounts. A little wayward but a sweet thing – long blond hair, piercing blue eyes which Mum said she was sure made her get away with more than most. Not to mention bright, a promising artist and...'

Sarah stopped listening as she gave way to a sick feeling in the pit of her stomach. A conjured-up image of his sister was formed instantaneously in her mind, then to six months before and the first moment when she saw the girl that had broken the peace at Graeme's leaving party.

'What is it?'

'Nothing. It's just the shock. I had no idea. Do you mind if we don't talk about Graeme anymore, Hannah,' she replied insistently, making a conscious effort not to snap. 'It's just, I feel that I need to not go back to talking about Graeme. Anyway, I really would like to hear about Marcus, tell me about him, your trip, your plans.'

'Are you sure you are OK?'

'Hannah, please don't fuss, I just need to catch up on more sleep.' Sarah made a further effort to look more attentive. 'So, where are you going first, on this trip?'

She tried to stay focused on listening, but the revelation about Graeme had shaken her to the core. Half an hour later, picking up on Sarah's lack of interest, Hannah called it a night.

Before they went to bed Sarah asked Hannah if she could stay for a few days. The trip that Hannah was taking with Marcus was scheduled for just two days' time. She offered her the apartment if she wanted it for the next six weeks, saying it would be doing her a favour to look after it. Sarah, failing to conceal her relief, hugged her, feeling she had been given some temporary breathing space.

As soon as she turned the lights out, with no distraction, she began to go over and over in her mind what she had been struggling to reconcile herself with earlier, what had been said about Graeme, then bringing her to how they had met.

1989

Sarah had no recollection of how long she had been sitting on the step when a man came and sat down beside her. He didn't say anything at first. After a moment he reached into his pocket to hand her a handkerchief.

'Are you going to tell me things can't be that bad?'

'Actually no, I imagine they probably are.'

'Yes, brilliant, thank you,' she snapped back. 'Don't give up the day job.'

'That could be an even bleaker outlook for me then.' In Graeme's later recollections, he said that when she looked up at him he knew that she was the one. What he didn't say at the time was that he remembered her from a couple of years ago when she came into the practice he was working at. Her mother had gone to see one of his colleagues. It was another of her periodic appointments to pacify Sarah's father when she accepted he was at maximum strain. The latest occasion being when she had been coming down from a manic high and would say that she would consider medication, talk through her options, which always resulted in a prescription that was collected, but would not long after be discarded. Sarah hadn't noticed Graeme at the time as she sat in the waiting room with her mother.

Two years on she sat on the step next to him, where she had come to a standstill not more than a few yards after leaving the charity shop. Her father had died a few days before, after no warning, from a heart attack. He was gone in a moment, the reality of which was now only beginning to set in. The previous week they had both been talking about her plans for the future, reminiscing about the past. He now lay in a morgue, a funeral only half agreed on. Giving herself the task of taking some of her father's belongings to the charity shop provided her with some respite from her mother's silent grief.

To that day she didn't remember Graeme's face as he sat on the step with her, just the initial reassurance that someone had stopped to talk. The first time she really looked at him was when he suggested they go to the nearby pub to find somewhere more comfortable to talk, offering the enticement of some of the best West Country ciders and ales on the planet.

At the time he said he was a doctor, but she wasn't listening and she had very little interest in someone that was a passing shoulder. She had had enough of doctors recently, who were unable to give her answers as to why her father, who never had a sick day in his life, had suddenly dropped dead of a heart attack. Being at the pub was better than going home, another couple of hours' respite from trying to communicate with, or raise the spirits of, her mother who had barely responded to her since coming back from the hospital. It had been the first time she had been able to open up to anyone. He listened, as he understood her loss, as if he knew her and what was going through her mind a moment before she disclosed it. He encouraged her to talk about the best things about her father, the good and difficult times, without compelling her to feel guilty for doing it so soon. She felt as if it were fate that he should be there.

It was only at the pub, when he went back for another round of drinks, she noticed for the first time the contrast of how they looked. He was immaculately dressed and clearly someone who looked after themselves. Her hands clasped around the near-empty glass, she was in a shabby Soviet coat, a bargain picked up from an army surplus store. But as they talked he didn't seem so different from her, especially when she found out that he had also studied at Cambridge. They talked of the same places they knew and mostly pubs that they had in common.

The afternoon merged into evening and as it had become darker they moved inside. She wasn't sure what the time was when she stood up, offering to buy the latest round, less cognitive of the fact that she had less than £3 in her purse. Unaware as she searched her pockets the landlord was having a quiet word with Graeme, who had been unsuccessful in preventing her from going to the bar. Taking her out of the pub she responded to his comforting arm and suggestion of a coffee by pushing him gently back against the wall of the walkway, kissing him, then on an impulse suggesting they go into the hotel whose sign they happened to be under at the time.

It was in the early hours that she woke up with shaky recollections of the afternoon. He lay next to her not stirring as she got up for some water. It wasn't until she peered through the window that she knew where she was. A hotel that she passed almost daily, only once having been in there for lunch. She gathered together her belongings, dressing quietly. She contemplated waking him but decided against it. Instead, she took a sheet of hotel notepaper into the bathroom and quickly began scribbling a note. 'Sorry I had to go.' She hesitated as she prepared to continue with the words 'thank you', but she wrote them nevertheless, unable to think of anything else. Her haste quickened by the sound of him turning over. 'Thank you for being there.' A failure to decide on anything further left her merely signing off, 'Sarah'.

On the side was his wallet, from which she took one of his business cards. She would send him the money for the hotel at least. The sound of her creaking down the antiquated stairs brought the attention of one the early morning staff, who quizzically peered around the kitchen door. She was greeted by the smell of breakfast being prepared as an unkempt-looking employee gave her a knowing wink, whilst he was carrying a stack of plates through to the dining room.

Once through the front door she hurried down the street, not looking back. She arrived home, feeling guilty as she saw her mother asleep in her father's chair, the television still playing loudly. She put a blanket over her and, as she stirred, told her she would make her a cup of tea.

Since the day that he had died, her mother barely moved

from the house. Sarah brought back basic food supplies from the local shop, although neither had any real appetite. Their well-meaning neighbour from the local church brought round soups and bakes that she then struggled to get her mother to eat. Sarah thanked the woman on the doorstep, who each time would offer, along with others who came to offer their condolences, to help 'if they needed anything'. Her mother never came to the door or asked who it was. On one occasion Sarah gratefully took the neighbour up on her offer by asking if she could pick up their order from the grocer's when she was in town, closing the door quickly as she could hear her mother's less than appreciative speculations as to the motivation for her offers of help and telling the neighbour to 'sod off and take Jesus with her'. After that Sarah would try and intercept anyone before they could ring the bell.

After a week, the house, which had always been kept so clean, had become cluttered and musty as the windows and curtains were kept shut. When her mother got out of bed she would just go to her husband's chair and switch on the television. Sarah had to cajole her into taking a bath, or eating some toast. Some days she considered letting in the neighbour from church, to see if such a confrontation would shake her out of it.

Instead, she tried shouting at her mother, using her father to motivate her. Family albums were taken out. She resurrected anecdotes of good times, tough times. Boxing up a few of her father's things was the only thing that provoked a reaction. She selected a few unsentimental items, a couple of jumpers that hadn't been worn, a coat that had had one wear after he contested that the sleeves were too short, and a couple of books. All the pent-up grief, and the revelation that Sarah wasn't even wanted, came out as she flew into a fury, pulling at the box, Sarah fighting for its possession as her mother raged her resentment, hanging on with all her strength as the fight gradually ran its course. Sarah was prepared for the anger, she welcomed it, but did not anticipate the resentment towards her. She told Sarah she had got in the way of the life they should have had, how she was ungrateful for everything that they had given her, saying her father wouldn't have had the heart attack if he wasn't as worried about her out all night drinking. How he had worked all the hours to pay for her education. She could see in her mother's eyes that it wasn't knee-jerk or grief, which she later apologetically contested.

It was a week before she took out Graeme's card. Its clean crisp printing. The last memory seeming anything but that. Thinking that £25 should cover it, she took an extra shift at the café a friend of the family owned, where she already had a part-time job. It was her choice to take the room. Her insistence. Finding the words to write was a greater task than on the morning she left. Especially as she had learned by his card that he was a psychiatrist. 'Glad that you were there. I wanted to send you this. Sarah.' On the card she could see that his practice was close by, somewhere that she had been with her mother, nevertheless she decided to send it by post. A week later they bumped into each other in the supermarket. He was awkward, aloof in front of one of his colleagues, who he fleetingly introduced her to. He wished her well as if she was getting over a cold, then quickly moved on, his colleague turning back with a smile as they exchanged words.

For the following two weeks after the funeral, Sarah stayed with her mother as they communicated through the medium of cleaning, sorting and television, as she gradually re-engaged her with life, the first being an answer to a question on one of her mother's quiz shows. 'What is the river that runs through Paris?' They suddenly began laughing at a hapless contestant answering in a panic who said it was 'The Nile'.

After feeling confident enough that she could leave her mother, she began preparing to go back to university.

Her books not touched in a month, she felt it was the right time to leave. Her spell of sobriety had also given her some renewed energy. Telephoning her friend Ruby provided her with welcome relief from the life that had been in suspension since the news of her father. The trivialities of who was seeing who, what had happened at the usual parties and even a new Indian restaurant opening up nearby, she found a comfort. A reassurance that everything would be as she left it.

With two days before she was due to return to Cambridge, she ran around making sure everything was in place, leaving instructions for delivery of orders at the grocer's, papers from the newsagent's, and lastly she called in to see her mother's friend who promised to let her know if her mother was struggling. It was getting late by the time she got home. Placing her keys on the table she saw a note with a name and telephone number. Graeme 783956.

She picked up the piece of paper, taking a moment to prepare for the inquisition when she went through to the sitting room.

'So, Graeme? He sounds nice.'

'He is, I mean was, anyway, it's nothing,' she joked, 'just a passing acquaintance.' Sarah answered knowing full well that any information was about to be followed by an inquisition. She kept details of previous boyfriends in Cambridge to herself. Any small disclosure of information Sarah made in mentioning someone was duly seized upon.

'Is? Was? Details please, young lady,' her mother had teased her. 'Who is he? What does he do?'

'Oh, nobody, a volunteer at the charity shop who wanted to give up a receipt for some of Dad's things.'

And her mother left it at that.

The next morning, as she was finishing breakfast, the phone went in the hallway. When she picked up, she heard Graeme's voice. He sounded to her as if they had known each other for a while. No hint of reservation in his voice that his call may not be well received.

'Yes. Hello, Graeme. How are you?' She tried to be indifferent but her voice broke slightly.

'I'm going to take you to lunch today. I'll pick you up around 12.00.'

'Actually, woah, that is a little confident of you. But, I'm set to go back to university tomorrow.'

'Cambridge. Yes, you said.'

'Oh. Yes,' she replied with no recollection. 'I remember.' Her nervousness intensified as she had forgotten just about everything they had talked about.

'There's a place I want to take you to. It's a cracking pub, great food. Pick up where we left off.'

'I don't know if that is a good idea,' she responded, not sure if he was trying to be funny, being very cool about what had happened or this was something that he did all the time.

'*De Brevitate Vitae*. Remember?'

'Sorry, what?'

'Life is short etc, etc. Seneca. "Indulge yourself" and all that. You started quoting the ancients.'

'Really? I said that? Wow. I didn't even know I knew that,' she laughed. 'Hang on, I thought the Stoics were about moderation.'

'Alright, perhaps that isn't exactly true, but they never tasted the steak and ale pie from the Rose and Crown. A whole philosophy could have changed off the back of Mrs Green's Friday specials board.'

'If you are trying to get me to laugh…' She broke out in a smile whilst maintaining a serious tone. 'I suppose just lunch. Just out of curiosity, that's all.'

'Mrs Green will be delighted, I'll see you at 12.00.' After he confirmed the address he promptly rang off as they were interrupted by a patient knocking at his door.

He was ten minutes late by the time he arrived at Sarah's house. Enough time for her to contemplate creeping regret, right up to the point when he pulled up outside. Unfortunately, her mother had caught wind of the conversation. Believing instead that she was watching TV and preparing to impart the woes of the weather forecast, Sarah only realised that her mother had been listening when she joined Sarah at the window. Her mother's interest increased when she saw his car – a red Mercedes. Sarah knew that underneath her mother was contemplating some comment about his being flash and such like. Before he could face the inevitable invite in and verbal thumbscrews, Sarah went outside to meet him. He had barely opened the door before she quickly encouraged him back into the car.

On the journey there, they talked about the weather, his car, then back again to the weather. With some relief they reached the pub. Once inside she insisted that Graeme go and find a table and she would bring over the drinks. Standing at the bar, the sight of the list of local ales and ciders brought about memories of the day they met. On the pumps she saw the names of drinks that she had a vague recollection of.

Now, in her sober state, she would have had the presence of mind to reject the offer of having a superb, yet lethal brew of 'Mad Mongoose' that she was sure she had tried at some stage. In an attempt to block out what would be the inevitable accompanying memories, she began asking the landlord, who was slowly drawing a pint of ale for her, about the brewery it came from. A smile came across her face as he told her about an 'earthy bitterness with an essence of citrus' in a way that seemed incongruous with a six-foot, bearded landlord in a heavy metal T-shirt. She thought what her dad would say, especially when, straight-faced, he presented the glass, concluding that it was 'a fruity little number'.

As she took her seat at a table in the corner, Graeme broke

what he could see was her prevailing awkwardness. 'Cirrus or cumulous or cumulonimbus?'

'Sorry, what?'

'The clouds? We should continue our detailed discussion about weather phenomena.'

'Yes, OK, very funny.' She picked up her drink to take a sip.

'So. Do you want to talk about when I last saw you? Are you OK?'

His remark caused her to blush. 'Um. Perhaps. I suppose. OK. That was not me. How I am, usually am. Not to say that I should feel bad.' Annoyed at herself for the realisation that she seemed to be offering an explanation, she continued spikily, 'Because blokes never feel bad, do they? Are you asking because women aren't supposed to...' She was going to say 'jump into bed with' but absence of memory brought her to a halt. She took another large sip of her drink. 'What is it with some men? I swear.' Floundering, she turned it around on him. 'What about you? Do you feel bad?'

'You really misunderstood,' he said, smiling bemusedly. 'Should I?'

'No,' she responded more calmly. 'Of course not.'

'I was asking how you were because you lost your father.'

'Oh.' Her third sip came in quick succession.

'But otherwise, yes, I wanted to see you. I thought that we had a good time. Well, aside from the devastating bereavement, and you nearly starting a fight with a biker that bumped into you, and me having to leave a substantial tip for the chambermaid.'

'OK, stop. I'm not sure I want to know.'

'It appears that two baskets of potato wedges and eight pints and a few slammers aren't as easily digestible as you thought.'

'Christ. Really?' She closed her eyes momentarily, cringing in embarrassment. 'I don't remember that. OK. Stop. Look,

I'm going to be frank. I don't remember a few parts about that night.'

'When you say "parts"?' he teased her.

'Alright.' She smiled. 'So whatever I told you, God knows what I told you, you should take it with a pinch of salt. But thank you, you know, for being there.'

'Not a problem. I'm glad I was. Probably not the best circumstances but… how about we start again?'

'OK. So. Just to get me up to speed. A doctor. So how does that go? Saved any lives this week?'

'Too many to count.' He smiled. 'So tell me more about your life in Cambridge. Being a mathmo. Now, that can't have been easy to admit to a stranger. You can see why I brought you out of the way of anyone who might recognise me.'

'Ha. That coming from a man who owns a pair of mother-of-pearl cufflinks and has ABBA cassettes in his car?' She raised her glass. 'Right back at you.'

Sarah thought back to that day in the pub. Sitting there until closing time, after which he dropped her back at home. They didn't talk about continuing to see each other until he offered to drive her back to Cambridge the next day. She thought about him most of the time, not giving in to the urge to call him if he failed to keep a promise of ringing her that evening. As he was on call most of the time she would catch the train back home to see him, spending the weekend at his apartment. It often felt surreal as she alternated between what felt like two existences, sometimes scoffing at how immature her life was in Cambridge and how she couldn't wait to start a life outside. On Fridays when he didn't travel up to see her she would buzz in anticipation for the weekend as she waited on the platform for the 14.45 train from Cambridge.

Her life in Cambridge during the week and her time spent away with Graeme couldn't have been more different. Her hometown felt as if it was being given a reintroduction, exploring new restaurants and bars, some of which had previously been beyond her means. She worked extra shifts at the restaurants where she had a part-time job, in an attempt to pay her way, but fell woefully short in her contribution, preferring it when they went to a local café where they would meet up for coffee, where she was more comfortable with the bill. But they would spend hours talking, sometimes into the evening.

Until then she had been happy living off modest means, owning just a bicycle and a shelf full of books. Although on the coldest of days she lamented the pitfall of not having a car. It was most acute when rattling over the cobbles on her bicycle, whilst trying to keep her shopping dry in her basket. Not to mention, numb fingers when she forgot her gloves and soaked trousers when a van hit the money shot of a deep puddle on the way to a lecture. But, from the minute she had walked into her college on her first day, even getting bellowed at by one of the porters for walking across the grass in the courtyard, she felt that this was where she belonged. In the two years she had been there, she had only had three boyfriends, none of which lasted beyond a couple of months. But Graeme, as she told her friend Ruby, was different, like no one she had met before. But to Sarah's occasional frustration, Ruby, the only friend of Sarah's he met, never got beyond saying in her impression of him that 'the jury was still out'.

On weekdays she would be wrapped up in scarf and gloves, the wind biting her face as she cycled through the streets, counting pennies for the necessities and taking grief from customers whose tips she relied upon. At the weekend, the comfort of his fresh leather-seated Mercedes, the restaurants and one weekend in a five-star hotel in London. It felt surreal when she dropped her bag back in halls upon her return.

In an attempt to keep up, one weekend she made all the arrangements. She booked a table at one of the best restaurants in Cheltenham, bought tickets for the literature festival and a night in one of the finest hotels on The Promenade. In an effort to not show that she was intimidated by its grandeur, she cast her eyes up around the lobby, only to be met with the sight of a pair of immaculate chandeliers lighting up the opulent Georgian reception. At the counter, feeling less at ease in her jeans and oversized jumper, she momentarily stumbled over confirming her name, making her go red. Even studying at one of the most prestigious universities in the world, with its splendid architecture, didn't compensate for the discomfort she felt after squeaking in her DMs across the spotlessly polished floors. At the confirmation by the receptionist of her booking, Graeme took over to upgrade from standard to superior room.

Although intending to pay for much of that weekend, Graeme didn't take her hint that they should go for a slighter cheaper wine or that she was too full for a dessert, baulking particularly at a soufflé that was at least two hours' wages. He watched her as he ordered the wine, then the fillet steak as she tried to enthuse about the good time they were having. All up, the meal at the restaurant was over a week's wages. After that, she relented to his suggestion that he should just pay when they went out.

Then a couple of months after they had first met, after an anxious rush to the chemist, the results of a test that she had barely been able to acknowledge told her that she was pregnant. The one night she had so little recollection of was the one for which she now hated herself for being so stupid. Having been so careful after that, she had been trying to put any legacy of that first night out of her mind. It was over a week after she took the test, when she was just beginning to come to terms with the bombshell, she decided to go and tell Graeme. Having promised to go and see her mother that weekend, she thought it best that she see him first.

The next day Sarah rushed through the station gates and onto the platform to catch her connecting train, which had just pulled in. Hurriedly leaping onto the train she hadn't been able to give Graeme a heads-up that she would be arriving early. Anticipating he would be at work, she used her last 10p coin to call his office where his diligent receptionist, Daisy, said that he wasn't due in for another two hours.

In the time it took to reach Gloucester she would have more than enough time to prepare how she was going to break it to him. Since the result from the test had begun to sink in, all she could think about was how he would react, and if she would be dealing with this on her own. In her memory she trawled through any conversations of anything that he had said that would give her a clue.

Her studies were everything, she couldn't ever see herself settling down. 'Commitment is for your patients,' she recalled, laughing awkwardly if they wandered by accident onto the topic of life plans. And she hadn't thought beyond that. Being accepted into Cambridge had been a dream, and even though she knew it was by the skin of her teeth, it was everything to her. He knew it, having graduated there many years before her. This was her last year. After that a loose plan, her top choice, was to carry on studying.

The impending reality check that she knew was coming, whatever she decided to do, would change everything, bringing into focus everything about her relationship with him. How little time they had spent in each other's lives outside their time together. She remembered making a passing joke in the car about him, saying her family couldn't take the shock if she introduced them to a public school boy, and worse, a Tory. Telling him they 'should keep it on the down-low' as a joke one night to emphasise the point – a term that she had picked up through watching an American crime show. It was one of many similar jokes that she had made whilst being driven in the expensive sports car, or being unable to afford to pick up the bill in the exorbitantly priced restaurant or when she pre-empted any possible future invites to meet his wealthy friends. When he said that he pitied his best mate who was getting married at the tender age of twenty-eight, she made a point of scoffing at anyone who wanted to settle down. Being 'squeezed into some Victorian Christian dynamic'. 'Settle? What is that? Coming to a halt, wearing a groove into a sofa, watching opiate soap operas, and waiting for your hair to fall out or rip it out yourself?' Then she recalled another one of his red lines: not wanting kids with snotty noses, who were just emotionally draining money pits. 'Settle? Once you settle, come to a halt, you never get out of it.'

Since finding out, she wished that her father had been there to call. She and Ruby talked of the multitude of his possible reactions. Her exams were only a few months away. She had her whole life ahead of her. Rationalising it exposed how little she thought she knew him, a number of variables all seemingly feasible. The only thing that she confirmed in her mind was that he should know. Then she would be able to move forward with whatever direction that was.

When Ruby pressed her as to how she really felt about him, she dismissed any idea that she should indulge in some happy-ever-after scenario. But, earlier when she had been sitting in the carriage on the long train journey with little else to do but think, she considered a future with him. A commitment that made her half repelled and half fantasise about. But when all was said and done she would know the minute she saw the look on his face. It was all in the first reaction. He had told her that. A conversation about patients' emotional responses now taking on a new context.

She had almost no sleep the night before and was struggling to keep her eyes open. Finally she succumbed to a nap for the last part of the journey, just after asking a lady next to her if she would give her a nudge as they approached Gloucester. The words that she had been rehearsing since the shock of the test now set to memory.

After alighting the train, getting closer to his apartment her rehearsed words gradually dissipated. Like grain running through her fingers, her sudden bout of anxiety brought her to a standstill outside his apartment. Her hands were trembling, making her question whether or not she should go to her mother's first. Get some sleep so she was ready to deal with his response.

As she prepared to ring the bell, one of his neighbours opened the door and held it open for her as she went inside. Without further hesitation she knocked at Graeme's door. She could hear music being played, smiling at the fact that he was at least going to be in a fit state and that he was in a good mood. With no answer she knocked again.

Her mind preoccupied, every thought came to a shuddering halt as a woman opened the door. A coffee in hand, and looking as if she was near dressed for the office, she gave Sarah an impatient once-over.

'Yes, can I help you?'

Sarah's immediate surprise and curiosity gave her a rush of anxiety. All of which she fought to suppress, in the face of someone who was treating her as an inconvenience. 'I'm here to see Graeme. I was looking for Graeme.' At her stammering request, the woman smirked, seemingly making a point of seeing through her discomfort. 'I'm Sarah.'

'Just wait a moment,' the woman responded impatiently, before pushing the door to. She then briefly reopened it. 'If you just wait here, I'll get him.' Before she had reclosed the door, she made a point of calling out loudly to Graeme, 'Dr Hughes, I think your services are required.'

After a moment, Sarah pushed open the door to see her making her way down the hall to Graeme's bedroom.

Unnoticed by the woman, Sarah followed her down there.

Before confronting Graeme Sarah hesitated outside his room.

'It's one of your waifs and strays. Sarah?' the woman announced. 'Scruffy-looking thing. Looks like some sort of refugee. Anyway, I've left her in the hallway. Who is she?'

'Oh. I know who it will be. It's nobody,' he replied casually. 'I'll deal with it. It's OK.'

'It isn't OK, Graeme. You shouldn't encourage them.'

'She isn't a patient, seriously, I wouldn't be that stupid. She's just a kid who's grieving. A mate's little sister,' he sniffed dismissively. 'You know when they find out that you are a shrink, they start banging on and you can't shut them up.'

'Well, whoever she is, you shouldn't let her think she can just turn up unannounced.' The room went silent for a second. 'I will see you later.'

Sarah ducked into the bathroom, her heart pounding as she waited for the woman to leave.

At the sound of the front door closing, she took a moment to compose herself before going in to confront Graeme.

'What the hell is going on, Graeme?' she challenged him angrily.

'Christ, you made me jump,' he joked in feigned exaggeration. 'This is a surprise, you are early.'

She was further angered by his indifference. 'Don't even think of saying that this isn't what you think it is.'

'No, it probably is. Look, Sarah, you and I, we've been seeing each other for what six or seven weeks. That hardly makes us married.'

'But I thought...'

'You thought that we were serious?' He picked a shirt out of the wardrobe, and began deliberating over a tie. 'I like you, no, really I do. If you thought anything else, that's on you.'

Tears began to fall down her face. 'You said... shit. It

doesn't matter. You arrogant…' she hesitated. 'What the hell was I thinking?'

'Did I ask you if you were seeing anyone else?'

'Sorry, what? I wouldn't,' she replied indignantly.

He held up a pair of ties. 'What do you think? The yellow one or blue one?' Before she could react he quickly continued, 'Come on. Lighten up. I'm joking, even I'm not that bad. Sarah, I do want to keep seeing you. As for Steph, she's a colleague and a mate. We just worked until late.'

'And she was in the guest room. Sure.'

'I didn't say that, but it's nothing, she is going through a tough divorce. But no, I'm not seeing her. Too high maintenance for one thing.' He feigned exasperation. 'We had too much to drink. You know how it is.'

'No, Graeme, I don't. Don't even… This is insane. No, I know this isn't on me,' she continued angrily. 'Who do you think you are? I heard you, you know that. Telling her about me. A mate's little sister?'

'Of course I knew you were there. I know what you are like.' He hung his tie loosely around his neck as he picked up a coffee. 'I was teaching you a lesson.' He watched her as he took a drink. 'I don't like being checked up on. Did it not occur to you that I may have been protecting you?'

'What? How?!' she responded incredulously.

'You know how private you are. You won't even introduce me to your family. If anyone was being non-committal it is you.'

'So, this is my fault? If you haven't noticed, my mother is struggling with my father being gone. It just isn't a good time to introduce you at the moment.'

'Listen, how about you stay here until I get back from work. I'll be finished by four, we can talk then. We don't have to end things. You might not believe me but that was the only time I have seen anyone else since we have been together.'

She listened and, despite her instinct to leave, she began focusing on how she should tell him. To get it over with, so she could know any ties to him were cut before she left. Everything that she had rehearsed dissolved in the face of the previous few minutes.

As she stood trying to find just the first few words, he continued, 'You're right. I'm sorry. My fault. I should have been clearer. But now we know where we stand. Honestly, I didn't know that you felt like this. I'm not saying I can't fully commit.'

'You think a lot of yourself, don't you, Graeme. Shit, I… there is something, something important that I need to tell you.'

'But whatever it is, it will have to be put on hold. Unless anyone has died or something.'

'No, of course, that would be the only serious option. And yes, great choice of words, classy.'

'Alright,' he laughed dismissively, 'I'm sure I can't wait to hear about it, but as I said, it will have to be later.' He picked up his keys from a dressing table. 'Oh the stresses and strains of being a student. I envy you. Wait until you hit the real world. Spare a thought for me, I've got a management meeting, in which I have almost no say, then a run of difficult patients, a paranoid schizophrenic, two, no, three depressives and an over-achieving neurotic.' She avoided him as he came over to kiss her. 'Sorry, but I really have to go, but hey, everything is good and I'll be able to give you my full and undivided attention tonight.'

'Very generous of you.'

'Look, I wasn't going to say but I have a surprise for you, for us. I was thinking that next week we could go away.'

'What, something that you are going to book at the office? You are so full of it. You know, you have done me a favour. It was a mistake coming here.'

'Don't overreact. We can just put this thing behind us. I promise Steph was a one-off. I know you want to stay. I will see you when I get back.'

He didn't wait for her to answer when she said nothing.

The apartment fell silent. The whirlwind of events over the last few minutes went as quickly as they came. It felt surreal to her, and that she had been on the very brink and yet not told him. A split second away from blurting it out and being able to get some sense of direction at least. Leaning out of the window, she saw him hurry to his car.

It was the first time she had been in his apartment without him being there. A typical bachelor pad, as he had described it to her before he took her back there for the first time. When she first saw it, she wasn't sure if she was comforted by the fact he hadn't bothered to make an extra effort in preparation for her stay, or reassured by the ease that they had with each other.

She took off her coat. Lifting up her jumper, she turned sideways, checking herself in the mirror. How long would it be before she would start to show? Two months ago, the minute she had seen him with someone else she would have left. Two months ago she would have gone back to Cambridge, got hammered with friends and got rid of every trace of him. Photos, gifts, tickets, anything. Now everything had changed. She ran her hand over her stomach. He or she was there. In that moment she felt protective of them, angry and resentful all at the same time, standing in suddenly what felt like a stranger's apartment.

'Christ. You bloody idiot.' She then leaned down to pick up her bag from the bathroom floor, taking a last look around the apartment before closing the door behind her.

Her promise to go and see her mother was abandoned. She didn't have the strength to face her. At the station she sat down to have a coffee, then, using the change she telephoned her mother to say that she wouldn't be coming to visit until the following Friday. Her mother saying that she would be fine but missed her made Sarah put her hand over the phone as tears began to fall down her face. If she had five days to get her thoughts together on what she would do, then she would be able to face her. Given that her parting words from the last visit were that her father would be proud, it seemed even more of a reason to delay.

On the Thursday, a day before she was due to go home, her friend Ruby came to tell her there were some policemen who wanted to speak to her.

Beginning with a sombre expression, one of the policemen said that it was regarding her mother. Before they could say anything else, her first question was to ask how she did it.

A week later she called Graeme.

CHAPTER 36

Two days after Sarah's arrival at Hannah's, Hannah had left for her trip with Marcus. Taking the opportunity of a lie-in, Sarah awoke just past ten o'clock. The apartment was quiet as she lay back, thankful there was no one waiting on her for anything. It felt strange to be there amongst the canvases and easel that had been put to the side to make room for her. Hannah had left a few instructions about the admin to be maintained whilst she was away and quirks in the heating system, even including potential noise from next door should Arsenal win, or for that matter lose, a match.

In response to Sarah's badgering to at least be tasked with something that might need doing, Hannah conceded that, if she really felt the need, there were a couple of repairs that she could tackle. As she had refused to accept any contribution towards the rent for her stay, Sarah insisted upon it. Hannah's parting words to her, as the taxi pulled up to take her to the station, were that Sarah could fill her boots. So long as she didn't start pulling down any walls, otherwise she could knock herself out.

That night, as Sarah lay in bed, her relentless thoughts were of Graeme, of what Hannah had told her and what he was doing at that moment. Hoping that he wouldn't turn up if he doubted Hannah, but at least certain that he had respected her wishes in not calling the children. So long as she wasn't getting a call from either of them, it was giving her a chance to buy some time. When she was devoid of answers of how she should deal with it, she would ease her restlessness by getting out of bed, not giving in to any temptation to go back to the casino every time the pressure brought the option into her head. It would soon come upon her when she had to find somewhere to live. She didn't belong where she was. The welcome and indefinite offer from Hannah they both knew would soon run its course when she got back. But the question of where she should go to next was met with a blank, as was finding the answer to when it would be right to talk to the children. Until then, she continued to exchange emails and photos, the time difference helping when it came to Seb, and Izzy's rural location made for a good excuse to email and telephone instead of using Skype.

The sum total of her current possessions consisted of a few clothes, toiletries and her purse. An hour later she began the task of sorting out her clothes, then putting in a load to wash. The side of Hannah's fridge was covered in photos and magnets from around the world. The man in the photos was Marcus, to whom she had been casually introduced the previous night. Judging by the pictures, she had been with him for a while, given that he had three different variations on his facial hair, from beard to clean-shaven and back to beard. In the photos she looked happy, relaxed. There were groups of friends. Hannah often drew quiet humour or, worse, derision from her family for living in a small rented flat – no husband and no children. But Sarah had once opined to Graeme that she thought Hannah was someone that wanted to explore the world and what it had to offer without being weighed down with the burdens of living in it. Hannah never said it but Sarah often wondered if she could see the sneaking admiration from others when she talked of her latest trip somewhere, thinly disguised by attempting to mock her for not taking life too seriously. Talk within the family about the pitfalls of being burdened by a mortgage and school fees, crippling schedules and children that showed a lack of appreciation was altered when Hannah was there. The belligerent teenagers were high-achieving heirs, and crippling house and car payments were instead about the wealth of possessions that the payments serviced. However, their status was demonstrated in its highest expression by the houses they owned. There seemed a general principle amongst them that if you were going to return home into a cauldron of discontent, then there had to be consolation in doing it via a five-bar-gated gravel driveway that was long enough to brace yourself for the periodic domestic challenges.

Sarah was pleased that she had the space alone, as she didn't want to talk to Hannah anymore about Graeme. In a strange way, despite everything it would have felt disloyal, most of all opening up her life for dissection, everything that she had been trying to avoid. The previous night when it had come to taking her medication, she noticed that there was only three weeks' supply left. The tablets that she had left she would stick to, and would have to find a solution as it came close to them running out. That could wait.

She knew that she couldn't call the children as she spent the morning considering the prospect of talking to them. She checked her emails to see if they had replied to her last one. Instead she found a message in her inbox headlining a reminder to not miss out on the latest odds for the up-and-coming Derby. Quickly, she put the phone in the drawer, before collecting a pad from the side of the fridge. Taking her tea with her, she went around the house putting together a list of repairs that she could undertake. Tomorrow she would think about where to go next. Giving herself a couple of days to make a plan and finding somewhere to live would be a start.

In preparation for the repair tasks ahead, she went to the hall cupboard to see what materials and tools she had. Inside, under a couple of dustsheets and a step ladder, she found a pot of paint evidently left over from the kitchen, a box of assorted tiles with cement, and a toolbox tucked away at the back. Inside there were a few hotchpotch screwdrivers, a hammer and a drill. On the top, a tray of assorted nails and screws.

Taking a break after her first task, that of replacing two cracked tiles behind the sink in the bathroom, she began considering if she should go the whole way and replace the lot, something that would keep her busy for at least a day.

Her calculations were interrupted as the intercom went. After recognising the name as being Hannah's business partner in the café, she buzzed her in.

'Hi there! I'm Sophie, I was hoping to catch Hannah before she left. She has her phone off again. Unbelievably, the cover that she lined up has just pulled out.'

'Would you like to come in? I'm Sarah, her cousin. Unfortunately, she left last night.'

'Sarah? Of course, she has mentioned you.' The look on her face suggested that if she had said her name was Gertrude and she was Hannah's aunt she would have offered the same acknowledgement. 'Can't stay, I'm afraid. A bit of a dash on.' She stopped for a moment and looked at Sarah quizzically. 'But, as I am here... I'm just asking. Are you staying for long?' Before Sarah had a chance to answer, she continued, 'Because as you have probably gathered, there's a few shifts going at the café.'

The suggestion took her aback. 'Well, I'm here for a week, a couple of weeks maybe, but that would be out of the question. For a start, I don't have any papers.'

'Papers?'

'My National Insurance, tax details... there's also...'

'Sarah darling,' she quickly interrupted, 'it is a few shifts for a week. I doubt they will mount a customs and revenue sting for £7.50 an hour plus tips.'

'It really is rather short notice and I don't have any experience.'

She looked at the tea in Sarah's hand. 'Right there. You have the requisite skills. 7 a.m. tomorrow. You will be a lifesaver. Thank you so much. A couple of days tops before I can get a replacement. Hannah will owe you big time.'

'I suppose if it is only a couple of days... For Hannah. OK. But I have to warn you that I...'

'Don't worry. Easy gig. Sorry I have to go, I have my car running outside. There is a prowling traffic warden I saw a couple of streets away. If he sees my car when he turns the corner he will break into a sprint.' She made off down the stairs, calling back her parting words, 'I will even throw in as many croissants, whatever, as you can possibly eat. What a star!'

The main door was closing when she heard Sophie's car hurriedly pulling away. After the flurry of activity, the apartment was once again quiet. Sophie's visit had been so brief it seemed almost surreal. Wondering how she had somehow agreed to this, the opportunity to back out wasn't something she could contemplate. It would keep her busy, no time to ponder bets.

CHAPTER 37

EARLY THE NEXT morning Sarah was greeted by Sophie at the café door.

'Hello again, darling! Thanks for coming, you are a lifesaver. Excuse me a minute.' She turned to a young girl who seemed to be unsuccessfully having a battle with a coffee machine. 'Just give it a whack, petal.' She returned her attention to Sarah. 'So, there's an apron behind the counter, there will just be the two of you on today. I have to go out but Charlie will show you around.'

The girl behind the counter, having delivered a hefty blow to the machine, raised a smile at Sarah. 'Hi. I'm Charlie.'

'I think she gathered that.' Sophie raised her eyebrows. 'She's not the sharpest but keen. Thanks again. A real star!' Before Sarah could answer she had left the shop.

'So, hello, Charlie,' Sarah remarked politely, now feeling the privilege of being allowed a word in. 'Good to meet you. She's a bit of a force of nature.' She smiled.

'Isn't she just. So, welcome to the empire.' She gave the

coffee machine another bang. 'This thing is on its last legs, the dishwasher gave up the ghost last night, and you have the early school rush. Apart from that it's great.' She tossed Sarah her apron.

'I don't know if Sophie told you but I've never worked in a coffee shop.' She gave the machine the once-over. 'I've no training as a barista. This is a spaceship to me.' She pushed one of the buttons, which emitted a loud hiss. 'Christ. See what I mean. So, you open at 7.30, then.'

'Yes, and don't worry it will be a cinch. It's the customers that are the real pain in the backside. I'll show you the basics and put you on tea.'

Once Sarah had filled the cabinet and completed two other tasks, including giving the tables a final wipe and checking sufficient condiments and cutlery were provided, she had a five-minute crash course on how to operate the machinery. Then a final statement to say there was some health and safety that was common sense. And she must not stick her hand on hot metal, and put tops on the coffee, as they didn't want some cack-handed twat suing them. And clear up spills and then something that she couldn't recall but said when she remembered she would let her know.

During the morning working at the shop, she hadn't had a chance to think about anything. Even the most taxing of customers were a welcome departure from thinking about Graeme. It was only later when she locked the doors and turned the sign, it came to the fore. When Charlie congratulated her on surviving the first day, she asked if she was just visiting Hannah or planning to stay. It was a question she was able to answer two weeks later when she agreed to stay for another fortnight.

CHAPTER 38

It was past 7.00 in the evening when Sarah walked through the door, her feet aching after a long shift. It had been three weeks since she started work, and in that time she had got into a routine, mostly coming back to eat, checking her emails then watching a film, or picking out a good read from one of Hannah's bookshelves, then finally crashing out in bed. All sports reports were avoided, turning the channel at the sight of a sports fixture, and when she felt things building up in her mind, she would go out for a walk. Television turned off, all devices put into a drawer aside from her telephone. Pubs she knew were a bad idea, and she limited herself to only two glasses of wine a night. Any weakening of her inhibitions would have her linked into a gambling site in a matter of minutes. Sometimes, even without thinking, she had automatically flicked onto the gambling site in an unconscious move. At times she contemplated the opt-out option they offered, to freeze the account for a month or six months, but always would baulk at the last minute. She would always hold her discipline. At the weekends when she wasn't needed, she took the time to go into the city to the museums. If she felt the need to get out of the apartment on an evening, she would go to the cinema around the corner, her only issue being that she had almost run out of her medication. In a shorter time than she had come off them before, she had been decreasing her dose for the last ten days. There was always the option to go to a doctor if she felt she had to.

Opening up the computer it was a welcome sight to see that she had an email from Izzy.

'Hey Mum!

Sorry, I haven't called this week as I have been having some long days. I promise, next week!

We are in Miletus at the moment. I want to tell you this. Mum, I am having the best time. If you ever worried I might regret it, I don't, not for a single second. Even though I understand Dad will be a long time in accepting it. I know what he did with my tutor. But, it's OK, I was angry, but it's done now. He hasn't replied to my emails so I think that it will still be a while. It's like he thinks I did it on purpose. But it's up to him, please don't say I talked about it with you. I only want him to be in contact if he is really interested.

So, on to a happier note! To my latest news...

It's two in the morning and we have just got back from a night out in the local town. One of the archaeologists here, Hasan, asked a few of us to join his family. His parents have a boat touring business. He took David and I out amongst the islets, past the bay. The waters here are beautifully clear, and the temperature, according to the locals, is now at its best, not too blistering as I am told to expect very soon. We moored in a secluded bay for a swim, where we ate the fish that David caught for lunch, along with some fresh peppers from the market he cooked on a smoking grill. I spent the rest of the afternoon on the deck reading about Aspasia of Miletus, which I was only a few chapters shy of finishing at sunset after which we sailed back. A day that I will never forget as we return to the sun-baked earth of the stadium we are excavating.

The food here is incredible, all the vegetables and fruits are seasonal and fresh from the nearby fields. Driving through the villages, you see a different country, remote from the cities. Passing the rustic houses and cows wandering through the villages, you suddenly find yourself faced with the architectural grandeur of the best of the Roman Empire. It can be surreal! You can find a magnificent temple, or an entire complex of marble baths, that had been funded from the coffers of the Roman Empire afforded by Hadrian. They are here, and when the soil is brushed away I imagine them when they once flowed with cool waters over the marble, now long abandoned amongst the dirt and dust.

As we explore the ruins, it is like every door to the past opens another. Then I discover another which comes to take their place. I am seeing it through the eyes of these ancients who I am gradually becoming acquainted with, who are guiding me through my travels. Writers, architects, merchants. Reading the words of Herodotus who tells me about the Persians scorching the earth I am now walking on, and sometimes contemplating what guidance Aristotle has to offer me, whilst I tread the same paths where he formed his ideas. They are taking me through their world. And when we uncover each layer, I see the lives, the endeavour, the reverence and the toil of the people that lived and breathed life into the city. When I am taking in a cold bottle of water in the shade from the sun, I see Alexander passing in his quest for deity, conquering those who stood in his way, routing the Persians back through the mountains as he headed to the ends of the earth. I see Cicero pondering matters of state, Strabo inking to scroll the maps that I follow. The people arriving to share tales of faraway journeys.

I think about the servants and the slaves and what they might have had to say as they built the city and served their masters. If only we could hear their thoughts about looking on at the privileges of the rich. When Aristotle walked amongst them on the roads they had back-breakingly laid. Or when they poured the wine from the unearthed amphora we found, for their masters or those better placed in servitude. I wonder how many hopes, desires were drowned in the weight of existence, as they fended off ill health or starvation. If they thought the Gods would ever answer their prayers. If they felt envy, love or contempt for those who owned their lives.

I have so much to learn, I have only just started and when I listen to the others, I take in as much as I can. To know I have infinite amounts to discover and understand, that is the best part of it. It has opened up a whole new world to me, that I feel drawn into, as if it was there for me all along. I feel I have made a dozen new friends and adversaries, all of them raised from the dust and pages of my books. The women, oh, what I am learning of the lives of most women. You know how I will feel about that…

Last week we went to visit Knidos. Again, it is at the far end of a peninsula that is almost deserted, apart from the two excavators we went to meet. Stone by stone, they are unearthing the ruins. Standing above the city you can now see the main temple taking shape. On one side the military harbour, on the other the trading harbour. The remnants of both lie just beneath the clear water, so you can see the breakers and the carved, lettered columns in the sand. I imagine the weary sailors approaching, expectant on the deals and a chance at some respite before heading out again. And upon news of the ships, from inside the buildings with their mosaic floors came those anticipating what wares were being brought to market. And the happy wine merchants on the shores eager to trade for the exchange of coin.

I took some lunch up to the theatre and tried to picture what it would have been like. A perfect spot with a breeze coming off the sea, and rest from the morning's exertions. I had been saving a fresh salad roll from the local baker near where we are staying. Along with my favourite, a flaky cheese borek. After taking in the smell of the contents that morning as we left the shop, I had been waiting for that ever since. David tells me, although I am not sure if he is just feeding into my romanticism of this place, that the cheese I am enjoying is from sheep and goats who roam the agoras and sleep on the steps of the theatres, which came from the stock before that provided the wool and milk for the thriving cities 2,500 years ago. I'm happy to go with it! So, anyway, from the top of the theatre I can only see three people now, where there were once over 70,000! Where the Spartan ships took respite between battles, the awe-inspiring splendour of the vibrant marble temples, where the people offered their incense and would have prayed for good fortune. And beneath my feet, the theatregoers pouring through the tunnels to see the actors in their final rehearsals. The celebration of a good day's trading, a chance to let off steam at their betters, the atmosphere buzzing as the people would have bustled their way to the places now around me.

I've been told about the mathematicians (you would know them better than me!), the artists who took their ideas, creations to the world. The architect Sostratos, who was from here, designed one of the Seven Wonders of the Ancient World. He set sail for Alexandria where he constructed the Lighthouse. I wonder how he felt as he left the calm seclusion of the inner harbour into the turbulent waters beyond the breakers. To think that ten years ago I sat in a classroom 2,000 miles away and was told about the Wonders of the Ancient World, one that came about because of the day a boat cast out to sea from this very place.

But for me, most of all, I picture the travellers who came to seek out the wonder of the beauty of Aphrodite. This is where the original was commissioned for, the celebrated, much coveted divine image of the goddess sculpted by Praxiteles. When I think of what came after it. The everlasting beauty of Aphrodite that the Romans continued to emulate, the legacy that has been given to us. Igniting the imagination in the hearts and minds of those that came after like Botticelli, Michelangelo, Rodin, Camille Claudel. So perhaps I am getting a little carried away…! But, anyway, it started here. (Do I keep saying that…?!)

Thanks for the book you sent out. I hope you soon get to come and see it for yourself, Mum. Sir Charles Fellows' intrepid excursions throughout Asia Minor. A hundred and seventy years before I wonder what he would have given for my car (which is running beautifully by the way!) instead of horseback! I find myself standing in the same spots that he took his sketchbook, the remote and rugged places that he explores. Many of the more out-of-the-way ones haven't changed. I understand when he says how he had difficulty holding onto the pages given the temperatures and gales that can kick up. Now we fly or drive to these places in a moment, and bring the outside world with us at every pace. If he might envy my camera, I think I definitely envy his chance for solitude and discovery of a lost world. Sometimes days from anywhere. Imagine as he sketched his rediscovered cities, evoked Homer and visualised presenting his triumphs to the British public. Again, David says my romanticism would soften at the prospect of a night in a draughty wooden hut, a tent and eight hours in a saddle exposed to the elements.

David has told me these winds will pale in comparison to those blowing across the plains of Troy! I didn't tell you but we are going there next month. To imagine the vanquishing of Hector and death of Achilles. And for you, I know, Odysseus embarking on his journey! You can see it for yourself if you want to, even bring Dad, if he comes around. He always said he wanted to see Gallipoli. The Dardanelles are just over the water, and David has a lot of contacts, so I'm sure that we can do that. Who knows, we might even be able to persuade Seb to join us!

Mum, really, it would be great if I could show you just some of this. I think that Granny would have thought so too.

You can see that you don't need to worry. I am having the time of my life and am happier than I have ever been. You remember you said about not chasing something I already have? I get it. I really get it.

Lots of love (even to Dad...)

Izzy xxxx

Attached photos of the boat trip and from the theatre (not a pith helmet in sight).'

After finishing the email, she delighted in the news from Izzy. Putting her irritation about Graeme's petulance aside, she thought how proud she was of her, and in her mind committed to replying the next day, along with calling by the nearby bookshop to pick out another book to send to her.

Earlier, having felt too tired to cook, she just had some bread and cheese that she had picked up from the express store on the corner. The news from Izzy gave her a lift, and a focus on the pressing need to make plans to move on. She decided that it was time to call Graeme the next day to sort things out. Having not spoken to him since the day she left him at the café, she felt that she was now in the best place to deal with him. It wouldn't get any easier. It was later in the evening, as if to add to that need to prioritise her plans, she had a phone call from Hannah telling her that she would be home the following week, Marcus having torn a ligament after falling over coming out of a pub after a day's climbing expedition.

She went to bed that evening at her routine time of 10 p.m., only to awake at 2 a.m. With the absence of any additional sedative for the last week, she knew she was unlikely to get back to sleep, and having to be up in four hours she couldn't now take anything. Tossing and turning, she was unable to get back to sleep. Like any time when she wasn't busy or engaged in something, the quiet void was soon filled with anxiety. After going through to the kitchen for a healthy nightcap she went back to bed. Still unable to sleep she tried a suggestion given her once by Lydia, to put on an audiobook. With little optimism she downloaded a couple of choices. Even though the content didn't sink in, the mellifluous voice of Juliet Stevenson seemed to do the trick, albeit over an hour later, when she eventually drifted off after a few chapters. After what seemed like hardly any break at all, her alarm went off.

CHAPTER 39

Sarah arrived at the café to find the closed sign up. Peering through the glass she could see Charlie on the phone. As she caught sight of Sarah she hurried over to open the door, continuing her conversation as she undid the lock. Responding to Sarah's look of curiosity she put her hand loosely over the receiver. 'It's that sodding electrical box, bloody thing has blown, again! I'm on the phone to the company to send someone out. Ugh, listening to the same bloody song, over and over. If I have to endure any more of this insipid new-age crap on another loop...'

Her attention was suddenly drawn back to the call as she listened to someone on the phone. 'Yes, I am aware you are recording my call, listen, do you have any idea what one Enya song on loop can do to a person's mind in twenty-five minutes?' She put her hand up in frustration as someone responded on the end of the line. 'If this wasn't the third time that I had had to call someone from your company out in a month I might be a little more "calm" and feigning offence at my tone isn't going to deflect from your company's ineptitude. If there isn't someone here by the end of the day I am reporting you to trading standards. I hope you have that on record. So, please, by the end of the day, thank you.' She was about to finish the call when she added, 'And this time try to send someone in a van, not a jalopy. Good day.'

'Wow. I wouldn't want to get on the wrong side of you!'

'Oh, they really annoy me. We were supposed to legislate for workers' rights not give a bunch of corporate arseholes rules to hide behind. They first wear you down with an attritional battle of telemarketing to get you to sign up, then try to placate you with a marathon of music when you call to complain! Which of course makes you either give up, or else you are losing the will to live by the time you get through to someone.'

'Hey, you are preaching to the choir. Forty-five minutes I spent waiting to have my energy contract terminated. Then another stretch telling them that my mind couldn't be changed. I thought saying that I was leaving the country would do it. Who'd have thought that my electricity company would become needy? I feel I am being emotionally blackmailed.'

'Leaving the country? Yes, you would think that might do it. So, with coffee off the menu, how about a fruit juice? It only went an hour ago.' Charlie reached into the fridge to pick out a couple of bottles of smoothie. 'Here, they will only go anyway.'

'Thanks.'

'You moved overseas? When was that?'

The question took Sarah a little by surprise. She had been working there for three weeks and had barely exchanged anything other than small talk or an occasional lengthy monologue from Charlie about her girlfriend or the frustrations of working in the café. Sarah had talked about Cheltenham and she was only visiting London to help Hannah out. 'Oh, it really isn't that interesting. Germany.'

'Germany! Whereabouts? Beth and I were there a couple of years ago. Berlin, what a city that is!'

'Isn't it just. No, it was Lower Saxony,' Sarah answered, hoping that that would satisfy her curiosity. 'Not nearly as interesting. So, after this I think I will take the opportunity to sort out that store cupboard. It is impossible to find anything in there.'

'Never mind that. So, where is Lower Saxony and do you miss it being back in Cheltenham?'

'Cheltenham is a wonderful town.'

'Beth's family are from Gloucester. Not sure you and I will hang out at the same places. But as her family are horsey, we do go to the festival every year. They can give you the best-informed preamble on every losing horse that I take their advice on. Last year they were right on the last horse, but I didn't tell them I hadn't backed it. Ugh. One winner out of six they had called and it was in a bumper of eighteen horses. The horse was 28-1. I had to be thrilled with them all the way home, having to pretend that I had won as well.'

'It made for a long journey back then.' Sarah smiled.

'The longest. Hey, do you and your husband go to the festival? Speaking of whom, I'd like to meet him. Hannah says he is a shrink. Most people shy away from them whereas I…'

Sarah interrupted Charlie abruptly. 'Sorry, Charlie, I would love to sit and chat but I have just remembered we are low on £1 coins. My fault, I meant to go to the bank last night. You can hold that thought and perhaps we can talk later?'

'Oh. Alright,' Charlie responded flatly to Sarah's obvious reticence.

'We can have a good chat later. On the way back from the bank I'll give our rivals some business and bring back some coffees.'

'That would be good. Thanks.'

'I won't be long.' Sarah grabbed her bag as she left the shop.

Standing in the queue in the bank, the sight of a woman in a sharp business suit with a Chanel bag took her back to the coffee shop in Belgravia. Instead of men behind her discussing the Nikkei, there was an elderly lady leaning on a wheeled shopping carrier, not making any attempt to be discreet about her curiosity over the woman's bag. Her strained expression couldn't make Sarah decide whether it was covetous or contemptuous. A mother behind her struggled to keep her toddler strapped into a pushchair quiet, her task made more difficult by the fact that another woman busy filling in a form at one of the peripheral tables was letting her toddler freestyle around the reception. With an aeroplane in hand, the child seemed unaware of everything around him, certainly oblivious of the child straining every sinew to join this extravagant air display.

It was fifteen minutes later she emerged from the bank, having been delayed further by a man coming in in a hurry and pleading on an emergency to jump everyone's place in the queue. His plane was leaving in a couple of hours and he had to pick up his currency. Aside from one murmur of discontent from the pensioner, the general consensus was that desperation like that couldn't be faked, their empathy also due to the fact that, as one person put it, 'we've all been there'.

On the way back she passed a post office, where there was an advert for an apartment. Enough room for when Izzy or Seb would visit. The price tag of a three-bedroom house in Cheltenham but it would be a start.

She then called into the rival café two streets away. In what Charlie would often bemoan as one of the environmentally toxic soulless chain cafés, Sarah set her sights on the apple pie that they universally stocked. A treat unrivalled by their own version. When she was at the counter ordering two lattes and what seemed a safe bet of an Americano for the workman, Sarah smiled as she knew that as soon as she presented Charlie with hers, the immediate comment following the thanks would be about the planet-polluting cups. Whilst waiting for the barista to fulfil her order, she delighted in the pie, taking the time to check for any emails from the children. Placing her phone back into her pocket she thought that about now Seb was most likely to be on the beach, after the injection of funds she had recently sent had freed him temporarily from his travel-funding spell of fruit-picking, and Izzy was down in a trench somewhere making her latest discoveries that she would soon be hearing about. As she planned to speak to Graeme that evening, she knew the phone calls to them would imminently follow, and how she was going to tell her and her brother about her and Graeme's separation. Every initial thought was subject to her anxiety of how they would react. The mess that she and Graeme had created, the mess that she wanted to shield them from. But most importantly the reassurances that she wanted to give them.

Every day she was coming to terms with the unravelling of her previous life with Graeme. If it was a bad night with her recurrent nightmares, her thoughts were dominated by that. But, they were becoming less frequent. Often she would wake and for a moment think that she was back with Graeme, every plan or routine still making an automatic basis for her waking moments. The jobs to be done, half expecting to turn over to see him there next to her.

Over the last few weeks it had sometimes seemed almost surreal to her that everything she had had with him had gone. What they had spent their last few married years preparing for, the possibilities fantasised about, trips, holidays, a new sports car for him and her own annex built for her 'hobbies'. For the first time she thought of the places where Graeme would drive her in the car and the 'hobbies' she would spend her time doing, and she felt no grief that this would never be. Not the expensive holidays with him or the Sundays where they would drive to pubs for lunch, or the extravagant piece of jewellery that had been hastily chosen for her birthday or Christmas.

The prospect of this life was now stale and colourless, and the only thing that came to mind was Graeme's voice, his words to her, about where they were going, what she would like. The new car that she had bought for his fortieth. She remembered how elated he was, not knowing that she had been saving for the past two years for this milestone. Instead of the model he had hinted at, she had gone the next one up. His prized car that a year later began to not quite have the full capacity to achieve the acceleration he wanted, and the interior had sustained a few marks from the kids.

A set of keys to the car that no one else was allowed to drive was then more frequently slid across the table to Sarah as an act of trust and wanting her to share the enjoyment, nearly always when they had a function or a lunch to drive to. After she made a minor scratch coming out of their local pub one Sunday afternoon, the following week he made a 'speculative' call to the dealers, as he was 'just looking at his options, just out of interest'. Days later, he had taken it in for a part exchange for another model. As she saw him drive up after work to face what he knew would be her opposition to the impulsive buy, she was overtaken by Seb and Izzy in complete awe of the spectacular red Jaguar that they had heard rumble over the stones.

That evening he announced a no-holds-barred trip to Provence where they had previously agreed they would retire to. After a recommendation from a work colleague, he said he had found the area that they would buy in, promising that it would be in five years and no more flash cars. They should save all they could. Then he said they should make an increased commitment to pay more into long-term investments. He would take care of it all.

Now, as she made her way back to the café, she looked at her watch and saw that she had been longer than she thought. Taking out her phone she sent Graeme a message. 'We should talk. Call me tonight. Sarah.' After sending it, it seemed stupid she should put her name at the bottom as she snapped shut her phone.

Sarah half smiled in coincidence as a smart Jaguar passed her in a rush, the driver pipping her horn at the ambling teenager crossing the road in front, who seemed unperturbed as he gave a dismissive look and slowed down half a pace. In the wake of the passing car she could hear an argument breaking out in a nearby shop. A man was being encouraged to leave by what looked like the shopkeeper.

The young man looked dishevelled in a sagging, stained tracksuit. The pale-looking employee tried to assert a calm authority as he ushered him out. Sarah looked overhead at the sign of the shop to see it was a bookmaker's. Visible through the door of the shop, flashes of lights from gaming machines could be seen. Behind the window, three TV screens with two men perched on stools watching avidly, one of them still, the other tipped on the edge, nervously twisting a pencil around in his fingers. Sarah's attention was then quickly brought back to the argument.

'Sir, I know that this is difficult. But you need to leave.' His voice had a slight detectable nervous fear as he showed a disingenuous empathy with the money he had lost. When the man continued to remonstrate, the employee took a phone out of his pocket.

'I'm going to have to call the police.'

'I'm owed!' the young man shouted. 'Those things are rigged. You know it. I know it.' Even under his cap Sarah noticed his eyes were bloodshot. He took a cigarette packet out of his pocket, his hands shaking as he searched for his lighter. 'Listen to me, you wanker. I am not moving until I get my money back. You are the manager and must have the keys to these things.'

'Sir, please calm down. I have CCTV and there are witnesses.' At which point another punter came out of the shop to talk to the man. 'Come on, mate, just calm down, you've just had a bad day.' He then turned to the manager. 'I'm sorry, my friend here, he's just lost a lot of money and this isn't like him. His wife has just gone and taken the kids. Please. There's no need for the police. I'll take him home.'

'Come on, mate. We can go and have a pint. This isn't worth it.'

'Get off. I'm fine. And you,' the man pointed at the manager, 'stop keep calling me fucking sir. Like you have any respect. You just steal our money with those fucking machines. £500 I've lost this morning. What about my kids?'

'Please. I understand. I just work here.'

'Just get me my money back,' he seethed. As the man moved towards him, the manager pressed one button, putting the phone to his ear. 'Police, please.'

Unaware that he had noticed her, he turned his attention to Sarah. 'And what the hell do you think you are looking at?'

'This is your last chance.' The manager tried to intervene. 'The police are on the line. Do I say they need to come here or should I say that you have cooled down?'

'OK. Fine. Don't shit yourself. I'm going.'

Before he had completed his exchange Sarah quickly moved on as he wandered in the opposite direction, her heart beating as she double-checked that he was walking the other way. Crossing the road she caught another glance of the bookies'. The screens still visible, suddenly being confronted by the familiar sight brought her guilt to the fore. There was the matter of the money.

Taking a shortcut back she arrived at the café to find the engineer on his way out the back.

'Oh. Hey. Have you finished already?' Although pleased to be back, she was still unsettled from the encounter.

'Easy job. Just one wire. No problem.' He put the tools in the back of his van. 'Any more problems just ask for me. My name's Todd.' He got into his van and wound down his window. 'Your mate in there. Single, is she?'

'Afraid not.' She handed him a coffee. 'Here, I got you one of these.'

'Cheers, darlin'. If you want to put a good word in she has my card.' He took a sip of the drink. 'Nice. Pucker coffee. Better than the cheap crap instant my last missus used to buy.'

'And who would think that you weren't worth the effort,' Sarah replied dryly. 'Well, you have a good one and thank you again.'

'No worries, love.' He winked at her as he placed the cup into a holder on the dashboard before driving away.

Sarah smiled as she could hear Charlie's latest playlist through the window of the café. Slightly above it was the usual painful accompaniment that Sarah was now used to. As Charlie was in full swing she was pleased that it was unlikely she would reignite their conversation at least for the day.

Sarah heard a noise behind her. Sensing someone was there, she turned around. It was the young man from the shop. 'Hand over your bag,' he seethed. The back gate swung closed behind him as he demanded it anxiously.

Sarah hesitated as she listened to see if there was anyone around. 'What are you doing?'

'Shut the fuck up,' he hissed. 'Just give me your bag.'

Her handbag was hooked under her arm as she held the coffees in front. 'I don't have anything of any value,' she responded desperately.

'Give it here.' He urgently yanked it out of her arm, the coffees crashing to the floor, one of which splashed up his leg, the hot liquid making him let out a cry. 'You stupid bitch.' He pushed her to the floor as the contents of her bag spilled onto the ground. Amongst her belongings was the bag of coins, which suddenly caught his eye. He reached down and grabbed the coins. 'Is this a joke?'

She picked up her purse that he now coveted. 'This is all the cash that I have. Take it! My friend is in there, no one has seen you yet. Go now or else you...' She stopped.

He snatched the purse from her.

'Please! There are photos of my children. Let me keep it. Just take the money.' She then quickly took off her watch. 'Here. You can have this.' She held it out. 'You said you have children. You can buy them something with that. I promise you, it is worth at least £500 or £600. It will surely at least cover what you lost today. I understand. Really, I do.'

'Seriously?' he snapped incredulously. 'You understand. Do you think I am stupid?' He leaned in. 'This bag, that watch. Of course people like you understand.' She struggled with him for the purse. As he did, it split open and the cards spilled onto the ground. He snatched up the bankcards, putting them into his pocket.

'Sarah!' Charlie dropped a box she had been carrying out to the back and rushed over to her. Before she reached them he was through the gate, slamming it in his wake to put off any would-be pursuer. Quickly going over to Sarah, she helped her up. 'Christ. Are you alright?'

Shakily Sarah leaned up against the wall. 'I'm fine. I will be fine.'

'Here.' She offered the support of her arm, noticing her purse dispersed onto the floor. 'I should have warned you, we have a few junkies around here.'

'Thanks, but really I'm OK.' She declined Charlie's assistance. 'He wasn't a junkie. Good job you were here.' She moved quickly to gather up the belongings that had fallen out of her bag, first scrambling for the casino card that had dropped out, quickly secreting it into the back of her purse, looking furtively to see if Charlie was watching.

Charlie took a look over the gate to double-check he was gone. 'I think he looked more scared than you did.' She then secured the bolt. 'We should call the police.'

'He will be long gone. Just let me get a drink first. You haven't got anything stronger than a coffee in there, by chance?'

'On the occasions that I have to complete a long shift with Sophie, what do you think?' She put her arm around her, joking to lift her spirits. 'Come on.'

CHAPTER 40

Taking Charlie up on her offer for her sister to come and cover the afternoon shift, Sarah went back to the apartment early. On the way home, it was the first time that she noticed a bruise coming up on her arm, her elbow sore as she had tried to hang onto her bag.

Recalling the desperation in his face had an uncomfortable familiarity to it, his anger and frustration. Instead, in his eyes she joined the band of outsiders who he knew viewed him with such contempt. The shame in his eyes for that moment she was repulsed by, yet connected with, knowing what was bringing him back to the same place, the same draw to the rollercoaster, the highs, the injustice of the lows. Guessing from the stained tracksuit and the obvious fact that he hadn't had a shower for days made the outward and clear division. No one would see them as the same. She wondered how long he had been gambling, how long it had taken, what he might have been. Why had he picked her and violated her life?

Locking the door twice behind her she made her first

priority to go to the fridge to take out a bottle of wine. Switching on the television, the news played in the background as she failed to suppress the memories of that morning. Why hadn't she just paid more attention as she went back to the shop? Why was she even thinking about it? After pouring the last of the bottle, she drifted off to sleep. Briefly awaking to the sound of her telephone ringing, she decided to leave it, and when it didn't ring a second time, she closed her eyes.

A couple of hours later, she got up from the sofa, having only drifted in and out of sleep. She picked up her phone to see the missed call was from Graeme, her sight now just about sharp enough to focus as she listened to the message.

'Just returning your call. I'm in all night. Also to let you know I will be back in the UK to take my things from the house. You should meet me there.' She began to dial.

'Hello, Sarah.' His tone was affectionate.

'Hi. Thanks for calling back,' Sarah replied coolly.

'It's good to hear your voice. I've been worried. You don't sound so good. Are you OK?'

'Just a long day. I got your message. I should have been in touch. It's just that I needed time. You're right, I think we should meet up, there are things we need to talk about. Other things that you need to know. The money, Graeme.'

'I saw that you took out £2,000. I understand. I probably would have done the same.'

'Alright. It isn't just that. As I said, we need to talk, you know, face to face. I've had time to digest what you have been saying.' She decided that it wasn't the time to talk over the phone about what she had found out from Hannah. Without premeditation the next thing that came to her mind was to say, 'You've made this so difficult.' Annoyed that she had made this show of emotion, she continued angrily, 'But what the hell were you thinking?'

'I've told you I'm sorry. If there is just any chance of us

getting past this. I still love you. If you are having any doubts.'

She didn't answer, unable to find the right words.

'No. I thought not. So, if it's OK with you, I will pack up your things from here and send them to be put into storage or you can tell me where you are? I just wanted to wait until I spoke to you.'

'Storage will be fine. Thank you.'

'They can be in the UK in a couple of weeks. I will give you the number for when you are ready to get them delivered. The house, we will deal with that when I come back to England. I suggest that we keep on the rental for at least the rest of the time on the contract.'

'Whatever you think.'

'If you don't want to tell me where you are, how you are doing...?'

She interrupted him. 'The house. We should start making plans.'

'It has been your home that you built. I am in no hurry to sell if you want to move back for a while. I have army accommodation for at least another eighteen months. That would give you another year, if you really needed that.'

'That sounds better and we might get a higher price in the summer. So do you not think we should put it on the market now?'

'Up to you. But OK, yes, perhaps you are right, that would be better to effect a swift outcome.'

'A swift outcome? Very nice, Graeme.'

'You know what I mean. It will be less painful for both of us not to draw this out. So, yes, selling it now is going to be a good call and we will get a good amount for it. Obviously you have the final say. If you agree, of course.'

'Of course. Why not?' she replied sarcastically, almost certain now he had already called the estate agents for a valuation.

'Good. So that's settled. And then there's Izzy and Seb. It's up to you what you tell them.'

'Tell them?' Her focus suddenly sharpened. 'Perhaps we should just say that we realised when we came out to Germany that we wanted different things out of life. No need for anything else at the moment.'

'At the moment?'

'Don't push me, Graeme.'

'Sorry, I didn't mean to. I feel that's the best thing to do. Just give me a heads-up if you are going to, you know… say any more to them. Thank you for this.'

'Don't thank me. I'm doing it for them. Do you want to speak to Seb or Izzy first? They will obviously want to speak to both of us.'

'I will call Seb,' he insisted. 'But just to keep it simple, as we agreed. They will know it was my screw-up anyway.' He quickly continued, 'I don't mean that as self-pitying.'

'What about Lucy? How is she doing?'

He was irritated at the mention of her name. 'We should just concentrate on us for now. Where we go from here.'

'Did you get her the help?'

'Yes. But I haven't seen her. Jane had agreed to take care of things. But, you obviously have to take my word for that.'

'So, about the house, I will take the train to Cheltenham. I can stay the night with Ellie. I will let you know as soon as I can get the time off, perhaps in a couple of weeks?'

'Time off?'

'I'm still in London. Staying with a friend for a couple of weeks.'

'A friend?'

'Yes, a friend. No one you need to know about. Listen, I'll speak to you after I've called Izzy tomorrow.'

'Take care of yourself. Sarah, I know it's too late for us, but I miss you.'

'I'll call you when I can give you a date for coming back.'

She placed the phone down and lay back on the sofa. The silence in the apartment made her thoughts amplify in her head. No more limbo, this was it from now on. Tomorrow she would call Izzy. In a moment she realised that she hadn't asked when he would speak to Seb. Before they called each other, best to do it at the same time. Too tired to ring him back and re-engage in another conversation, she decided to call in the morning.

CHAPTER 41

'Hello. Dr Hughes's phone.' A young woman in happy spirits began speaking. 'He is rather busy at the moment.' A sound in the background could be heard as she tried to suppress a laugh. The voice was then muffled as she couldn't hear what was being said.

'This is his wife Sarah. Who's this?'

'His wife?' Before she could finish answering, Graeme had taken the phone.

'Sarah, hi.'

'Who was that?'

'A colleague. I'm in work.' He lowered his voice. 'This isn't what you think, before you jump to the wrong conclusion. I'm at the office, and that is one of my new officers. I just asked her to pick up as I was a bit incapacitated.' She heard another laugh in the background as he appeared to cover the receiver and move to another room. 'Don't read anything into this. It is a major, a new doctor that has just arrived. Call my office number if you want.'

'It's fine, Graeme. You can do what you like. We didn't agree on a time to call Izzy and Seb. I'll call Izzy at 9.00 our time. Tell Seb that I will ring him tonight, or if he wants to call me earlier, I will be waiting.'

'This really is it, then? You've decided no going back?'

'You make it sound like I was the one who made the choice to end our marriage.'

'I really loved you, Sarah. If I could change what happened. I'm sorry for this. For everything.'

'You probably are now. I imagine you were just about after I found out.' Tears began to well in her eyes. 'I'll be in touch after we have spoken to Seb and Izzy.' She tossed her phone onto the sofa, feeling the finality, her emotions conflicting. A life they had shared together had been severed. But there was something she hadn't expected. The feeling of a huge weight being lifted.

Sarah contemplated every question that Izzy would ask, and her resentment towards Graeme grew. How she would have to keep his confidence. Their agreement that it was a realisation that they wanted different things, knowing that she was as keen to conceal the revelation of Lucy as he was. On every level wanting to spare the children the exposure of what he had done and, for her own sake, the look that she was almost certain Izzy would give her. Pity and anger at why she hadn't taken a grip on her life earlier, lines would be drawn against Graeme.

And then beyond the children, what would happen when the wider family were told of their split? She would see what they had thought. Graeme's mother's refusal to see it as anything other than her failing. The comments over the years about her illness. How Sarah had once overheard Lydia say that she thought he was effectively taking on another patient.

Now, at the news of their separation and the absence of the children from the immediate sphere, she thought that all the reservation that his mother had shown over the years would be levelled at Sarah, given the chance. Even if she had Lucy standing in front of her, she would say that her son's attention was drawn to her because of Sarah's deficiencies.

Avoiding an encounter with his mother was best for the benefit of both parties for the near future. Another consoling factor at their separation was at least she wouldn't have to be subjected to her indefatigable drip of undermining barbs, that her son had never quite married as well as he should. His mother adored her grandchildren and would often say that they were Graeme's likeness through and through. His brains, his talent, his drive. The acknowledgement of Sarah's education had long since been buried, under the evergreen reminder that she had reached her potential with her 'little boutique'. According to Lydia, the children's success with their gregarious nature and vivid intellect was purely Hughes genetic stock. However, Seb's recent reluctance to bring an imminent conclusion to his travels, and the news that Izzy had dropped out of medicine, would in her mind no doubt bring utterances of a shift in that theory.

Anxious about the call ahead, the apartment felt increasingly claustrophobic, the option of turning to some respite in the afternoon's betting markets gaining greater appeal. Grabbing her keys from the side, she took a walk out to the park, everything that had happened with Graeme returning on a loop in her mind. The immediate prospect of the sale of their home and of building separate lives.

Walking through the park, the sight of families together, with whom a year ago Sarah would have felt a shared existence, now transformed into a different meaning for her. She was certain there had been relief in his voice, knowing he hadn't been honest with her, most likely resenting her when having to lie, worst of all perhaps contemptuous of her stupidity in not taking the hint and just leaving him.

A recollection came to her of a few years before when he had spent the night tending to one of his patients in the hospital. A fifty-year-old woman who had made a half-hearted effort at killing herself. Sarah recalled his frustration at being called out in the night after a long day, venting that if the deluded woman had taken the hint that her husband just didn't want her, she would have saved herself years of self-destruct. Sarah now remembered him asking her directly. Why did she think that was? Sarah was now sure, as she thought about it, that when she had said perhaps love, or children, that it had no relevance to them. She hadn't considered it, not for a second. She hadn't seen it coming, the path to Lucy. Now, beginning after the conversations she had with Hannah, she had been left repulsed by it. At best she pitied him, at worse she felt degraded.

The best thing for her was to separate her fears, her anger, and focus on pure practicalities. Then there was the separation of money and decisions that would have to be made over their savings which they had been paying into for all those years. The money that they had talked of enjoying, that she now wondered if there was a point where he knew he was merely paying lip service to.

The issue of where to live had a ticking clock, no longer having the luxury of putting it off and dealing with it as and when the time was right. The rental property pages and internet listings would now have to be given full scrutiny. She dismissed the notion that the property would find her, or she would just know when the time was right. As Graeme would always say, such things were childish imaginings of serendipity conjured up by soap operas. Something that he was at least right on.

However, there was no such place in her mind for the long-term, not a town or a city, a new start or going back to Cheltenham. When contemplating the latter, she didn't like the idea of the post-break-up rallying that would be staged by well-meaning friends. Even contemplating such fuss and attention felt overwhelming. It had to be a simple and unfussy start and find a small flat nearby. To regroup, assess her options before any significant commitment.

Some of her things would have to inevitably stay in storage for a while, but before she was faced with making the choices, she decided upon a list of necessities. Thinking about her possessions that had been packed away, she tried to recall what she had most missed out on. After including her paintings, photographs and books, the list ran dry, aside from the keepsakes from the children, which were a certainty. But nothing else immediately came to mind. Which in a complete sense felt liberating.

The apartment around the corner became woven into her possibilities. A modest amount of furniture, a few belongings and God knows what to do beyond, but to never go back. It would be an end to being kept in the dark, sacrificing too much of her own ambition and relegating her own desires. Most of all she would have complete control again. Until their house was sold, half of its rent could cover the flat. What investments they paid into could be shared.

As the details and complications emerged of what could lie ahead, she would have to be ready for whatever obstacles, orchestrated or not, she might have to overcome, even though she doubted Graeme's desire to make this awkward, given the vulnerability of his position.

Sarah came to a halt, turning around to go back to Hannah's. She passed the apartment that had previously caught her attention on the way. The calculations that she had begun on the walk began to take shape. She made a mental note of the phone number and would call tomorrow for an appointment. Soon she would be able to give Seb and Izzy an address, a place for them to stay, realising that she was getting ahead of herself as she was already picking a fresh colour for the sitting room that she could just about see from the road. It was a start.

Once back at Hannah's, she opened up the computer, now focusing completely on the task ahead. The thought of gambling was near absent as she began to take stock of their finances, to get an accurate total on their investments. Even though she hadn't checked them for some time. When they stopped sending the bank statements on paper, she hadn't bothered to ask Graeme for the password. He made a point of saying every month how they were doing. With five years to maturity it was enough to know they were there.

The first thing would be to put a down-payment on the apartment if all came good. Looking at the rent, that would be at least a month's advance. £1,500. Better to call Graeme and give him a heads-up. If she took another amount after their last call he might go into a spin and take the money out. The thought made her uncomfortable, more because she knew her own ability to cover things up in concealing her losses from him. When he asked where the money for the shop went, she would have to tell him. Although, that would be counter-balanced in their share.

Not wanting to speak to him, Sarah called the German apartment, knowing it would be a message to pick up later. 'Hello, Graeme. Just to let you know I might have found a place to live. I'm just going to transfer some money for a deposit. Don't panic. We can talk about the rest when you call me back. If you get back today.' She couldn't resist the last comment, annoyed at herself that she had shown such emotion.

Sarah brought up the first of two accounts that she hadn't checked for over a year. Navigating to the account page she entered their usual password for their other accounts. It came up as incorrect, then the one for his computer came to her mind. Lysander. That also failed and then, with her last remaining attempt, she tried the same Lysander1234, which logged her in. She rolled her eyes as he had questioned her about how she got into his computer. The addition of the four characters he clearly thought was uncrackable.

As the statement appeared on the screen, she rocked back into her chair. Having been £20,000 from the last year it was now £3,100. A list of outgoing payments. From a year ago. £1,200 every month to Lucinda Knowles. The last ten months, ten payments of £250 into a separate building society. She brought up the other account. A lesser one which had been £16,000 last year was now almost gone, standing at £250. This time the money had gone into an account in his name, a bank that she had no recognition of using. She brought up the bank's website. Without any deviation, he had the same password. All the withdrawal amounts were for online ordering from Amazon. The last being for nearly £300. Her heart racing she quickly opened up their website, but the name he was using was one she couldn't find. All the money they had been saving almost gone in a year. Before Seb left, she remembered how Graeme had told her that he had transferred £5,000 to him for travelling, and then how she had chewed out her son for not showing a little more gratitude for the money his father had given him. Instead, she could see it was for Lucy. Of course Graeme had been keen to talk to Seb first instead of Izzy. She recalled the atmosphere between Seb and Graeme for the couple of months before he left, and how he had gone away a month early. The pressure Graeme must have put on him. If she had just opened her eyes she would have seen what was right in front of her.

Before Graeme could speak to him, she called Seb.

After a few rings he picked up. 'Hey, Mum! You're calling late! Is everything alright?'

'Hello, darling. I know, I'm sorry, I know it's late, but I need to talk to you about something. Have you spoken to your father? He said he was going to call you tomorrow but just on the off chance.'

'No, I was out and just got a message to call him. What's happened?' Seb responded, concerned.

'There's something I need to say to you. I know why you went away early. Your father told me. I'm sorry that he put that on you.'

There was silence on the phone.

'It's alright. I know everything, he told me about Lucy, that you knew. I wish you could have told me. There is something else, it doesn't affect you and Izzy. But we are separating. I'm sorry to just drop this on you. I should have said something earlier. You shouldn't have had to carry that with you. But, just so you know, you don't need to feel you have to protect him.'

'Protect him? I wanted to tell you. Dad said that you couldn't take it. I didn't want to make you ill again.'

'I imagine he did. Sorry, Seb, that he did that. I understand. Is that why you left earlier? Why you didn't tell me about the money?'

'I was going to go away anyway. As for the money, he said this girl had taken an overdose, the money was to help her. I'm sorry but I couldn't even look at him.'

'I understand. It's OK.'

'When I saw them together, at first I didn't believe that he would do that. Then it was a couple of months ago, she got in contact with me. You obviously know she is not much older than Izzy. It's disgusting. He is so selfish. I would have reported him myself if it hadn't been for you and Izzy. He's such an arsehole. Sorry, Mum, but he is.'

She began to well up. 'No, it's fine. He is.'

'I won't have anything to do with him, or her. I promise you that. Don't let this pull you down.'

'I won't. Really, I'm OK. He is still your father. It is down to me to sort this out,' Sarah reassured him.

'No, I don't mean Dad. But I'm not saying that I want to see him anytime soon either.'

'Sorry. What? What, who are you talking about, then?' Sarah replied, confused.

'The boy, my supposed half-brother,' Seb replied irritably. 'It's just you and Izzy that I care about.'

Her mind spun as she took in what he said.

'I mean. Lysander. A stupid bloody name. As I said, I don't want to know. I take it he hasn't told Izzy.'

Still digesting his words, Sarah was half paying attention. 'I don't think so.'

'Well, if she hasn't said anything to you, then, no, I think we would have known about it. She wouldn't hold something like that back. I'm sorry I listened to Dad. I should have given you more credit. Just so you know, I didn't do it for him. I promise you I didn't know about him, you know, the baby, until recently. I swear.'

'It's OK.' Trying to take care not to stumble, not to falter, she continued, 'I understand. But I am fine. You shouldn't worry.' She could hear the words coming out of her mouth but was still barely able to process what he was saying.

'He promised that he would get this Lucy another doctor and Germany was a new start for you and him.'

Sarah was barely listening as the pieces began to fall into place. From somewhere in her mind, she had a recollection of Lucy by the fountain. The pram next to her.

'Are you still in Germany? I'm worried about you.'

'No, long story, but no. I'm at cousin Hannah's.'

'London? I wasn't expecting that, no, that's good. I'm glad you have her. I doubt Dad is going to try to get past her.'

'That would be something, wouldn't it? But you should know I'm getting a place in London. Just a small flat but big enough for you and Izzy as a base when you come home. For as long as you like.'

'Thanks, Mum. I'm glad you are leaving him. Really, I'm not just saying that.' He stopped as he heard Sarah trying to contain her emotions at the other end. 'I hope Hannah has got some stuff in that will help. You know I noticed the green tin, don't you?'

'No point denying it.' She choked out a laugh, drawing on every reserve to keep from the well of anger and grief that she was suppressing. 'You don't have to worry about me. You or Izzy.'

'You are our mum. Of course we will. Let me know when you are moving and I will come back and help.'

'Thank you but no. Hey, I might even come out and see you in a few months. I know it's late so I will call you tomorrow. I want to hear all about what you have been up to. You are getting pretty good with that camera.'

'Thanks but they take themselves here. But yes, I would love it if you came out for a visit. We could get Izzy over too. She's told you all about David and her Raiders of the Lost Ark thing that she has going on, right?'

'Yes. She's doing really well. Proud of both of you. I miss you.'

'We aren't going to get too deep here are we, Mum?' he joked. 'Only, I am in shared digs.'

'Absolutely not. It sounds like you are having a wonderful time, anyway, so...' She hesitated. 'Listen, I had better go. I have to call Izzy. And, Seb, I'm not going to tell her about, about, you know, everything. Not until I can see her face to face. Please don't say anything to her or your father. I'm not ready for that either. I want to do this in my own time. When your father calls, it would be better if you said we hadn't spoken.'

'OK. If that's what you want. He doesn't even know that I know about the boy. I haven't been able to face him to be honest. She seems fragile, this Lucy. He's treated her like dirt

431

and she still wants him. It's really sick. As I said, we are behind you. Don't protect him on our behalf. I know Izzy would feel the same.'

'Just let me worry about how to deal with it. It's something that you need to leave to me.'

'Whatever you do, whatever you decide, you have us behind you, Mum.'

'Thank you, darling, but I am alright. You do what you have to, but don't rule anything out with your father. He does love you, and see how things pan out. Don't feel that you are betraying my trust if you want to see him. Just one more thing. This boy. Have you seen any pictures of him?'

'I just saw one photo. She sent it to me last month. She found me on Facebook. Are you sure you want to know?'

'Does he look like you?' Sarah asked tentatively.

'Please. It doesn't matter. Don't do this to yourself. Please, Mum.'

She took a couple of deep breaths as she realised what Seb was saying. 'If you want to see him, you know, as he is your... you are related.'

'I don't,' he quickly interrupted. 'No. I don't.'

'OK but perhaps later if you want to then I don't mind. As I said, I will be fine. Now go back and do whatever it is that you are doing. What is that?'

'Just about getting in.'

'Oh. We will speak tomorrow. You get some sleep.'

'Take care, Mum. Just look after yourself and call anytime if you need anything.'

'You too, darling. And, Seb... Thank you.' As she heard the line go dead she broke down, crying out in release of the anger at Graeme, listening to her son's burden and his pity. Beside herself and unable to organise in her mind the multitude of conflicting thoughts and memories she was trying to get on top of, she reached for a bottle of wine.

Her anger and agony amplified, she then drank one glass then another in quick succession. Opening a second bottle saw her through her new and imagined confrontations with Graeme and how Seb had held onto that, concealing it through all the exchanges they had since, his words, and then his evasion over the photo. Her imagination crafting an image of a child, she now felt shame and loathing of herself for hating his existence, and of the contempt that she had held for a girl who would have been desperate. Her focus turned to telling Izzy, but she failed to find the words, just knowing how she would react. The man she looked up to would be lost to her as he had been to Seb. Their family was gone.

She would have to decide what she was going to tell Izzy. Halfway down the bottle of wine she tipped it into the sink. Every time she thought of picking up the phone, her heart raced. Seb had had time to prepare and, despite his concern, would most likely have felt relief at the revelation. If Lucy had contacted Seb, then if she was so inclined, she might decide to tell Izzy.

Sarah opened up the computer, needing a reset before making the call. She would have to have complete control over her emotions, have a calm façade. She needed something that would give her a reset. Opening up the familiar page, the lights flashed and the money was laid down. Every account that she could find in his name, she transferred to her account. As Graeme's wages had just gone in, she took the entire amount and put it into her old business account. In a flurry of bets she wagered on nearly as many markets as were listed. Football, rugby, volleyball, cricket, tennis, basketball, any league, anywhere in the world. Teams that she had bet on before, teams that she only recognised by name. £50, £100, £200, she placed at such a rate that she had to pause to take stock of what she had bet on. Bringing up different sports scores pages and opening several tabs, she waited as each score registered, expired bets replaced with new ones. The account showing insufficient funds was soon replenished. With the first turn of the wheel or flash of a score she blocked out the last couple of hours. Everything except the burning undercurrent of her anger at Graeme.

Losing track of time, it was dark by the time she was moved by a growing headache. On the way to the kitchen her phone rang. It was Graeme. She ignored it. It rang again. At the end of the second ring a message came up. 'Sorry, I missed your call. Give me a ring back. I have decided not to wait, I am coming back this weekend.'

She opened the phone, angrily typing a reply. 'I won't be there. Take your things. I know about Lysander.' The phone rang again and again. A signal for a succession of messages sounded before going silent. She took some gratification at his desperation. Knowing that he would be beside himself, no doubt his first call after that being to Seb. She left the phone in the hallway, closing the door.

An hour later the phone rang again, continuing relentlessly, breaking her attention away from a match on which she had placed a large bet at the beginning. £2,000 on the home team who were at that moment winning. She quickly answered it.

'Oh, Mum! Thank goodness. What is going on? I've just had Dad on the phone.' It was Izzy.

'OK. Calm down. I can't hear you very well. What has he told you?'

'Sorry, yes I'm not getting a good signal here, and we are in a bit of a windy area. Anyway, Dad said that you aren't well again. You've been blowing thousands of pounds. He said that I shouldn't speak to you. Did you hear what I said?'

'Just about. But no. I'm fine. Thousands of pounds?'

'Yes, £2,000 from the account and everything else. On shopping, like a fortune in Berlin, he said. You went away like when you told me about, years before, and have been drinking heavily. Now you have left him. He said that I shouldn't call because it might make you worse. He said he had it in hand, you need rest. What does that mean? Are you going into treatment? He told me that you were and he would let me know when it was good to call.'

'He said what?' Sarah raised her voice to make herself heard. 'No, darling. Of course not. Listen, Izzy. It's a long story. It's rather complicated. I will tell you everything when I see you. We have decided to separate. It will all be OK, please try not to worry.'

'You're separating? Oh.' She hesitated. 'Wow. I see now. What did he do?'

'I know this isn't the answer that you want but it is complicated. We can talk when you can get a better connection. Izzy, I would rather we did this by Skype, not over the phone. Please accept what I am saying. I am fine. I promise.'

'I'm coming home now.'

'No, absolutely not.'

'You can't stop me. I'm flying back. This place has waited 2,000 years to be discovered, I don't think another week will make much of a difference.'

'OK. But if you can wait, I can fly over to you for a couple of days for the weekend. But as I said, there is nothing for you to worry about.'

'I know this isn't about money. There has to be more to it.'

'We should talk face to face but we can sit down at the weekend. But nothing affects how we both love you children.'

'We are not children! Where are you at the moment?'

'Cousin Hannah's.'

'Oh that's good. She will look after you.'

'So I've been told. But, I don't need looking after, Izzy.'

'I will catch a flight back as soon as I can. You can't stop me. We are taking a break in the dig anyway. Edward Dawson, our sponsor, has just flown out and is giving the project another

£20,000! There is a party they are giving for him. I think that it was down to plying him with raki on the last visit that got us the new funds. Sorry, I imagine that is the last thing that you want to listen to.'

'No, I do! That's great news. So, take a rest tonight and enjoy the party. If you insist on coming back at least let me book you a flight. Just give me a moment.' Sarah began a search for flights on the computer. 'Just a second, bear with me. Here. There is a flight leaving at ten o'clock tomorrow morning from Izmir. You arrive here at 11.30 UK time, or there's one here twenty-five minutes later, and that's a better airline. No arguments, Izzy, but I am booking this.'

'I won't give you my details.'

'I applied for your passport renewal last year, I know all of your numbers off by heart.'

'You are an incredible nerd, you know that, Mum.'

'Yep. I know. I will email you the ticket after we finish talking.'

On the other screen a flash of a goal. The teams were now level with a minute of injury time to go. £2,000 gone in an instant. 'Look, Izzy, we should wait until tomorrow. Please stop fussing.' She looked again at the score on the screen.

'Oh. OK. No problem. Love you.'

After putting down the phone, another roar sounded. Her team had scored a winner in the last seconds of the game. £3,800 was about to appear in her account. Now feeling guilty at her short treatment of Izzy, she quickly completed the details on the flight purchase, buying her business class as a treat. As soon as the confirmation of the booking came through she flicked back to the gambling site. She thought how good it would be to see Izzy, despite what she had to tell her. Her attention was immediately drawn to the sight of a fixture with one of her more lucky teams who were due to kick off in the next ten minutes.

With the time until morning to go, her imagination conjured up an image of what this child Lysander looked like. Now she had Lucy's name, she could look her up. For some time she lay back, contemplating the prospect of seeing for herself. Knowing from Seb who she would see in him. She flipped the computer back up to go back to her account. As would happen sometimes, the website was temporarily down. She tapped her fingers impatiently, constantly refreshing the page, over and over. Sarah opened her old Facebook account and typed in Lucy's name.

The posts had stopped in the last year. The pictures that were there looked of better times – parties, friends, who were striking poses that mirrored Izzy and Seb's pages. Now, there were no celebratory raising of glasses or holiday shots, or restaurants, or recirculated comical memes, deep quotes of Nietzsche, intense emotions or romantic destiny that she had previously posted. Now she was somewhere, waiting for Graeme to begin the life with her that would never come. He would always keep her close enough, and keep her distracted so she couldn't fully break from him. He had saved her.

Sarah closed the lid, the four walls once again feeling stifling. Picking up her keys, she took a cab to the casino.

Sarah sat at the roulette table anxiously rotating a chip through her fingers. The wealth that she was now staking, which had changed hands against the house over the last few hours, was to take a single spin. The time had come to make a single choice. Red/Black. After three consecutive wins at the table, it had to be now. A feeling in her gut, as with the last three spins. This was her opportunity. She had been right then, she was right now.

Others around her were already selecting their bets. After several hours having barely moved, her body ached, her head fragile to the intrusion of the people that came and went around her. The last few hours of her ever-shifting fortunes she had become exhausted by the spikes of ecstasy and the pits of desperation to stay in the game. But this was to be the last bet.

She focused on the table. Red/Black. Impatient with her own hesitancy in committing to placing her stake, she continued to turn the chip. Looking once again at the roughly stacked chips in front of her, she surveyed the amounts of her long-fought gains. Tonight, the luck had been hers.

The sum that she had coveted when she had taken her seat had been surpassed in the previous spin. But one more win would make good everything she owed, and set her up beyond her previous expectations. After months, this would be where it would reach its end. It would be over. She would never come back.

In choosing her bet, there wasn't any temptation to go to the fated numbers she had used so many times before. The numbers entwined with her past, dates, events, from her greatest fortune, love or happiness. Each had become meaningless in turn, as they had taken their share in her losses. As if they conspired to hurt her.

The people that she had lost, the people she had left, were in her mind gaining momentum in a relentless tide of thoughts. When she had been struggling to rebuild a swathe of losses she knew what they would say to her. Memories of them were becoming almost intolerable. After this turn, she would be able to indulge them beyond anything they had had before, to give them everything.

The croupier picked up the ball. It was now time to commit, her head buzzing with conflicting instincts as to where she should place the wealth of chips.

She closed her eyes. In a moment of certainty, the colour came to her. Black. The strongest feeling she had all night. In a swift move, adrenaline coursing through her veins, she urgently slid the stacks of chips across the green baize.

A man next to her, who had chosen the same colour, reacted to her move by spontaneously taking in a deep breath in admiration, then raised his glass in acknowledgement.

'Fortune favours the brave and all that.'

Unaware of the attention around her, she anxiously waited for the ball to set to purpose. Others around the table, whose attention she had quickly gained, joined in with the expression of excitement or anxiety. Two of whom then changed their mind from red, as if to be part of the big occasion that lay ahead.

The difference of a millimetre drop would release her from this torment. She blocked out contemplating the alternative outcome. Her stomach churned as the croupier set the ball in motion.

'*Mesdames et Messieurs*, no more bets please.'

Under the lights, the bold colours glimmered in the wheel's polished veneer, holding the attention of the surrounding gamblers. Those around the table gravitated to the thrill, now urging their favoured fortune, willing their deserved fate.

In that moment, she didn't consider that it was an amount she and Graeme had paid for their first house. Or know that she would never see him again.

The numbers came into focus. The familiar metallic clank echoed around the bowl, as the ball bounced from one bed to the next. Sarah let out a cry as it came to rest.

CHAPTER 42

SARAH WOKE UP on the sofa after a couple of hours sleep, having got in at past 5 a.m. Her first thought past her recollections of the previous night were of collecting Izzy from the airport. It was just about her and the children now. Today all accounts would have to be settled.

Making herself a pot of coffee she began her first task. All the luck celebrated by others in the casino the previous night had dropped away in the cool air as she stepped onto the pavement, heading back alone to an apartment that wasn't even hers.

For the last time she opened her gambling website. She began the process of closing her account. In a final click, the first step to a new start had been made.

She knew that her battle had just begun, and in the coming months she would most likely try a hundred, a thousand times to find any excuse to reopen it. She anticipated it would just be another variation on every addict's story she had read about. Like after a drunken binge, then pouring the rest of a bottle down the sink, after spending the morning convulsing over the toilet, when the episode would be forgotten by the next week.

Sarah had spent the last few weeks tentatively reading stories of reformed gamblers, addicts. Many with a different path, all laying bare the cost. When they resonated, she closed down the page.

But she had to face up to it, the thought of what could have been the alternative outcome of last night making her nauseous. There was never going to be a good time. But if she was certain of anything, it was that if she continued, she would be the same. She would lose everything. No maybes, it would be inevitable.

The particular story she went back to was one that she had begun reading a couple of weeks ago, as it had stayed with her the most – a gambler who had lost everything who was offering advice. This time she would read it to its conclusion. Typing in the address of the support website, she scrolled to the place of the gambler's story.

For Sarah, it was the start of a journey that she didn't want to fully accept at that moment. That she couldn't return to the websites, the gaming tables, or even have a flutter at the horses on a day out. Knowing that every time a sports report was broadcast on the radio, or she saw a match being played on the television the temptation would be there. The memories, the good, the bad would flash to the fore, when she would have to fight temptation, when her mind would conjure a vivid burst of possibilities of once more having the high of a big win. All would always be just a few clicks away. For the time being it would have to be a day at a time, sometimes an hour at a time. She soon finished reading the gambler's account, hanging onto the first words of the advice. It would be one day at a time. Today she wouldn't bet.

After going through her financial accounts, she felt shame

as the lists of deposits to the website were before her. Ever-increasing sums that now looked grotesque in their desperation and greed. Figures that had become purely a means of being able to stay in the game, fund the expectation of that big win, and day to day propelled her into a world of separation. For those few precious highs that kept her from the suffocating silence. The funds that she now assessed had been replenished by other people's losses.

The excess amount was to be shared between the children, her business account restored. The money cashed in to get there had changed its meaning. But it was the chance for her new life to begin. One day at a time, piece by piece until she could find clarity. To stop the noise. To get off the merry-go-round. And then when she was ready she could choose her way forward for treatment.

There was Lucy. The previous night on the way to the casino, after seeing her Facebook page, she contemplated leaving a message. Because she knew when Graeme's attention was turned to his self-preservation she would have her eyes opened. She wondered for how long Lucy couldn't or didn't want to leave him, to not see him for who he was. How she must have hung onto his words and promises, how he manipulated her to control her. If there was anyone who could break the fantasy that she had, she knew it wouldn't be her. Sarah didn't want to meet her, or see her son, not ever. But if it wasn't her to talk to Lucy, then it had to be someone else. Instead, she thought of Tom, who would still have his contacts in the UK.

Now, she had to carry out something that she knew had to be done from the first day she learned about Lucy.

Sarah opened up the website of the Royal College of Psychiatrists upon which Graeme's house of cards rested. It took her ten minutes to write an official letter, as she carefully and precisely documented the details regarding Lucy. They would no doubt soon be in touch. Rereading it twice, then a third time, she copied it to Graeme then clicked send. She then turned her phone off as she knew a call from Graeme would be imminent, she would speak to him when she was ready.

CHAPTER 43

WITH PLENTY OF time until Izzy's flight came in, she could get shopping in for the next couple of days, before taking a train to Heathrow.

The later flight that she had chosen she could see was keeping to schedule. She left the house with an hour until the plane was due to land at Terminal 2. The flight tracker having shown it on time, she caught the underground and managed to run to catch the express from Paddington to Heathrow.

Buying a newspaper at the station, she flicked through the pages as she sat on the train, taking in little of the stories as she waited in anticipation of Izzy's arrival. She put in her earphones and put on some music, the same playlist as she had made for packing the loft. She thought of how it was going to feel going back to their house in Cheltenham when she was ready to collect her things. If she wasn't going to accept the children's help then she knew that Ellie or Chloe would be more than happy to pitch in. Once they had got over the news she was yet to tell them. A revelation that she was seeking to delay, as it was most likely that they would say she was better in her hometown. They might be right but not yet.

In quick succession to that notion she now considered that, given the situation with Lucy and the boy, he might set up somewhere else. His hand would be forced. Despite her tough exterior this was going to hit Izzy hard. Her daughter was her priority.

Sarah arrived at the terminal with just enough time to grab a coffee. As it would take Izzy at least half an hour to get through she still had twenty minutes. Giving the barista her order she was happy, yet anxious, to see Izzy. But most of all happy. Glad that her daughter had been away when this had broken. Once they had talked about Graeme and she could give her reassurances, Sarah could hear about what her daughter had been doing. The details of the dig, to focus on the best things that were happening in her life. Perhaps even taking Izzy up on her offer of visiting for a week when she was settled into the apartment, with no spectre of Graeme's expectations or those that she had previously bound to herself.

On the table next to her she noticed a couple's attention drawn towards the television inside. As she turned she could see through the glass a plane wreckage, smoke rising through the air, the aerial footage from a helicopter broadcasting the pictures, underneath a rolling bar on the screen giving the breaking news: Turkey Plane Crash. Her stomach churned as she leapt to run inside. One of the waitresses began turning up the news at the request of the customers. 'A jet plane has crashed on the edge of the Madra Mountains, in the province of Izmir... We haven't any more information as yet and will bring you more details...'

'Have they said anything else?' Sarah desperately asked the man next to her.

'No. A terrible thing.'

She ran out of the coffee shop to the arrivals board. It

445

couldn't have been Izzy's flight because she had seen it on the flight tracker. Finding the flight number she saw the flashing indicator on the flight information. 'Landed.' The relief washed over her. Her heart still pounding from the fright, she made her way quickly to the arrival gate, the adrenaline-induced terror of the last few minutes taking its time to dissipate.

An earlier flight was coming through as Sarah looked anxiously through the doors. Needing to release her exhilaration she began striking up a conversation with a couple next to her. His parents were coming back from a cruise. He joked with Sarah that they were hoping they hadn't been hitting the margaritas too hard during the trip. Sarah then spent the next five minutes, hardly pausing for breath, talking about Izzy and her dig and listened then with interest about their trip taken to Ephesus, all the while keeping an anxious lookout for her, even though she knew that it would most likely take her another fifteen minutes or so before she would be through. Half an hour later the couple's parents came through and they wished her a good visit with her daughter. Shortly after, it appeared that Izzy's flight was finally making its way out, mostly identified by various obvious souvenirs, such as a bag of Turkish Delight and an Istanbul T-shirt.

Another twenty minutes after the last of the flight had made their way through, her joy at Izzy's return now turned to frustration as she went to turn on her phone to see if Izzy had missed the flight. In a sudden panic she realised that she had left her bag in the café. She hurried back there. Immediately her heart sank as there was no sign of it. Walking through the door, the waitress waved happily for Sarah's attention, then from under the counter she produced Sarah's bag.

'Oh! You superstar! I would have been in real trouble.' She began searching for her phone at the bottom of her bag, which she retrieved with some relief.

'You've saved the day.' Sarah thanked the waitress once

again. The coverage of the plane crash continued to broadcast in the corner.

The same man that Sarah recognised from before sighed as they continued with the report. 'It makes you count your blessings.'

'Doesn't it just,' Sarah replied. Half looking at the television the barista took an order from the next customer. Turning it on she noticed a multitude of messages on the screen, and a string of missed calls from Izzy and a voice message.

As she waited for the message to play she took another look at the TV. Izzy's voice began to sound.

'Hey, Mum. Do you ever have your phone on?! It must be your age...'

Sarah looked at the screen closely. A name at the bottom of the TV screen was now added to the bar. Dawson Enterprises, the disintegrated remains of the wreckage now shown in great clarity from the fading smoke.

The rest of the message continued to play. '... you forgot to email the flight details! But anyway, you won't believe this but Edward Dawson, you know, that ridiculously wealthy sponsor, well, one of the other girls told him about my flight and he has offered me a lift! Ha, a lift, in his private jet to London City airport. So I will get the tube to Hannah's. I should owe you one! Keeping it short as we just about to take off! What a life, Mum. Try not to be too jealous. We can catch up on everything when I get back. And, Mum. Love you.'

Sarah dropped her phone and sank to her knees.

EPILOGUE

A Gambler's Story

On that first day, never say never because it will get you through that day. It is a confinement to which you have the keys. Doing this in your own way, but knowing that just that one lapse, one wager, will be a hook to another. Stand firm, not to take this bet, not today. Do whatever necessary to take yourself away from it. To not sit still, be strong enough to repel the insidious temptation that illuminates the possibility of the prize, the highs, because if you embrace it, if you yield, because you think it is under control this time, it is too late. The spiral set in motion, the delusion you chase will pull you down to the ugly depths of guilt and regret.

For whatever reason you started – fun, grief, personal loss, suffering, unhappiness, the thrill of the game – you are where you are. Understand why you started gambling and take it from there. Don't let the past anchor you; you've probably punished yourself enough, with self-loathing and guilt. But you won't overcome it through self-pity or off the backs of others. It will most likely be one of the toughest challenges you will ever face. If you can, get help, you will need every reserve of your strength. There is always someone who will help.

The best way you can, prepare your defences, when the compulsion that you wove into everyday life brings you an ever-present reminder. Be strong. Like when the anticipation of Wimbledon begins building in the week before, the sound of the first serve, the ecstasy as the ball just clips the line for the triumph you knew was coming, or when the talk amongst your friends is of the impending cup final, hold firm. Or, if when you feel you are ready to accept an invitation from friends to a day at the races, be prepared. When, amongst the roar of the crowd, you see the horse you were sure you would have backed head a flagging contender to take the trophy, and you are struggling to watch the jockey sharing the victory with the happy punters in the buzzing enclosure, remember the ones that didn't win. On the plus side someone else will be buying the champagne. Make sure you are aware of the upcoming matches that, for you, have to be avoided. Perhaps even the sight of a sport that had only ever been for betting will evoke mixed emotions in their occasional mention on a sports report. It can be when you least expect it, like as it was for me, at just the sight of a Yankees baseball cap on the high street. It brought back memories of Derek Jeter hitting a home run to the roar of the Bronx crowd, I won a fortune on that, but I also relived the agony when a week later, the sure-fire Alex Rodriguez got caught at the wall to take back what I had previously won, and then empty my account. Personally, I haven't watched baseball, basketball nor an American football game since. It is too raw. I blew a loan of £10,000 which I lost on a baseball game by a single run. The shortstop run out at the plate. Game over. It was the last bet I made.

Let's look at the bookies' world. The orchestrated, polished veneer luring every coin through a slot, grateful of every pay cheque that's cashed. When you begin to free yourself, when that clarity and rationale returns, you will see better the theatre, the reality. Like learning the magician's secrets, behind the gloss, the enticing riches, the machismo and the swagger of sure-minded punters, who are in the know, like you, who have the smarts, the luck. To take your place amongst the winners. Behind the false flattery, where they peddle the successful lifestyle in the relentless string of adverts, that keep throwing up odds before, during and after the match. Where you are enticed by indifferent celebrities, who will later be rubbing their hands at the impending coin of the losers, seek to inflate your expectations, play to your ego by telling you that you could be a winner in just one click away.

Although, to be fair, they owe a big thanks to society's own pressures of conformity. It makes their job easier, and made it easier for me to hide. Society wouldn't expect me to be a problem gambler, probably even a gambler at all, because there are types. I'm not a bankrupt aristocrat playing the tables of Mayfair, a housewife playing internet bingo, a twenty-year-old man putting my benefits into a fixed-odds terminal, or a businessman syphoning off company funds. So, I was dismayed to realise that I could develop an addiction, impervious to stereotypes. You will afford me that joke. You probably know better than anyone the need for a sense of humour, it is what got me, will get you, through this hell.

This is what the gambling industry tells you. The best way they can tap into your psyche, the best way to get you to part with your cash. They tell you gambling on sport, that's about men, for the lads that want to be part of the success. Men are men. Risk-takers, fearless. The highs, being part of the glamour of the success of the best team, your team, the round of drinks to celebrate your nous, the cheers, the money for that day that surpassed a week's salary, and the envy of those that didn't listen to your tip. The lights on the screen displaying in large figures your casino win, a game you knew inside out. You are a winner. You are with the funny guys, the hard men, the men who women want to be with, the people that you are aligned with.

They have an even more puerile perception of women. Women don't gamble, not the nurturers, the homemakers. They have harmless fun. Enjoying the cosy, fluffy kinship of their friends, linking into people they barely know, starting with pence, as it is nothing. How could that lead to anything else? Women gamblers? There doesn't exist a woman who borrows beyond her salary to feed her compulsion, or another who sits behind her desk ticking off the minutes until the meeting is finished, so she can go and recoup her wages at blackjack on the computer she shields from her colleagues, or those that stake their family's home against the turn of a wheel. Women have been assigned a role. They are the fallback, the failsafe, the responsible ones. They are the gambler's glamour, the prize, the ones to be impressed.

For all that seek the dream, the big win, there isn't a void in your life, or the need for a distraction, or the need for escape, or an ego that needs to be stroked, or a means to a success that will always be beyond you. Roll your eyes every time someone says the house always wins.

In case you haven't been paying attention, or noticed the small print, the house is very concerned about their responsibilities. There is an alternative way out that is offered. They should use one of their sound effects to complement it. Such inspiration should come with a drum roll. And here it is. You can 'Stop'. There you have it. The blunt colourless option to this tantalising arena. Just 'Stop'.

Of course they are never going to show a glimpse of what your life could be without gambling. What it really could be for you. To start the life of possibilities, opportunity, the space to see what is around you, to see what you have, to be loved without feeling the guilt, the shame, the nights where you can sleep, or talk of your favourite sport with a passion that doesn't take the fortunes, the health, the happiness of you and your family along for the ride. To not lose your job, or see your family walk out of the door. To not wake up each morning and be burdened by the weight of choices, to keep you well, alive. No. It's just 'Stop'. Another stacking of the odds.

In the pub, when the bell goes for closing time, the television is switched off, the empty beer glasses collected, the desperation of the win that never materialised is front and centre. To return home empty-handed to the partner you have to deceive because there is nothing left. Ignoring them as you brood over the fact it was the striker's fault who had failed to score a sitter in the ninetieth minute. He clearly wanted a transfer. Or the idiot of a referee, who was biased, had sided with the home crowd. But there would be no need to say anything, not yet, because mid-week Manchester United were playing and there was no way that they could lose. Just one more loan and that would be it. Just one. Calculations already being made, as the partner you imagined treating on the back of your win is on eggshells, and dreading the start of the game, or the return from the pub. Or your mates, who you were seeing less and less, were getting on with their lives, becoming increasingly intolerant to your moods.

I'm not much of a loss to the bookies. A drop in the ocean. They have a ready supply of willing replacements with wages, pensions, student loans, benefits, money for food, housekeeping, child support cheques, other people's money, homes and sold possessions, they are happy to gratefully accept. It's a feat of some measure to conceal that behind the wink of an actor and the promise of the good life.

I would like to say that after five years I am over it. It

has eased, and after a year I gradually got back to watching the sports I liked before gambling. I go to the rugby, and the occasional day at the races. You will find your own limits as I have come to accept mine. But I know I can never go back. Not a £1 each way at the races, not so much as a lottery ticket. But my life is great, I am in control and there is no better feeling.

You have the challenge of having to draw on every bit of strength, courage, to face down your demons, to recover the life that has been buried under the weight of loss, shame and debt. To have hope, pride, love, dignity, once again fill your life. I wish you all the best.

ABOUT THE AUTHOR

Rachel Atherton-Charvat was born in Norwich. After graduating in Modern History, she qualified as a history teacher and taught for several years before becoming a freelance sports photographer, contributing to numerous publications including The Times. She has spent many years travelling and living overseas and has exhibited her landscape and urban photography in the UK, Cyprus and the USA. Red/Black is her debut novel.

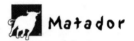 Matador